The Dawn of
Tamus
Tower

BY
MARTIN PATRICK

Patrick Press *Publishers*

Patrick Press *Publishers*
Brighton, UK BN3 5QJ

First published as paperback one volume edition 2007

www.lulu.com

ENEMIES OF THE REALM first published in
Great Britain by Patrick Press 2007
THE ROAD TO BRIMMA first published in
Great Britain by Patrick Press 2007
THE PASSING OF THE CLOUD first published in
Great Britain by Patrick Press 2007

First published in one volume 2007

ISBN 978-0-9556788-0-6

Printed and bound in Great Britain by Lulu Enterprises UK Ltd,
London, W6 7BA

This is a work of fiction. All characters, events, and places are of the author's imagination and not to be confused with fact. Any resemblance to persons, living or dead, or events is merely coincidence.

'Those that have survived must ensure this grim saga is never forgotten,' said the old friar. 'The future generations of this realm must learn of this episode. You must therefore tell these sorry tales; the tales that mark the dawn of Tamus Tower...'

CONTENTS

THE ROAD TO BRIMMA

THE PASSING OF THE CLOUD

PREFACE

This tale continually evolved until it became an account of a rather large saga. Initially, I intended only to write what is now Part One, *Enemies of the Realm*, and originally, the book was named *Tamus Tower* and consisted only of this part. This naturally grew, upon me realising that the tale was far from finished.

My original aim was to complete a story that offered a considerably open-ended conclusion to what might subsequently unfold. However, as the tale developed and new elements to the text manifested as crucial factors to the story I realised that to simply leave it where Book Two now ends would be contentious at best, indolent at worst.

It took me several years to complete the entirety of this work and structure it into its final form. Work began in earnest during late 2003, although much of the earlier half of that year was spent drafting parts of the story. I had an ambition to write a fantasy novel from as early as 2001. A basic plot existed in my head as far back as then but it wasn't until 2003 that I felt truly ready to begin outlining a rough story.

Perhaps, however, the true genesis of this tale stemmed from a desire that grew inside of me in 2004, whilst reading somewhat dry English case law and legislation, to mix my legal studies of that time with a creative project. I therefore decided to continue working on what I started in 2003. However, in 2004 I was a Police Constable and was too preoccupied in this arduous role to truly focus on such an undertaking.

Nevertheless, upon joining the Police I continued to write; jotting down notes and ideas whilst living in a now decom- missioned training camp in Ashford, Kent. Ultimately, I resigned from the Police service and it wasn't until late 2004 that I felt happy with my outline for Part One – which I believed at the time to be the entirety of the tale I wished to tell.

An almost year long lapse between writing, starting in early 2005, kept the seminal figures of the tale in limbo, waiting in the Grange Abbey for many months. Most of the later half of that year I spent alongside Endal during the later stages of his ambitious goal, and it wasn't until early 2007 that any of the friar's party had as much as trod onto the Plains of Falgor. The vast body of Book Five and Six was realised in a period of intensive writing during the early half of this year where a great momentum had kicked in, enabling me to write for hours on end often into the early hours.

Throughout writing this book I have had various commitments, chiefly as a learner, that have most onerously absorbed me. I slogged on, often by night, and finally completed all six books in July of the year I write, 2007. The next few months were spent 'fiddling', a task almost as tough as writing itself, until I was personally content with every aspect. Almost every chapter was drafted several times and some proved tougher to crack than others in terms of achieving the desired pacing.

I found writing much of this book a blissful experience but there were countless moments of stress and frustration. At one point in late 2006 I gave up on the project, fearing I didn't have enough energy inside of me to do the book justice. It also got to the point at times where I felt the story was playing out of its own accord; my efforts as a writer merely to commit to riding what became a great wave of imagination rushing through my head.

Various points perhaps need to be raised regarding metaphor, allegory, meaning, and message. There is little in this tale in the way of metaphor or allegory. I would suggest one should not try to read too deeply into the book. Although there are certainly themes and meanings to most of what happens in the story it was principally my intention to write purely escapist fantasy. Message and meaning come only with the intrinsic aspects of the story and only indicate factors related to the story itself. Some of the characters' names, for instance, portend future events in their translation and definition. For example, *Aku-Mi* translates from Japanese roughly as Evil-Beauty. Although Akumi is not inherently evil as a character she is ultimately overcome by an evil force. I do not wish to reveal any more of these intrinsic messages but will stress that they are often there. I would like to also add that there is no religious connotation to the inclusion of the character named Jobe.

The story is full of sundry characters. Varied, often intentionally archetypal, figures constitute the majority of those established in the story. I truly hope there is someone for every reader to love and hate. Strong female characters play a central role in the plot. This is something I didn't initially envisage but the personalities of these characters became so abound with resolve as to warrant that they developed lives of their very own.

I imagine that each reader will subjectively have their own favourite book out of the six that constitute the novel. Each book represents a specific stage of the story and different readers will no doubt have different predilections.

This is an adult tale and it was my ambition from an early stage of writing to depict physical combat graphically and with more rawness than is often the case with fantasy literature. Early drafts of various violent moments proved too graphic, descriptive, and perhaps superfluous. Hence, I was careful not to overly pursue this intention of mine to portray fighting for what it is: bloody and exhausting. However, a large element of this tale is still undoubtedly to do with swordplay, battle, and conflict in its wider context.

Martin Patrick Poole
Brighton, England
December 2007

ENEMIES OF THE REALM

BEING THE FIRST PART

OF

The Dawn of Tamus Tower

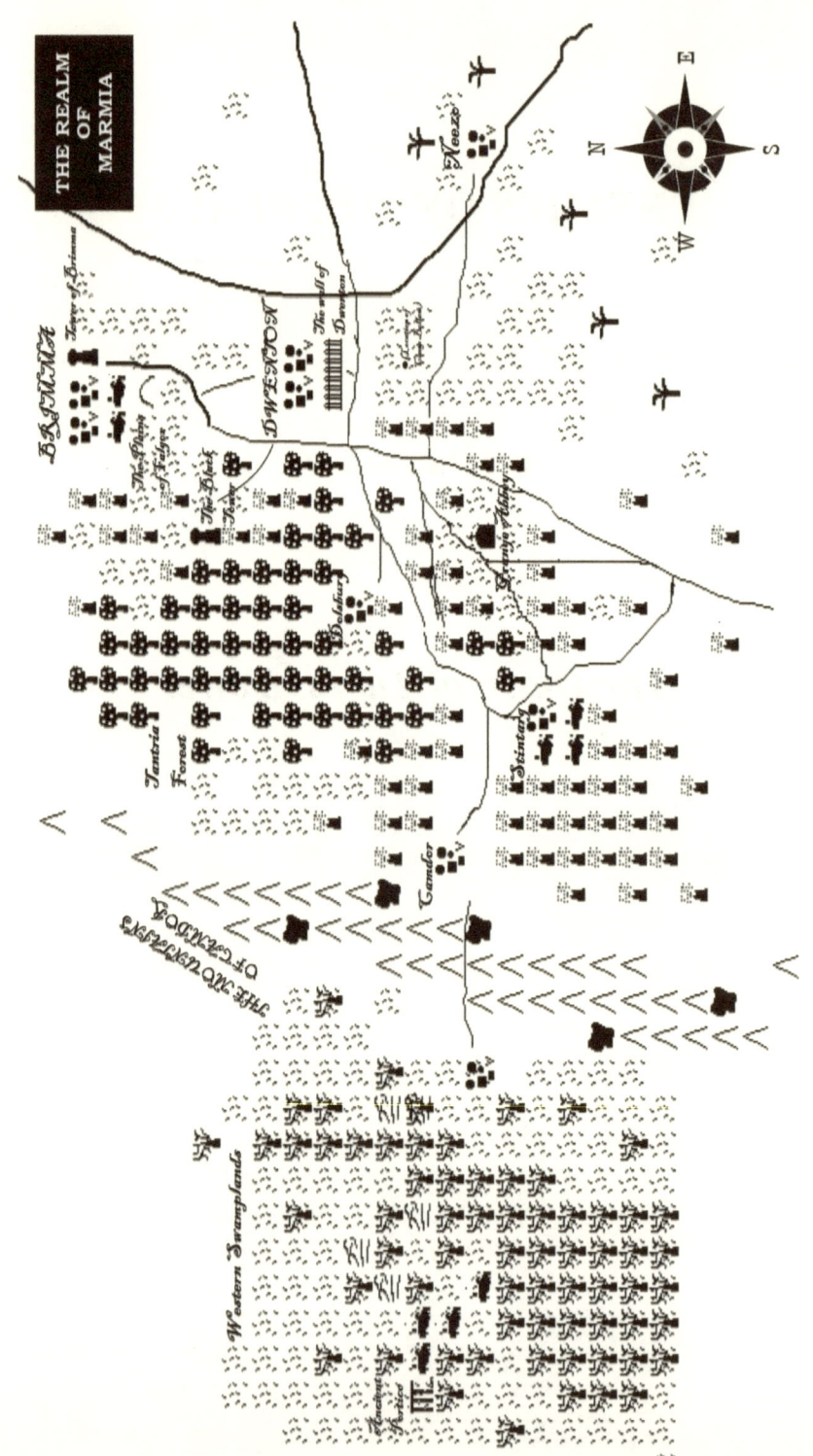

BOOK ONE

CHAPTER I

BOLLAM'S DARK DESIGN

Golandin couldn't sleep. His mind was awash with worries and regrets. The bearded, aging warrior rested awkwardly on his sturdy wooden bed. His heavy silver armour pressed against his skin with his weight. A longsword lay by his side and his helmet rested on a bedside table. The small room was partially lit by a single flickering candle that gave enough light for him to make out the bare walls around him. It was late and the full moon poured eerie shades of white illumination through the small window across the other side of the bedroom.

A small fire burned calmly to his side; the flames of the fireplace further lighting the room with orange glows of heat and conflagration. The crackles of burning wood kept Golandin's mind alert as he stared blankly at the drab ceiling. He was in a state of shock and confusion. They all were, all of those men that had been forced to accept defeat in a war that had raged on for decades. The victorious side, led by the warrior Tamus, had finally finished off any last major segments of the rebellion. Its power was now complete and order had been restored in the realm of Marmia.

For men like Golandin it was now a case of accepting this and giving up their arms. It was now a question of removing the weapons of war and starting a new life, one of conformity to rule and order. The state had finally put an end to the attempts by men like him to take power over these lands. His fight was over.

Golandin knew as he rested on the white sheets that he was not going to be able to drop his weapons and go back to the life he had sworn to never return to. He was one of the veterans, the battle-hardened extremists. He knew most of his kind would now be dwindling away back to those places they had come from. The news that had been announced today of their armies defeats all across the realm and of the killing of their leader, Warlord

Twinicia, on the field of battle had effectively ended this war. There was no hope for men like Golandin now; the Tamus Empire had shown its strength in one final chess move.

Golandin continued resting in the candlelight. It felt as if his struggle had been for nothing and his mind was filled with anger. There was suddenly a loud knock on the door to the room.

'Enter,' Golandin yelled fierily.

The wooden door cranked inward and a figure came into view. He was a slim, middle aged warrior who sheathed a shortsword beside his waist and wore a light chainmail tunic. Long, scraggly, thin blonde hair hung from his wrinkled, pale face and rested on his shoulders.

'This won't do!' he yelled as he closed the door back shut.

Golandin sat up and faced the man. 'Who is left downstairs Arthir?' the old warrior asked.

Arthir looked to the ground and replied cautiously. 'Everyone has gone,' he said dryly. 'I tried to convince them but they aren't stupid. They know all is lost and I couldn't hide the facts.'

'And so it is over,' Golandin remarked whilst staring into space.

The fire crackled softly whilst the two men looked at each other knowingly.

'The village will likely be a dangerous place to dwell,' Arthir said. 'We cannot trust anyone anymore, and Tamus soldiers will no doubt be closing in on all the lands we had held up until now.' Golandin didn't reply.

'There is nothing else to be done Golandin. We are finished!'

There was a loud cry from beyond the room, coming from the streets outside. It was followed by deathly silence.

'Chaos is kicking in all across this village now. The word has spread! We are defeated and all those who are identified as remnants of our forces will be arrested,' Arthir went on.

The village they were in was Dolsbury; a small hamlet in the rural plains of Marmia. It had been captured by their side early on in the war and had been held ever since, but now the war was lost places such as this were dangerous for men like these. They either had to flee or blend in with the small population of the village and become civilians once more.

'I suggest we decide what our next move is and soon,' Arthir said.

Golandin stood up and grabbed his helmet from the table. 'We cannot trust the people in this village. When there was hope they embraced us, but now they will happily expose us to Tamus if it means safety for them,' Golandin said with certainty.

Arthir nodded.

'I won't bow down to Tamus! I won't remove my armour and drop my sword!' Golandin yelled furiously.

Arthir appeared withdrawn and didn't respond.

'We must get away from these parts soon, our men have fled and it is now only the two of us,' Golandin said.

'Where is there for us if we refuse to yield to this new order of things?' Arthir asked.

'I know not but I will not flee just yet, like some wounded animal!' Golandin replied.

Arthir smiled, like he was impressed by his ally's steadfast attitude.

'Shall we go for a drink then?' he joked.

Golandin looked up. 'Yes… in our armour and colours we shall have one final drink at The Lamb Inn and show whoever's in there that we for one have not gone underground!' he announced.

Arthir appeared to agree although it was clear he was more fearful of the unfolding situation than his friend.

Without delay they left the room and raced down the narrow staircase of the small village house. They found themselves in a room of abandoned garments of war. Empty bottles of cider and ale spread out across the wooden tables of the front room and swords, bows, armour, and supplies of food extended out across the floor. This was the image of retreat and taking flight. For men like Golandin it was a sorry sight. His emotion was broken and downtrodden but he wasn't prepared to show it.

'To the inn!' he yelled.

They left the house and entered a poorly lit street. It was silent and motionless. The cold night air whistled over the thatched roofs of the small dwelling of houses and shops. They felt alone and a feeling of complete abandonment seemed to strike them as they marched up the muddy dirt track towards the inn at the end of the road.

The sign to The Lamb Inn was clearly visible amongst the dark tones of the street. Its white paint and golden writing were striking from every angle. The warriors approached the doorway, knowing it would be open even at this hour, and opened the sturdy oak door. The interior was warm and bright from a large fire in the corner and several glowing torches on the walls. There were several figures sitting in huddled groups amongst mostly empty tables. A single barman stood resting at the bar, surrounded by shelves of bottles.

'I knew you'd turn up,' the barman smiled.

'Of course we did Bollam,' Golandin replied. 'We are not ones to miss an evening's drink!'

As the two walked to the bar those scattered around the inn looked towards them in intrigue and concern.

'What now Golandin? What now?' a voice wailed from the fireplace.

Golandin looked towards the fire and studied the murky figures dotted around the space. 'We go our separate ways, or fight on in small groups. Either way is fruitless if you still wish to win the war. It's over,' he replied truthfully.

'And where do we go? What place is there we can run to?' another asked.

Arthir came in: 'Drop your weapons and go back to your lives, go back to your homes. Tamus will only deal with those who still fight on.'

There was a mixed grumbling of response and then the inhabitants started to continue glumly drinking amongst themselves. The barman had already poured two pints of the local ale and placed them by the warriors as they leant against the bar.

'Ah thank you,' Golandin said.

He clutched the wooden ale mug and took a long and relieving swig of the beer. Arthir was soon to follow.

Some time went by as the characters continued to slowly swig the ale and talk of memories of the war. The barman knew these men very well and had agreed all along with the cause they represented. Many had wanted a change to the way of things even though Tamus was proving a very popular Emperor. Marmia was a liberal and free realm but men like Golandin, Bollam, and Arthir craved the power rule over the realm would offer. The rebels were trying to take a piece of the pie by force. This had been all the war was really about; those who wanted power taking on the empire that had created a society of freedom and democracy. In this respect Golandin's cause was hardly the moral stance.

The conversation turned from war stories to that of what nows. The three men looked reserved. Arthir gazed into his ale mug and looked up with a thought.

'If we all regrouped and turned this into an underground resistance surely it would prove possible to fight on?' he asked.

Golandin shook his head and turned to his war buddy. 'We'd be better off turning to crime and just forming a guild of thieves!' he mocked.

'Well I am only considering options!' Arthir snapped. 'Besides, what other plan do we have? Or is there no plan anymore?'

Golandin seemed to be getting angry. Arthir was looking to him for the answer and he knew he didn't have it. Golandin was of a high rank. He'd escaped the field of battle and fled back to this village with the core of his own group of rebel troops. Arthir was lower ranking but still a war veteran. Every other rebel leader had been caught or killed on the field. Golandin and Arthir had merely slipped the net.

'I have no answer Arthir,' said Golandin, trying to calm his tone.

Bollam stood facing them from the other side of the bar. He was a pale, thin character with greying black hair tied back in a ponytail and dark, almost black, eyes.

'I think you need to face facts Arthir,' the barman said. 'With your Warlord dead and the bulk of your armies in ruins there is little chance of salvaging your rebellion. It's too early at this stage to start seriously talking about going underground. Besides, I doubt you'd get many takers.'

His words appeared to pour water on the rebels' desire to speak anymore about what to do. Instead, they continued to prop up the bar whilst some of the other former men of war started to leave the inn as they walked from their fireside tables.

'Any ideas?' Golandin sniggered, staring directly at Bollam morbidly.

This was the moment it happened, a thought was planted into Golandin's head.

'You know,' Bollam started, 'there is more than one way to rid a realm of her Emperor and ultimately that was your aim in this war.'

Arthir laughed. 'You are talking of other ways to win the war than that of fighting his armies?' he asked.

'Well, yes. Now it's over men like you must start considering more alternative options, if you are to continue at all that is,' said Bollam.

Golandin was intrigued. 'So what other ways are there?' he asked.

'I am no warrior; I am just an innkeeper. However, as an inn-keeper I hear things,' Bollam went on. 'You know… things that are often very interesting. We get all sorts in this pub, being in a village right on the edge of the front lines and all. I've had characters in here saying things, speaking of certain people…'

Golandin interrupted: 'What have you heard that is of interest to us?'

'Well, word is there is a character new to these parts staying with monks at the Grange Abbey. He's meant to be a particularly skilled assassin. I have no idea why he's in these parts though but based on what I heard the other day he's here and quite the notorious name in certain circles,' Bollam responded.

'An assassin?' Arthir smiled. 'Is there really such a thing bey-ond paid thuggery and myth?'

Bollam laughed. 'In this subject Arthir you are particularly ignorant. Assassins are around the place, offering a service, but they are hard to come by and only answer to those they see fit.'

Golandin listened attentively. 'What is known of this assassin?' he asked.

Bollam was about to speak but Arthir jumped in: 'Who cares Golandin? An assassin! What rubbish. It is a waste of time dwel-ling on this,' he ranted.

'Shut up for a moment please Arthir!' Golandin barked. 'Let him finish for God's sake!'

Bollam came in: 'All I know is he's notorious within, as I say, certain circles and is meant to be exceptionally skilled. He goes by the name Endal. That's it.'

'Endal,' repeated Golandin. 'Hmm.'

Arthir took a final gulp of his pint and looked to his friend.

'I wouldn't waste time dwelling on this information. Besides, no assassin could get even remotely close to Tamus or even his great tower for that matter, regardless of their skill,' he said.

'I am open to all options right now and as a ranking soldier in what was our army I have a responsibility to at least try and salvage some hope in our cause,' Golandin bellowed aridly.

'Yes but this... even if it turns out true how much would such an assassin charge? Hah! More than we could offer I am certain,' Arthir replied.

'You guys know I am for your cause and you also know I am not exactly a poor man,' Bollam suddenly came in. 'I would be prepared to offer a contribution if you were to, well, pay a visit to this man.'

This appeared to spark a sudden reaction in Golandin. 'You are to be commended for this Bollam,' he praised.

Arthir was shocked by Golandin's new tone. 'Hold on, we are not even decided on this, surely?' he questioned.

'My friend, what do we have to lose? Is it not worth us paying a visit to this Abbey and finding out for ourselves if there is any truth in this information?' Golandin swiftly replied.

'No assassin would have a chance killing Tamus!' Arthir declared adamantly. 'If it were possible why didn't we ever think of seeking one's services before now?'

'Well, as Bollam has already stated, it is rare to even hear of an assassin nowadays let alone find one,' Golandin said.

'It also needs to be stressed that any normal assassin would likely laugh at this job,' Bollam said. 'A normal assassin would have no chance killing Tamus. However, I bring this up because from what I hear Endal is no normal assassin. He is a legend. It seems that his presence in these parts may well be fate.'

Arthir was silent for a few moments and then nodded. He spoke:

'I guess this may well be a long shot, but it's one that is better than having no plan at all besides giving up entirely on our cause.'

The plan seemed sealed at this stage of conversation. The three men drunk up and there appeared to be a mutual agreement that this would be worth pursuing.

'I will travel to the Abbey right now. After all, I cannot sleep and we were going to head in that direction anyway,' Golandin said.

'We were?' Arthir asked.

'Yes Arthir,' grumbled Golandin. 'We were.'

'In that case I will give you two thousand gold from my safe, surely enough for Endal's charge and perhaps even a little for you two to have fun with,' Bollam announced.

Golandin was impressed by the willingness of his friend to lend such an amount.

'This is a worthy cause friend and your act today will not be forgotten,' Golandin made clear.

'All I ask is this: If you find this man and he accepts this contract, if he manages to kill Tamus and his empire falls, I wish to be a part of the… new leadership. Is that clear?' the barman asked in a serious tone.

Golandin smiled and quickly answered: 'My friend, if that occurs then you will be a part of the inner circle, I assure you of this.'

The three men laughed together as they contemplated this distant pipe dream.

Golandin became quite intrigued by Bollam. 'Ignore me if I am wrong but I get the impression you have some level of faith in this Endal, a level of knowledge perhaps you are not admitting to?' he dwelt.

'Let's just say that from what I have heard, and from whom I have heard say it, this assassin is our best bet. This guy is serious, I mean the real deal.' answered Bollam.

Golandin appeared to understand. 'Then we will not speak of this any further. Only the three of us shall know of this and it must not be revealed to anyone until the time is right,' Golandin affirmed.

'I am in,' Arthir said.

'As am I,' smiled Bollam.

The three looked at one another and after a moment's silence Bollam left them. He then returned with a bag containing his gold.

'Two thousand gold. I suggest you go now,' he said.

Golandin took the brown purse and placed it carefully onto his waist belt. 'We will, farewell Bollam… for now,' he said.

'Farewell friends and good luck,' Bollam replied.

Arthir patted Bollam on the shoulder and bid farewell and without delay the warriors left the inn and raced off up the dark street. Bollam started to polish a glass he'd picked up from the bar. As he rubbed it with a white cloth he sniggered to himself, firmly believing he'd just got a good deal.

Golandin was deadly serious about reaching the Abbey as soon as possible. Arthir went along with the situation he found himself a part of. They both had hope in this stranger they'd never met. In this world the word of those you trusted meant everything and the information they had seemed credible. It was a case of taking the gamble and hoping for a desirable outcome. They had nothing left to lose after all.

'We shall head south out of this village and across Tantria Forest. The Grange Abbey is just beyond those vast woods and we should be there within hours if we keep a good pace,' ordered Golandin.

'It will be morning soon. As long as we are far from this village by sunrise we should be safe from Tamus, as I'm sure his troops are already closing in,' Arthir warned.

'We shall be long gone by sunrise, and as soon as we reach the Grange we can go our separate ways,' concluded Golandin.

They marched on up the dirt track in good speed. The occasional villager peeped out from their window as they overheard the hushed voices and watched the armour clad fighters storming up the road.

CHAPTER II

A WARM RECEPTION

The carriage raced its way along the meandering road with little hassle. The flat ground allowed its wooden wheels to rotate without much resistance. Tamus sat inside; peering out of the side window and studying the dark woodland of the night. His carriage was in the middle of a convoy of several. Each one was powered by large white horses. Soldiers armed and poised for anything manned the other coaches.

Tamus wore a dark regal robe. His long, dark black hair covered the majority of his face as the wind blew into the carriage from the open window. Beside him was a young girl. Her radiant beauty captivated the Emperor as he caught the occasional glimpse of her at the corner of his eye. Her bright silver armour and dark, ruby red cloak were the focal point of the cab. She had a lightly tanned complexion and warm blue eyes. Her straight, shoulder length blonde hair contrasted with the dark shades of Tamus.

The two sat together in silence. They were alone in the carriage as its movement occasionally rocked them forwards in their seats on the purple padded surface.

'It is finally over Sylvie,' Tamus smiled.

The youthful girl turned to face her leader. 'Yes, the war is finally over, and Marmia is finally at peace,' she softly responded. Her voice was soft and innocent, like her appearance.

'We have so much to celebrate Sylvie, the times ahead will be all we dreamed of for Marmia,' Tamus declared emotionally.

Sylvie smiled to herself whilst her Emperor started to lecture about what great things would now be possible. She deeply admired Tamus and had sworn to protect him against any threat. Her family had served his for decades, long before there was any order in the realm, but it was she who was now chiefly responsible for his most intimate defence and safety.

'As soon as we reach the tower I shall declare a week of celebration!' Tamus yelled excitedly. 'Did you hear that lads? A week's worth of partying!' There were a few cheers from several soldiers amongst the convoy outside.

The journey to the tower was soon complete. The row of large carriages reached a large bridge that crossed a still lake that snaked across the south of the capital city of Marmia, Brimma. The large, urban city circled around a single tower, which rose up to heights that seemed to touch the clouds. The vast structure of the great tower could be seen from miles around. Its borders were fenced and gated off to the rest of Brimma by hordes of Tamus' most elite guards and defenders. This was the heart of his empire.

The structure of the tower was as old as the very land itself. None knew of its origin. The ancient tower had been there far longer than the city that now surrounded it. Brimma had been built in this rather isolated location solely because of the urge settlers had had to be close to the alluring construction.

Those that controlled Brimma controlled the tower and used its olden interior as a place to establish their court and rule. Now Tamus was finally irrefutability in control of Marmia he could truly claim his right to dwell in the tower and watch over Brimma. It was already being referred to as *Tamus Tower*. The mighty erection had become an icon of rule and order. Its omniscient presence served as a potent symbol of the Emperor's power.

The night sky was faltering as the morning sun slowly became apparent from across the distant mountain tops of the east. The dense, rolling plains surrounding the south of the city started to reveal themselves to Sylvie as the girl stared from her window. She felt a deep sense of pride and was emotionally on a high. She had been with Tamus since the tender age of sixteen, defending him from any rivals on the fields of battle. Now at twenty one she was fervent in her passion to protect him. The ardent girl loved him and all he stood for. Marmia was free and her Emperor admired across the lands.

Sylvie had been trained from an early childhood age to act as the protector of the Emperor. It was a role passed down to her from her father who had passed away some years ago, before ever seeing Tamus come to power. She'd had a lifetime of training. Her sword fighting skills were sharp and honed, and her knowledge and ability as a leader and bodyguard acknowledged throughout the lands.

The convoy crossed over the bridge, passing various checkpoints and soldiers. It then entered onto a main road heading straight into Brimma and towards the main gate into the tower. This was the moment Sylvie kicked into action. Her red, drooping cloak flickered as she stood and swiftly turned to face the coach door. Tamus grinned at the sight of her silver broadsword resting on its waist belt as he caught a glimpse of the shimmering blade from behind her cloak.

'What would I do without you?' he remarked.

Sylvie replied swiftly: 'What would Marmia do without you, Emperor?'

She believed he was worthy of her services and sincerely meant what she said. Her tone touched the middle aged man.

'Thank you Sylvie. It means so much to hear that from someone as able and righteous as you.'

The convoy had passed under the main gate to the tower and stopped in a courtyard. From here the stone tower tracked up into the heavens and large walls surrounded them from the rear and sides. This was some fortification. Sylvie got out of the coach and Tamus followed. A group of armed and armour clad soldiers were already waiting outside.

'Hurray for our Emperor!' a soldier yelled emphatically

There was a loud volley of cheers and shouts in support of the man many believed was in the process of turning Marmia into a truly great and prosperous realm. Sylvie stood by his side, slightly humbled by the attention the troops were giving her whilst they looked in the direction of Tamus and caught a glimpse of her. She looked to the ground playfully as Tamus soaked in the moment for its worth.

'You deserve this Emperor, you have led us to final victory,' the girl said tenderly.

Sylvie was a very attractive girl and many had questioned how such a girl could possibly be worthy of the role of defender of the Emperor. This confusion from certain parties about her had been put to the test time and time again during the war. Each time the highly skilled warrior had proved herself more than worthy of the role. By now Tamus trusted her more than anyone else, even his close personal advisors.

He looked to her whilst the cheering resumed around them.

'You have served me well Sylvie. And just to think I was called mad for trusting a female warrior to act as my closest defence! You have proven my intuition right,' his sentiment touched the girl.

She simply bowed in response, then looked around only to realise the soldiers had turned their attention to her. A voice suddenly bellowed out from the crowd:

'Hurray for Sylvie! Defender of the Emperor!'

A loud holler of praise sounded out around the courtyard as the girl was bombarded with energetic eulogising. She was touched and tears of happiness formed in her perfectly blue eyes.

The celebratory mood did not falter. Eventually, the Emperor and Sylvie entered the tower and climbed several flights of its countless steps. They reached a high level and entered what was the throne room. An elegant dining table was ready for the return of Tamus from his trip to witness the final battles of the war.

Servants surrounded the myriad of chairs and regal characters awaiting the entrance of the Emperor. Soldiers stood around the far corners of the chamber and Sylvie acknowledged their glances as she came into the room. They all knew her and answered to her. She was in charge of Tamus' security and therefore had the rank to order his troops if she saw fit.

'The Emperor is home,' a voice called.

A series of trumpets were played, forming a warm melody as Tamus strolled to his chair at the top of the table. Those around the table had been standing by their chairs, holding back until Tamus took his seat.

'My friends, I am humbled by this warm reception. Today we shall celebrate this great moment for Marmia!' Tamus announced.

In reality the ruler was tired. He had been travelling all of the night and had been on the field for much of the day before. He needed to rest his weary head but this morning was unlike any other. The odd time of day for a large gathering of faces didn't seem to alter the festive and joyous mood. Everyone was on a high and only Tamus seemed to mentally acknowledge that it was such an unearthly early hour of day.

'Let us sit and feast, let us celebrate!' the tired Emperor roared with faltering energy.

There was cheering and a quick succession of applause. The countless figures around the large table then took their seats as conversations started to kick in. Sylvie was seated near Tamus but not directly alongside him. This currently empty chair was allocated to General Dorwor, supreme leader of the armies of Tamus and a proud and aged warrior. He made a habit of informal punctuality, rarely meeting the prompt timings of the rest of the Emperor's court.

Hordes of advisors to Tamus sat around Sylvie speaking of the good times ahead and what now needed to be done. Her mind didn't dabble with the politics of the realm, nor the deeper issues. Her job was to protect their saviour and make sure his safety was never compromised.

Her powers were limitless in this task. She led an inner circle of protectors that were always on the scene, around Tamus, but never quite in view. They consisted of the finest of soldiers and warriors, several also female. Tamus had a deep faith in female protectors, believing they were less susceptible than men to the cravings of power that often sparked betrayal.

The mood was warm as the table of followers feasted and drank whatever was placed onto the wooden surface by the swarms of servants. Tamus sat mostly silent, soaking in the atmosphere and occasionally acknowledging those around him. Suddenly, his attention was drawn towards the doorway of the hall he had entered from. As the entrance crept open General Dorwor marched in through the forming gap. He headed straight for his chair whilst several onlookers greeted him.

'This is the man we should be thanking! Here is our real hero!' Tamus humbly announced.

With his words applause rung out as the large, bearded general took his seat next to the Emperor. His white hair was thinning and wiry and his eyes worn and tired. He wore dark toned fabrics of brown and black that mostly covered his chainmail armour.

'I am grateful for your words Emperor,' he said softly.

'Your tactics on the field destroyed the enemy Dorwor, you led Marmia to victory against her enemies,' Tamus continued.

The general, who now sat in between Sylvie and Tamus, smiled whilst staring at his plate of food.

'We are victorious Tamus but the enemy still exists in pockets. Many will give up and fade back into the realm but I am certain others will fight on. The battle is not yet truly over... but yes, these are minor issues and I am foolish to dwell on the mopping up parts. Victory!' Dorwor bellowed.

His words sparked Sylvie's interest as she sat next to him. She was well aware that pockets of rebels continuing to fight on meant there was still a threat to the Emperor. She was more than prepared to continue valiantly protecting him.

'Yes, yes, Dorwor. You are right to remember these factors but they are, as you say, small issues. The war is won!' Tamus declared merrily.

The general nodded whilst grabbing a mug of beer and taking a gulp of the cold beverage. Loud crossed conversations kicked in once more as a few moments of silence passed. The general looked to Sylvie and spoke:

'And how is the Emperor's most trusted?'

The girl didn't seem surprised by Dorwor's dry, sarcastic tone.

'She is well, General,' she replied swiftly.

The general quietly laughed to himself. It turned into a chesty cough.

'Good, I am relieved you are not too tired,' he said.

Dorwor had always secretly questioned why Tamus felt Sylvie and those she led were better suited to protecting him than he was as the leader of his armies. He trusted the girl in charge of the Emperor's closest defence but made no secret of the fact he believed he was better fitting for the task. Sylvie rarely let the general bother her, simply seeing him as an ally and powerful figure. She respected him but never let his attitude impact her focus.

'You proved yourself on the field yesterday, General,' she said. 'The Emperor is very pleased with you.'

'Yes I gathered,' he replied. 'But between you and me the enemy still stirs Sylvie. A leader of theirs, Golandin, was not caught or killed on the field. He got away with other key figures.'

The general edged in on Sylvie and continued in a whispered tone:

'With these people still at large I will not rest. Until such men are caught we cannot take any chances. I trust you will know what to do. Our armies will not stop searching for these enemies of the realm until they finally are caught. It's only a matter of time but until this time let us remain on alert.'

Sylvie seemed calm at the news. Her facial expression remained fixed and merry.

'As our armies continue to search I will continue to maintain the Emperor's protection. This news won't impact his safety, General. I will keep a close eye on things,' she whispered.

Dorwor nodded. 'Of this I am certain Sylvie. So let us continue as we are, Tamus need not to know of these issues, agreed?'

'I agree, General,' she replied.

Dorwor smiled then turned back to face the Emperor and those around the table. The merry mood was unscathed by the whispers of less positive concerns and he resumed swigging back on his mug of ale.

A further character suddenly entered the scene of the great banquet. His thin, awkward figure strolled along the side of the table until he reached his chair beside Dorwor.

'Oh,' grumbled the general, 'You!'

The pale, scrawny male took his seat and studied those around the table. No one appeared to acknowledge his belated arrival. Even Tamus showed no interest as he feasted.

'Hello Ellis,' smiled Sylvie.

The sketchy looking advisor to the Emperor partially nodded his head in response. He wasn't interested in conversing with the girl and soon gnawed at his chicken legs oblivious to those around him.

Ellis was a member of Tamus' council. He advised the Emperor on everything from how best to lead his army to how to properly wear his robes of state. He had been with Tamus ever since the beginning of the victorious campaign against the rebellious armies of Twinicia. The Emperor trusted him but General Dorwor had always despised the wet character. They seldom met; this was the first time they had sat side by side in many months.

Sylvie was indifferent to Ellis. She hadn't really had any dealings with him and just considered him another member of the court. She soon focused her attention back on what Dorwor had said about rebels still at large.

The young girl sat back on her chair in contemplation. She was confident of the Emperor's safety and didn't dwell further on the news. Her focus turned to the food heading towards the table. Servants were bringing forth chocolate cakes and other delicacies. There was still much to celebrate.

CHAPTER III

STRANGERS AT THE ABBEY

Surrounded by olive trees and rich green pastures old friar Jamus wiped his brow as the warm midday sun bombarded his body. His brown, drooping robe was hardly the best attire to wear in this heat when working hard in the fields. Other monks soldiered on alongside him as the party of workers dug the earth and planted new seeds. Their Abbey was isolated and self sufficient, relying on the crops they maintained and the animals they kept. A flowing stream darting out from Tantria forest offered all the water they desired. Their lives were devoted to the worship and teaching of the word of their God and they lived a simple existence in this rural place. Jamus led these devotees, being the head monk; a position passed down to him from his late father and one he had deep pride in.

The labour was hard and Jamus had been at it for some hours. He decided to rest for a few minutes and sat amongst the grass and soil.

'Let us rest brothers,' he announced.

The fellow monks joined him in peaceful meditation as they sat together.

'We have done much work today and deserve some rest,' Jamus added.

The monks sat for several minutes and silently soaked in the sun. There was a warm breeze that lightly stroked across the landscape as if Mother Nature herself was comforting her world. Jamus was at peace with his surroundings and at one with the natural world. The long green grass stretched out across the flat plains. Jamus studied it as he sat motionlessly amongst his fellow monks.

Whilst he concentrated on the horizon he started to make out two blobs of dark tone within the green shades of nature. He realised they were moving ever closer to his position. Within minutes it was clear the blobs were two figures walking towards the Abbey's outskirts.

'Brothers, we have company,' said Jamus.

The monks looked in the direction Jamus pointed.

'Let us greet these travellers, they seem to be coming to the Abbey,' the friar said.

Before long the figures in the distance had closed in and were now only several metres away. The monks had watched the two men walk ever closer towards them in intrigue. It wasn't often they had visitors and they rarely saw anyone passing by these rural, distant parts. Friar Jamus smiled in their direction as they became visibly clear. He stood up to greet them as the rest of the monks stayed put in the grass.

'Hello there travellers,' Jamus said.

The two figures walked closer until they stopped by his side.

'Hello Sir. I am Golandin and this here is Arthir,' Golandin pointed to his friend beside him.

'Greetings to you, I am friar Jamus of the Grange Abbey. May we be of assistance?' Jamus asked.

Golandin looked to Arthir then back at Jamus. The pair looked tired; they had been travelling for many hours to reach the Abbey.

'We have come for we seek someone. We have been informed he is here at the Abbey,' Golandin said.

'Oh?' Jamus was intrigued. 'Whom do you seek?'

'We only know of one name for him, Endal,' Arthir came in.

The wise friar looked to his fellow monks briefly before responding.

'We do not know of an Endal. However, you may be referring to a man who is currently staying with us in the Abbey. We know not his name for he does not speak to us. He came here about a week ago and has simply helped us work the land. In return we give him shelter and food. We know nothing of him.'

Golandin smiled. 'Well that sounds like Endal to us. We wish to see him,' Golandin said.

The friar nodded. 'He is in the Abbey, likely in his room at the far end of the second floor. Go ahead and check if he is the man you speak of,' he said.

Golandin thanked the friar then turned and started to walk towards the Abbey house alongside Arthir. As they passed Jamus he studied them closely, remembering their faces and appearance. He was absorbed by them and what they wanted with the man staying at his Abbey.

Golandin's pace was swift and Arthir struggled to keep beside him as they marched off of the fields and onto a dirt road that snaked its way up to the Abbey door. The building was a small, church-like structure. It was of stone and an attractive thatched roof appealed to the eye. Surrounding the building were stacks of hay and a small stables alongside the edge of the road. A single black horse stood patiently under its low, coarse covering.

'I will do the talking Arthir,' Golandin insisted.

'I am aware of that Golandin, half of our journey here was taken up with you repeating you knew what to say,' Arthir sniggered.

'We just need to get this right that's all. If Endal is of the skill and notoriety that we have been led to believe he won't be particularly desperate for work. We need to sell this contract to him,' Golandin said.

The two rebellious warriors seemed ever so nervous as they reached the sturdy doors to the Abbey. They felt as if they were about to confront a dangerous character. Even though the pair of them were battle-hardened fighters, the allure of this character had turned them into an edgy couple of visitors.

The doorway opened up as Arthir pulled the door outward. They crept in through the entrance and studied the interior. It was bare and dull. A few paintings hung from drab white walls. Golandin spotted the staircase ahead.

'Second floor, let's go,' he murmured.

They sneaked up the narrow staircase, which eventually spiralled around itself onto the first floor. The warriors moved onto the next set of steps that continued up to reach the final level of the Abbey.

'He said far end, must be at the top of the hallway,' Arthir noted.

They passed room after room and peaked inside. Each door was propped open by a wooden chair. The rooms looked identical, each consisting of a bed, small table, and set of shelves. This was the humble life. As they continued on Golandin was first to spot the door at the end of the corridor. It was closed.

'He's in that room,' he cautiously announced.

Arthir studied it. 'Only one way to tell friend,' he said.

They moved on and stopped directly outside the brown timber entrance.

'I'll knock and we go from there,' Golandin worded softly. 'Remember, I'll do the talking.'

Arthir acknowledged him. Golandin wiped his forehead and after a moments pause raised his left arm, placing his knuckles on the door. He then knocked three times and put his arm back down by his side.

The men awaited a response, some sign of there being a person inside. There was none. A few seconds went by and Golandin decided to strike the door again, this time more loudly. They waited.

'Is there someone inside?' Golandin shouted nervously.

At that there was a sound from within the room. The noise of fiddling at the door momentarily shocked the men. They stepped back from the door in anticipation. The door then churned open. It slowly pulled back into the room, revealing a dark figure standing in the doorway. He stepped out of the doorway slightly and studied the two men that surrounded him.

They were silent at first, taking the image of the assassin in. He wore a black robe that drooped down to his shins and a dark black cloak. His hair was also black and long, covering parts of his pale face and neck. A set of blue eyes revealed themselves from the strands of hair. He had thick stubble but no beard and looked relatively young, clearly younger than Golandin and Arthir. However, there was some ancient presence about him, as if he were a great figure of timeless origins. He had the intensity about him of a wise seer.

'Hello, err, Endal?' Golandin stammered.

The name seemed to spark the figures interest as he studied them. He didn't reply, but looked into Golandin's eyes attentively.

'We are here because we have been advised you are a skilled assassin. We are looking to hire you for your services,' continued Golandin.

The dark character was quite short and smaller than they'd expected. Both men were forced to look slightly downwards at him as his eyes stared straight back up. He remained silent but seemed alert and didn't show any sign of confusion. Golandin went on:

'We need your services Endal. We will pay you well, very well. Are you interested?'

The figure answered in a deep morbid tone: 'What is it that you require of me?'

His reply appeared to please Golandin, being a slight confirmation that the figure was in fact such an assassin.

'Shall we discuss this in your room? It seems strange talking in a hallway like this!' Golandin laughed.

There was little response. However, the figure then took a few paces backwards and turned to walk further back into the room. Golandin and Arthir cautiously followed, closing the door behind them.

They took a seat on the bedside as the assassin stood near the window looking out at the fields and forests beyond.

'We need you to kill the Emperor, Emperor Tamus!' Golandin said firmly.

He expected a shocked response from the stranger. After all, the task was clearly the toughest that could possibly be asked of such an assassin. However, instead of this the man just continued to look out of the window and eventually responded:

'And how much will you offer me?' his tone was the same as before.

Golandin looked to Arthir then back at Endal. They had agreed to offer fifteen hundred gold but the atmosphere of the room seemed to impact Golandin's decision.

'Two thousand gold,' Golandin announced.

This amount was enough in this realm to happily live on for quite some time. Endal turned around and looked towards them.

'I accept the contract,' he declared.

Golandin was surprised. 'So that's it? I mean you accept? Don't you need more information, like why we want him dead?' he asked.

'This is your contract and I accept it for the sum offered,' Endal replied.

Golandin was taken aback by the decisiveness of Endal. He had expected to be questioned by the character since the task being put to him clearly had vast implications. However, he didn't challenge the response; it made the situation considerably simpler than he'd anticipated.

'So you will do this? Go and kill Tamus?' Golandin was somewhat mystified.

'This is your contract and it will be done as you desire of me,' Endal answered.

'When by?' Arthir came in.

'Within a week I shall return to you having completed the contract and accept payment,' Endal said.

Arthir nodded and turned to Golandin. Both men were perplexed at the resolute clarity of Endal.

'You will need to know where we shall be...' Golandin was interrupted.

'I will find you,' he said.

'We will be in hiding until you have completed the contract Endal! We are rebels, on the run! Tell me how?' Golandin continued.

Endal smiled slightly, the first sign of any emotion from his distant and deathly face.

'I shall find you once I have completed the contract and accept payment,' he repeated.

Golandin knew not to question him further, sensing a deep level of power and wisdom coming from the dark assassin. Both he and Arthir could tell from his general presence that he was of particular skill, seeming otherworldly in nature.

'Well in that case my friend let us conclude this meeting. Once you've killed Tamus come to us for payment and we will be waiting for you,' Golandin concluded.

With that he stood up from the bed, followed swiftly by Arthir. Golandin raised his arm out to shake Endal's hand. The assassin looked down to his hand then up into Golandin's eyes as if baffled. The clumsy warrior quickly withdrew his arm and turned with Arthir to the door and walked out of the room. Endal stood still and watched them enter back into the hallway.

'Good luck Endal,' Golandin said awkwardly. 'We will look forward to our next meeting!'

Endal slightly bowed his head in acknowledgement at the sentiment and with that Golandin patted Arthir on the shoulder and the two men walked away from Endal's view and back down the hallway. The contract had been made.

There was an odd sense of closure as the warriors walked back down the steps of the Abbey, leaving the assassin where they found him. It had seemed all too easy and simple yet somehow decisive.

'There is something about that guy,' Golandin commented.

'Do you think he's got a chance?' Arthir asked.

Golandin appeared unsure. 'You know, we went into this thinking it was just a long shot, some final option, but meeting that guy... I just don't know Arthir. I suppose we will just see won't we,' Golandin smirked.

Neither man knew what to think. The task Endal had accepted seemed impossible and a part of them felt foolish even believing for a second they would ever see the mysterious assassin again.

'Put it this way,' Golandin continued, 'if he does succeed we will happily pay him! If he fails we will never need worry about this again and furthermore, we won't have lost out.'

'Yes, it all feels rather easy huh?' Arthir sniggered.

Golandin nodded then replied: 'I guess its just natural for it to feel so easy since, after all, all we have done is put a task to him. What intrigues me is how he thinks he will find us!'

'We can only assume he has abilities we cannot begin to imagine or even comprehend. He seemed certain finding us would be no issue,' said Arthir.

They were satisfied with their meeting and continued discussing impressions of Endal and what they felt his chances could possibly be in completing the contract as they left the Abbey and eventually headed off into the fields from whence they came. They now knew it was simply a case of going underground and waiting for Endal.

As they faded into the forest friar Jamus carefully watched them pass by. He and his monks had been continuing their work in the fields but Jamus had spotted the warriors leaving. He was interested by them and didn't take his eyes off them until they finally vanished from sight amongst the feral trees and hilly grasslands of the western path they now ventured.

CHAPTER IV

FROLICS IN THE NIGHT

Hazati was late. This wasn't unusual and friar Jamus had expected it. He sat in his cosy armchair looking into a smouldering warm fire. The rest of the Abbey was in darkness as the nightly shades spookily hid landscape under a dark drape. By now his monks were all in their quarters; sound asleep after the hard days work.

Jamus was waiting up late for the arrival of his old friend. He occasionally dropped by for an affable chat but sometimes there was also business to be done. However, this was not one of those occasions. The two just wanted to catch up. A message from Hazati had reached the Abbey some days ago informing Jamus of his coming. He was quite the creature of the night, due to arrive at midnight. This did not bother Jamus for he often couldn't sleep and found himself seeking company at such unearthly hours.

There was a sudden knock at the door. The friar got up from his chair and went to the door of the ground floor room. It was a side entrance to the Abbey, used by those in the know. Jamus wrestled the worn, decrepit door open and smiled as the image of the tiny old man struck him.

'Hello there Hazati,' he welcomed him in.

Hazati strolled into the room and placed his large straw hat on a tabletop. He was a very old yet agile swordsman, trainer of assassins, and master of concealment. However, his appearance was humble. He resembled an old beggar, wearing a plain brown robe and loose leather belt. A longsword hung from around his back. He had short dark hair and a small, stubbly, greying beard.

'Thank you for seeing me at such short notice friar but I was in the area and expected you'd likely still be having problems sleeping,' the old man chuckled.

The friar sat back down in his armchair whilst Hazati sat on a soft chair opposite him beside the raging fireplace.

'Well you are right about the sleeping,' Jamus remarked. 'I often still struggle and sometimes don't bother trying!'

'Ah, well it's good to see you're still well though friar,' Hazati said.

His voice was soft and soothing to the ear.

'Yes I am well enough dear Hazati. So tell me then, how are you?' Jamus asked. 'It has been a while since your last visit to the Abbey.'

'Oh I am fine thank you,' said Hazati. 'I have been up to the usual I suppose, paying close attention to my trainees although I can hardly really call them that now. They are fully ready, able, and formidable assassins that is for sure. I have little left to show them but will continue guiding them until they get bored of an old man!' Hazati laughed.

'Have you had much work recently? From Tamus?' Jamus asked.

'A few jobs yes, very small. The general often still seeks our help getting rid of certain troublesome enemies of Tamus. However, our fight seems closer to an end now, after the news of victory,' smiled the old man.

The friar nodded whilst rubbing his hands together. 'You and your assassins have served the Emperor and Marmia well Hazati. That is for certain,' he said.

The men had known one another for many years. Jamus was once a warrior just like Hazati but had surrendered to the ways of the monk. Hazati respected his friend's change of life and had remained in touch.

Hazati had helped Tamus over the years, using his skills to help the war effort and train others in the ways he knew so well. Those he had trained were mostly orphans; their roots lost and forgotten.

'I am grateful for your words friend,' Hazati thanked Jamus.

'And how is the delightful Akumi?' the friar inquired.

Hazati smiled. 'Ah she is well Jamus, very well. Her skills have now surpassed anyone I have ever trained. She is swift and deadly yet also still as sweet and tender as always,' he beamed.

'I am glad to hear it. She is such a pleasant child,' Jamus said.

'Pleasant yes, but not so much a child!' Hazati shrieked. 'More a young adult nowadays!'

The two old men laughed together in innocent mockery of such distinctions in maturity.

'And how are things here at the Abbey Jamus? Any news?' Hazati asked.

'Oh, well no not really, apart from some odd visitors we've had over the last few days,' Jamus noted.

'Odd you say?' Hazati was intrigued.

'Yes, well, we don't ever really get people coming here. So therefore I was rather surprised when a lone traveller came to the Abbey early last week. He arrived late one night and seemed in need of shelter yet didn't speak a word, deadly silent...' Jamus began.

'Oh?' Hazati sounded.

'I gave him a room and for the next few days he helped us work the fields, although we didn't ask this of him. He would then retire back to his room and reappear the next morning. He never spoke. I was fascinated by him for he seemed very out of place and I could tell from my past days that he was a skilled warrior,' the friar continued.

Hazati remained interested, sitting up whilst the friar spoke on.

'Some days later two others came to the Abbey, seeking someone. They were certain he was staying in the Abbey and so I assumed they must have known him. And so I let the men go into the Abbey to meet him and after a short time the men left. All went on as normal, the stranger remained in his room after they'd gone and attended dinner with fellow monks. The next morning he was gone.'

'Strange people,' shrugged Hazati. 'Many often seek solitude in an Abbey; perhaps his friends catching up with him triggered him to move on.'

'Yes I suppose so, but it was all rather odd. We just rarely get visitors coming by that's all,' laughed the friar.

'He was very odd though, I mean rather alarming at first,' he continued. 'He arrived in the night on a black horse, clothed entirely in black, and knocked on the doors. Upon opening them he simply bowed and, although it was quite clear he wished to stay, he never spoke. The next morning he helped us sow seeds, in hot sun, whilst wearing this black robe. Very odd! And as I say, I could tell from my old ways that he was no traveller, he was skilled and battle-hardened.'

'It is likely these men were all just retreating from the front lines,' Hazati suggested. 'You describe a typical example of one of those rebel thugs my friend.'

'Yes, it's very likely that was the case, but when those other men came asking for him I couldn't help but feel confusion though,' Jamus sniggered. 'You see, I used to have a horse, Kendal, and when they asked for their friend I, at first, thought they were after the horse!' The friar chuckled to himself in reflection.

'You did?' smiled Hazati warmly.

'Well yes, oh I do tell jokes badly! Excuse my nonsense Hazati,' Jamus said. 'I did so for they asked for Endal, presumably the strange character's name, and so I thought I heard Kendal!'

The friar giggled away to himself whilst Hazati sat silently. His mild, relaxed mood altered in a sharp instant. He remained silent and motionless, staring down at the floor between him and Jamus. The friar stopped chuckling and looked up, intrigued by Hazati's deeply serious expression.

'What is wrong Hazati?' he asked.

'Endal you say?' Hazati bellowed. 'Endal!'

'Why yes Hazati. They named the stranger Endal. What is it?'

'And you, you are certain? This is no mistake Jamus?' Hazati went on. His tone was serious and fierce.

'It was Endal, I am certain of it. What in the world is up?'

Hazati looked to the fire and then answered slowly: 'From your description of him and all you have said it would seem quite clear that this Endal is the Endal I am thinking of. He is an assassin, but not just any assassin. He is something of a dark legend.

Endal is somewhat a myth yet it is apparent he exists, a sinister and highly skilled assassin. Ever since I can remember the name Endal has been notorious but only to those, like me, in the right circles of knowledge. I have been told about this figure but have never known of him active… until now it would seem.'

The friar sat up, now as serious as Hazati.

'It is said Endal comes from another world yet chooses to dwell here, accepting contracts from clients as he pleases and selecting only those that excite him,' Hazati said. 'In assassins' circles he is a rumour yet a feared one. Nothing else is known about him. All that seems clear is that he exists and remains active. So the question is what was he doing here and who were those that sought him?'

Hazati was now a troubled man, clenching his tired fists as he studied the burning flames.

'Hazati, they supplied me with their names, perhaps rather stupidly now I hear this information,' Jamus said. 'One called himself Golandin, the other Arthir. I watched them leave the Abbey, they didn't stay long. They headed off in the direction of the village Stintarg to the west; I can only assume they may have gone there.'

Although a veteran of decades of war Jamus now lived a humble life and his memory of names had faded. He wasn't in the picture anymore and had no clues to who they were.

'This information may prove vital Jamus, well done for remembering it,' Hazati remarked. 'Those names mean little to me although I feel this situation requires urgent attention. If this is the Endal I fear and he left hours after they spoke with him it would seem a contract was accepted. Endal has gone to complete a contract, their contract. But what would be of any interest to Endal? What contract might he have been willing to complete?' Hazati was in deep thought.

The old man pondered for several seconds and then suddenly stood up from his chair.

'Friar Jamus, I must leave. I have much to do.'

'I understand Hazati, it was good to see you again and I hope you can get to the bottom of this.'

'Jamus, I fear the only contract Endal and men like Golandin at a time such as this would be interested in is one of great magnitude. I believe Endal has gone to kill Tamus!' Hazati announced.

Jamus was alarmed. 'Oh my! Oh my! I had no idea Hazati, no clue to this…' Jamus was silenced.

'Do not worry Jamus,' Hazati assured. 'You had no reason to expect this. However, I know of Endal and must now get moving, not a moment to lose. I must speak with people in Brimma and get back to Neezo.'

The friar stood up as Hazati raced for the door.

'Farewell friar, I shall be in touch.'

'Best wishes Hazati,' Jamus replied.

The old man grabbed his bristly straw hat and wrapped it around his head, tying string from it around his chin. He opened the door and vanished into the night, the door squeaking back shut; keeping the warmth of the fire inside.

CHAPTER V

THE STUDENTS OF HAZATI

The river flowed peacefully down the winding stream. Surrounding the clear reflections of the rushing waters were clear azure skies and lush pine forests. The fresh morning air soothed the lungs and the moist atmosphere awakened the senses. Several birds sung in unison as the morning sun impassioned the wilderness with golden light.

Akumi lay in the green grass soaking in the serene moment. Beside the cute, petit girl rested Jobe. His long, brown, pony tailed hair spread out roughly across the flattened grass as he rested his head on the ground.

The two trained assassins were at peace. Their light leather armour and small but deadly blades were only an appearance. Their minds were pure, innocent, and eager to help others. They believed in Tamus and were blissful at the news of the end of the war. It meant peace and the sealing of a free and liberal Marmia.

Akumi's stunning looks were reflected as she sat up and looked down into the water. She made out her clear reflection. A warm set of brown eyes centred her fair complexion. Her straight brown hair waved its way onto her shoulders. It was tied in a bun, ready to limply fall down over her back at her desire. She was a young girl but felt ready to prove herself as an assassin, believing she had a duty to rid Tamus of all the thugs of men that cried for a continuation to war and bloodshed. This was precisely the sentiment of her closest friend, Jobe. He was her age, a young adult barely aware of the ways of life but willing to test his skills. He had tanned skin and a slim body, covered in leather armour and a brown coat.

Akumi wore a red cloak that concealed her blade. Its scarlet tone seemed out of place amongst the jade theme of nature. Her slender body was clothed in light leather body armour that snaked its way down her arms to the elbow. She wore fingerless gloves that she started to fiddle with as the reflection was obscured by clouds darkening the strengthening sunlight. She then started to fiddle with her black boots. She was beginning to grow anxious for the return of Hazati, wondering what would next be required of her and the other assassins he'd trained. Jobe was still resting flat on the grass. He was staring at Akumi as he lay, studying every strand of hair on the back of her head.

'What is up Akumi?' Jobe asked daintily.

'Nothing Jobe, I am just eager to hear from Hazati what is to be required of us next,' she answered. Her voice was soft and delicate.

'Yes I know how you feel; we have been waiting to prove ourselves for so long now! He will return soon no doubt,' said Jobe.

From beyond the riverside a figure popped up behind Jobe. He'd come from the nearby house; the only structure for miles around.

'Ah, what a view,' smiled Harkor.

He walked closer to Jobe and dropped himself down into the grass playfully. He resembled Jobe yet had darker hair. He also had a thin goatee beard, with strands of his straight locks dangling down over his face.

The three assassins remained together on the riverside for some time. The sun slowly rose, bringing greater light and warmth as the morning evolved. Akumi seemed attentive and alert whilst her friends continued relaxing behind her. She studied the river flowing by her feet.

The water was swift and the sight put her into a meditative state. In this heightened awareness she was first to spot a figure from across the river moving out from the tree line of the pine forests beyond. She could tell it was Hazati straight away, his triangular straw hat a dead giveaway. The old man trundled on through the grass with his walking stick prodding the ground before him.

'He is here,' Akumi smiled.

Jobe looked up. 'Ah good,' he said.

Harkor stood up and brushed a few dead leaves from his attire.

'I hope he's in one of his chirpy moods,' joked Jobe.

Hazati crossed the river via a ramshackle wooden bridge further up the stream. He eventually moved down the field to bump into his party of assassins.

'Hello master,' Akumi greeted him. He nodded in acknow-ledgment.

'Follow me,' he ordered the three of them.

The master then walked on towards the small house near the riverside. The young friends looked to one another in intrigue and obediently complied, following him along the field and into the tiny abode. There was only one floor; a wooden decking the foundations for stone walls, which propped up a low flat roof. Inside the single room were several sleeping mats and stocks of food. Hazati turned to face the assassins as soon as they'd all entered into the room.

'I got here as swiftly as I could but without a horse I was delayed,' the old man stated. 'My meeting with the friar proved interesting and means great things for us. It seems an assassin has been contracted by a couple of high ranking rebel warriors that are clearly not giving up the fight. The assassin in question was staying at the Abbey and Jamus supplied me with the details of the men who spoke with him.'

Akumi and her friends were hypnotised by the information coming from their master.

'On my way here I ventured north to Brimma, the capital, and sought an urgent meeting with General Dorwor. He is the man who has given us tasks in the past. I informed him of this news and gave him the names of the men who came to the Abbey. It seems that those men, Golandin and Arthir, are known by Tamus. They are high ranking rebels on the run. They were the ones who spoke with the assassin in question, Endal.'

The old man paused for a moment. 'From the information we have it seems very likely these two rebels have paid Endal a large sum to complete a contract. Now I need to explain to you that Endal is no ordinary assassin. He is exceptional and unique.'

Hazati went on and explained to the three who Endal was in the mysterious manner much alike to when he described him to friar Jamus.

'This assassin is highly skilled and very dangerous, even to us,' Hazati made clear.

Everyone continued to listen carefully.

'We know little of this man except that he is to be feared. Those like Endal do not simply take on contracts because they have been offered to them. Endal will only have accepted this contract if it was something grand, that which would have excited him. For these reasons I believe Endal has been contracted by Golandin and Arthir to kill Tamus. It makes sense when you bear in mind who Endal is.'

This announcement sparked a sudden emotional reaction.

'This cannot be allowed! We will stop this!' Jobe yelled.

'And we shall get him first yes master?' Harkor asked knowingly.

'Yes Harkor, we have been asked by General Dorwor to help track and stop Endal before he can potentially get to Tamus. We must do this,' Hazati said.

Akumi remained silent, deeply concerned that someone as skilled and seemingly infamous as Endal was likely now out to kill the man they all treasured and had sworn to serve.

'We shall help the armies of Tamus in this cause,' the master continued.

'Those stinking rebels! How did they even find this Endal?' Jobe cried.

'Rumour likely spread of an assassin in the area and it just so happened to be one as notorious as Endal,' Hazati said.

'What kind of man must this be, to accept such an iniquitous contract?!' Harkor grumbled.

'The kind that we do not understand. Endal is dark and his roots a mystery. Many believe he is alien to this world,' said Hazati.

Akumi had remained silent for long enough. She felt a deep sense of duty, already aware that her skills were of a particularly high standard. Hazati and the others knew this. She was the strongest of the group and her master was well aware that her abilities were becoming distinctively extraordinary.

'And what of Golandin and Arthir master?' the girl asked curiously.

'Dorwor will go after them Akumi. We have been left to deal with the assassin. Others will also be after him but the general has a special faith in us. We will not fail Tamus!' Hazati declared firmly.

'We will not falter master,' replied Jobe.

'Dorwor's troops will see that the remnants of the rebel factions are dealt with,' Hazati said. 'It is up to us to now track Endal and stop him. I must stress this will be no easy task and it will test every one of you to the very limits of your individual skills. I never intended for you to go into such a dangerous and challenging assignment as this but fate has sealed it so.'

'We are not afraid and will serve you well master,' Harkor replied.

'I am pleased you are all so eager,' the master said. 'Akumi, you are quiet. What are you thinking?'

'I am just taking it in master. I am ready and prepared for this task,' she claimed.

Hazati seemed satisfied with the response his speech had invoked. He felt confident his assassins were ready for the challenge but also knew there was now no choice. They had to go after Endal. The master spoke:

'We shall move out right away, no time to lose. Endal left the Grange Abbey about a day ago on horseback. This means he will now likely be in one of the three villages in that area of the realm. We shall go to these villages and seek information. Let us move!'

With this there was no delay. The group raced for the exit to the quarters, collecting bags and stacks of supplies that lay out over the ground.

'We shall hire horses from the stables on the road leading north through Tantria forest. From there we will reach the first village, Dwenton, within several hours,' the old man ordered.

Akumi was first to follow Hazati out of the door and back onto the field. Jobe and Harkor were close behind. The four of them then marched off towards the old jagged wooden bridge.

As soon as General Dorwor had heard his old pal Hazati had arrived at the tower gates seeking his counsel at this unearthly hour he stormed out of his late military briefing. The tired, sturdy soldier marched down the hallway passing countless guards that stood fast and tall as he passed by. He reached a large spiralling staircase that bent its way down the tower back to the ground level. Dorwor raced down each set of stone steps in an almost steady jog. His steel armour plates rattled as his descending body twisted and turned with speed.

Eventually, he reached the ground level of the mighty structure and walked across the courtyard. Several guards stood with large halberds poised in readiness for him to arrive beside them. In between them stood a bent and ragged old man, leaning on a brown wooden stick, and holding his large straw hat. Hazati smiled as the general got closer and halted in front of him.

'Hail Hazati, and how is the old man?' Dorwor sniggered.

'I am well, General, but need to speak to you regarding an urgent matter.'

The general knew that when Hazati said a matter was urgent it required his utmost attention.

'Right, well come with me, let's walk and talk,' he said swiftly.

The two moved away from the hordes of guards around the tower's courtyard and headed off back into the tower itself. Upon entering Dorwor pointed to a series of benches just beyond the door and once they reached them both men took a seat side by side inside the vestibule. They were alone.

'I can sense your mood; tell me what is troubling you?' Dorwor asked.

The aged warrior was swift to reply. 'Friar Jamus of Grange Abbey has supplied me with information. It indicates that a notorious, highly skilled assassin known as Endal is in the area and has been contracted by two men, Golandin and Arthir.'

Dorwor recoiled. 'You know of these rebels? They have yet to be caught!' he yelled.

'They spoke with Endal at the Abbey two days ago,' said Hazati. 'According to friar Jamus they left soon after arriving and Endal left yesterday morning. I know of Endal my General and listen well: He is no ordinary assassin. He is somewhat a legend in our circles. His skill is said to be unrivalled and his powers otherworldly.

'It is my firm belief Endal would only have accepted a contract from these men if he had felt attracted to it. Someone of such skill as Endal can be very selective. From Jamus' account it seems Endal accepted the contract, seeing as he left the next morning... my General, I believe Golandin and Arthir contracted him to kill Emperor Tamus and it would seem Endal has accepted that contract.'

The account stirred Dorwor. He restlessly stood up. 'You are to be commended for discovering this information Hazati. I shall not rest until we have caught Golandin and Arthir and discovered this for certain. However, regardless of knowing for certain we must plan for the worst case scenario and assume the Emperor is in danger,' he said.

Dorwor started to pace up and down whilst Hazati sat humbly.

'Golandin and Arthir went in the direction of the village Stintarg, Jamus noted they were heading that way from the Abbey. It is at least worth a try to go there,' Hazati suggested.

'Yes, I will order the masses of the Tamus armies to search the entire realm for these men!' Dorwor screeched. 'We shall go to that village and all the villages these rebels could possibly be, they shall be found Hazati. But what of the assassin? Hazati will you help your Emperor and help us track and stop this Endal?'

Hazati seemed ready to respond to this. 'I vow to stop Endal and protect Tamus, General,' he said.

'As I suspected,' smiled Dorwor. 'We shall track the rebels and find this Endal before he can get so much as near Tamus. He is only one man Hazati and now we have this information he won't stand a chance!'

The general was certain and confident. However, Hazati remained cautious; knowing the full power and threat Endal posed.

'Hazati, I have faith in you to stop Endal. We shall assist, of course, with as many troops as is required. Every village will become a bastion and every road a convoy of our armies until this assassin is caught or killed.'

'I will not fail in this task, General,' Hazati replied.

Dorwor smiled at the confidence of his ally and then looked around their surroundings.

'We must move, things to do and as you say, no time to lose,' he said. 'I will not forget this Hazati and I shall keep in touch.'

'Farewell, General,' the master said whilst getting to his feet.

Dorwor then left him by himself as he marched away back towards the spiral staircase of the tower. Hazati walked in the other direction, back through the doors of the tower and out onto the busy courtyard.

As the old man ambled away he noticed a girl heading towards him coming from the opposite direction. Her blonde hair and blue eyes stood out amongst the crowd of darkly toned troops around her. Hazati knew the face only too well. It was his good friend Sylvie, protector of Tamus. He had hoped to bump into her during his swift visit. She noticed him and ran over to greet her beloved friend.

'Hazati!' she shrieked.

She softly hugged him and stood to his side. 'Hello my dear,' the old man chuckled.

'What brings you to the tower?' Sylvie asked excitedly.

'You will need to speak with General Dorwor Sylvie,' Hazati said. 'I have just spoken with him about an urgent matter. Tamus could be in danger, an assassin may have been contracted to kill him.'

Sylvie slowly nodded whilst taking the news in. 'I see... an assassin?' she was perplexed.

'Yes, a highly skilled and quite infamous one, known as Endal. I discovered this earlier today and came straight here to inform the general,' he replied.

'Do you know who is responsible for seeking this assassin?' Sylvie asked.

'You will need to speak with Dorwor Sylvie. I have told him everything I know. I am very sorry but I need to get back to Neezo, myself and my assassins are going to help track Endal and stop him. The general has asked it of me. You will learn the facts upon talking to Dorwor,' he said.

Sylvie seemed calm although the news was something of a surprise. The celebratory mood of the past few days was suddenly being tested by this credible intelligence but she instantly felt certain she, regardless of anyone else, would make sure Tamus was kept safe.

'As Tamus' protector Sylvie you will be his final defence,' Hazati said. 'Stay extra close to him and please do not underestimate Endal. You are highly skilled and devoted but Endal is no normal threat. He is exceptional.'

Sylvie remained cool. Her composed behaviour was normal in the face of such situations.

'No one will get through me Hazati. The Emperor shall remain safe.'

The master smiled. 'I don't doubt it Sylvie, with you by his side,' he said. 'Now I must go, Tamus shall get through this! Farewell.'

'Goodbye for now Hazati,' Sylvie said affectionately.

Hazati bowed and then continued to walk away from the tower, straight towards the courtyard gate that led out into Brimma.

Sylvie didn't hesitate and walked straight into the tower destined for Dorwor's quarters. She was eager to get the full picture and get straight back to the Emperor. The girl raced up the stairs, passing swarms of fully armoured soldiers racing into the courtyard, likely at the news of the threat to Tamus. Sylvie passed them by on her journey to the higher floors. She could tell Dorwor was already starting to order his armies into action.

Before long the blonde warrior reached his war room, on the high level of the tower. As she walked into the room a large table full of maps separated her from the general who stood studying the imagery of the realm of Marmia in all its might. He was surrounded by his minions, lower ranked officers eager to carry out his orders to the letter.

'General, I have briefly spoken to Hazati about what is happening,' Sylvie announced as she walked closer to the general. 'I want a full account.'

Dorwor looked up from his maps and nodded slowly. 'Yes Sylvie I will explain all I know. I was awaiting your arrival,' he said.

She got closer to him and Dorwor shunned everyone else around him away to give them space around the war table. Dorwor hurried to fill Sylvie in and proceeded to tell her all that Hazati had said. She listened carefully as the large military man spoke on for several minutes. As the information poured into her brain she realised the full extent of the news, knowing it was now vital to keep Tamus as safe as possible. She knew not to underestimate her enemy.

'I shall keep Tamus safe, General,' she commented. 'Just make sure you find Golandin and Arthir. We will keep the assassin at bay.'

Dorwor had explained all he knew to the girl. He outlined his plans to send soldiers after the rebels responsible and to man every village and roadside in order to search and check travellers and keep movement restricted. She took his briefing in and then kicked into a decisive disposition.

'I will need to remain around Tamus for now and instruct my people to start hunting for this Endal,' she said. 'I need to get planning. Thank you for updating me, General.'

Dorwor looked down at her. He seemed confident the girl knew precisely what to do.

'I will leave you to it. Let's keep one another informed. I will leave it to you to inform Tamus of this news,' he said.

She was well aware that he had expected her to break the information to the Emperor.

'I will speak with him now,' she said, 'and will keep you informed of my actions, General. Bye for now.'

'Okay, well goodbye for the time being then Sylvie,' he replied.

Sylvie walked from the table. She was a girl on a mission. Her mind was now focused on giving Tamus the greatest of security she could offer and making sure no one could possibly get near the Emperor.

It wasn't long until she had further climbed the stairs of the tower and reached the highest level. The peak of the tower touched the clouds. This was the Emperor's chamber. At this uppermost tip the bulk of Marmia could be overlooked on a clear day. The Emperor's view of his realm reminded his subjects of his watchful eye.

Sylvie reached the doorway into the chamber at the top of the progressing staircase. Two guards stood by the side of the door and acknowledged the girl with a military salute. She passed through the entrance and walked along a narrow aisle between benches, lit by burning torches hanging from the walls. Her pale complexion and blonde hair were given an orange tint by the flames as she glided along the throne room heading for the balcony at the far end. She knew Tamus would be standing there, perceiving his lands.

The girl's mind was transfixed on proving to all those around her that in this time of danger she alone could protect the Emperor. She felt confident that, regardless of the assassin, her resolve to protect Tamus would prove impossible to defy.

As she contemplated this she reached the end of the hall and stood facing a balcony. Its door was open and she could make out the blue skies beyond the stone terrace. Tamus stood facing the buildings and land far below. Sylvie crept closer, a sense of vertigo striking her as she got nearer the edge.

'Ah Sylvie,' Tamus smirked, 'you have caught me watching the realm.'

He laughed to himself and turned around to face the girl he had sensed coming to him.

'Hello Emperor,' Sylvie bowed. 'I'm afraid I have some bad news and will need your attention.'

Tamus became more engrossed. He leant against the edge of

the balcony and gave his protector his full concentration.

Sylvie stood by his side on the terrace of the tower for several minutes giving Tamus a full account of the news. She supplied him with all the information she had and made it clear that she was certain he wasn't in any real danger, maintaining she would protect him against any threat. She explained what was now happening, including Dorwor's plans and the role of Hazati's assassins. She then started to explain her intentions.

'You must remain in the tower Emperor. Tamus Tower will be the safest place for you until Endal is dealt with and the conspiring rebels found. No one could ever breach this place and in the meantime we can track the assassin,' she said.

Tamus turned back to face the navy sky and misty, faint ground spread out across the visibly angling horizon.

'Ah, Tamus Tower,' he bellowed, 'named as if my very body were carved in the stone itself!

'If this is your wish Sylvie I will do as you ask and trust your ability to protect me. With you around I need no other to remain safe.' He smiled warmly.

She was honoured and knew her Emperor's trust in her meant she could not fail him.

'I will not let you down. The assassin will be stopped,' she affirmed energetically.

'I know Sylvie, I know he will,' Tamus smiled.

He turned to her and softly placed his left hand on her shoulder affectionately. The two looked into one another's eyes. Sylvie was captivated by the moment. Tamus studied her caringly. It was clear he deeply valued the extraordinary and beautiful girl before him.

CHAPTER VI

A CLASH OF BLADES

Endal blended in with the darkly lit woodland as the morning sun only just started to rise into the sky. The early morning was fresh and cold, with a light breeze whistling around amongst the trees. The dark assassin raced along the rough dirt road on horseback. His black horse was fast and mysterious. Together, they formed a captivating and spooky image. A dark rider was riding a dark horse. Endal wore a drooping hood that entirely hid his head, turning his face into a void of darkness.

The woodland around Grange Abbey was dense and eventually Endal was forced to slow down. The black horse steadied as turns and bends became the norm on this bumpy trail. He was heading for the nearest northern village and hoping to reach it by the afternoon. The assassin had camped out in these woods beyond the Abbey for a day. He had been in a focused, meditative trance; preparing for the grand task ahead.

Although a relatively small dwelling Dwenton was one of the most significant trading towns in Marmia and particularly busy and bustling. Endal intended to reach it as his first port of call. Here he could rest and continue on towards Brimma the next day. He was well aware of the newly named *Tamus Tower* and already expected his journey would likely ultimately lead him there.

Endal was clearly a mysterious figure. He had travelled to Marmia out of intrigue after staying in other realms beyond its borders. For many years he had lived the life of a drifter, moving from Abbey to Abbey and relying on the unconditional embrace of rural monks. He lived alone and knew no one. His past was shrouded in myth and rumour. He never spoke of it to the very few people he ever conversed with. What was clear was he'd been active in the past and his name had become notorious. He'd killed many and served many now forgotten kings of men in distant lands. He'd invoked fear within communities and fallen empires alike, become a hero to those that craved such power, and remained a name of intrigue and caution over decades. His exceptional skills were extraordinary and his name was tantamount to the highest order among fighters and assassins.

Although seeded in speculation it was often said Endal had come from some other place, some other world or even dimension of reality. His powers and skill were unlike any others as was his mystifying presence. He seemed alien to those that met him and beyond the contemplation of anyone that ever tried to get close. Endal was a living legend.

As his horse trudged on up the winding path Endal's hidden facial expressions became less distant now no one was around to see them. His face became more human and emotional as if during this time of solitude his veil was somehow lifting. The figure momentarily looked like he was nothing more than human.

His skills were the result of endless training, fighting, warfare, and teaching. He was a bitter and dark character. His mind was numb and his thoughts rested solely on the contract and a meditative state of no mind and no thought. He didn't dwell or contemplate. He was above it. Endal was an evolved being, operating at a higher level than man.

This contract appealed to Endal for it was a challenge. It was a task that tested even someone of his ability. He had been caught during a phase of boredom and desire. This was why he'd so freely accepted such an imposing and demanding task. He hadn't been approached for an epoch and this moment marked his first time active in many years. The rumours that spread around Marmia of his presence at the Abbey had led to this and Endal was personally eager to prove to himself above any other that he could complete this mammoth objective.

The figure had become astringent and numb through a lifetime of bloodshed. His roots were entirely unknown. All that was known was he'd been around ever since anyone could remember, lurking the lands and remaining a name only said in hushed tones.

The hooded figure continued riding the trail. Dry soil was kicked up behind the back legs of the horse and rose up forming brown clouds of earth. The thudding of horse shoes striking the ground rung out across the woodland in booming resonance. The foliage was becoming more and more visible as the morning sunlight strengthened with time.

As Endal studied the road ahead he spotted a single figure sitting to the side of the path a few hundred feet in advance. The figure noticed Endal heading their way and stood up and positioned themselves in the middle of the clearing. Endal noticed the armour clad figure pull out a sword from their waist belt and stand fast in the face of his oncoming horse. Endal smiled to himself from underneath his black hood. He could tell the character was a lone bandit, hoping to strike lucky.

Endal stopped his horse a few feet in front of the bandit who was dressed in loose fitting leather armour and a green cape. He could just as easily have ridden swiftly by the man but this was a sign of weakness amongst these types of men. Endal had every intention of giving the bandit his chance.

'So you're prepared to hand over your money then stranger?' the bandit sniggered.

As Endal leapt from his horse and stood to confront him the bandit seemed less cool, more alarmed, and visibly intimidated by the appearance and behaviour of his random catch.

'Hhh... hand over 'ya money!' the bandit stammered cautiously.

His sword was poised and its tip aimed directly towards Endal. The assassin stood motionlessly, his left sword arm resting limply by his side. His hand gently stroked the handle of his deadly katana blade that remained hidden inside his dark robe.

The bandit was nervous but clearly an experienced robber and warrior. He was probably a retreating rebel eager for funds. He slowly shuffled closer to the dark hooded stranger in front of him.

'Hand it over or you will feel my blade stranger!' he screeched. 'And also that horse, I will take it!'

There was no sign of a reaction from Endal who remained still and silent. The bandit looked to his side, noticing his hand resting on the tip of a sword handle. This was a sign to him that the stranger was clearly looking to defend his property.

The bandit sniggered. 'So you fancy a scrap hey?' he mocked. 'Well here I come!'

He walked towards Endal with his sword in both hands. As he closed in he swung it from his right side at Endal. The sword sped across the air aimed at Endal's neck. In this moment Endal bent low, calmly avoiding the sword as it swept over him. The bandit's side was exposed to Endal as he finished the swing of his sword move. Endal revealed his shimmering blade from out of his robe and shuffled forwards. He placed the sharp edge into the bandit's side then slid it across his torso until the tip reached his belly.

The speed and force of this move forced the bandit to spin around in shock and reflex and drop his sword to the muddy ground. Endal faced him with katana raised. The bandit stood in terrified shock and confusion as large quantities of thick, warm blood oozed out of the deep, clean incisions. The long cut opened up his entire torso within seconds and split further as the skin tore. Endal then drove his katana deeply into the man's gut and then out again. The bandit fell to his knees and then collapsed front ways onto the soil beneath the black boots of the assassin. He was dead before hitting the ground. The blood steamed in the morning air.

Endal placed his blade back inside his robe, its edge perfectly clean and blood free. The exceptional steel was stainless and blood merely dripped off from the sharp tool of war. Without any hesitation Endal remounted his horse and rode on as if no event had even taken place. The cool, mysterious figure hadn't even as much as felt a drip of sweat over the encounter. He had been in autopilot, his skills merely teased by a rapid moment.

His horse sped on as the light of day now fully embraced the wilderness around them. Dwenton beckoned and the path was beginning to lead to new surroundings. Beyond the wood were flat grassy fields and hilly pastures. The black rider would be a sight to behold amid such serene places.

Akumi walked along the flat field with a purpose. The waist high crops hindered the four assassins as they moved at Hazati's swift pace. He was in front, several feet ahead from Akumi who followed him just in front of Jobe and Harkor. The two young men were talking together about their sword fighting styles and skills. Harkor was giving Jobe advice, being the superior swordsman out of the two.

'When you swing always be prepared to back away if the strike misses,' Harkor said. 'Never let your guard down. If Endal is as good as we are told you will need to remember never to expose yourself. The key is to wait for him to strike. Catch him off guard.'

Jobe took a mental note of the advice from his friend. He looked up to the slightly older Harkor. He had helped him all through Hazati's training. The three of them had a strong bond. They had been taken in by Hazati at an early age and trained as assassins. He'd been a father to them and given them his knowledge and skills. None of them had ever known their true families. Hazati had found them alone and fending for themselves. They had come from homes destroyed by war.

Akumi watched Hazati cut through the crops with his wooden stick as she followed his path. They had been travelling for several hours and by now the midday sun beamed down onto them without lapse.

Jobe and Harkor decided to catch up with the girl and raced ahead to walk beside her.

'Akumi, Harkor has been giving me some great sword tips! I'm sure you could give a few,' Jobe playfully intrigued.

They all knew Akumi was the strongest fighter in the group. Her skills were exceptional and even Hazati knew she was significantly skilled.

'You fight well Jobe,' she said, 'but make sure you watch the enemy's sword and not the enemy.'

'Yes, I will remember that. Thank you Akumi,' he replied. 'I just wish I could be as strong as you. You are so fast! Like the wind!'

Akumi giggled, putting her hand to her mouth in modesty as Jobe pretended to be her when in a sword fight. He jumped around wildly and started to roll forwards in the grass.

'Swoosh! Akumi's speed is unmatched. She glides like the wind and can't be caught!' Jobe yelled.

Whilst his antics amused his audience Hazati looked back at them with the slightest expression of disapproval. His judgemental eyes caught Jobe's and he immediately ceased his larking and walked back alongside Akumi. The girl smiled to herself. She was very fond of Jobe and always found him great, humorous company.

Hazati knew the lands well and had already decided where the party would go to as a first port of call. Dwenton was Marmia's leading trade town and full of those with sharp eyes. Hazati believed such a town would be a likely place for Endal to head to.

It was also a town luckily near to them as they travelled westwards across the outskirts of their home dwelling of Neezo. He had contacts in Dwenton he hoped would have stories to tell of a strange person hanging around the village.

As the old man led his trusted followers amongst the wide open field of crops he noticed a series of houses up ahead. One was on fire. Dark smoke scattered up into the clear blue sky in puffs of menacing shades. The image became clearer as he walked on further towards the spectacle.

Men on horseback rode around the house encircling it as it burned down. The fiery engulfment consumed every inch of the old cottage. A smaller building stood to its side untouched by flames. Suddenly, one of the figures hurled a lit torch into the haystacks inside the small storehouse. Akumi and the others had spotted the eerie sight and rushed to Hazati's side.

'What's going on?' Jobe shrieked.

The four watched as the gang of men ran havoc around the burning buildings. From the other side of the house several of them came rushing around into view. They were holding two people. It was clear one was a woman, the other a frail, bearded man. They were thrown to the ground and surrounded by the gang. Hazati grumbled.

'This is not our business. We must pass by,' he ordered.

The men proceeded to push the old man back and forth as he stumbled to his feet. They mocked him and formed a circle around his feeble body.

'We can't just ignore this!' Jobe yelled.

Hazati continued to grumble to himself, annoyed they had stumbled into such a display. The gang of thuggish looking men were clearly pillaging this small home. They were likely retreating soldiers from the rebel factions; bitter and frustrated by their defeat and eager to cause havoc across Marmia. Suddenly, one of them, likely a leader, walked into the circle and stood beside the two terrified strangers. He pulled out a large longsword and pointed it at the neckline of the old man as he sat panting beside the woman.

'We can't let this continue!' Akumi shrieked. 'Master, let's help those people.'

Hazati was insistent. 'No Akumi, we have no time for this. It is not our business. Let us move on.'

Jobe fiercely shook his head in protest. 'We are meant to help the people of this realm and our enemy is currently directly in front of us!' he yelled.

'Master, let us stop these rebel thugs,' Harkor came in.

He seemed less emotionally concerned about what was going on but equally as eager to intervene as the others. Hazati looked to his three battle ready apprentices proudly. Regardless of his order they sensed what was right over what was logical. They wanted to help those in trouble and felt a duty to protect. These assassins had a morality about them, they were focused and intended only to target those that threatened the peace. This had been Hazati's aim and the very reason they had been trained.

'Go on then, sort this out. Get those thugs running and assist those two people,' Hazati said calmly.

There was no delay. Akumi raced off towards the burning flames and Jobe and Harkor followed closely behind. Hazati stood fast, poised against his walking stick. He was eager to watch his assassins in action. It wasn't long until a few of the retreating rebel troops spotted the three warriors running towards them. One, on horseback, yelled out:

'We've got visitors!'

This sparked a reaction from the gang of twelve men. They all turned to face Akumi's charge as did the couple cowering down beside them. The leader stood by the two civilians with his longsword still ready to prod the old man. He wore a dark red bandana and had long dark hair that flowed down his back and shoulders in straight strands.

'Deal with these glory hunters,' he smiled.

'Get them!' a second in command commanded loudly.

By now the fires were raging in full force. The heat of the flames was immense and the reflection of orange fire covered the shimmering blades of the swords the warriors clutched in readiness for a fight. Dark smoke pillared up into the sky around them as a light breeze gently swayed it forwards in the direction Akumi and the others ran from.

Akumi paused as they reached the gang head on. The rebels slowly crept forwards to greet them.

'What can we do for you then?' a largely built warrior smirked.

He held a large battleaxe in both hands and stood nearest Akumi.

'Do not harm these people,' Akumi pointed at the trembling couple sat beside the leader's blade.

'Friends of yours?' the axe man asked.

'They are defenceless and you have already done enough,' Akumi continued.

Her tone was serious and forceful. Her will to be heard seemed to shock the masculine soldiers she conversed with.

'My my,' the leader bellowed, 'what a cute little thing you are. If you like you can watch as we slit their throats. I will then bring you back to my tent!'

There was loud laughter followed by a volley of sexual comments aimed at the young, attractive assassin. Jobe responded:

'Back away and leave these people alone or we will attack you!'

The bandana clad man in command of the party sniggered. 'Attack us, feel free,' he smiled.

Jobe looked to Akumi and then Harkor. The three were ready to engage; knowing that if they didn't the soldiers would kill the innocent couple and then attack them for threatening them. There was no choice but to fight.

Akumi was first to jump into action. Her sharp katana glided into the air as she raced towards the axe man. He didn't flinch and walked towards the speeding girl. He swung his axe from his side towards her waist. She leapt into the air, vaulting over the incoming steel chunk, and slid her sword across his chest and shoulder in one flawless move. The assassin landed on her feet behind him as the large man dropped to his knees, completely stunned and about to die. Jobe and Harkor moved forwards side by side as several soldier came at them. Swords clashed and the sound of steel blades striking each other rung out over the noise of burning wood and hay.

Each strike from a soldier's sword was blocked and deflected effortlessly by the two sword fighters. Harkor held his weapon with one hand, the other arm resting by his side. He looked like a fencer and seemed entirely unchallenged by the swarm of attackers swinging at him. He blocked a strike with his sword and in a flash flicked his blade past the soldier's outstretched arm and drove it into his gut.

Jobe sidestepped a swing and cut another rebel across the waist.

Their strikes were deep and perfectly aimed. Deadly and precise, the blades penetrated the loose leather armour of the soldiers and killed them in seconds.

Akumi didn't hesitate after defeating the axe wielder and pressed ahead, now alongside the flaming farmhouse. A man tried to stab her, poking his sword at her body. She struck his blade from his hands and spun on her feet, swiping her clean katana across his gullet. Another raised his sword, about to swing it down at her. She moved close to him, her body pressed against his, and in a hasty exhibit staked him in the heart with her light killing blade. He fell beside her lifelessly as two more raced directly towards her. Their war cry was wild and feral, driven by adrenaline and a will to kill.

The assassin bent low, her body arched, and drove her sword across the thighs of both soldiers as they ran into the tip. The pain and shock of the deep cuts caused both men to drop their swords and yelp in agony. Akumi rose up and pierced the torso of the one to her left side whilst kicking the other to the ground. She pulled her sword from the body of her victim and turned it towards the man to her right, now on the ground after her high well executed kick. She walked towards him with blade poised, looking down at him with fiery eyes.

'No please! Don't!' the soldier panicked.

Akumi hesitated. She was about to stab him in the neck, finishing him, but his fearful voice didn't go unheard as her compassionate side was appealed to.

'Don't do it,' he stammered.

'Stay down,' Akumi firmly demanded.

She walked past the fallen soldier without striking. Her mercy seemed to amuse the leader as he watched whilst standing by the fearful couple.

Jobe placed his well timed strike into another soldier that momentarily stood facing him. The sword dug into his lungs and punctured his ribcage. Another body struck the grass. Harkor's swift, simple stance and style looked to intimidate the two thuggish rebels that had stood confronting him. He smiled as they hesitated to attack him. He then walked forwards towards them. They desperately launched their strikes.

The swordsman blocked the first and his blade cut the attacking sword in half. He then placed it into the soldier's neck, cleanly cutting it and killing another. The other attacker tried to drive his sword directly into Harkor's chest. The assassin effortlessly dodged the blade by pouncing to its side. He studied the man as he brought his attacking arm back into a stance and then swiftly marched frontwards with his sword cutting into the rebel's chest side-on in a bladed clothesline. He then swirled it around him and pressed it into the small of the man's back. Blood spattered out of the soldier's mouth and he fell down dead.

Jobe had no problem defeating the last remaining soldier besides their leader. Their swords clashed and the two parried for a brief few seconds until the assassin slid his sword across the thug's belly. He stood surrounded by bloody bodies and looked to Harkor who had been watching him floor the last of the soldiers.

Akumi didn't attack the leader. She was waiting for him to make a move, hoping he would run away with his tail between his legs.

'Get away from them,' she ordered.

The long haired soldier was angry. 'You little bitch!' he snapped.

He withdrew his longsword from its position aimed at the old man's neck and closed in on Akumi.

His sword struck hers as he proceeded to bombard her with blows. Akumi deflected each strike and bent low to avoid a swing aimed at her head. The man continued to attack. His strength and skill was far greater than the other defeated soldiers and Akumi could sense he was a hardened swordsman. His solid, sturdy sword pounded against Akumi's katana as she blocked strike after strike. Jobe and Harkor watched from beside the couple they'd rescued.

Akumi frustrated the soldier as strike after strike failed to make contact with her body. He yelled out in rage and sped up his volley of attack. In a sudden instance of opportunity the trained and honed assassin found a moment to strike. She deflected his sword and struck his sword arm to one side. She spun around so her back faced him and plunged her blade into his stomach as she pushed it into him from beside her waist. Her eyes were lit up by the dazzling fire. She remained on one knee, motionless as the impaled soldier remained standing. He dropped his sword and bent forwards limply and increasingly lifeless. Akumi pulled the blade from his body and edged away. With that the leader collapsed front ways into the grass. He was still alive, murmuring in agony.

Hazati appeared from nowhere, slightly grumpy. He had seen the entire fight and had slowly started to walk towards the scene from his observation point in the fields. Akumi wiped her sword and put it back in its sheath about her back. She looked down at the leader who panted in shock and agony. She started to feel a sense of guilt and an urge to help him.

Hazati could sense her emotions creep in as she stood staring. He suddenly brought out his ancient steel from beneath his tattered robe and plunged it into the man's back, killing him instantly. Akumi gulped in shock and looked to her master for explanation.

'You are an assassin Akumi,' he howled angrily. 'Kill and show no mercy!'

He then walked over to the soldier she'd let live. He was sitting upright in the grass clinging to his cleanly cut thighs.

'Kill!' he repeated.

Without warning he stabbed the man in the back as he sat half conscious in shock. The sword sank into him like a knife through butter and the old man brought it back up and into his robe. Akumi was speechless. She was shocked by her master's sudden merciless edge and ruthless direction. It had been the first time she'd seen him kill in this manner.

'They were defeated! They... they,' she stumbled her words in disbelief.

'Akumi, you are a killer! These men were an enemy. Do not falter at any stage of a fight. If they fall and remain alive, kill them! If they plead for mercy ignore them! This is the way you must be, otherwise Endal will rip you apart where you stand!' Hazati yelled.

It was clear he was annoyed and troubled by her emotional responses to what had happened. He'd known for years she was exceptional but also knew she didn't possess the cold mind an assassin needed and now feared she wasn't truly ready.

Jobe and Harkor remained silent. They understood Hazati's lesson to Akumi and, although surprised by his actions, had no desire to get involved.

'If you are to even as much as stand a chance against Endal you must drop all emotion!' Hazati went on.

Akumi knew not to invoke more temper in her beloved master and bowed in acknowledgement of his instruction. As the assassins stood over the bodies the couple they'd saved got to their feet in relief and intrigue.

'Thank you strangers, thank you for saving us,' the old man said.

Hazati smiled and gave the bearded fellow a slight bow.

'We must go,' he announced.

He turned and walked back into the crop fields, the smouldering ruins of a cottage and dead bodies behind him. His assassins looked to one another and snapped out of a slight trance they'd been in during this sorry spectacle of bloodshed. Akumi smiled at the couple and then they followed the master on into the field. They left behind two baffled strangers, deeply thankful for the help they'd received from mysterious travellers.

CHAPTER VII

A BRIEF STAY IN STINTARG

The darkly lit room would have to do. Golandin's life seemed to somehow revolve around these dim spaces. Not that there was much to offer outside in the cosy western town of Stintarg. Beyond this ramshackle inn there were only lifeless narrow streets surrounded by decaying waterside property. The town rested beside a large lake on the western edges of Marmia and the beginnings of other lands. A small sandy bay separated sea from land and Golandin's window view allowed him to behold the wondrous vista of tiny waves rolling across the sizeable pond.

He and Arthir had reached Stintarg two days ago. Golandin had decided to rest here until he was prepared to venture further west. Arthir hadn't been so casual and had moved on and bid farewell to his friend; he intended to get home as soon as possible and hadn't felt any urge or reason to stay in Stintarg. Golandin was now on his own amongst busy waterside fishermen and sailors. He felt safe.

His mind was focused on Endal and what the assassin was currently up to. He craved some up to date report yet knew all he could do was wait for his return within the week. Since two days were now up since the meeting he imagined Endal would be near Brimma and Tamus Tower, working out a way to breach through the Emperor's mighty defences and reach him. As his thoughts dwelt on the possibilities of what may happen and what he would do in Endal's boots he felt a sudden urge to take a walk around the town and perhaps buy a small rowing boat to take onto the sea. It was now mid afternoon and there was plenty of golden sunlight left to keep the scenery visible.

Golandin didn't delay and left his bare and simplistic room for the tiny staircase down. There was no one around this lifeless local stop for passing travellers desiring rooms to reside in. Only a feeble elderly gentleman remained indoors, resting by a reception desk and reading a book. Golandin passed him by and walked through the protesting door that chafed across the stone ground of the entranceway. Outside, a flat street turned to his left and right. He went left in the direction of the sand and plodded down the pathway.

As the warrior moved towards the water of the lake he realised he could hear the faint sound of horses racing along dry mud. The noise of the fast movement got louder. Golandin turned and looked up the street in intrigue.

The bearded man was struck with the sight of an army of armoured soldiers advancing in disciplined ranks on horseback. The large party were coming into the village and heading down the street right at him. He stood to one side, leaning against the wall of a house, waiting for them to pass by. They stopped before reaching him and the lead horses halted just outside the door to the inn Golandin had come out from. He watched as the soldiers leapt from their horses and grouped up near a largely built man.

'Search every house, search every boat!' the large man bellowed.

'Yes, General,' came a reply from one.

Golandin instantly disliked the look of this. He imagined the Tamus troops were hunting around for retreating rebels, like him. It was at this point he remembered his face was known to Tamus and on top of this he was still clad in worn armour and carrying his sword. He turned around and continued to walk towards the tips of the lake, hoping he could slip away out of the town as they searched.

The soldiers split away from the general and had begun to race into buildings all over the street. Several stormed into the inn to the surprise of the old man sitting by the desk.

'May I help?' he asked in a tired tone.

'We are searching for someone, a traveller. Who is staying in this inn?' a soldier asked.

'Oh, well just one. He left here only two minutes ago,' the old man replied.

With that the soldiers ran back out into the street.

'General, the innkeeper reports someone left here a few minutes ago,' one yelled.

The general smiled whilst he stood in the middle of the street overlooking his men. His eyes were fixed on a single figure walking down the pathway towards the edges of the calm waters and out of the town. The general noticed his attire and appearance. It was only when the figure looked back at him momentarily that he also noticed the rough beard.

'That's him,' he said to himself. 'There's our man! It is he who just left the inn. Stop him!' The general was certain.

The troops around the general ran after the target. The general walked on following slowly. Golandin didn't immediately realise they were coming towards him. He resumed his pace and stared out across the blue lagoon. He then suddenly heard one yell out to him to stop. He turned and realised his predicament. There was little he could do. In front of him was only water. Behind him was an army of soldiers. To his side were walls and locked doorways. He turned to face his pursuers. They were now right by him with weapons poised.

'What is your name old man?' one asked. Golandin didn't supply an answer.

'His name is Golandin, isn't it? Captain Golandin to be precise, although I don't have much respect for rebel ranks!' the general announced whilst coming forwards from behind his men.

Golandin laughed. He could now recognise the face of his old enemy. General Dorwor had always been around. The two men had been a part of the war since the early days.

'What is it that you want Dorwor? The war is over and I am heading home, away from these parts. I am resting here in this village and will be gone tomorrow,' the former captain explained.

Dorwor stood beside his soldiers as they faced Golandin.

'If it were only so simple Golandin. Yes, the war is over but clearly for some the battle continues. For you it seems the war has become personal, wouldn't you say?' Dorwor asked.

Golandin didn't quite cotton on to the general's wit.

'I am tired of fighting, as must you be. For me the war is over,' he answered.

'Yet you go out of your way to hire an assassin to kill Tamus? It can't have been cheap,' smiled Dorwor.

Golandin swallowed hard. Out of nowhere his hope diminished and he felt as exposed as the lake behind him. How had his secret plan been so quickly discovered? He lost all reason and turned to run. The soldiers swiftly ran forwards and encircled him before he'd had a chance to gain any ground.

'Unfortunately for you that friar you had dealings with is very good friends with a contact of mine, a contact whom sides with Tamus!' Dorwor laughed.

Golandin knew he'd slipped up. He'd been sloppy and realised his false hopes were in reality a shield. Why had he even as much as remotely believed his plan would have worked? He felt foolish and ready to surrender.

'I trust the assassin failed then?' he asked.

'He will do, but has of yet not been traced,' Dorwor said smugly.

Although this meant there was still at least some hope Endal would complete the contract, Golandin felt no faith in him and simply felt regret for even plotting such an action in the first place.

'You are under arrest for plotting and conspiring against the Emperor. Surrender your sword and do not resist,' the general ordered.

There was little Golandin could do unless he felt ready and able to defeat the army that now surrounded him. He had no wish to die so complied. He dropped his steel to the ground beside his feet and stood limply as two soldiers clutched him from either side.

'Good,' commented Dorwor, 'now let us ride.'

Within the hour the rebel prisoner had been ridden to an isolated prison north-east of Stintarg. Golandin had been thrown in a cell and left to dwell on his fate. Before long two guardsmen entered into the damp chamber. Dorwor was close behind them.

There was very little light in the dark room. Golandin's life surely did revolve around such shady places. He sat beside the two guards and faced General Dorwor who studied his eyes and placed his crossed arms on the table.

'So start talking Golandin. Who told you about Endal? Is his contract to kill Tamus? Who else is in on this?' Dorwor grumbled.

'I cannot deny I was at the Abbey. I cannot deny I spoke with Endal. Yes, I put it to him, to kill Tamus!' Golandin croaked. 'It was an act of desperation. A last move on my part. I wasn't prepared to walk into the night Dorwor. It was a chance I took and now regret.'

Dorwor nodded to himself. 'Who told you about Endal?' he asked.

'It was a rumour I acted upon. I heard word of a lethal killer roaming the lands, that was all. It turned out what I heard was true and to my shock the assassin accepted the contract.'

'How much did you pay him?'

'He didn't take money. He insisted he would find me once killing Tamus to receive payment.'

Dorwor appeared fascinated by this and looked to a fellow ranking soldier that stood near him listening to the prisoner.

'That at least explains the money we took from you! He won't have much luck finding you now will he? Unless he comes willingly into this prison,' Dorwor laughed loudly.

'Where is Arthir? We know he was with you at the Abbey,' Dorwor pressed on.

Golandin didn't seem willing to say much. 'We went our separate ways once leaving the Abbey.'

'Where is he going?' the general probed.

'I have no idea!' Golandin snapped.

Dorwor got up and gazed down at Golandin as he leant against the table. 'I want names rebel! Who told you about Endal? It wasn't just a rumour... someone else is in on this! And where does Arthir call home? That is where we will find him,' he smirked.

'Shouldn't you be busy looking out for Endal? I've said all I will say Dorwor,' Golandin responded.

'I suggest you talk. If you don't I will make sure you never leave this place... the rest of your life will be in this or some other dark, grim hell hole. However, if you give me names I might consider all this a case of foolish error and let an old war enemy go back to wherever he calls home...'

Dorwor's proposition surprised Golandin. He sat up, knowing an offer when he heard it. His mind didn't recognise loyalty. When a good offer was put to him he never turned it down until weighing it up.

'Golandin look,' Dorwor said, 'I know you didn't have the money to pay Endal for this. The picture we've been given of him suggests he only thinks big. By big, and considering we are talking about killing the Emperor here, I mean big money! Real big money! Who is putting the money up for this? Who gave you that gold sack?'

'Why go after Arthir if you are so willing to just let me go if I supply this information?' Golandin sharply asked.

'None of you will go unpunished. This will not be allowed. What I am saying is if you supply this information your punishment will perhaps not be as harsh as to spend the rest of your life in some cold, rat infested dungeon!' said Dorwor.

Golandin was silent for some moments. He was thinking and weighing up his position. He suddenly sprung up.

'The landlord of The Lamb Inn in Dolsbury has a sharp ear for all sorts of things. He also has a lot of money. I also remember hearing Arthir comes from Camdor, further west.'

The evil deed was done. He had betrayed his fellow plotters for a promise of a heavily reduced punishment. He knew Dorwor was a man of his word. He also knew both men he had named would have done exactly the same thing if they were in his situation. He felt no guilt. They had all been prepared for the plan to fall foul.

General Dorwor looked to his close party of fellow soldiers and advisors. They hung around the cell in pockets. Golandin's words sparked a collective reaction. Once Dorwor nodded nothing else needed to be said. The Tamus masses were on the move again, some headed for Dolsbury to their north, others for Camdor in the west.

'We will speak again Golandin,' Dorwor concluded. 'For now enjoy this cell. We will let you know how your assassin does but I wouldn't keep those hopes up if I were you!'

Golandin merely quietly whinged to himself and then replied: 'He has a chance... I've seen him,' he smiled.

Endal's allure still captivated his memory and the thought ignited distant hope in the old warrior. Endal was now all he had left to rely on. He prayed the dark assassin would be able to pull it off.

'Oh don't be so sure,' smiled Dorwor. 'We have our plans too. Endal will run into a few treats, mark my words... if he ever even reveals himself again that is! If he's smart he'd have dropped this contract by now, that's for sure.'

With that the general marched out of the cell with his party of soldiers and advisors close behind. The iron door slammed shut, leaving the captured former captain alone and in the dark.

CHAPTER VIII

THE TRAVELLING TRADER

The view of the dark stranger riding into the outskirts of Dwenton appeared to attract much attention from the workers spread across the fenced off fields. His dark horse trotted up the flat road towards a stable just outside the gateway to this bustling trade town. Endal moved along without as much as glimpsing at any of them. People were so captivated by the man that they stood in amazement facing him and momentarily paused their labouring. An old man leant on his rake and stood by the roadside as Endal passed him. He wasn't impressed by the arrival of his type and grumbled in protest as the black horse brushed by.

The hooded assassin continued on up the path until the stables were reached. A single small barn with adjacent field represented the location. Several horses already wondered around the clearing and as Endal halted just outside the house an old woman crept out of a tiny wooden door. She took an intrigued look at his horse and gazed at the figure as he pounced off the animal.

'It'll be one silver for the day sir,' she moaned.

Endal strolled over to her and handed her the money without hesitation. He had already got it prepared, knowing the woman's price. She took hold of his coin and backed away from him as she glimpsed into the void of darkness from within his drooping hood. She sensed evil and fearfully edged away back into her hut.

Endal then turned and watched as a young boy grabbed his black horse by the reigns and tried to lead him into the stable yard. The horse would not budge.

'Go Harwind,' Endal announced.

With that the horse ceased to resist and followed the amazed boy into the field. Endal started to walk towards the gate that sectioned off the inner part of the town. It was a sturdy entrance guarded by a couple of soldiers standing to either side of the solid structure. Around it were high stone walls and watchtowers. This was an important dwelling for Marmia.

The hooded man went straight up to the door and removed his hood as a guardsman came out of a shed to study him.

'What is your business in Dwenton traveller?' he asked.

'Trade,' he whispered. 'I seek bargains. I am merely a travelling trader.'

The cautious guard studied the shaggy face of the stranger. His dark stubble and long black hair contrasted with his military short cut and cleanly shaved skin.

'On 'ya way then,' he said.

He nodded slightly at another soldier who then started to turn a wheel to his side. The gateway rose and the entrance opened up. Endal stood until the space was enough for his body to pass under and immediately walked through once the moment came.

He was struck with the manic mania of the bustling market town. His darkly clothed body suddenly merged in with large busy crowds of people standing around merchant stalls that started within feet of the gateway. Endal walked along and studied his surroundings. Countless people barged by going in all directions. There was a loud continuous sound of haggling, conversation, and activity. Sellers stood behind the constant line of market stalls yelling out at passers by and promoting their products.

Endal spotted everything from wine to steel cutlasses. Suddenly, a large wheeled trailer rammed its way down the road, forcing the hordes of shoppers to edge to one side of it. A fat man sat on top yelling at people to move as it sped down the path. Endal glided to its side and stumbled across a sign to an inn. He intended to stay the night here and decided to go inside. It was now late afternoon and the dim clouds were beginning to darken as the sky slowly turned black with night. He had been on the road for many hours and was in need of some rest.

The interior was as alive and loud as the outside as droves of drunken men propped by the bar and countless tables around the ground floor. Endal noticed to the end of the room a man at a separate desk to the bar. He walked over to him.

'I seek a room for the night,' he said to the man.

'All full traveller,' he answered. 'You won't find any rooms in Dwenton at this time of day.'

Endal didn't respond and turned to walk out of the pub. As the dark and sinister looking man passed beside the wild, jostling crowds at the bar his appearance suddenly seemed to spark some attention from the local tradesmen and farm workers. One, obviously waiting for the moment, came out from the crowds and confronted Endal as he stood in his way in front of the door.

'Why don't you join in the fun and have a drink on me,' the drunk yelled. 'Our pub not good enough for the likes of you?'

His voice was croaky and the broad man staggered on his feet. He put his half empty mug of ale up to Endal's mouth forcefully.

'Have a drink!' he ordered.

Regardless of the man's intentions Endal only ever responded one way to any intrusion of his personal circle. He raised his left arm up and knocked the mug of beer away from the drunk's grip. It flew across the room and struck a wall. Endal then jabbed the man in his belly with such force he bent double. Endal's knee struck him in the forehead as he bent down and took him off his feet. The sturdy guy fell back and then to Endal's side. His body went through a wooden table and the unconscious drunk rested limply amongst the broken wood.

There was a swift reaction to the stranger's aggression. Several of the drunkard's crowd came forwards to confront Endal. There was a wild bloodlust in the air, these men were out to hurt someone and Endal was the target.

He flicked out his shimmering katana from his black robe and stepped towards them as they got closer. The sight of his steel shocked these simple townsfolk and they backed away in fright. With that the assassin put it back in his robe and walked out of the tavern and back into the flowing crowds of the street. He was soon lost in the sea of people and forgotten about by the intoxicated males.

Endal walked along the road until the crowds dwindled and the path led off into other directions. He noticed a large church up ahead. Its tower was the tallest point of Dwenton and a majestic structure. He walked along a narrow track amongst residential houses until he reached the church doors. They were unlocked and he went inside. The church was large and his footsteps echoed around the open space of the main chamber. There was no one around. An altar at the far end and wooden stools to his sides made up the decor. He sat down and rested himself on one of the benches. This would have to do. The assassin stretched out and lay down. He was more than used to sleeping on solid surfaces and the warmth of the building was all that was important. He calmly let himself relax and remained alone and undisturbed for several hours.

Little did the sleeping warrior know that around him a panic and growing whirlwind of concern and precaution was kicking into place. Word of the assassin had spread by now and Tamus soldiers were rushing into all the towns. Dwenton had been reached and the garrison informed of the hottest news in Marmia. All around security was being tightened and searches conducted. As the nightly hours went by the incoming wave of guardsmen overcame Dwenton. General Dorwor's masses were converging on the lands and informing the inhabitants of whom needed to be found.

Beyond the walls of Dwenton another distinct party were also gaining on the town, eager to reach it before the morning.

Hazati halted. His lead horse stood fast on the road. Akumi and the others stopped a few feet behind wondering what had sparked the attention of their master.

'What is it?' Akumi asked.

'A body on the road ahead,' the old man moaned. 'Let us continue on to see it.'

'A body?' Jobe seemed concerned.

The four horses trotted up the muddy track until they stumbled into the lifeless corpse stretched out in the middle of the path. Hazati climbed off his brown mare and bent down beside the body to investigate. The other assassins were swift to follow his lead and stood over him in interest. Hazati clutched the caped body and turned it over to rest front ways. It lay in a pool of dark and dried up blood, which stuck to the mud and stained clothing. The master studied the gashes.

'From his wounds this man was killed by a sword. He was cut cleanly and deeply. This was the work of a skilled swordsman,' he commented.

'It's flawless, straight and complete,' Harkor added.

'Yes it is,' said Hazati as he stood back up.

Akumi looked into his eyes attentively. 'Endal would have come from this direction assuming he aimed to reach Dwenton from the Abbey,' she said. The old man nodded.

'This was a bandit, a mugger,' Jobe said. 'I bet he tried to mug Endal!'

'We cannot say for sure what happened but from the wound it is clear this man was killed by a skilled blade. He has only been dead a day at most too,' said Hazati.

The path they were on was the main route to Dwenton from the south and west. They had joined it further south as it was the swiftest way to the trade town.

'We should press on and reach Dwenton. If this was the work of our target it means we are on his tail. He may still be in the town,' said Hazati.

'Lucky we got these horses from that stables back along the track hey!' Jobe smirked.

The party got back on their mounts and followed the master's lead as he darted onwards along the rough track. Jobe seemed eager to hear Akumi's opinion.

'Do you think that could have been his doing?' he asked her.

'There aren't many who can kill so cleanly with a blade in these parts. It would seem likely considering he probably would have come this way,' she said.

Jobe was excited. 'We are close to confronting him! I bet he's in Dwenton!'

Akumi smiled politely at her friend's excitement. She was more focused, her mind resting on her training and skill and the importance of stopping the man they pursued. Harkor was just as alert and followed his pals silently.

The track meandered on through challenging terrain and frustrating bends for the horses. It snaked around foliage and then hit flat pastures. It crossed a tiny river and led around fields of red roses. However, this varied landscape wasn't visible to the riders during this nightly hour they travelled. The starry sky and white moonlight was all they went by. Their astute and trained eyes were honed and used to seeing in the dark and this enabled them to press on regardless of the lack of helpful visible light.

CHAPTER IX

SHOWDOWN IN TANTRIA

Endal was awakened by a loud thud. It had come from outside the holy building he rested in. He sat up on the solid low bench and looked around the church. It was still creepily silent and eerily lifeless. He had been asleep for several hours and felt refreshed after his long rest. He could tell by the light seeping in through the tinted windows that it was early morning. The sun was beginning to rise but there was still the dark and moody atmosphere of early morning. The assassin got up from the bench and stretched his arms above his head. He then turned his neck to the left and right and snapped himself into an alert state. He had no intention of spending anymore time in this town and his thoughts turned to resuming his journey to the capital city of Brimma where he was confident Tamus would be.

The thud from outside repeated itself as Endal walked down the aisle of the old building towards the exit. Once he passed through the wooden doors and looked around the surroundings of the church he realised what the noise was. Several people were erecting a ramshackle tower across the clearing beyond the church grounds. They seemed to be struggling with the heavy piles of material and the task appeared to be getting the better of them. Endal proceeded to walk away from the church back in the direction of the main gate out of the town and the stables he had left his horse.

There was a misty haze over the town that reduced visibility. The fog seemed to sweep across the lands, with a dark overcast sky above. There was also a light breeze that whistled around the rooftops and set a mysterious mood. Endal was at one with this setting. With his dark hood now over his head the black figure crept down the main street and appeared from amongst the fog to those that were coming in the other direction. Endal's focus was on his surroundings and it didn't take him long to realise that several soldiers were ahead near the gate and standing in the street. They appeared alarmed and fascinated by the dark figure as he walked closer towards them and became more visible now he had passed the grey haze. Endal analysed them and their behaviour. It was clear they seemed cautious of him but as the trained assassin got nearer he realised they were not about to let him pass unchallenged. The group of six armoured troops were ready to pull out their swords and formed a rough line in the path. Suddenly, one ran off back towards the gate whilst the others stared carefully at the stranger. He showed no signs of holding back and walked straight up to the line of men and halted before them. He noticed the soldier who had ran off excitedly speak to an even larger group of warriors near the gate and point in his direction. They all started to head towards him.

'What's your business here?' one asked, stepping closer from the line.

'I am leaving and have been looking for bargains,' Endal replied. 'I didn't find any.'

Another soldier appeared from a house to the side of the road beside the line of troops. He was half dressed, like he'd just got up and noticed the commotion. His ginger hair was curly and ungroomed and his pale skin worn with age.

'Arrest this man, he's going nowhere,' he ordered.

The soldiers were swift to follow the command. They edged in on Endal and the nearest spoke:

'Surrender any weapons and come with us sir. We are hunting for an enemy of Tamus and you have raised our suspicions. We will need to question you.'

Endal responded by revealing his light katana and holding it in a stance, showing no signs of withdrawing it. The soldiers responded by revealing their swords in unison.

'Drop your sword or we will strike you down!' the ginger haired officer yelled.

Endal acted pre-emptively and swung his blade at the nearest Tamus soldier. The sharp edge sliced along the exposed belly of the man, whose armour only partially covered his chest. He yelped in shock. One stepped forwards and thrust his sword at Endal's chest. The hooded assassin deflected the strike and struck the blade from the man's hand. He then poked his steel directly into the guard's neck. He fell in a frenzy of gushing blood. The

troop whose belly had been sliced was now on his knees before
Endal, clutching his wound and yelling in pain. The other troops
stood around; unsure what to do. As a sign of strength and will
Endal raised his blade and looked around at the troops
surrounding him. By now a larger group had reached the fight
from the gate and stood closer to their ginger leader. Endal didn't
seem intimidated by the large numbers that now confronted him.
He looked down to the man on his knees and suddenly swung his
sword across in an arc and cleanly cut the soldier's head from his
body. The head spun in mid-air and landed near the body of the
other victim he'd slain. The headless corpse limply collapsed into
the dirt beside him.

This aggressive and cruel action sparked collective rage
amongst the soldiers. In a frenzied charge they came racing at
Endal. As they closed in his blade flawlessly glided around
making contact with exposed parts of their bodies. Before they
could place a strike they'd been struck with a deadly deep
incision. Endal's dark figure danced around with immense speed,
dodging swings and deflecting any sword that came at him. One
soldier came forwards with a large steel shield. He hid behind it
whilst closing in. Endal pounced to the ground and rolled
forwards, now beside the soldier. He skimmed his sharp blade
through his thigh, separating leg from body. The man fell flat on
his face in shock and pain as blood oozed from the slashed limb.

Endal followed on by charging into the body of troops around
him, who now backed away in fear and confusion at the hooded
killer that confronted them. His steel hacked at them with
terrifying speed and flawless precision. One after the other they
fell dead or fatally wounded. The road was becoming littered
with pools of blood and hideously crippled bodies.

The seemingly unbeatable swordsman proved too much of an
adversary for the large group of highly trained and armed Tamus
troops. They were now falling at his assault and backing away up
the road closer and closer to the closed gate. None dared attack
Endal, now merely desperately defending against his lightning
strikes. It proved impossible to stop them and with each soldier
Endal targeted a body fell to the ground. Their armour made no
difference. His blade penetrated it thanks to his strength and its
sharpness. He also seemed totally aware of where the chainmail
and steel plates were most weak and where they didn't protect.

There was nothing anyone could now do. They'd erupted the mythical assassin's fullest might. The ginger lead troop had backed away with his men but now found himself leaning against the gate. He was close to yelling to the troops beyond the walls to open it up but knew this would make little difference now. It would take minutes for it to rise, minutes he didn't have. He watched as Endal finished off the last few soldiers that stood before him. One launched a wild strike at him, sword first in a charge. Endal strafed to avoid it and slid his sharp edge across the man's head, skimming the top of his skull and disabling his brain. The body continued to run forwards and collapsed into a pile behind the assassin.

'What are you?' the ginger haired man yelled.

Endal walked towards him. The soldier suddenly revealed a small knife from his belt and hurled it at him. It was a good and accurate throw. The knife came racing at the assassin but was deflected and cut in two by his sword. He advanced on his last remaining opponent and thrust his blood clenched steel deeply into his stomach, bowing slightly forwards to angle it effectively. The blade passed the man's body and penetrated the wood of the large door of Dwenton. It impaled him against the gate and his lifeless body bent forwards.

Endal pulled his weapon out of the body and let it slide down the side of the large doorway and rest upright on the ground. Endal clutched the body's cloak and wiped the edges of his katana clean of blood. He looked around and smugly put his blade back into his robe. With that he noticed a wooden wheel to the side of the gate. It could be opened from either side. He walked over to it and proceeded to turn it until the exit started to rise, eventually forming a gap large enough for him to creep out of. His dark outline sneaked out of the entrance to the fright of the two guards that were still manning the outside of the gate. They were the same two that had initially let him enter.

'Oh God!' one yelled in shock at the revealed sight of the massacre.

They had been aware of the fighting beyond the gate but had been ordered to keep it closed and man the outside.

One poked his large halberd at Endal. He sidestepped to avoid it and grabbed the soldier by the collar. His arms locked around the guard's head and snapped the man's neck cleanly. The other raced at him only to be met with a high kick. Endal's boot struck him in the face and sent him to the ground. He tried to get to his feet but received a volley of punches from Endal's fists as he rolled around to get up. He grabbed his sword from his waist belt and tried to raise it in defence. Endal clutched the handle and the two struggled for control of the blade. Endal proved the stronger and swiftly turned it around on him. He then pressed it into the guard's chest until there was no longer any resistance. The dark assassin stood up straight and stepped away from the warm bodies. The stables were only a few feet ahead and he could already make out his black horse eating grass in the misty field beyond.

Hazati was first to spot the black rider race from the road out of Dwenton. The figure zoomed westward along a path continuing on past the turning into the town. They then turned north.

Hazati halted in alarm. 'That's him!' he yelled out.

His assassins raced close to his side and studied the lone rider venture off up the trail. It was surrounded by tall trees on either side and his outline was soon lost in the fog. He had headed back into Tantria forest. The vast woodland ensnared the northern road for many miles.

'That was him? That was Endal?' Jobe asked frantically.

'Yes, get ready,' Hazati seemed nervous. 'I can tell that was him, I just sensed it.'

'Well let us give chase!' Harkor said.

'We need to be very careful,' the old man answered. 'Don't underestimate this target. Regardless of your skills you must fear him.'

Akumi was silent, now listening attentively to the reasoning of her master.

'We will follow him but at a distance, for now...' Hazati paused.

'First, let us check the Dwenton gateway. Tamus troops should be around here by now and I want to check for them.'

'Yes master,' Jobe replied.

The four raced on and turned at the crossroads to head for the gate. As soon as they turned it was clear the gate was half open and two bodies were lying beside the walls. The nearer they got the clearer it became: beyond the gate were more bodies, many more.

'This is insane!' Jobe commented, having now reached the large door.

The four leapt from their horses and peeked into the town. By now the morning light was strengthening and groups of towns-folk were appearing and running to the scene of the massacre. A few guardsmen were alive, mostly in agony, and were being aided by the gathering crowds.

'We've seen enough,' said Hazati. 'Let this stick in your minds and remind you of the strength of our enemy.'

'He did this? On his own? There are at least thirty bodies here! How can one man defeat thirty soldiers like this!' Jobe shrieked.

'Through skill and ability you don't have Jobe. This is our enemy,' Hazati warned. 'Let us move on.'

Akumi studied the wounds to the bodies nearest the gateway. The image of so many fallen troops seemed to ignite something in her. She was beginning to realise how much of a task this was going to be. However, she was deeply confident of her skill and didn't show any signs of hesitation. Harkor and Jobe appeared cautious and looked to her as Hazati turned to get back on his horse.

'This is crazy... Endal must be some kind of demon to do this!' Jobe said to the girl.

'Which is why we must defeat him,' the girl responded. Harkor nodded to himself.

The party remounted and rode back along the road before turning north to go forth up the trail Endal had raced off from. There was now no holding back as Hazati led them full speed up the pathway surrounded by dense foliage and cascaded by a depressing rolling vapour. It looked almost like smoke, flowing around the air and rising up into the tree line.

'We must keep a track of him and attack when he rests,' Hazati commanded whilst riding ahead. 'This road leads straight to Brimma and won't reach there for hours. He will need to rest at least once and this is when we strike. We will pursue him and hit him when he has his guard down.'

'It makes sense, killing him in his sleep so to speak,' Harkor commented. 'It will be swifter than fighting him that's for sure.'

As the assassins rode on in a swift pace along the track the conversation continued loudly as they shouted over the sound of rushing hooves.

'There are four of us and one of him,' Jobe spoke. 'We also have Akumi! Why don't we just tackle him head on once we catch him?'

'Because of the fact he is dangerous, even for us,' Hazati grumbled. 'We must go about this carefully Jobe.'

Jobe was eager to prove himself and his adrenaline was rushing now he felt they were getting closer to a confrontation with the target. Harkor and Akumi were less forward and although just as pumped for a fight able to maintain a disciplined frame of mind before their master.

The pursuit went on for the whole morning. By the time midday had come around they had followed the black rider through the tiny trail for a couple of miles. It had passed over a steep hill and wound through a small marshland. By now they had the lone assassin in sight several hundred feet ahead. As the morning fog had slowly cleared his dark figure became more visible.

Hazati made sure they didn't get any closer. Endal's pace seemed slighter slower than theirs had been and so Hazati had slowed them down accordingly. The old man knew that in reality the black horse of Endal's could outrun any other in these lands but the rider had simply decided to adopt this slower speed than what would otherwise be flat out.

They raced on with him occasionally in view and often obscured by twists in the road, which meant bushes and trees concealed him. It was a carefully calculated distance that Hazati maintained. He knew that there was a good chance Endal would spot them but they could merely ride on if he did and act like they were simply travelling by.

More hours of the day crept by as the chase continued. Endal hadn't stopped once so neither had they. Their horses were being pushed to the limit as the pace refused to falter. It wasn't until late afternoon when the road struck a rich section of pine forest that the lone rider stopped his horse.

The muddy path became surrounded by knee high grass and dead dry leaves. The air was cold and with each breath the warriors took distinctly observable puffs of vapour left their throats. Up ahead were tall pine trees scattering out over a flat clearing beyond the roadside. The sparser woodland stretched out way beyond the path. Endal turned his horse to go off the track and slowly moved into the woods. The ground was covered in moist fallen pine needles. Hazati paused and gave a hand signal to his assassins to halt and pay attention.

Endal was just about in view and the old man's eyes homed in on him from in between the gaps in foliage. He appeared to stop in a clearing just off the track. Hazati spotted him directing his horse to a small isolated stream near the clearing and then sitting down on a large log amongst green grass. Finally, their target was having a rest.

The assassins got off their horses and sneaked into the woodland to the side of the path. They were well hidden by the foliage as they edged deeper into the woods and closed in. Once they got within fifty feet of the target Hazati became poised to act and stopped.

'Jobe, get a bow,' he whispered irritably.

The young assassin knew what to do and crept back to their horses resting on the path to grab his bow from a bag tied to a pack on his mount. He was skilled with the ranged weapon and had the trust of his master. Jobe then shuffled back into the woods and knelt beside Hazati.

'Get as near as possible to him and strike. We have a good chance of ending this right now,' the old master stated.

Jobe nodded and crept away deeper into the woods towards his prey. Hazati looked to Akumi and Harkor and gave his own nod, combined with the slightest raising of his eyebrows.

The three followed closely behind Jobe. The bowman bent low and edged on through the bushes that kept him concealed. He carefully watched Endal as he got closer to him. The hooded man was sitting still on the log with his head bowed in what looked like a meditative state.

Jobe managed to reach a point as close to Endal as he wished to go. He was covered by a large bush and had a clear line of sight when he leant to the side. His heart was racing and his adrenaline pumping. He felt as if he was in a dream, the fact he was suddenly so near Endal hard to believe after so much time spent thinking about this moment.

Behind him his allies positioned themselves amongst further trees and bushes. They were poised to react to Endal and eager for Jobe to strike him. Briefly, Jobe looked to Akumi who knelt down a few feet behind him. She smiled towards him and continued to focus on Endal up ahead. Jobe seemed nervous and turned back to face his target. He raised his large, fine bow and clutched one of his arrows from a stash tied around his back. Whilst he put the arrow on the string of the bow and prepared himself to fire Hazati whispered out:

'Quickly Jobe, do it now.'

Jobe didn't hold back and leant to his left, exposing himself partially into Endal's view, and aimed the bow directly at his enemy. He pulled back on the bowstring and stretched the strong cord back as far as the bow would flex. He focused on the dark figure that was about fifteen feet ahead of him and carefully perfected his aim and angle. There was a second or two of hesitation as he finalised his shot and then suddenly he let go of the arrow and let it launch with immense speed from his bow. It silently glided through the clean air towards Endal.

The hooded assassin seemed to be instantly aware that an arrow had been fired at him. It had only been for the skill of his hunters that his instincts had not detected them close in on him until now. Endal dived to one side and managed to avoid the arrow as it flew over the log and penetrated a tree behind it near the small stream. He leapt to his feet and brought out his katana.

His eyes instantly spotted Jobe and he faced the young assassin. Jobe was unsure what to do and dropped his bow to the grass in order to clutch his sword. Akumi and Harkor raced around the bushes and appeared to Endal's side whilst he faced Jobe. Hazati crept into the clearing and stood back staring at the mythical assassin they'd suddenly stumbled across.

'Endal,' the old man grumbled.

'Can I help you?' the hooded figure's voice was dark and grim.

Hazati studied the character that had been the source of much fear throughout the lands ever since he could remember. His worn eyes faded from Endal's view as he bent his head down to conceal his face behind the tip of his straw hat. Hazati pulled out his ancient steel and stood motionlessly.

'You will not kill Tamus, we will not let you. Your time is up Endal,' Hazati stated firmly.

Whilst their master confronted the dark assassin the other assassins stood silently in awe over their target. They were edgy and unsure what was going to happen.

'Hazati,' Endal said softly. 'I won't be stopped.'

Hazati seemed confused about how Endal knew his name but whilst he studied the mysterious enemy he had begun to sense powers beyond his understanding. The old man imagined that Endal knew a great deal more than anyone probably expected. In those lucrative circles of knowledge Endal frequented a wealth of information was no doubt at hand.

'Kill your target!' Hazati yelled.

His assassins instantly closed in on Endal without fear. They were eager to prove themselves. Harkor was first to strike, rushing forwards deliberately to get the first move. The highly skilled swordsman got close but didn't attack, remembering to wait for Endal's strike and therefore for him to expose himself first. Endal studied him and swung his katana towards him as he stood in a stance. Harkor raised his sword to deflect the strike only to realise Endal had paused his swing and altered the angle. His blade swooped under Harkor's raised steel and sliced its way up his chest. The swordsman stumbled back in shock at the lightning speed of the sly move.

'No!' Jobe shrieked, running at Endal in fury.

Endal turned to face Jobe as he closed in.

'Jobe get back, don't attack!' Akumi yelled.

The girl had been right behind Harkor and seen the insane speed of Endal's strike. She was taken aback by it and now too concerned over Harkor to focus on Endal.

Jobe seemed to snap out of his undisciplined fury and stepped back as Endal faced him. Akumi knelt by Harkor in concern. She was equally concerned that Jobe was alone facing off against Endal until she noticed Hazati close in after momentarily holding back to watch his assassins.

'Endal,' he called whilst coming at him from behind.

Endal pounced around and raised his katana at the old man.

'I'm okay Akumi, it's not deep,' Harkor said whilst sitting himself up. 'His speed... it's not natural!'

Harkor got up and appeared able and willing to fight on. Akumi didn't hold back any longer and closed in on Endal as the four of them stood around him.

'I have killed enough people today. You four will merely add to a large statistic,' Endal smirked.

There was no response from the now highly focused attackers. Hazati made a move. The wise and masterful swordsman launched his sword at Endal. The hooded figure blocked the strike and immediately spun around to block a further strike from Jobe who launched his first attack. Harkor was next to attack and placed his sword low hoping to sweep Endal's legs. Endal jumped high into the air and spun over the four attackers, knowing he was vulnerable in the middle of them. As he landed Hazati was first to launch a strike and his sword clashed with Endal's.

The two assassins locked horns as their swords struck one another in a frenetic parry of swings and blows. Each strike was blocked by the other's blade until both men stepped back from one another. Endal had no time to relax as Harkor's sword flew towards his neck. Endal's katana met Harkor's sword and the two weapons proceeded to battle with each other as strike after strike was deflected.

Suddenly, Jobe came from another side and tried to catch Endal from behind. Endal launched his leg up and fiercely kicked the young assassin in the face whilst continuing to deal with Harkor's onslaught. Harkor had been forced to alter his fencer-like, one armed stance and now found himself on the receiving end as Endal launched a volley of sword swings.

Unlike Endal, Harkor was unable to deal with the speed of this confrontation and found himself getting cut across the thighs and arms, then waist. He stumbled back as the intimidatingly dark figure's katana danced around in front of him and suddenly struck his blade from his hand. Endal spun around and kicked Harkor firmly in the chest, sending him flying back and bumping against a tree.

Hazati launched several fast attacks. His skill seemed to truly test Endal as he was forced to back step whilst blocking the swings from the old man. Akumi had been holding back, unsure of the right moment to confront her target. She was more concerned with the state of Harkor as he sat upright against a tree limply. She looked down to Jobe who was unconscious and then back to Hazati.

The old man didn't let up and desperately tried to breach Endal's guard as he assaulted without pause. Akumi seemed eager to step in but reluctant to whilst others were attacking him.

She somehow intuitively knew this fight would ultimately be down to her.

Endal suddenly ceased blocking and deflecting Hazati's strikes and stepped forwards in retaliation. His katana arced downwards as he slammed it down from above his head. The move caught Hazati totally off guard and by surprise; he had just launched his own strike but Endal had speedily strafed to one side in avoidance.

His katana came down in a flash and struck the old man's straw hat, cutting through its front tip, before landing on the top his right shoulder. The blade cut into his flesh deeply and forced him to yell in pain and shock. Endal then drove his palm into the old man's chest, further stunning him and forcing him to fall to the ground in reflex. Hazati dropped his sword and lay clutching his wounded shoulder, which already started to profusely bleed.

'Akumi! It's up to you!' he yelled, crawling away from beside the dark assassin in defeat.

This was the moment Akumi had been waiting for. It was a straight one on one showdown between her and Endal. The dark figure seemed intrigued by Akumi's stance and behaviour, having been aware she'd been holding back until now. He noticed her shimmering katana that resembled his and smiled to himself. He then decided to remove his hood in order to get a full view of his surroundings. Hazati and Akumi looked on and studied his face as the hood was withdrawn. His long black hair wrapped around his head and his dark stubble gave him a rough and ready appearance. Akumi panted heavily in anticipation for the showdown. She was nervous yet didn't fear her enemy. She was silent, as was he.

Endal edged closer to her and this sparked the girl's fighting instincts. She lifted her blade and closed in. Endal swung at her as she got near. His katana swooped over her as she bent low to avoid it. As it whistled over her she raced across Endal's side with immense speed whilst bent low. She was aiming to slide her blade across his waist line whilst his outstretched body swung his sword.

To her amazement he reacted to her positioning by swiftly pouncing to one side, away from her, and rolled across the grass before getting to his feet to face her again. Akumi stood back up and held firm as Endal got close.

His blade struck hers and the two katanas clashed with ferocious pace and highly fuelled power. The sound of sharp steel striking sharp steel whistled out across the clearing and seemed to entice the birds to fly away from the trees above. Akumi managed to deflect a strike and launched her elbow at his chest. Endal leant back to avoid the blow and then pressed his palm into her chest, pushing her back with force and sending her to the ground. She instantly sprung back to her feet and launched an assault that appeared to force Endal to jump back and retreat to near where his horse stood by the water.

Akumi's katana glided around, forcing him to carefully block each of her well placed strikes. Her pace was swift and he quickly realised his skill was being truly tested trying to block her moves.

There was nothing either could do except fight on and wait until one of them made a mistake. The pace of the swordplay was so much as to blur the katanas. Their speed became impossible to follow with the eye. Endal halted near the roadside and as Akumi's katana came at him strafed to avoid it and turned across the girl's back until the two were leaning against one another.

'You are skilled,' he commented dryly.

Akumi didn't respond and spun around to face him at the same time as he spun around to face her. Both katanas met but the sheer pace of the swords striking against each other proved too much for either to handle. Both assassins lost their grip of the weapons and both blades spun off into the air, falling into the grass.

Akumi knew this wasn't just a sword fight but a matter of assassinating her target. She proceeded to launch a volley of lightning paced punches at Endal. He raised his arms in defence but one caught him in the chin. He stumbled back in amazement and shock at the girl's ability. Akumi leapt into the air and placed a flying kick into his chest. He fell back and tripped on a stone, stumbling over onto the grass. He turned around and pressed his arms against the ground to support himself as he got up but Akumi was quick to leap onto him.

She pounced on top of him and wrapped her arms around his neck tightly. She also wrapped her legs around his waist. Endal fell back to the ground and lay front ways down as the girl wrestled with him. She put all her strength into her tight grasp.

Her arms quickly started to strangle him as they wound around his neck. Her strong legs pressed deeply into his waist. Akumi was improvising, desperate to claim her target.

A few seconds of struggling went by as Endal madly fought to get free. Akumi seemed locked around him, totally transfixed on not letting him break away. However, her determination didn't seem to be enough. Endal suddenly elbowed her in the waist with such force that it instantly winded her and forced her to retreat from on top of him. She rolled to one side as Endal got up.

She didn't let the pain show and stood to face him. He walked towards her. The girl swung more fast jabs at him but this time Endal was more prepared. He grabbed her by the wrist and bent it around, forcing her to go with the pressure. She spun into the air and hit the ground firmly. She leapt up only for the same thing to happen again when she tried to attack him. The third time she went for a kick only for Endal to avoid it and drive his fist into her chest. She stumbled back and was hit with a fierce strike to her throat as the dark assassin placed his outstretched arm into her neck.

She was on the ground but noticed she was lying right by her sword. She clutched it and sliced it across Endal's thigh as he stood over her about to kick. He yelped and fell back. Akumi got to her feet and followed him as he rolled away in brief retreat. Before she could strike he'd reached his own sword and got up to face her. She was on the offensive and swung her blade with full speed. He deflected it and spun around with his katana poking out from the side of his waist. It stabbed Akumi in the side and forced her to retreat back from him. She'd been injured and it stung like nothing she'd ever felt. Endal came at her and struck her katana from her weary arm. She was white with shock and pain and stumbled back as he pressed closer. She knew her wound was bleeding too much for her to ignore and fearfully dropped to the ground before him in defeat. He smiled and raised his katana up in a poise that pointed it directly down at her chest. It looked like it was to be the girl's last moment.

The sword descended towards her decisively but was knocked to one side of the girl's exhausted body. It poked into the soil beside her head. Endal looked up as Jobe's sword held his to one side. The weary assassin had just come round. The two stared at one another until Jobe decided to act. He raised his sword up, hoping to strike Endal's chest. The boy let out a loud war cry as his sword raced upwards at his target. Endal was able to pull his katana from the mud and swing it back to knock Jobe's steel off course. He followed this through by raising it up and stabbing Jobe directly in the neck. The katana went straight through the flesh and as it was pulled out a wild gush of blood spattered down from his split gullet and poured onto Akumi as she lay below them.

'Akumi,' Jobe whimpered, falling down beside her lifeless. The girl tried to cry out in shock but her voice failed her.

Endal suddenly became troubled by his thigh and clutched the cut that bled, staining his dark robe. Akumi was staring up at him; still conscious, but feeling faint all over. Her hands were clasping her waist and she knew she was about to pass out.

Endal looked around. Harkor hadn't moved from his slouched position against the tree but he realised Hazati wasn't where he'd last seen him. With this thought he realised the old man had finally got up and crept forwards to face him.

Endal focused away from Akumi and raced at Hazati. As the two locked horns once again there was a sudden loud cry from the roadside.

'There! Look!' a soldier on horseback yelled.

An army of heavily clad Tamus troops raced from a convoy of horsemen coming up the road and into the clearing. Hazati desperately parried several strikes from Endal. Suddenly, as the dark figure became distracted by the army racing at him from the muddy track, the old man managed to land his sword into Endal's side. The steel pressed through the robe and partially entered into the assassin's flesh. There came a howl from the notorious assassin and he stumbled back.

With a sudden rush he ran towards his horse. The soldiers were closing in but he'd still had enough time to reach his mount near the stream and clamber onto it. In a wild retreat the rider yelled out and the black horse bolted through the woods and back onto the path. A lead soldier yelled out and the bulk of them turned to pursue the enemy of the realm.

Within moments the rush of troops had zoomed on up the track; leaving only a vast cloud of upturned soil. The rest came rushing to the aid of Hazati and his assassins. They were all wounded and utterly exhausted. Akumi lay motionless. She felt as if she was about to lose consciousness. The confrontation with Endal had proved an arduous, gruelling experience.

CHAPTER X

PATH OF THE FEMALE RIDERS

Akumi stumbled up from the grass wearily. She was breathing heavily and held against her cut waist with great pressure. She looked around as the troops converged on the clearing. As the figures dismounted and came closer she couldn't help but notice one in the middle of the group. The blonde girl stared back at her and smiled before leaping from her horse and walking towards her.

'Are you okay?' the concerned girl asked as she got close.

Akumi picked up her katana and calmly responded. 'I am okay, will need a bandage for this cut. Who are you?'

'I am Sylvie, protector of the Emperor. I led this convoy from Brimma. We were hunting for the assassin. Once we reached Dwenton and discovered what Endal had done we raced up this road as fast as possible. You must be Akumi, Hazati's finest assassin I hear?' Sylvie was intrigued.

Akumi nodded humbly. 'We pursued him closely and attacked here,' Akumi said. 'He is so skilled!' The girl was visibly shocked by her encounter.

Sylvie seemed shocked herself, knowing full well how skilled Hazati and his assassins were themselves. Akumi then turned to her friends.

'Jobe!' she shrieked.

In her weariness she hadn't realised until now that her close friend had been so seriously hurt. Several soldiers knelt around him desperately trying to give him aid and assistance. Akumi budged through the men and knelt by him.

'Jobe!' she cried. 'You saved my life!'

It only took a moment for her to know he was dead. His head lay amongst a pool of blood that continued to ooze from his cut neck. He was pale and lifeless. Akumi was teary eyed but didn't burst in tears. Instead, she just knelt by him silently.

Sylvie turned to Hazati. He shunned off a few soldiers seeking to attend to his shoulder wound and slanted against a tree by himself, looking around distantly. The blonde girl walked over to him.

'Hazati are you...' she was interrupted.

'I am fine Sylvie,' the old master muttered.

He was clearly frustrated and bitter about what had just happened.

'His skill is exceptional,' he said, turning to face the girl. 'He is unstoppable. Endal won't be defeated.'

Sylvie was careful with her response, knowing that Hazati's words always required the fullest of attention. 'But you injured him though, didn't you? I saw you strike him before he fled?'

Hazati nodded slightly. 'I have never fought so hard, and he would have brushed each one of us aside if it had not been for the fact we outnumbered him four to one. His wounds are not serious. However, mine is.'

As he spoke Sylvie noticed blood drip down from his shoulder with growingly greater pace.

'You must let us see to that wound,' she said.

A few troops stood by waiting for him to let them attend it. He nodded, knowing it was foolish to act like he needed no aid.

Akumi was in a daze. She walked away from Jobe and with sudden urgency ran to Harkor. Her mind was numb and she'd failed to remember about him and her master in her trancelike state of confusion and shock. Harkor was sitting up, being attended to by a few of Sylvie's troops. They held a water bottle up that he sipped from slowly. He was now conscious.

'Harkor, are you okay?' Akumi yelled.

He was frail and looked her in the eyes as she sat by him and held his hand thoughtfully.

'I'll live Akumi,' he smiled. 'Is Jobe...?'

Akumi looked to the ground. 'Yes,' her teary eyes exploded with grief.

Harkor reached his arms out to her and the two softly hugged one another. Hazati studied them as he stood across the other side of the clearing. He knew they'd now be feeling low and emotionally as frustrated as he was. In many ways the old man felt deeply guilty. Sylvie stood by his side.

'I should have known better,' he groaned. 'I should have

known Endal was beyond our skills. I should have known my assassins were no match for him. I didn't listen to my heart.'

'You should be proud Hazati,' Sylvie insisted. 'You confronted him and he is wounded. You and your assassins put up one hell of a fight against him!'

'But it wasn't enough to stop him,' the old man whispered.

'We now have a fix on him and will pursue him till he falls. He is only one man. Now we are onto him he is on the run. It will only be a matter of time,' she replied.

Hazati didn't say anything back. He knew that it was likely only he who could truly comprehend Endal's power. He knew that her faith was misguided and that Endal was something quite other than just one man.

Akumi and Harkor backed away from one another. The girl got to her feet. 'I am going to see Hazati,' she said.

She bounded across the grass and reached her master in seconds. As soon as she reached him, knowing he was wounded but standing, she wrapped her arms around him. The troops cleaning and wrapping bandages around his shoulder backed away as the two joined together. The old man patted the girl softly on the back as she hugged him. He was marginally shorter than the girl and had to raise his arched back up to meet her.

'You fought exceptionally against Endal. I am very proud of you Akumi,' he said.

The teary girl stepped back and gave him a bow in acknowledgement of his words.

'Master, Jobe is...'

'I know Akumi,' he affirmed. The two were silent for several seconds.

'You must get that seen to Akumi,' said Sylvie, looking to her cut waist.

'I will attend to it with some bandages. It's okay,' she replied.

Sylvie appeared convinced she was okay and that the wound wasn't troubling her. Hazati suddenly moaned in pain and clutched his shoulder. Akumi moved to his side in concern.

'His wound is deep, the muscle has been damaged,' a soldier stated. 'Sir, we will need to get you back to Dwenton where we can see to it. You won't be holding any sword in that arm until it has been seen to.'

Hazati nodded to himself knowing quite clearly that the injury was troubling him.

'Go master. You injured him, I saw it! I will pursue Endal and finish him. You have done enough and need to rest,' said Akumi.

'Akumi, this is over,' he ordered. 'Forget this and go home. Take Harkor with you. Endal is too much for you, this is up to Tamus. It's no longer our fight.'

Akumi was stunned by her master's new stance.

'But master...'

'No Akumi, this is my order. I don't want to see you or Harkor die over this. Endal will prove unstoppable. He will kill Tamus. Don't be another victim.'

His words sparked a reaction from Sylvie. 'Hazati, no matter how tough Endal is he won't succeed... I assure you,' she came in.

'Sylvie, you too; don't be another of his victims. The two of you need to stand aside. Endal is too strong,' he moaned, suddenly yelling out in more pain.

Akumi and Sylvie looked to one another as Hazati pushed the soldiers back as they tried to see to his wound again.

'Master, I will not walk away from this. Jobe died for our mission. Endal cannot kill Tamus. If he succeeds Marmia will fall into chaos once again. I can't stand aside knowing this. Please understand,' Akumi passionately spoke.

Hazati was weak and sat down on the grass. 'I knew you'd be like this Akumi, stubborn. You put up a good fight against him and it seems you may well be a match for him at least. If you insist on this I cannot stop you but I want you to know this: I believe Endal will prove unstoppable.

It is up to you what you do from this point on. I hope to see you again Akumi, and you too Sylvie. Do what you feel is right.'

The old man suddenly went limp and fell back. Akumi and Sylvie raced to his side along with a few troops.

'He has passed out from the blood loss. We will take him and Harkor back to Dwenton. They will be fine,' one of the soldiers said.

The female warriors seemed satisfied with the soldier's words and watched as a bunch of them carried Hazati and Harkor to a carriage back on the roadside. It was heading back to town. Akumi then noticed them take Jobe's body and put it in the same carriage. Sylvie gently stroked her arm in affection.

'Will you ride with me and continue? You know that Hazati speaks sense...' she inquired.

'Yes, he speaks sense but is just concerned for us. Deep down he knows we are going to fight on, we have to. We must stop Endal,' Akumi was firm.

Sylvie was pleased and looked to their horses. The soldiers had brought Akumi's mare across from the road and placed them beside Sylvie's. The two proud, white animals stood side by side. By now the carriage was heading off and the remaining troops were getting ready to follow Sylvie into the pursuit.

'We need to go now, we can still catch up,' Sylvie said.

Both girls now had the same path to tread. Akumi thought of Jobe. A fire burned deep within her. He'd saved her life and died fighting Endal. She knew it was now up to her and Sylvie to continue that fight. It was her duty to go on and act but it was now also personal. She wanted revenge.

'Let's get moving,' she announced.

The two girls raced to their horses.

BOOK TWO

CHAPTER I

THE UNMASKING OF THE INNKEEPER

Arthir knew what the signs indicated. The large group of troops on horseback racing across the fields towards his remote farm could only mean one thing. The weary rebel knew that Tamus was onto him. The plan had somehow been foiled. His first reaction was to grab his sword from the table near the window he stared out of. He was alone in his farm, which rested on the outskirts of a nearby town. Someone in that town must have tipped the soldiers off and pointed them in the direction of the ramshackle dwelling.

The overcast sky suddenly opened up. A swift downpour of rain started to bombard the crops and roof to his shack. The sound of fast falling water striking the timber joints seemed to kick Arthir into action. He knew he had no chance of escape, his farm surrounded on all sides by flat fields, and he had no horse to mount. He darted to a corner of the room and raised a rug from the ground. Under it was a small trapdoor. Arthir was going to try and hide. The sneaky character had clearly rehearsed this moment. He opened the door with a key he had tucked away in his pocket. The entry groaned open revealing a dark space under the floor. In the small room were several candles and a torch, a collection of books, and food and water. It was clear he would be able to spend a long time here.

The man lowered himself down into the dingy space and quickly pulled the door shut as he fully clambered in. A lever attached to a string then pushed the red rug back into place above the door. The homemade contraption clearly worked well and the hiding place became well concealed.

The incoming army had reached the farm within moments of the rug being tugged. A gang of soldiers leapt from horses and raced to the door of the small house. It was kicked in within seconds and the troops charged into the interior.

'Arthir, show yourself!' one yelled.

They looked around the mostly bare room and then a few went upstairs to check the low roof. A wardrobe was violently shaken and searched as were several boxes in a far corner.

'He doesn't seem to be home,' a soldier said, leaning against the table.

A leader paced up and down the floorboards as his men stood around waiting for further orders.

'No... he doesn't does he?' he said back.

As the man spoke he looked at the rug and smiled. He looked to his men and pointed at it whilst miming an order to them to lift it up. Two troops came forwards and lifted it, instantly revealing the trapdoor.

'That old one, a trap door under the rug,' the leader whispered dryly.

He gave a nod to his men as they prepared to tackle the small door. One pulled at the handle but the lock was firm. Another poked at it with his sword hoping to penetrate the wood. It was too thick.

'Arthir, we know you are down there,' the lead troop yelled. 'Come out now or we will burn you out!' There was no response.

The lead troop studied the floorboards around the door.

'Starting a fire is too easy,' he said to himself.

'O'Brien, put a rope around that handle and attach the other end to your horse. Let's wake this man up,' he ordered.

The soldier quickly followed the order and grabbed a loop of strong rope from his horse outside. He came back and tied it around the handle of the trapdoor and fed it back to outside the farm house through the doorway. The leader held the front door open and watched as his man tied the other end to his horse and mounted it. A group of other soldiers stood around the trapdoor waiting to confront Arthir.

There was a nod of confirmation and then O'Brien yelled out to his horse. The animal raced forwards in full speed and as they moved the rope line tightened until it was perfectly straight and rose up into the air. The knots held firm and the rope did not falter. Instead, the trapdoor snapped from its hinges and lock and grinded across the wooden floor until it was pulled into the field outside. The horse soon stopped. The gap revealed Arthir cowering in his cave. He looked up with his sword poised.

'Go away, you won't take me alive!' he yelled.

The soldiers prodded at him with their blades until one knocked his sword from his grasp. Another then grabbed him by the hair and slowly forced him up from out of the space as he pulled. The disarmed rebel reluctantly complied and came out of his hiding place.

'You are under arrest for conspiring against the Emperor. You will be taken from here for questioning,' the lead soldier announced.

Arthir was silent. He was now bitter and desperately eager to find out how the plan had been exposed. He suddenly found himself being led outside. The rain was still pouring.

Across the lands another convoy of Tamus troops was racing towards a building. This one was a pub. It was The Lamb Inn to be precise. This convoy of horsemen included General Dorwor who led from the front as they stormed into the town. His white mare was an intriguing sight for the villagers as he and his soldiers bounded down the narrow lane towards the taverns swinging signpost. The large metal notice was easy to spot and Dorwor quickly had a fix on his destination.

The soldiers reached the outside of the tavern and dismounted in unison. The streets were empty and eerily silent.

'It's the innkeeper we are after. His name is Bollam,' Dorwor grumbled. 'I once drank in this pub and remember his face.'

With that Dorwor cranked open the door and marched into the bar. His troops swarmed the tables and stools of the inn and converged on the barman who stood in the corner of the lifeless room.

'What is this?' he protested.

Dorwor closed in on him and leant against the bar. 'Where is Bollam? We are here for him,' he said.

'Bollam? The owner? He is up...' the barman was interrupted mid sentence.

His voice was overpowered by howling laughter coming from a figure that appeared from the staircase behind the general.

'You are after me Dorwor?' the figure sniggered.

Dorwor turned around with sword drawn. His soldiers edged

towards the man coming down the stairs.

'Who are you?' Dorwor asked cautiously.

The figure was concealed in a hooded black robe. His voice was croaky and intimidating.

'I am Bollam, well, that's a name I have gone by over the years anyway. I come here on occasion to maintain the identity of the owner but often… go away on business,' he laughed. 'In reality I just use this identity to get the gossip. My real name is Vortor.'

Dorwor gulped. He knew the name well and immediately realised the plot went deeper than he'd realised.

The figure only vaguely resembled Bollam but it was clear he'd been able to slightly alter his appearance through some magical ability. His skin was now paler and worn. He also seemed shorter, now hunched forwards slightly as he stood.

'Sir? You are not…' the barman was confused.

Vortor laughed out loud. 'You and all the staff have fallen for my disguise,' he said.

'Who is Vortor?' a troop asked.

'He is a very powerful mage and an enemy of Tamus,' Dorwor said. 'He disappeared for several decades; we thought he'd gone. Clearly, he was just lurking in the shadows.'

'That's right,' Vortor replied, 'and I am pretty certain I know why you are here for me Dorwor. I expected the secret to quickly become the realm's biggest story. I don't need to deny anything. I made sure that our passing assassin friend, Endal, was pointed in the right direction by the rebels whilst he dwelt in these parts. I couldn't resist.'

'Vortor, you are under arrest,' said the general.

Vortor laughed. 'It would take more than just you bunch, I assure you,' he said.

With that the soldiers closed in at the general's command. Vortor faced them from the bottom of the staircase and before they could get near yelled a few arcane words and raised his arms. A bolt of white, streaming light glowed from his palms and raced out into the chests of several of the soldiers. They stumbled to the ground in pain. A few more troops charged towards him but were hurled back by an invisible force as he aimed his arms towards them. They struck wooden tables and smashed them on impact as they were tossed around the room like rag dolls.

The general did not approach Vortor. Deep down he knew the

mage's powers were beyond the control of him and his men and yelled out before his soldiers foolishly tried again to close in on him: 'No one attack, stay back!'

The group of warriors sat up limply, several being supported to their feet by allies.

'A sensible move Dorwor,' the dark mage sniggered. 'I will let you live another day so you can no doubt try and catch me another time… we can have more fun that way. Now I must leave here and keep an eye on things. So long, General.'

Vortor calmly strolled to the door of the pub and left the building. Dorwor immediately turned to the barman.

'You had no idea about this?' he asked aridly.

'No sir, I had no idea,' the timid man answered.

He seemed genuinely shocked by the sudden unmasking of his boss.

'We can only go after one target,' Dorwor said. 'We need to get back to Brimma and find out if we are any closer to tracking Endal.'

His soldiers appeared to acknowledge his words but were also busy attending to their sore bodies. Vortor's strikes of energy had exhausted them.

'We will be seeing Vortor again I sense, so there is no need trying to follow him,' the general continued. 'Let us get back to Brimma.'

CHAPTER II

THE BLACK TOWER

Endal bolted from the scene like a wounded animal. His horse raced across the mud, kicking up dry soil and creating clouds of earth as his back legs hurried forwards. The horseman then turned off the road and bounded into the woodland. It was becoming less dense now, with large gaps between the high trees, and the assassin could clearly make out plain fields beyond the forest. He knew he was being pursued and gave no attention to his wounds that continued to sob and bleed unchecked.

The pursuing horde of Tamus soldiers were not far behind. They had spread out and looked to be following him in a line formation that covered every angle he could turn away in. They were fired up and eager to catch up with their prey. One seemed to lead the charge. He was several feet ahead of his men and held a large javelin that tipped forwards ahead of his horse.

The chase went on for several minutes without much ground being made by the soldiers. They couldn't catch up with Endal but were able to match his pace at least. By now the woodland was becoming sparse. The ground became flat and the grass more prevalent as the foliage turned to clearings. There was little sunlight left as dark gloomy clouds covered the sky in menacing opulence. There was a morbid tone to the new surroundings. Meagre mist rolled across the grass beneath the soldiers as they raced along on horseback.

Endal's dark figure suddenly came to a halt as a structure became apparent ahead of him. It was a strange, dark structure in amongst the rolling fields and occasional tree. He then pressed forwards again until his horse refused to go any further. The troops could clearly tell Endal was desperate to get his mount in line but the animal would not budge and turned away from the building in reluctance. His head bowed and the rider was forced to leap off from his saddle and instinctively pull out his sheathed katana, knowing he had no chance of outrunning his pursuers on foot.

'Here be our chance lads,' the lead troop yelled. 'Make him pay!'

With this command the troops separated out and shrieked with passionate war cries as they closed in on the enemy. Endal stood firm with his weapon raised. The lead soldier brandishing a long javelin was first to reach him. His spear pointed directly at the assassin as he closed in for the kill. Endal bowed down and rolled forwards to avoid its tip as it jetted by overhead. He got up to his feet and hurled his katana at the soldier's back as he rode onwards; about to turn around to attempt another strike. The blade split into the man's spine as it spun across the air. The troop instantly drooped forwards and fell from his horse. Endal raced to him and pulled his weapon from the large gash to his lower back. He then stabbed him with the blade several times in the back, finishing the job.

At this point another rushed forwards to take the dark figure on. He swung his sword down at the enemy beside his horse but in a flash Endal had blocked the strike and slid his blade across the soldier's waist as he passed him by on horseback. The horse ran on but the soldier stumbled from his mount and hit the grass head first. Two more soldiers were swift to follow the attack. One stopped his horse and tried to strike Endal with his blade whilst still sitting up on his ride. The assassin managed to quickly disable his opponent with a swift blow to his torso. He quickly followed this through by deflecting a strike from the other soldier who attacked his other side. The foolish warrior had overstretched in order to reach the assassin and fell from his horse as Endal blocked the strike. His next and last sensation once hitting the grass was feeling Endal's cold katana penetrate his abdomen and slice up his insides.

Endal looked up at the remaining soldiers. The bulk of them had yet to attack and had instead all halted around him. He was surrounded and staring at a circle of fired up yet nervous enemies. He initiated a counter attack to their surprise and shock. He walked forwards and started to strike at one of the soldiers nearest him in the circle. He cut him up without any effort. Behind that soldier was another on horseback. Endal brought him down in two swift sword moves and pressed forwards.

The soldiers now finding themselves beside Endal were desperately trying to turn to face him but found themselves getting cut across the thighs and ankles as their enemy took advantage of their exposed positions around him. There was suddenly a panic amongst the troops as Endal carved his way through the circle. It was three troops thick at each point and by now Endal had gone through the three soldiers on horseback in front of him and wounded all those that had been beside them.

He calmly walked up the field and away from the shocked troops. He suddenly then felt faint and limp all over. The throbbing gash to his thigh had abruptly taken its toll on his body. The cut to his stomach was a lesser hindrance but also still bled. He had been losing blood unchecked and now his rush of adrenaline had reached its climax he felt totally exhausted.

The soldiers had turned to face him and were unsure whether to attack. This hesitation did not last long though. One came forth from the crowd and raised a bow. He desperately aimed an arrow at the enemy. This had been the first chance the archer had got at firing a shot at his target. He pulled the string back and let go. The weak and frail assassin stood with his back turned to the soldiers. He was close to fainting. The arrow struck him in the small of his back and its head penetrated the skin. Endal yelped out and fell to his knees. He seemed to spark back alive with this sudden wake up call and tried to get back up. He couldn't manage and instead plucked the arrow from his back in defiance.

As he turned to face the archer he realised there was now a line of them ready to fire. He raised his sword and with a final attempt to defend himself glided it across the air as a volley of arrows raced towards him. His katana managed to cut and deflect several of them but it proved impossible to stop the whole barrage. Two impaled themselves into his torso. The shock of receiving the blows sent him falling back into the grass as he continued to sit on his knees. He dropped his blade and lay motionlessly.

The troops leapt from their horses and excitedly closed in on the assassin.

'We got him!' one shouted out.

There was, however, little time for celebration. A volley of balls of fire suddenly struck dead several of the soldiers nearest Endal. The bolts of orange flame came from a lone figure that had swiftly appeared from the field behind them; just in front of the eerie structure Endal's horse had refused to get close to.

'A mage!' a soldier shrieked.

The sight of flames darting from his palms and instantly killing several of the soldiers created a manic alarm amongst the troops. The dark hooded figure walked forwards and passed by Endal's horse that had remained standing where their master had left them. Two troops seemed eager to challenge him but before they could even charge towards him were met with further rapid bolts of flame. The spell appeared to strike their hearts and kill instantaneously. The figure got closer to the flock of soldiers who now were beginning to show signs of retreat as their horses became uncontrollable at the sight and presence of the hooded mage.

It became clear the figure was an old man. He was laughing to himself as he gained in on the soldiers. The line of four archers turned to face him and raised their bows. In a flash four more bolts of orange flame struck them all dead. This was the last straw for the remaining troops. They turned and fled in an undisciplined panic. Many horses were left behind; the soldiers that had ridden them now dead in the field. They all kept a distance from the figure but didn't seem bothered about staying in his general area.

The figure watched as the soldiers fled away and halted nearer the woods ahead. As he watched them stop he noticed more coming from the woodland, many more. A whole army seemed to be forming and he could distinctly make out two figures on white horses leading the reinforcements.

'You have brought the enemy to my doorstep Endal,' the mage sighed.

He looked down at the assassin as he stood beside him. Endal was lifeless but the mage didn't look concerned. He whistled out and suddenly Endal's horse darted towards him. Harwind suddenly showed no fear towards the mage, like the whistle had been a sign from him of friendly intent. The mystical figure appeared astutely in touch with the animal.

He picked Endal up and carried him over his back. He also grabbed Endal's katana that rested beside the assassin in the grass and placed it back into Endal's robe. For a small and elderly man the figure seemed strong and able. He then placed him onto the horse and sat himself on the mount in front. Endal drooped out sideways on the horse's back. The mage yelled out and the horse made for the structure he had come from. The black tower was the only prominent landmark for miles around and one that rarely saw such activity about its walls.

The animal bounded for the structure as the army of Tamus soldiers continued to form up from beyond the woods. There was a sense of desperation as the numbers increasingly grew and grew. There seemed to be a delay in their advance as the two leading female warriors spoke with the retreating soldiers who'd witnessed the mage's rage.

As this went on the black horse soon reached the tower that they clearly no longer feared. The mage yelled out an archaic word and a doorway opened up to one side of the large and murky construction. They raced in through the gap and it quickly closed back shut.

The interior was bare and dark. The mage halted the horse and leapt from him with great pace. The ground was of flat stone and the horse's hooves patted the surface, creating a light echo of bellowing thuds. The mage brought Endal down to the cold floor and studied him attentively.

'It would seem all of Marmia is after you,' he sniggered. 'I best make sure you can continue the fight.'

He placed his palms together and closed his eyes. He then started to hum loudly. As he did so a yellow tint of light had begun to form around his body. It looked like his aura was becoming visible. Endal's horse ran to a far corner of the empty clearing in fright. The wizard had begun to chant further words and the light became a radiant glow around him. He then placed his hands on Endal's chest; the energy started to flow from his arms and into the assassin who remained unconscious.

The process went on without interruption. The mage suddenly plucked the arrows from the assassin's wounds and continued to chant out loud. The spell lit up the whole interior of the tower structure with its orange and white glows. It revealed the entire space. To each side of them were curved walls and above them the extent of the height of the erection became apparent. There were no floors, just a single space that was roofed by the tip of the phallic shaped tower.

With a sudden shriek the mage ceased his spell. He recoiled back and sat beside Endal. The light dimmed as the dark shades poured back into the confined room around them. He was panting heavily and seemed eager. He smiled as Endal suddenly opened his eyes.

'Welcome back,' the mage smiled.

Endal took a few seconds to fully gain his faculties. He stared up into the high reaches of the structure and then sat himself up. He looked at the mage beside him.

'Vortor,' he whispered.

'Hello Endal,' the mage replied. 'It was lucky you came this way. You stumbled across my land. This tower is where I dwell. You needed assistance and I came to your aid.'

Endal acknowledged Vortor's words without any oral response. He studied his body, which seemed entirely healed and no longer troubled him.

'I healed you,' Vortor said. 'Not a spell I often use! You'd received some knocks, which is no surprise considering you are being pursued by all of Marmia!'

The mage's voice was dim and croaky. He was as evil and dark as the assassin that sat beside him.

'I know your task,' Vortor went on, 'and I want to see you complete it. This is why I have assisted you.'

'It has been a while since I last saw you friend,' said Endal, 'and I greatly appreciate your help. It is fate that I reached this tower.'

'Yes, it is the Dark Lord guiding you,' replied Vortor.

Both gave slight nods at the comment.

'But tell me this brother,' Vortor seemed intrigued: 'who is it that you were hurt by? I have never known of a man who was able to touch you with the sword or of an army that was able to as much as delay you.'

Endal placed his dark hood back over his head and looked to his ally. The two figures both simultaneously got up to their feet. They looked like clones, both wearing black robes with baggy hoods covering their heads and faces. They were an intimidating and frightful sight. Like the scene of some dark carnival, their figures were as black as the gloomy shades pervading them.

'A female assassin who hunts after me was able to do this. She slid her blade across my thigh. She is exceptionally skilled; the best I have ever fought,' Endal answered. 'My battle against her fatigued me and the wounds I'd received slowed me down. I was unable to fully deal with those soldiers. I had lost a lot of blood.'

'Who is this girl assassin?' Vortor asked.

'I know not, but her master is Hazati,' said Endal. 'I battled with him as he fought beside her. There were also others but they proved inferior.'

'Bah! Hazati! Damn that name!' Vortor raised his voice in disgust. 'I knew he would have something to do with this. General Dorwor is relying on him to stop you it seems.'

'This girl is still pursuing me; although I defeated those she was with, including Hazati. She will likely be eager to face me again,' Endal went on.

'You will defeat this girl Endal. In that I have no doubt,' said Vortor. 'And Hazati... he is dead?'

'Not dead but injured,' replied Endal. 'He shouldn't be troubling me any further.'

Endal spoke softly in whispers. His tone of voice was calm and open as if Vortor was someone he had a kinship with. The two were clearly old allies.

'I see,' Vortor grumbled. 'Well I now wish to show you something. I think you will like it.'

The mage had begun to walk towards the far corner of the space. It was gloomy and Endal lost sight of him as he faded into the darkness. He followed on and halted once Vortor had ceased. He stood beside the stone wall and looked down at a small trapdoor by his feet.

'Outside these walls is the bulk of the Emperor's army. They are continuing to form around us as I speak. However, do not fear. This trapdoor leads to a tunnel. The tunnel will take you to Brimma. From there you can proceed with your task,' Vortor smiled.

Endal seemed unsure but Vortor quickly assured him:

'Trust me old friend. I have used this tunnel in the past to reach the capital. It is quick and secure.'

'What will you do?' Endal asked.

'Stay and bide you time. I am too weak and tired from healing you to go to Brimma. My time has come Endal. Go and complete your contract!'

The two evil characters stared at one another for a moment in recognition of the situation. It was a moment where other men would have shaken hands or exchanged fond farewells. However, these two were otherworldly and quite inhuman. There was a mutual understanding betwixt them and that was enough.

'There is no room in the tunnel for your horse. Leave him here,' said Vortor.

'Thank you for your assistance,' concluded Endal.

'Go forth and slay Tamus,' Vortor smiled. 'With the fall of the Emperor a wave of fear will rock these lands, and as soon as it does my powers will feast off the emotion. My energy will form like the genesis of a distant star. Through portals I have carefully constructed an army of darkness will enter into this realm. You will make it so Endal.'

The dark assassin bowed his head. He was indifferent and showed no reaction to the dramatic announcement. To him the task of killing Tamus was merely a contract; one in which his dark mind was transfixed on completing.

He opened the trapdoor and slipped down into the narrow tunnel below. It started at the point the trapdoor was positioned and led off deep down into a void of darkness. A torch hung from the stone wall to one side and the assassin grabbed it. Vortor laughed and lit the torch with a spell that created flames that raced from his palms.

'Godspeed Endal,' Vortor yelled out as the assassin started to walk into the breadth of the passageway and into the darkness.

Once the assassin had faded away into the depths Vortor laughed to himself.

'And if I fall on this day you will be my avatar Endal,' he laughed. 'You will lead the dark forces! They will seek you. It is your destiny my dark child of the night!'

CHAPTER III

REVEALING THE SHORT CUT

'If we wait any longer God only knows what they will have formulated to defend themselves,' a soldier yelled at Sylvie as she studied the tower from the vantage point they had in the field.

Sylvie was reluctant and looked to Akumi who stood beside her.

'So, we have a mage and Endal to deal with now! Any ideas?' she asked the assassin.

Akumi was stroking the tip of her sword and studying the terrain dutifully.

'Endal is injured. The mage came to his assistance. From what I know mages tire quickly. He will likely already be weary from the spells he cast at the soldiers. We should move now,' she said.

Sylvie nodded. 'Prepare to attack the tower!' she yelled.

The army of troops on horseback responded by forming up into tight lines and clutching their weapons. There were now hundreds of them and further troops were still converging on the area. Sylvie looked around and studied them.

'We can end this now,' she commented.

'Let's press forward,' replied Akumi.

Suddenly, a company of troops came racing towards the two girls from the woods behind them. They pushed through the lines of soldiers ready to charge and it quickly became clear General Dorwor was leading the group.

'Do not give the command!' Dorwor yelled as his horse screeched to a halt beside Sylvie.

'General?' Sylvie remarked. 'What is wrong?'

'We have just come from The Lamb Inn in Dolsbury, we were heading back to Brimma but heard of what happened in Dwenton on the road,' said Dorwor, looking down at Sylvie from his horse. 'We caught up as quickly as we could. We were after Bollam, one of the conspirators. It turns out Bollam is behind this whole thing, and it turns out Bollam is actually not Bollam at all but a mage, a very powerful mage... Vortor.'

'Vortor?!' Sylvie was alarmed.

'Who is Vortor?' asked Akumi.

'He is an enemy of Tamus and has been for decades. He is one of the last mages to dwell in these parts and probably the most powerful ever known to Marmia,' Sylvie replied.

'He is also enemy number one as far as I'm concerned,' added Dorwor. 'He is using Endal to complete a task he has been eager to carry out himself for years. But he never tried it. He is as evil and powerful as Endal I assure you.'

'How do you know he is behind this?' Akumi asked.

'He told us when we confronted him in the inn,' the general answered. 'He then brushed his way past us and vanished outside in the street.'

As the general spoke he studied the intimidating black tower ahead.

'We've known about this place for a while,' he said, 'but it is said that to go near it uninvited is folly. There is some spell at work.'

He then looked further at Akumi.

'Who are you anyway?' he grumbled.

'She is one of Hazati's assassins, an exceptional one might I add,' Sylvie remarked.

'Where is that old man?' Dorwor asked.

'We confronted Endal earlier,' said Akumi. 'He killed one of my party and injured Hazati and another. They are back in Dwenton being attended. He is okay.'

Dorwor groused with the news Hazati was no longer in the fight.

'So you have fought Endal and survived the encounter?' Dorwor asked. 'Tell me Akumi, can you beat him?'

'I don't know, General,' Akumi said humbly, 'but I will not stop until he has been defeated.'

'Hmm, you are too modest my girl!' Dorwor bellowed. 'Endal will fall by nightfall. That I assure you.'

Sylvie then came in abruptly: 'We cannot delay any longer. General, we must attack the tower!'

'Wait!' Dorwor yelled. 'Now listen, I am hearing word of a mage aiding Endal and taking him to that tower. It's clearly

Vortor. He warped himself here or something, whatever folk like him do! I want to stress that he is very powerful. A sword is useless against him!'

'Endal is wounded and Vortor will be weary after casting so many spells. He will not be able to fend us all off. We cannot hold back,' said Sylvie.

'How wounded is Endal?' asked Dorwor.

'He must have lost a lot of blood from his encounter with Akumi and her group, and was struck by a few arrows from our soldiers. I would say he is close to death without being properly attended to,' said Sylvie.

'Vortor will heal him if he is not dead already. I have heard the mage can even resurrect the dead at will. We must assume Endal is alive and fighting fit. We must assume the worst,' said Dorwor.

The three discussed tactics and after a few minutes of consideration Dorwor seemed to finally agree that they needed to attack regardless of the dangers. There wasn't really a choice. They positioned themselves a few feet ahead of the mass of soldiers poised to charge and Sylvie was given command.

'Charge!' she yelled as loudly as her feminine voice would allow for.

The masses of Tamus troops erupted into a ferocious army of assaulters. Their horses bounded across the grass in unison as they let out menacing war cries. The leaders kept in front and crossed the field in a matter of seconds.

Before they knew it the tower was prominent ahead and no longer in the background. They gave no thought to the rumour that the structure was protected by some sort of spell.

Vortor had been keeping an eye on the army beyond his walls and was not surprised when he saw the masses of troops charging towards the tower. He'd set himself up on the high roof of the structure and peered down at the land below. There was no obvious way of getting to the top and the mysterious mage felt safe on his high ground.

There was no force field or spell guarding the tower apart from Vortor himself. He waited until the attackers had reached the walls themselves before casting any spell. Dorwor was first to spot the entrance and analysed it knowing the sturdy door would prove difficult to breach. The soldiers formed up around the walls and studied every section to the alien construction.

Vortor suddenly yelled out and a volley of bright green bolts blasted from his palms and raced down into the army below. The green energy struck individual soldiers amongst the crowd and burned through their armour and fatally charred their chests. The volley was repeated with at least ten bolts of the green light flying down from the top of the tower. They were accompanied by the distinct sound of mocking laughter coming from the old mage that could be heard down below.

'That's Vortor!' Dorwor panicked. 'He's on the roof.'

'We need to get inside the tower!' Akumi stressed.

'There is no way in,' a soldier yelled in response to her words.

It certainly did seem impregnable. The flat stone walls had no weak point and the door was solid and thick. How ever Vortor was able to get inside it was certainly not through the use of a key. It was as if the tower was a sentient being that only answered to the mage that hid inside.

Vortor waited several minutes until he cast another spell. The attackers seemed at odds with what their next move was to be and he was amused at the sight of them cowering in huddles by his walls, fearing more strikes from above.

He yelled a string of words and pointed his arm out at a bunch directly below him whilst gazing over the low wall he leant against. A line of white lightning split from his palm and struck the ground. It was constant and as Vortor's arm moved it moved along the grass. It burnt through horse and man with effortless energy and cut through the soldiers' lines with sadistic ease. There was sudden panic at this and droves of troops broke from the path it snaked around in. Horses became uncontrollable and kicked off their riders. It was utter bedlam. The animals had only gone this far because of Vortor's distance from them high above. It was not the tower they feared but him.

Dorwor was becoming growingly frustrated and wild with what was going on. He watched as the lightning tore through the ranks of his men and turned them into fearful, helpless masses.

'We need to retreat!' he said to himself, loudly enough for Akumi and Sylvie to hear.

'Wait, I have an idea,' Akumi persevered. 'We have grappling hooks?'

'Yes I have some,' Sylvie said with intrigue.

'I have rope, enough to scale this tower. If we can get the hook to reach that roof and attach itself to the low wall around it I can climb it,' Akumi suggested.

Dorwor overheard the girls. 'Your sword will do nothing against Vortor. Even if you got up there he'd send you flying back down!' the general screeched.

'I will go too,' insisted Sylvie.

Dorwor watched as the lightning suddenly ceased. He then heard Vortor laughing evilly from above. His spell had left a trail of death and destruction as the burnt earth and charred bodies smoked away with fresh heat.

'We need to get the hook up there!' Akumi yelled.

'That I can do,' Dorwor laughed. 'Give me the rope.'

Akumi had tied a grappling hook to her pile of strong rope and passed it to the general. The largely built and strong warrior looked up at the towers roof and then to the hook.

'Stand back,' he said.

He pounced from his horse and started to swing the rope around and around. The hook spun with great pace in circles as he danced with momentum. His men were beginning to cotton on to what was going on and watched with great trepidation.

After a good few more full swings Dorwor let out a loud cry and let go of the hook and rope as he threw it into the air. It jetted up with grace and climbed with great speed. The hook made the distance with a few feets' worth of excess and slotted against the low wall that circled the top of the black structure. The rope dangled down from the tower's side. Akumi raced to clutch it and announced it was safe to climb. She and Sylvie looked to one another.

'You don't need to come up Sylvie,' the assassin assured her.

'I am coming,' Sylvie smiled.

Vortor was too busy belly laughing at his dominance of the situation to notice the grappling hook pressed against the wall behind him on the other side of the wall. He was overlooking the bulk of the troops encircling the tower.

He decided to cast a new spell; a quick succession of luminous red balls raced from his hands and claimed those they struck. They hummed with magical intensity as they glided through the air. His spells were a light show of colour and for an onlooker the display of fireworks would have been a sight to marvel.

However, for those at the receiving end of his works there was only a deep sense of fear.

Akumi took the lead and grabbed the rope. She placed her feet on the wall of the tower and started to rise up its surface. It looked as if she was walking up the stone. Her arms held firmly onto the rope as her legs clambered upwards. She moved slowly and carefully and seemed at ease with the dangerous feat. Sylvie was soon to follow her and proceeded to climb up with a few feet of distance behind the assassin.

She looked as confident with the task although was unsure at first. Akumi was much faster though, and her pace grew and grew as she gained more and more height. Eventually, with half the tower climbed, she went all out and scaled the remains of the structure with such speed as to make it seem effortless.

Once at the low wall she grabbed hold of the stone and flipped over it onto the roof. She carefully studied the dark hooded mage ahead of her. His back was turned and he seemed too occupied with his spell casting to notice much else. Sylvie was slower to reach the roof but it wasn't long until she'd reached her ally. Akumi had patiently waited for her to arrive, knowing not to underestimate the mage and attack without backup.

'If only we'd brought a bow and arrow up!' Sylvie commented upon viewing Vortor's position.

'Too late now,' Akumi said softly. 'Let's get closer.'

The two females crept forwards and edged towards the mage. Both had their swords at the ready. Vortor was leaning against the wall and laughing. He seemed less amused by the fact the troops were suddenly less fearful. Those that had broken from the ranks had come back. They appeared less intimidated by him. He was about to cast another spell but knew he was now very tired. He had used a large amount of his energy to cast his spells and was reluctant to push himself. It was in this moment he became aware of a presence behind him. He slowly turned only to spot at the corner of his eye Akumi bent low with her katana out and poised. They were now only feet from him.

Vortor shrieked in shock and surprise and pounced around to fully face them. Akumi was decisive and raced forwards to close the gap between him and her. She unfalteringly raised her katana and brought it down in a swinging arc that slid across the entirety of the mage's chest. It flawlessly ripped through his robe and skimmed across his body in a perfect line. He whined in shock and pain and stumbled back onto the low stone wall behind him. He sat with his back against it and looked down at his gushing wound.

Akumi and Sylvie studied him carefully. He remained defiant and looked to them with sheer hatred.

'You won't stop Endal. Tamus will be killed and Marmia will fall into absolute chaos! This is when the dark forces will strike, at the weakest moment of this realm,' Vortor laughed out loud but then started to cough up blood.

He wiped his brow and continued: 'You Tamus fools will suffer! You will suffer!'

Akumi walked closer to him and carefully pressed the tip of her katana against his neck.

'Where is Endal?' she asked.

Vortor smirked. 'He has gone my girl, long gone,' he said. 'You won't stop him now.'

'Where?!' Akumi yelled.

Vortor did not reply and instead laughed out in defiance once more. Akumi withdrew her sword. She seemed deeply at odds with what to do. Vortor suddenly stopped laughing and instead moaned with pain before falling silent. His head bowed forwards lifelessly. The notorious old mage was no more.

His death appeared to alter the atmosphere. The grim ambience abruptly gave way to a feeling of peace and normality. His presence had faded; his influence on the lands had passed. Both girls looked down at him and then suddenly jumped at the sounds of an entrance flicking open. A small trapdoor on the roof of the tower had become unlocked as the magical force keeping it closed diminished with Vortor's demise.

Back on the ground the soldiers and Dorwor marvelled at the sight of the tower doorway opening up. It edged outwards, forming a gap wide enough for them to charge into. Dorwor gave the command and the hordes advanced into the structure. The adrenaline of the charge was met with an anticlimax. The interior was bare and dead and no one was home. The open doorway allowed enough light to pour in to reveal the entire space. There was nothing inside of any significance except a lone horse cowering in a corner.

'That's Endal's horse,' said Akumi as her and Sylvie raced

down from a tiny interior staircase above.

It had brought them back to the ground level, coming from the roof trapdoor and going around the side of the tower in a spiral until ending on the base.

'Is it dangerous?' Dorwor asked ignorantly. 'It looks evil to me! Those eyes aren't right.'

'It's a horse,' smiled Sylvie upon reaching him.

'Hmm, but Endal's horse!' Dorwor remained unsure. He looked to Akumi. 'You got Vortor?'

'Yes, Vortor is dead,' Akumi said.

'We sneaked right up on him,' added Sylvie. 'He was too busy casting spells and laughing to notice us creeping up behind him. Once he had realised we were close Akumi struck him before he could react.'

'The tower must have relied on him to remain closed up I guess,' said Dorwor. 'This is a great day for Marmia! Vortor is finally no more!'

The general cheered along with countless troops around him. Akumi walked to Endal's horse and gently stroked the animal. He was shy and fearful. The girl continued to stroke his neck as she spotted a black bag tied to his saddle. She stepped closer to the pack and started to fiddle with the string that did it up. The animal then suddenly made a bolt for the door and galloped through the crowd of soldiers, snaking out through the exit and into the field.

'Stop that horse!' yelled Dorwor.

'Oh let it go,' Sylvie said. 'It's just some horse.'

Regardless of their opinions it had gone, shooting out of the tower and into the fields. It was making for the woods. Akumi watched it carefully as she looked out from behind the doorway.

'Where did he go?' she asked herself.

The question was answered almost immediately.

'Hey, we've found a trapdoor. It's unlocked,' a soldier shouted out.

Dorwor and the girls raced over to inspect it. It didn't take long to put two and two together.

'He abandoned his horse and entered this tunnel,' said Sylvie. 'Question cracked.'

'Well let's get cracking,' Dorwor smirked. 'We have defeated Vortor and Endal will not be far ahead. We can follow this tunnel as far as it goes. He must have gone this way.'

'Hold on, General,' Akumi announced. 'There is no use us all going. More lives will only be lost.'

'Akumi is right,' Sylvie said.

'The only reason Vortor was so swiftly defeated was due to his primary weakness,' Akumi continued. 'A mage can do little against a warrior when they are up close to them. He made a mistake not paying attention to his surroundings. Endal has no such weakness. He is too much for your men, General.'

Dorwor appeared to understand but showed signs of reluctance.

'We don't want any more dead soldiers,' said Sylvie.

'My men want to go after Endal,' said Dorwor. 'They are fired up for blood. I trust the two of you will be going after him down this tunnel. Well take ten of my best men with you.'

Sylvie was about to speak.

'I will have no argument about it!' Dorwor stated firmly.

Both girls accepted his stance and the compromise was set. The general yelled out to his men and ordered that those around him, his personal guards, went with the girls.

'Take your orders from these two and get Endal. Tamus is counting on you,' he commanded.

The troops stepped forwards and joined Akumi and Sylvie as they stood around the trapdoor.

'You will need torches and fire down there,' Dorwor said.

His men had already brought forth several pre lit torches and handed them to the party.

'Perhaps this very tunnel even leads to Brimma,' said Sylvie. 'It would make sense and we should assume the worst.'

'Then go now and do not delay,' Dorwor said swiftly. 'Find Endal and end this. I will take our army back to Brimma and tighten the tower defences. Good luck.'

'We will see you soon,' Sylvie said.

'Goodbye, General,' said Akumi.

With that the girls dropped into the tunnel and were followed by the ten troops. As they raced along the narrow passage the orange glows of their torches got fainter and fainter from Dorwor's view. The further they passed into the blackness of the underground space the dimmer they became. The bearded warrior studied them until they vanished into black. He then turned to his troops.

'Let's get moving men,' announced the general. 'We must get to Brimma.'

CHAPTER IV

A DARK MAZE

Endal was back on top form and his wounds were a distant memory. He ran along the tunnel in great speed; his torch's light flickering up and down against the narrow walls with the movement. The passageway was eerily silent and totally straight. It was as mysterious and alien as the tower itself had been.

The assassin knew to trust Vortor. He had had dealings with the old mage in the past and his notoriety was in the same league as the dark assassin's. They were both feared amongst men and both said to be of otherworldly origin. The only real difference between them was Endal had no ideology or axe to grind. He merely accepted contracts as a means to prove himself and home his skills. Vortor, on the other hand, had believed in a Dark Lord and craved chaos. He could not face the fact Tamus had finally decisively won the war and was using Endal to do something he had known he'd likely have failed at. The two characters had a mutual understanding. A dark energy pervaded both their minds and souls. It linked them together.

The path went on and on. It occasionally turned slightly but never to any extreme degree. It mostly remained straight. Endal imagined it would go on for a long time, knowing full well that Brimma was a few miles away yet. After running along the tunnel for the best part of an hour the assassin slowed his pace to a walking speed. Even he needed to catch his breath.

Back along the beginnings of the lengthy extent of the tunnel Akumi and Sylvie were leading the party that were racing to catch up with the dark assassin. They were moving with immense pace and the armour clad soldiers seemed to struggle to keep up.

'This is one grim place,' one yelled out.

His voice created a loud echo that bounced off the narrow passage walls.

'Let's just hope it doesn't turn into a maze!' another joked.

'It won't,' Sylvie remarked calmly as she jogged ahead of them. 'This clearly leads to a specific place.'

The party trudged on without any breaks. They maintained the pace well, being driven by the urgency of the situation. For what felt like an hour they pressed on further and further along the dark passage. The air was warm and thin to breathe. Dust and dirt was rampant in the atmosphere and with every breath they could feel the grime enter their throats. There was also a strange smell of dampness and something rotten.

Eventually, Endal upped his pace back to a calm jog. He had walked for several minutes and had also stopped to take a rest for a short moment. The space appeared endless and he was eager to press on. It was at this point he suddenly spotted faint light ahead. It was dim at first and merely a dot amongst black but as he moved further on he had slowly begun to make out an expanse. The tunnel entered into a wider room. It was only slightly larger than the breadth of the passageway but at the end of it was a door.

Endal tested the wooden entry once he'd passed by the room. It was unlocked and once he'd opened it he was hit with the sight and sound of rushing water. A much wider tunnel initiated upon the point of the doorway. It only went in one direction and was filled with water that looked to be coming into it from smaller sections to its sides. Light poured into the tunnel from gaps in the ceiling. Endal studied the nearest. It was a drain hatch. He could make out a blue sky from beyond the metal bars. The lines of light poured down continuously in a pattern of separation along the extent of the tunnel. This was clearly some sort of sewer.

Back within the confines of the passageway Endal's pursuers were closing in. Their pace hadn't faltered and they had covered the distance faster than the dark assassin. They had managed to close the gap and as they ran onwards Akumi suddenly spotted the faint light of the room to the sewer system.

'The tunnel is coming to an end,' she said.

'Thank God for that!' a soldier laughed loudly.

They continued on until they got close enough to the source of the dim light to identify it as a small room that led to a door at the far end. They crept in, panting heavily and with hearts racing.

'The light is coming from the gaps in that doorway,' noted Sylvie. 'This must be the end of the passage.'

The female warriors shuffled closer to the door and Akumi swiftly tried the lock. The handle squealed downwards as the door opened inwards. They poked their heads around the corner to assess what lay beyond the room.

'Some sort of sewer,' said Akumi. 'Light is coming in from those holes.'

Initially, even this taster of daylight shocked their eyes. Being in the dark tunnel for so long had made their night vision astute.

'We will still need these torches,' said Sylvie.

The party moved into the larger sewer tunnel. Beside the rushing water was a wide side walkway, which allowed them to walk forwards parallel to the hurrying water. As they sneaked onwards Akumi noticed small passages leading off from its sides. Her mind was deeply focused. She sensed their enemy was near.

They pressed on cautiously. The loud sound of gushing water and the constant drips of moisture falling from the walls and plodding into the streaming surge created an undeniable tension.

The moment then unexpectedly came. In unison they spotted a black silhouette appear from one of the side passages just ahead of them. Akumi knew instantly that it was Endal.

'That's him!' she whispered.

This was not the time for stealth. Endal had sensed someone was near and had hid in one of the side passages to the sewer tunnel. He'd come out to check if anyone was close. They were. Swords were drawn in an instant. Endal dropped his torch into the gushing waters and held his katana up high. He faced them head on in the middle of the flat stone walkway.

Akumi was about to announce something but the gang of soldiers behind her and Sylvie suddenly barged their way ahead to confront Endal.

'You're a dead man Endal!' one yelled out.

'Wait!' Akumi yelled. 'Don't attack him! He is too much for you!'

'Listen to Akumi men,' Sylvie ordered firmly. 'Don't get any closer to him.'

Several of them started to comply with this reluctantly but two were already near enough to make a move on the assassin. They didn't seem interested in following the girls' orders.

Endal stood motionlessly, waiting for them to attack. His hood was still up; giving him a ghostlike appearance in this dark space.

He was just a black shape.

'You can't be all that,' one of the eager soldier's yelled.

The other stood to his side. They were uninterested in the yells from their fellow troops to get back and listen to the girls. With sudden aggression one of them charged at Endal and swung his large broadsword towards his body. Endal deflected the sword and knocked it from the soldier's grasp. It fell into the flowing water beside them. The assassin then poked his katana into the soldier's abdomen. The deep stab was fatal and the man dropped and rolled into the pouring liquid racing down the sewer. The other soldier became wild with anger and swung out fiercely. There was a second's worth of parrying until Endal's katana slid across his neck and then drove through the bone. The soldier's head was instantly decapitated and bounced against the stone wall before splashing into the drink. His body fell awkwardly to the ground beside the dripping katana blade.

The eight remaining soldiers were shocked by the ease in which the dark figure had claimed their friends.

'What the...' one cried out in confusion.

'He is too much for you! I must deal with this,' Akumi affirmed sadly.

'Vortor is no more Endal,' announced Sylvie emotionally. 'Tamus is secure. You have no chance. Why do you persist?'

There was no response from the assassin. He remained in his stance and seemed entirely indifferent to their comments.

'We need to attack him at once,' a soldier suggested. 'In a rush.'

'Stay back! Please!' Akumi ordered.

She edged forwards with her blade fixed on her enemy. Sylvie appeared to instinctively follow the assassin's lead. She brought out her shimmering silver sword and held it in both hands.

There was sudden mocking laughter from Endal as he watched them close in. He then abruptly pounced from the walkway and over the flowing water of the sewer to the other side of the tunnel. He ran ahead across its pathway and into a side passage out of sight.

'We must go after him,' a soldier bellowed.

With that there was a wild charge. The troops dived over the water and sparingly made the distance. It was not a particularly hard jump to make in the rather narrow space. Akumi and Sylvie knew to follow suit and gave up trying to control the soldiers. In unison they pounced over the water and hit the other walkway.

Endal raced up the side passage and paused at the point it turned off in two directions. The space was tight and claustrophobic. It was lit only by the light oozing in from the sky beyond the sewer. He spotted a soldier racing up from the passage to confront him. He wasn't paying much attention and didn't even realise Endal's katana was poised to penetrate him. He ran into it and yelped out. The cold steel cut into his ribcage and mangled his guts. Endal withdrew the blade, causing the warrior's body to leak blood. The assassin slid the blade across his chest, finishing him off. He then ran deeper into what was now a maze of tight passages leading off into sub tunnels and other places.

'Stick together,' yelled Sylvie. 'Don't split up.'

She hoped her voice could be heard by those around her. She followed Akumi as they marched up the passage Endal had fled from. They stepped over the body of the soldier he'd slain and studied every angle. The other soldiers had gone up different passages in the hope of flanking the assassin. Instead, they'd ran into paths leading to other places. One went upwards and linked onto a walkway above the sewer tunnel. Another turned and met a tunnel leading away from the main one. It was a complex collection of narrow spaces and one in which getting lost was no difficult task.

Endal sneaked silently deeper into the maze of passageways. He intended to reach the surface in the hope he was now quite near Brimma and could lose his pursuers.

'Everyone regroup!' Sylvie yelled. 'We can't afford to get split up.'

The blonde haired girl and Akumi kept together. It seemed too late to get the soldiers back into their ranks. They'd darted off in differing directions and were now fuelled by their adrenaline. As the girls reached a wider tunnel and stepped over a small gap in between the two walkways they heard a man yell out in agony. The scream echoed around the stone walls until there was silence.

The girls knew to follow the sound. They raced down a passage it had likely come from to find a dead soldier sitting upright against a wall. Blood oozed from deep throbbing slashes to his flesh and spattered the ground in spurts of dark red.

'Regroup!' Sylvie yelled out again. 'He must be close.'

They moved on up the tunnel they'd stumbled across. It turned and led into another main passage that looked to lead off into dark infinities in either direction. As they stared into the black voids they heard another loud shriek. It had come from beyond the darkness of the tunnel. They turned right and headed for the scene.

'No... you will die!' a voice gargled. It was followed by another loud, agonising yell.

'Endal!' Akumi screamed wildly.

She started to run up the tunnel. It was wide and seemed to be becoming brighter as they moved further along it. The female assassin was desperate to confront her enemy. The fact soldiers were dying around her drove her into a state of deep devotion to her task.

Sylvie raced to catch up and the girls briefly stopped once they'd come across bodies. Two more soldiers had fallen under Endal's sword and their lifeless bodies were huddled together in a pool of blood. There was nothing the girls could do. They ran further onwards along the brightening tunnel.

CHAPTER V

THE GLINTING WATERS

'It looks like daylight,' commented Akumi. 'The tunnel is leading to an exit.'

The dim light was becoming brighter. The tunnel's end was a circular iron gateway that led to the outside world. Iron bars partially blocked the incoming light meaning it entered the sewer in a lined pattern as it poured in between each sturdy, rusty pole.

'Hold up,' a voice yelled from behind the girls.

They turned to check who it was as they continued to jog towards the exit. Two soldiers appeared from the darkness.

They reached the door after a few seconds more charging. The afternoon daylight was at first blinding for their sore eyes. Akumi studied the bars. They had been cleanly sliced and several of them lay on the ground beside the locked hatch.

'Endal must have come this way,' she said. 'He struck through these bars.'

'Where are the others?' Sylvie asked the soldiers.

'Mostly dead,' one groaned morbidly. 'But we don't know where the rest are.'

'We can't afford to try and find them,' Sylvie said. 'We are too hot on Endal's tail.'

Akumi bent low and edged through the gap Endal had formed in the bars. Sylvie and the two soldiers followed. The tunnel popped out from the ground like a rabbit's burrow. They studied the world beyond the iron bars as they crept into the outside. It had brought them out onto a hillside.

The mighty hill led down into a vast lake and beyond the lake stood Brimma. Its bristling architecture and countless buildings dominated the landscape. However, the main focal point was the vast and soaring structure in the middle of the city. Tamus Tower was in full view.

The four warriors studied every angle around them in the hope of spotting Endal. Suddenly, Akumi locked her eyes on a black figure creeping down the hill amongst bushes.

'There he is,' she said softly. 'We must stop him before he reaches the lake.'

With that they ran down the hill. It wasn't particularly steep but was peppered with foliage and small growing trees. The black figure of Endal kept popping in and out of view but there was now nowhere he could flee to.

Endal looked back up the extent of the hill and instantly spotted his pursuers. He then noticed two more soldiers pop out from the tunnel exit eager to catch up with their group. Endal looked to the lake. He was now only a few hundred feet from it. The hill led directly down into the blue, glinting waters. The mighty city was reflected in the still lake; two cities could be seen, one the lucid, watery chimera.

The water was calm and several small rowing boats floated on the surface. They were tied to a tiny wooden pier that led out into the water. The assassin knew there was no point trying to flee from his pursuers anymore. He would have to confront them head on at some stage and the lake was now beckoning.

Endal stood motionlessly and studied his opponents like some cornered animal. The clouds above were darkening and a wind had begun to howl. There was likely going to be rain. Akumi stood in front of the soldiers and Sylvie remained by her side. It didn't take long for them to catch up and find themselves staring at the dark figure on the water's edge.

'This is as far as you are going to go Endal,' Sylvie called out.

Akumi didn't say anything and instead raised her sword. She briefly looked at the four soldiers eagerly poised behind her.

'He is too skilled for you,' she said. 'Do not approach him.'

The men were at odds with what to do. One came forth.

'This is now personal. He killed a few of our friends in that tunnel!' the soldier said forcefully.

'And he will kill you if you attack him,' said Akumi.

'We won't chicken out of this,' another grumbled.

With that the four troops charged forwards and ploughed past the girls. They yelled out war cries as they ran at Endal. The assassin didn't flinch and as their swords got within striking distance his katana split the air and made contact with skin. One collapsed instantly whilst the other three backed away slightly.

Endal edged forwards and deflected a strike from one to his left. He then poked his blade into the soldier's torso and withdrew it. The man let out a desperate yell in agony and stumbled down lifeless.

The girls couldn't watch and darted into the brawl before Endal could kill the others. The men didn't appear to want to back away and got near to the dark assassin again.

'Wait!' Akumi shrieked.

It was too late. As soon as they'd got within range of Endal's katana the shimmering blade had sliced them cleanly across the chests. Their swords dropped and they fell down in synchronicity.

Akumi jumped in without hesitation. Suddenly, the two assassins had locked horns again. Their katanas struck one another in a volley of parrying blows. Each strike was deflected by the other. This was a deathly dual, with each move of the assassins' a carefully calculated defence. Any mistake would be fatal for either fighter.

The speed of the blades dancing in the air momentarily shocked Sylvie as she studied them. She then entered the tussle. Her sword was larger than the katanas. It was a silver broadsword and one which glistened in the daylight. Her stance was intriguing, like an animal bending low at the knees and arching their back slightly forwards. She was astutely poised.

Endal stepped back slightly from Akumi in preparation to take on two opponents. He looked into Sylvie's eyes briefly. Endal could sense she was another skilled warrior. Without warning Sylvie moved in. This marked the first time the two had battled. The defender of Tamus, a highly decorated warrior, was about to take on the notorious assassin.

Her broadsword swung out at him. He was forced to evade it by taking a few steps back. The dark assassin then retaliated by edging back nearer her and swinging his blade out in the hope of catching her throat. Sylvie ducked low and the sword glided over her head. Upon rising back up she thrust her sword forwards at Endal. It was aimed at stabbing him in the stomach. The momentum of the broadsword and the girl's strength forced Endal to again retreat back. He seemed reluctant to try and deflect her sword. As he dodged her strike Akumi came from his side again. She was faster than Sylvie and her style was much more like Endal's. The two assassins were like minded in their ways of sword fighting. Sylvie's style looked to slightly confuse the hooded killer, at least to begin.

Akumi and Endal manically attacked one another. Neither seemed to tire as their speed and skills were put to the test. Sylvie sneaked closer and studied Endal. She appeared hesitant to attack him when he was occupied taking on Akumi. The two assassins battled on. It looked perfectly even until Endal suddenly managed to deflect Akumi's blade in such a way as to force the girl to bend sideways with the momentum of her deflected steel. He then struck her in the back of the head with his elbow. The girl fell down momentarily dazed. Sylvie leapt in.

Sylvie's ruby red cape blew with grace in the wind. The outstretched cloak made the girl look twice her size as her outlines expanded. Endal carefully analysed the girl before making any move. She was still bent quite low and angled her sword upwards to face him. In a flash Endal closed the distance and his katana made contact with the girl's broadsword as she struck against his strike.

The assassin tried to trick her and suddenly brought his sword down under hers and attempted to flick it back up to strike her. She turned to face him sideways on and narrowly dodged the tip of his blade.

Both retreated back and as Endal got poised for another assault he noticed movement across the hillside. Several hundred feet away was a road that snaked its way down the hill from the south and hit a bridge that passed the lake and entered into Brimma.

The dark assassin made out an army of horsemen race onto the bridge and cross it with immense speed. Leading them was a large man whose horse was several feet ahead of the convoy. This seemed to alarm Endal and at that very moment Akumi sprung back to her feet. The female assassin clutched her katana and raced to Sylvie's side. Endal took a look at them and then back to the army converging on the city.

'General Dorwor is home,' Sylvie commented.

Endal looked at her coldly and then without warning bounded for the lake. He raced up the wooden pier and dived straight into the water. Both girls ran after him without hesitation. They raced up the pier and halted at the water's edge.

'We have to stop him!' Akumi wailed.

'I will catch up with Dorwor,' Sylvie said. 'He needs to know that Endal is near the city.'

'Okay Sylvie,' Akumi replied quickly. 'I'm going after Endal. Oh, and thanks for back there. Endal would have had me if you hadn't have jumped in when you did.'

'Don't mention it,' Sylvie said. 'I have never fought anyone like him Akumi. He is exceptional.' Her voice was suddenly more serious.

'I know,' said Akumi, 'which is why we must stop him. I will see you in the city.'

Akumi leapt into the water. Her body cut into the lake like a flawless incision. She was gone. Sylvie turned and ran for the bridge. It was now vital she reach the tower and safeguard the Emperor's protection.

Akumi was a naturally skilled swimmer and shot through the clear, warm water with grace and speed. As soon as she had gone underwater she had spotted Endal. He was now about half way across the lake and had begun to swim on the surface in a front crawl. The girl stayed underwater and scuttled like a fish in pursuit of food. She was certainly the quicker swimmer of the two.

Endal could see the tower with great clarity. There was little in between him and his goal. The lake was halted by a mighty stone wall that went across the width of the waters, covering the boundary of the capital city. He hadn't lost his cool at this stage but knew that he didn't have much time to play with. He wasn't interested in battling his pursuer and was more eager to lose them. He had a plan.

CHAPTER VI

RALLYING AT TAMUS TOWER

Akumi was catching up. She planned to swim up and strike Endal from underwater. However, her plan soon looked flawed. Endal abruptly went back underwater and headed down into the dark depths of the lake. Akumi knew that to pursue him she would first have to get another deep breath of air.

She reached the surface and inhaled. The girl then swam with all her might down into the abyss below. The water was clear for a while but then became dark and murky. As she went deeper more fish became apparent, swishing around her and narrowly avoiding contact. She knew roughly where Endal had disappeared but once she got deeper she realised that on the muddy base of this lake were vast collections of rugged rocks and coarse plant life. Schools of fish continued to dance around the low depths as Akumi pressed on just above the rocks. The ground was scattered with pebbles and seaweed. She swam around carefully, checking every angle.

There were literally an unlimited amount of places for Endal to potentially hide. Each large rock formation created cavernous gaps and crannies that could hide any number of dark, grim secrets. She was careful not to poke her head into them for fear of being struck by a well placed katana blade. As the seconds went by Akumi got more and more worried. She needed to accept defeat. She had lost him. The girl needed air and knew not to push it any further. She had begun to climb back up to the surface.

As the slim body of the female assassin rose to higher depths Endal carefully studied his surroundings. He had hid in amongst the rocks and hadn't been spotted by the girl. He was able to hold his breath for an inhumanly long time and was not troubled that there was still some length to go until he would reach the wall. He moved out from his position and swam onwards as near the rocks as possible.

Akumi stared up at the sky momentarily as she took several deep breaths. She was at odds with what to do. Her focus then turned to the bridge and this reminded her that Sylvie would likely now be in the city with Dorwor. She decisively concluded that it was no use hunting for Endal in the rocky underwater maze and that it would be best for her to regroup with the others and be around Tamus. Endal had eluded the determined assassin on this occasion.

Sylvie ran up the bridge and was allowed to pass the tall gate without protest from the guards who knew her face well. An army of soldiers had converged on the dirt track leading into Brimma from the gate of the city and the troops peppered the streets. Sylvie ploughed through the crowds to reach Dorwor who she could spot standing amongst several of his officers. As the blonde haired girl appeared from the masses of sturdy men the general looked up.

'Ah, Sylvie,' he smiled.

She halted by his side and immediately broke into the matters at hand: 'We couldn't stop him, General. He has reached the city. Akumi is on his tail but he has probably already crossed the lake.'

Dorwor roared something out loud that his men could immediately understand. It was a command that meant precisely what Sylvie had said; Endal was near the Emperor. The soldiers made for the tower without delay. The general started to walk swiftly up the narrow street towards the vast tower and Sylvie followed him.

'I will create an impregnable wall of defence around the tower Sylvie,' he muttered. 'This Endal character won't have any chance. He cannot defeat three hundred soldiers!' The general laughed out loud.

'I am going straight to the Emperor,' said Sylvie. 'I am sure you are right but I will not take any chances. I will call up all of my people and we shall not leave the Emperor's side.'

'Feel free to call up all your bodyguards,' Dorwor smiled. 'They can all watch from the tower as my men kick Endal's head around the courtyard!'

There was a sudden yell from behind them as they marched

nearer to the tower.

'I lost him,' Akumi announced whilst running to catch up. 'He went underwater and vanished. We have to assume he is in the city.'

'I know Akumi,' Dorwor replied. 'Don't worry! We won't let him get any further. That is certain.'

After jogging up a few streets and passing a forming crowd of concerned citizens being shunned away by soldiers the three friends of the Emperor passed through the small gate to the grounds of Tamus Tower and were met by hundreds of faces eager for orders. The gate was shut firmly behind them and bolted with large iron bars. Archers took positions on the walls around the tower and hordes of troops stood around the general and the two girls by his side.

'Men this is it! The moment has come where we finally crush this bug that wants to harm our Emperor and show it what Tamus is all about!' Dorwor addressed his men with great passion. 'Take up positions around the tower and be poised to fight. Endal is near and we must be ready to take him on. Whoever brings me his head shall instantly become a general!'

As he finished there was a roar of acknowledgement and a sudden foray of movement as the soldiers took up positions. The tower was defended by a single tall wall that went around the sides of the structure in a rough square. After this there was a flat courtyard and tiny stables, and then the doors into the tower itself.

Sylvie looked to Akumi. 'I'm going to Tamus,' she said. 'I have a team of well trained bodyguards ready to take my orders. I want to be by the Emperor's side.'

Akumi nodded. 'I will stay down here. I need to be here when he comes,' she said.

The two girls hugged one another and separated. Sylvie made for the doors to the tower. From this close the structure seemed to rise into the very sky itself. There were certainly many steps for her to take.

General Dorwor paced up and down the courtyard whilst studying his men and stroking his sword. Akumi watched him for a moment and then turned to the wall around them. Soldiers massed on the boards that gave them a view over it and allowed for arrow fire. She then sat herself down and started to tie her wet hair back. Her hair bun had succumbed to the liquid and her long locks naturally drooped onto her shoulders. She was drenched and caught the eyes of several soldiers making comments about her and then giggling to themselves. She smiled to herself. After all, if anything, being soaking wet made her more alert!

Sylvie entered into the darkness of the tower after passing the sturdy doors. She marched across the entrance hall and straight up the dimly lit spiral staircase that snaked up the sides of the unique structure. Her Emperor was awaiting her and her closest soldiers were perched to follow her command. As she walked upwards her red cloak became continually illuminated by burning torches that hung from pegs at each turn in the stairs. The flames flickered with the breeze as Sylvie's movement brushed the air.

Before long the blonde girl had reached the highest floor of the tower and once again found herself outside the large door to the Emperor's throne room. Two guards withdrew their large halberds from the entrance and bowed respectfully before the girl. She entered into the large hall and immediately spotted Tamus leaning against a small altar, awaiting her presence.

The room was scattered with guards dressed in black leather armour and robes. These were his personal protectors and Sylvie was their leader. These bodyguards were the Emperor's most trusted and Sylvie had every faith in them. As she walked towards Tamus the bodyguards immediately stood to attention and formed in lines.

'Stand easy,' she ordered.

She halted beside the altar and gave Tamus a slight smile. He seemed more alert now his most dependable subject had appeared. He rose up from his slouched position and stood to face her. He wore a thick, drooping white robe and his long, dark hair rested roughly upon his shoulders.

'Ah, at last you return to be at my side,' he said. 'I trust you had an eventful trip...'

'Hello my Emperor,' Sylvie replied politely. 'It was certainly eventful. I encountered the assassin and have just returned from the lakeside where I fought him. Endal is exceptionally skilled. He is in the city. We must now prepare for anything.'

Tamus was unsurprised by the information. 'I suspected this thing would escalate to this,' he said. 'Hiding in my throne room like I am the game and he is the Emperor hunting me! You have done all you can Sylvie and I am proud of you. I am ready to follow your orders.'

'You expected this?' Sylvie asked.

Tamus smiled at the question. He could tell the young girl was probably quite ignorant when it came to the realities behind the figure of Endal.

'I did Sylvie,' he said. 'I didn't want to tell you this to begin for fear of worrying you, but I know all about Endal. Over these years of war that have passed I have heard about many things, not just assassins.

'I don't confess to know as much about him as others but have always been aware of his existence, and his ungodly powers. I am not surprised he continues to elude you and Dorwor. Endal is a force of his own. He, and a few others like him, represent the last remnants of a gone age; an age of mystery and foreign, otherworldly interventions with the business of man. My girl, the force that demands my blood may prove unstoppable!'

'Endal will be defeated,' Sylvie insisted, shaking her head at his words in defiance. 'Vortor was killed, and so Endal, too, will prove mortal.'

'Vortor?' Tamus nodded. 'That old mage huh? I've not heard his name mentioned in an eon. So you encountered him?'

'Dorwor was first to encounter him,' said Sylvie. 'It turns out he was one of the conspirers. He hid under a false identity as an innkeeper in Dolsbury. He intervened when we had Endal in our grasp and retreated to his tower. I scaled it alongside Akumi, one of Hazati's assassins, and she killed him.'

'Interesting,' said Tamus. 'The old names are coming together it would seem: Vortor, Endal. It would seem the old mage desired to see me fall. He obviously sought relations with the rebels solely as a means to get them to go to the assassin. My guess is Vortor didn't wish to ask Endal himself! Perhaps he feared Endal would reject the contract if he sensed something afoot.'

'Well he is gone now,' said Sylvie. 'And soon Endal will be joining him.'

'Let us hope so,' said the Emperor. 'And as I have said, I will now follow your orders. I am deeply grateful for all you have done. I can think of no other I would rather stand beside at this moment.'

'Thank you Emperor,' Sylvie said, slightly touched. 'For now we must stay put and observe what goes on outside. It is all we can do.'

The warrior's drive and allegiance to Tamus had never been stronger than it was right now. Her dedication to protecting him was rock solid and now she was beside him her determination to make sure he wasn't harmed became a personal drive.

Back on the ground Akumi continued to sit in contemplation and relaxation. There really wasn't much any of them could do but wait. As she looked up into the overcast sky she noticed some of the troops overlooking the wall beside the large gate shouting down to someone on the other side.

'Who are you?' one yelled.

Akumi couldn't make out the response but soon heard the soldier shout back: 'Who? Speak louder.'

The soldiers appeared to hear a response and then one turned and eyed the columns of troops dutifully.

'General Dorwor,' the man yelled out.

Akumi looked to where she had last seen the general. He hadn't moved far and had turned from his position sitting on the ground with a few officers to respond: 'What is it?' he roared back.

'There are some people outside asking for you. They say you know them. They want to enter,' bellowed the soldier.

'Well what are their names?' the general was aggravated.

'Sorry, of course,' the soldier grumbled. 'They say they are called Hazati... and Harkor.'

Akumi instantly stood up and looked to Dorwor. 'Let them in,' he yelled, beginning to walk towards the gate.

The soldier nodded and without delay the gates churned inward and opened up, revealing two figures standing side by side with their horses behind them. Akumi walked alongside Dorwor.

'Looks like you're going to be reunited,' Dorwor chuckled.

Akumi was so excited to see them she had already begun to run to the gate and suddenly found herself in front of her two friends.

'You're both okay!' she exclaimed happily.

Before either had responded Akumi had clamped her arms around Hazati and given him a warm hug. The old man seemed alert and focused like he was fully recovered. His walking stick still kept his hunched posture upright. He laughed and gently patted his apprentice assassin on the back.

'We are fine Akumi. And you?' he asked.

'I'm okay master, and relieved you are both here,' she said.

Akumi gave Harkor a hug and noticed he was cautious of anyone touching or knocking into his waist. She was delicate and thoughtfully kissed him on the cheek.

'Are you still hurt?' she asked.

Harkor smiled. 'I'm okay Akumi, just still a bit sore.'

The three assassins walked back into the courtyard and the gate closed back behind them. General Dorwor had kept his distance, allowing them to catch up before he jumped in.

'There is so much to tell you both,' Akumi said. 'So much has happened.'

'We can catch up soon Akumi,' Hazati said. 'All that matters right now is that we focus on defending the Emperor. We heard Endal was in the city as soon as we passed across the bridge. This is all we need to know for now.'

Hazati noticed Dorwor waiting for them to get closer to him as he stood a few feet ahead. 'I hope your men are prepared for a small war, General,' the old man commented dryly.

'Welcome back Hazati,' said Dorwor. 'Oh, and we're ready for Endal. Don't you worry about that.'

CHAPTER VII

THE GENERAL'S LAST STAND

The temperature of the water seemed to hit an icy low when one reached the rocky bottom of the lake. Endal had managed to swim underwater right up to the wall of Brimma. As soon as he had reached this stone structure he moved upwards and headed for the surface. Before long his head had popped up from the water and his body floated carelessly.

He took in several deep breaths and carefully looked around. He'd been underwater for several minutes and hadn't spotted any of his pursuers for some time. He was still cautious though and remained alert. For all he knew they themselves were still underwater and hunting for him.

The assassin studied the wall and started to swim alongside it in intrigue. He had no intention of entering the city via the bridge, knowing it was likely now a fortified and closed entrance. His aim was to find another way in and some other means to get beyond the intimidating wall.

As Endal contemplated how he was to get beyond the fortification that enclosed the city he continued to slowly swim up the side of the lake parallel to the aged stone. Within several seconds he noticed a small entrance pop up on the side of the wall. It was on the level of the surface of the water and beyond it was a narrow sewer tunnel leading into Brimma.

Endal swam to the side of the barred entrance and studied the rusty iron poles. It would be impossible to cut through the strong railings with his katana and he had no other means to force entry. Unlike the bars to the previous sewer tunnel these were thick and strong; untested by years of erosion.

He continued to peek into the tunnel as he bobbed on the water in vain. It was in this moment the assassin heard a distinct sound. A horse was galloping in the distance across the lake. He turned to look for the source. Across the water, and coming from the hilltop, a single black horse was rushing forwards. It didn't take long for Endal to realise it was his own.

The mysterious Harwind had tracked where his master was; his will to reach him along with an unfaltering natural instinct had brought him here. Rider and horse were reunited. The assassin wasn't only pleased to see his ride again; he was relieved. He smiled to himself at the knowledge that inside a pack tied to the horse's saddle were explosives he had made long ago in the Abbey. There were also tools and gadgets amongst the charges that would prove very useful now they were truly required. The black horse had saved the day.

Endal kicked as fast as he could as he initiated a front crawl to get back across the lake. His horse stood by the edge of the water staring out at his master getting closer and closer. In this precise moment it started to rain. A shower poured from the dreary clouds above and fell vertically with no wind to spoil the trajectory. Thousands of ripples instantly formed rapid patterns of circular movement on the surface of the lake. The weather had been deteriorating all day.

The journey back to the other end of the water took a few more minutes and suddenly the assassin clambered out of the drink and stood drenched beside his horse. The animal looked pleased to see Endal and bowed its head as the man gave it a warm stroke and pat on the back.

'You have done very well my companion,' said Endal.

He then unwound the straps to the large bag tied on the horse's back. He noticed the knots of the thin strings had already been slightly loosened. He didn't seem concerned. It opened up to reveal a couple of swords, a silver shield, food, water, and a large quantity of a strange reddish concoction.

'Here we have it,' Endal said. 'Perfect.'

The assassin retied the bag and lifted it from his horse. He then placed one of the flaying straps around his shoulder and brought it up to burden. As he tested the weight he noticed within a gap in the fabric a sack of horse food. He took it out and poured its contents onto the ground. The dark mare appeared to acknowledge the gesture with a head movement.

'I must go now,' he said to his horse. 'You stay here and wait for me. I will return.'

There was no way of telling if his words were understood.

What was clear was that he spoke in a tone that suggested he was certain the animal could comprehend him.

Endal found himself in amongst cold water again as he lowered himself back into the lake. He turned and supported the bag to bob on the surface as he started to backstroke forwards. It was clear he was finding the pack heavy and the task of getting it across the stretch of water would take a good deal of energy. The rain was getting heavier and the constant thudding of raindrops striking his head forced him to close his eyes as he kicked onwards. The crossing seemed twice the distance when there was something heavy to drag along.

The wall became larger and larger in view as Endal pressed on. He didn't cease and kept his pace until he'd reached the other side. The sewer entrance looked unconquerable. The iron was thick and unchallenged by the many years of waterside attrition.

Endal kept his black pack on the surface of the water with one arm whilst keeping himself afloat with his legs. If the bag was to sink it would disappear into a murky black void below. The assassin feared if it did go under he'd no longer have the strength to retrieve it after his trek across the tarn. The red powder was in two sacks and Endal gathered up a quantity of it into a glass bottle. Within the pack were several of these bottles and fuses along with large matches.

He made tying the fuse to the bottle of powder look easy and placed his creation just inside the tunnel behind the bars. His hand was able to prod in between them. He flicked a match and lit the fuse. It sparked and hissed as a small flame sneaked its way down it with a green glow. Endal swam back several feet and leant against the wall.

There was a loud bang and brilliant white flash. The sound echoed into the tunnel and a scurry of birds suddenly flew up from above the tip of the wall in protest. Orange flame then raced out of the tunnel in a small fireball and dropped into the water, instantly flickering out into nonexistence. There was black smoke and the smell of sulphur. Endal swam back to the tunnel and analysed the impact. The entrance had been obliterated. There was now nothing to stop him clambering into the gloomy sewer.

The first thing he did was lift his pack into the tunnel and out of the water. He felt relieved once the strain of keeping it afloat finally passed. He then crawled in and lay flat out on the stone.

He needed a quick breather.

'What happened happened Akumi. You cannot dwell on it now,' Hazati insisted.

Akumi sat beside him on the ground whilst Harkor stood swinging his sword arm around and stretching his body.

'I know master,' replied the girl. 'It's just that I can't help but feel we should have been able to protect him.'

She was dwelling on Jobe's death. Although she'd been putting up a rock solid front she had been deeply grieving his death since leaving his side. She had lost one of her few true friends.

'Don't blame yourself. He knew precisely what he was doing,' Hazati said.

It was clear Akumi saw her master as a father figure. He had been by her side since she could remember and now he was at the tower she felt a sense of security.

'We must make sure his death was not in vain,' Hazati continued. 'We must make sure Endal is stopped.'

Akumi nodded and then looked to the ground glumly. 'The Emperor is surrounded by hundreds of soldiers. We are here, as is Sylvie, and the general, yet I still sense Endal is confident,' she said.

'Endal is not invincible Akumi,' said Hazati. 'You have now seen the true extent of his skill but don't forget that even Endal is only one mortal man.'

As Hazati spoke he kept his deeper thoughts to himself. He knew only too well that Endal was quite possibly something other than man. His origins remained a mystery.

'From what you have told me Vortor fell easily enough,' Hazati continued. 'I remember a time when men spoke of that old mage like he was invulnerable! You proved them wrong!' Akumi nodded humbly at his reassuring words.

The old master had been impressed to hear his student had defeated the dark mage. Like the general, Hazati had known about Vortor ever since he could remember. The news of the mage's role in this tale had deeply intrigued him. However, as with his thoughts on Endal, Hazati's deeper deliberations remained in his head. He feared that what Akumi had told him the mage had said to her and Sylvie before his death may prove to be a warning, speaking of far greater troubles to come than even this.

The three assassins continued to banter and prepare for battle. Akumi flexed her muscles and when a group of troops began to pass out food and water they quickly devoured the offerings. This was the picture for most of the inhabitants of the tower. All that could be done was to prepare and wait.

The silence of the scene was suddenly interrupted by a bass heavy boom. The noise thudded through the streets and echoed around the walls of the tower courtyard. The sound had come from just beyond the walls.

'Prepare!' Dorwor yelled.

Hazati and his assassins raced to the wall and climbed up onto the board that allowed them to peer over the high structure into the city beyond. Smoke was rising from the far side of one of the narrow roads in front of the main gate into the tower. As they studied the dark smoulder a black figure abruptly walked across the street from one side of houses to the other. The figure vanished back behind the buildings in an instant.

'Endal is here,' said Hazati.

Several soldiers started to shout out in panic and adrenaline at the sight of their enemy.

'Archers prepare,' Dorwor commanded from the wall side. 'As soon as he is in view again pepper him with arrow heads!'

A large group of troops came forwards and raised their bows.

'Be alert,' Hazati addressed his assassins. 'This is the showdown.'

Hundreds of faces continued to stare at the roads beyond the wall. White houses were the only spectacle. The smoke had faded and there was now nothing to behold. This moment of calm was to be the last the tower would see for some time. Without warning there was a sudden volley of loud explosions that rung out from all over the streets to one side of the tower. Orange flames howled up from the ground and raced across the air in moaning conflagration. One building collapsed in on itself with the force of the fire that had begun to rage around its foundations.

'He's going to blow us up!' a single unknown troop wailed out desperately.

This was certainly a dramatic entrance. Without even raising his sword Endal had sent the wind up the tower's defence. Fire had now started to spread and engulf several white houses.

Several civilians carrying young children ran from the scene in fear and confusion as the peaceful streets of Brimma turned into a fierce front line.

Dark smoke blew from the flames and formed vast black clouds that moved towards the wall. Within seconds the incoming blur of darkness converged on the soldiers and entirely blocked their view of the streets ahead. The western wall was suddenly blind. Soldiers coughed away and bent low on their platform to avoid taking in the thick smoke. The assassins were swift to cotton on and cowered behind the sturdy bricks of the wall as the cloud blew by above them.

'How did he get into the city?' Harkor protested.

'He was bound to find a way,' Akumi said.

'He has explosives,' added Hazati. 'He probably blew his way into the sewer and entered into the streets via a manhole. That would have been the only way I can see.'

Akumi was hesitant to keep low for long. The smoke had gradually begun to weaken and as the bulk of it raged up into the sky she raised her head and looked beyond the wall. Her brown eyes caught a glimpse of the dark assassin running away from a section of the wall a few feet along from them.

'He's placed a charge on the wall!' she screamed. 'Get back from the wall!'

There was an instant collective acceptance of her words from the panicked troops and the entire side of the wall started to turn and flee from the raised platform beside the wall. However, there was no time. A deafening rumble roared as a white flash reported the large explosion. A vast orange fireball expanded from the flash and ripped a large segment of the wall into pieces of flying brick and smoulder. Debris shot outwards from every angle and struck several fleeing soldiers with ferocious force.

The three assassins had managed to avoid the blast as they bent low to its side. The force of the explosion had gone in one direction and utterly destroyed several metres of the wall. The explosion itself had consumed many of the retreating troops and sent them high into the air. Some were on fire and rolling around desperately as others lay around dazed.

From the highest point of the tower Sylvie and Tamus studied the scene from their balcony. The smoke had risen up and gone beyond their altitude. Back below Dorwor emerged from the wreckage of the western side of the wall and clambered to his feet. He was covered in dust but remained unscathed.

'Regroup on me! Get up men,' he roared with passion.

The soldiers still standing on the other side of the tower wall were unsure what to do with themselves now it was clear Endal was coming from their opposite side.

'Keep your positions! Don't move!' Dorwor yelled.

Hazati seemed eager to yell his own commands and stood up as the smoke passed over him.

'General, get your troops to form up around the sides of the tower. Abandon the wall!' he screeched as loud as his worn voice allowed.

Dorwor appeared to acknowledge the suggestion and as he studied the bodies around him he realised most of them would not be getting back up.

'Form around the tower!' he screamed.

As he yelled out Akumi noticed a dark silhouette pass through the charring ruins of the wall unchallenged.

'Dorwor, watch out!' she cried.

The general looked around and back stepped as his soldiers initiated their move to the tower. Akumi and Harkor bolted to reach him. Dorwor then noticed that just beyond the fading smoke in front of him a single hooded figure stood with two katanas poised in either arm. It was the general's first glimpse of Endal. He showed no sign of fear.

'For Tamus!' Dorwor bellowed.

He raised his large sword and charged at Endal in a loud war cry.

'No!' Akumi shrieked. 'Dorwor, don't!'

The large general ran up to Endal and swung his sword towards the figure's hooded head. Endal flawlessly dodged the strike by leaning back. As the general's sword ended its swing his body became outstretched. Endal drove one of his katana blades into the man's neck and cleanly cut through the Adam's apple, followed by the throat. The blade sliced through neck skin and came out the other side, decapitating the general in a flash. His head fell to the smouldering bricks and his body collapsed forwards and smashed onto the hot dust. Endal then turned and ran back into the streets.

'The general is down!' a terrified voice rung out. 'Avenge the general!'

No order was required as a large quantity of the soldiers standing by the tower broke off and ran after the dark assassin. Akumi and Harkor reached Dorwor's body and retreated back to avoid the charge of furious troops. Nothing they could say would stop them from running after Endal.

It became clear at least half of the tower's garrison had now run from their formation and into the streets in a wild horde. Once the last of them had passed the wrecked wall Akumi and Harkor looked down to the general. Nothing could be done.

'He died defending Tamus,' Harkor commented.

Akumi was just silent. Hazati came stumbling forwards and looked as the soldiers charged into the street ahead.

'This is falling apart,' he said. 'We need to fall back and get to the Emperor's side.'

As soon as he had finished his sentence the words were followed by three ear-splitting blasts. More explosions erupted in the streets. Endal had lured the soldiers into a well timed trap. They had ran into an ambush. As Endal had scuttled away he had dropped three of his bottled bombs. They went off one after the other, directly within the mass of troops charging down the narrow space.

CHAPTER VIII

CONFLICT IN THE COURTYARD

Endal watched as the fires consumed his pursuers. He hid by a pillar and looked up the street. The first explosion had gone off in front of the troops and the other two within their huddle. Now there was only smoke and dust. Some of the buildings beside the detonations collapsed and their debris added to the destruction and carnage. There were countless screams of agony and protest from beyond the grimy smoulder. Endal walked out from the pillar and stood in the middle of the road with his katanas edged forwards, glimmering in the flames.

He marched up the street and as the smoke passed he studied the scene. Most of the soldiers lay lifeless and charred by flame. Some were crawling around in pain. None were standing. He calmly walked past the bodies and met no resistance. He moved on and within seconds was back inside the tower courtyard. Hazati and his assassins had retreated back to the side of the tower where the remainder of the soldiers still stood in formation.

'We can't abandon these soldiers,' said Akumi as they stood beside the door into the tower. 'We need to stay here and take Endal on.'

Hazati noticed Endal eying the tower from just inside the courtyard. His hand still clasped the handle to the tower door but his grip was loosening.

'His explosions must have claimed all those troops who went after him,' Harkor dryly noted. 'So many just died.'

Hazati's hand let go of the door handle and his arm moved back down to his side.

'We shall stand our ground as Akumi says,' he said.

Endal started to edge forwards. There were still around a hundred troops left who had not been killed or wounded by his bombs. These troops stood firm beside the tower in tight lines.

'Endal!' Hazati yelled. 'You have reached the end of your

journey. Come no further and you will live to tell this tale. Tamus is safe. Be gone!'

Endal didn't seem moved by the old man's words. He continued to creep ever closer to the first line of soldiers. Hazati looked at the archers whom stood by the side of the tower behind the last line of troops. They were ready to fire but were unsure what to do without orders from the late general.

'Archers fire!' Hazati screeched.

A hail of arrows leapt into the air and swiftly turned to rain down on the dark assassin. Endal ran forwards and dived to the ground in a front roll to avoid the sticks of death. They landed just behind him and impaled the dry soil. In this move Endal had got too close to the first line of soldiers for the archers to fire again. The hooded figure got to his feet and raised his swords. The first line of troops moved in and there was combat.

The soldiers bore shields but they didn't appear to help them. The first troop raised his and swung his sword out from its side. Endal deflected the blade and poked his other katana into the troop's chest from above the defensive steel.

Another came at him and was sliced across the thighs before raising a sword. Endal bent low and crashed into another's shield, sending them off balance and forcing them to trip up. Endal grabbed their shield and hurled it at the forming circle of soldiers around him. It struck one and sent them to the floor.

For the soldiers in the other lines the battle looked like troops entering a meat grinder. Whenever one got close to Endal they were cut or hacked and either fell down dead or retreated back in agony. Endal's speed was beyond their ability to tackle. Numbers meant nothing.

Endal was in a dance. His swords glided through the air and struck skin and bone. Whenever a sword came near him he was able to narrowly dodge it or calmly deflect it with his own. He was a master of dictating how a battle would flow. His every move sparked the soldiers around him to attack in a certain desired manner. Endal read them and acted accordingly. The whole thing looked like a choreographed display.

As well as this it was clear the assassin was using more than his swords to kill his attackers. They continually tripped up and were caught off balance. Endal used his elbows and legs to strike and his swords to finish off. Within only seconds the bodies were forming up around him and the line started to resemble a pile of corpses. Akumi and Harkor were eager to jump in but Hazati held them back knowingly.

'In this crazy scuffle you'd be as likely to get hit by a soldier as you would Endal,' he whispered.

It was true the troops seemed driven by fear and anger more than skill and discipline. Their attacks were wild and uncoordinated. Endal hadn't moved from his position. Two came at him at once and were knocked off their feet as Endal dropped to the ground and forced them to trip over him. He pounced back up and stabbed them both in the lower back.

Tamus watched from the balcony with intrigue. Although it was impossible to make out detail from this high vantage point it was clear the assassin was gaining ground. Sylvie appeared unconcerned as she stood by his side.

There were suddenly no more troops from the first line standing. They'd all fallen and had either never got back up or had limped away into a far corner to bleed. The second line of three looked less confident than the first. The soldiers immediately in front of Endal were reluctant to attack.

'I can't watch this any longer,' yelled Akumi. 'We must confront him now!'

'Don't be foolish Akumi,' Hazati spoke. 'Stay back.'

'Master, he is unstoppable,' Harkor said desperately.

'Enough!' Hazati howled.

Endal faced the second line and appeared to be fondling with something under his blood stained robe. The soldiers were either too afraid or blind to notice but he had lit a fuse. He hurled a bottle of red powder at the formation. It blew up as soon as it reached the men. Endal dived to avoid the blast, which looked like a puff of red light followed by flame. It instantly wiped out those around it, cutting through both the second and final rank of troops. Those around the blast backed away from it instinctively.

'Flee! He is a demon!' a voice screamed from the smoky haze.

'No one is to flee!' Hazati answered forcefully.

His words didn't seem to have much impact. As Endal stood up and eyed the troops, who now all huddled in a mass behind where his explosion had ripped into their lines, they started to look troubled. They appeared less interested in attacking him and more interested in keeping a distance.

'Maybe they should just run away,' said Harkor. 'If they get close to him they will be killed anyway. What's the point in them fighting him anymore now?'

Hazati had no response to this.

'It's up to us now,' Akumi commented.

The old man grumbled to himself and then spoke: 'Soldiers... do as you will. This is now a battle between us and him. You have fought well but this is no longer your fight.'

The troops were locked in conversation in a mass state of panic. They'd heard the old man and one had taken on the role of speaker. He replied:

'Endal is a demon! We can't defend the Emperor against demons!'

There was no time to reply to this view. Endal wasn't about to delay his assault. He walked forwards towards the tower door and therefore directly towards Akumi, Harkor, and Hazati.

'This is it,' Hazati said. 'It's us and him. Remember to watch his blades. Don't be caught off guard.'

Endal closed in on the assassins and watched as they in turn gained in on him. Akumi moved frontwards first with Harkor closely behind. The girl raised her katana and initiated yet another clash with her rival.

Her blade struck one of his and then swayed to her side to block his other from striking her chest. Harkor shuffled around Endal's side and swung his sword out to hit his legs. Endal pounced into the air and flipped backwards to avoid the swing. As he landed Harkor followed through with another strike that Endal struck clear. This went on until Akumi came to Harkor's side. The two assassins launched a barrage of speeding sword strikes at Endal. The hooded killer was forced to retreat back as his katanas danced and his body ducked and weaved. As this went on Hazati came around and stood behind Endal, ready to strike.

The dark assassin knew he was now surrounded and as Hazati went to stab him in the back he fell to ground and kicked the old man in the shins, knocking him over flat on his face. Akumi tried to stab Endal as he lay under her but was met with a firm kick into her stomach. She fell back herself and Endal frog leaped to his feet.

Harkor waved his blade around in the hope of striking Endal but as his sword arm moved in on him one of Endal's katanas cleanly cut his hand off at the wrist. Harkor screamed in shock but his pain wouldn't be long lived. Endal then bent his arms back and thrust them forwards, instantly stabbing Harkor's chest with both katanas.

There was a moment between the two as Harkor stared into the dark eyes of Endal with his last seconds of life. His head then bowed and his body went limp. Endal pulled his swords from the body and kicked it backwards to the ground. He then turned to face the others.

Hazati had rolled to one side and got himself up only to realise one of his assassins was down. Akumi had been seconds away from getting herself to her feet but she'd realised Harkor was down and became too upset to attack again so soon. Harkor's body lay by Endal's side as he stood in between his opponents.

'What evil consumes you Endal?' Hazati asked, deeply saddened.

Endal turned to face Hazati. They looked at one another for a moment. Endal had no intention of responding. Akumi stood up and just stared at Harkor's body. She morbidly looked at his severed hand that rested beside his corpse. She'd lost yet another friend and suddenly a rage once again started to burn deep within her. Her eyes turned a blood red as her body started to feel a rush of intense adrenaline.

Endal didn't spend anymore time staring at Hazati and suddenly the two had locked horns yet again. Endal drove Hazati back and back until the old man stumbled into the wall that now only partially surrounded the tower. Akumi raced to catch up. She was enraged and felt a new sense of invulnerability inside of her. It was as if in this moment she'd evolved.

'Endal, this is between you and me,' she yelled firmly.

Hazati had managed to defend himself against Endal's strikes but was panting and pressed up against the stone wall. Endal turned to face Akumi. As he did so Hazati became relieved and momentarily let his guard down as he fought to catch his breath.

Endal then raised one of his sword arms and evilly turned the katana to face behind him. He then thrust it backwards forcefully into Hazati's gut.

'Hazati!' Akumi screamed wildly.

The old man yelped as the blade entered his body but as soon as the steel had made contact his energy entirely diminished. He went pale and blood oozed from his mouth and dripped down his chin. His sword dropped and his body slid down the wall until he was left sitting upright, head bowed. Endal pulled his katana from the old man and grimly smiled as Akumi stood with tears forming around her large brown, anime eyes.

He seemed intrigued by the girl and studied her reaction to his sly trick and clear lack of warrior etiquette.

In a rarity he spoke: 'Killing is an art form. It is never right nor wrong, only an act. Do you not see child?'

Akumi was wordless. Emotion had got the better of her and she could now only think of racing to Hazati's side in the vain hope she could save him from his wound. Tears were flowing from her cheeks and her eyes became consumed by water. She had never experienced despair like this. She slowly looked away from her master and to the hooded figure that had spoken. His words were as cold and lifeless as him.

'You can't be human,' she said frostily. 'What are you?'

'I am an avatar,' he remarked. 'You could say I am a God in human form.'

His words sent chills up Akumi's spine. 'A God who kills so mercilessly?' she questioned.

'Killing and death are part of life and part of the world we live. If you don't understand this then you will never become a truly masterful warrior,' he replied.

Akumi refused to listen to his words. She was sensing a spell of allurement taking hold of her as the mysterious figure spoke on. Her mind snapped back to thoughts of proving herself.

'If you're a God then I must be a Goddess for I swear I will kill you for what you have done,' she stated firmly. 'You will not kill Tamus or anyone else.'

Endal didn't reply with words. Instead, he laughed in a mocking manner and raised his swords. Akumi lifted her steel. She felt focused and ready. It was as if she had suddenly sensed her true power.

The remaining troops had now all but left the area. Many of them sat mourning by the bodies of dead friends. Others watched the spectacle of Endal fighting, with no intention of getting near.

'You are in an interesting predicament,' said Endal. 'You see, Hazati is not dead... but he will be, unless you help him now that is. Fighting me will only squander valuable time.'

Akumi looked back at Hazati, her mind at odds with what to do.

'If you don't see to him now he will surely die,' said Endal, 'and if you waste time battling me he will die. However, if you see to him now he will likely survive. I will let you attend to him. Let us pass by one another?'

Akumi wasn't thinking clearly. Her only thought was on Hazati and attending to his bleeding wound. He was still alive and occasionally rolled his head. She looked up at Endal.

'I must attend to my master,' she said.

Endal smiled from under his hood. 'Then see to him. I won't interfere.'

With that Akumi raced to Hazati, entirely dropping her guard, and Endal walked onwards towards the tower door. Several soldiers noticed and became fuelled by a sudden duty to challenge the demon they so feared. Akumi paid no attention as she stroked Hazati's forehead. All she heard was swords striking armour and blood gushing out of arteries. Endal swiftly put down the three soldiers that approached him and reached the tower door.

'Master,' Akumi whispered, 'are you okay?'

The old man clearly wasn't and the girl knew it. She ripped cloth from his robe and started to dab his wound. She then noticed his water bottle in a robe pocket and brought it to his lips. He was still conscious and groaning in protest at the injury. The girl pressed more cloth against the gash and started to tie around it to put pressure on the bleeding. Hazati took a few sips of water and the rest was poured onto his cut skin.

As Akumi attended to her master there was another fierce bang as Endal blew the tower doors open. They had been locked from the inside. The emotional girl just ignored it, too focused on Hazati.

'Don't you leave me too,' Akumi said tearfully. 'I need you.'

'Akumi...' Hazati managed to stammer.

The girl listened attentively, leaning as close to his body as was possible. 'Master?'

'Akumi, go! All is lost. Forget this battle. Endal is too strong for you. Go, live life, and don't look back.'

'But master... the Emperor?' Akumi was confused.

'Forget the Emperor! Forget this! Endal is too strong. I should never have… have…' he paused.

'Master?'

Hazati moaned again before speaking: 'I should never have led you all into this. I should have known to stay away from him. I am sorry Akumi.'

'We had no choice master,' said Akumi. 'We had to defend the Emperor.'

'The Emperor…' Hazati smiled absently, 'yes the Emperor. We had to do our duty for Tamus.'

Hazati looked into Akumi's eyes. 'You have been an exceptional student my girl,' he said. 'Do as you will. You no longer need a master. I am proud of you, Akumi.'

These were to be the master's last words. The old man smiled and then his head bent forwards. He died in his students arms. Akumi, the last of the assassins, burst into tears.

CHAPTER IX

THE SPECTRE STRIKES

Sylvie had never been as focused as she was right now. Behind her Tamus sat on his throne eying the large door to his hall. Sylvie stood in the middle of the throne room beside vast ornaments and exquisite plants. Her elite team of bodyguards were spread out all across the large space. They wore dark black and mostly held sharp and curved cutlasses.

'Endal will meet his end in this very room,' Sylvie shouted out. 'Where he thinks he's about to complete his contract he will fall and die!'

There was a roar of confirmation from Sylvie's highly trained troops. These were the cream of the armies and their allegiance to Tamus was unfaltering. Most of them had been with the warrior since the beginning. They had been tested time and time again in the past but this was the big one.

Tamus didn't say much at this stage. His usual wit and love for conversation had faded as he'd watched the assassin get nearer and nearer to him. He was now prepared for combat; with his sword of state by his side. This was The Sword of Tamus and held only by the Emperor. Named after him, the first true Emperor of Marmia, it was a symbol as well as a deadly weapon. It was said to be unbreakable and its roots centuries old. Gems sparkled from its handle and the perfect steel was as light as a feather. Tamus had carried it ever since he could remember and used it long before his faction had ever come to power.

The doors suddenly slammed open forcefully. A bottle was rolled in after the forced entry and stopped just inside the room.

'Get back!' Sylvie warned.

'And so he enters,' said Tamus. 'The dark figure is before me!'

The bomb went off and a white flash and screeching boom smashed the glass of the countless windows bringing light into the high hall of the tower. There was no fire since there was nothing to catch alight, only the stone ground.

'Like a demon, he rolls in through smoke,' said Tamus. 'Alas! Here he comes to claim me. The spectre strikes!'

The smoke cleared and Endal strutted into the room, his katanas placed about his back and a line of sharp blades now sticking from the sides of his arms and elbows.

Two of Sylvie's elites confronted the intruder and glided their cutlasses forth as they appeared from his sides. Endal struck one in the chest with an open palm strike and clutched the other's sword arm. He bent the bodyguard's wrist and forced him to bend and roll with the pressure. He flipped onto the ground. The other guard recovered from Endal's strike and got close again. Endal deflected a sword strike and struck his arm into the troop's chest sideways on. The blades that stuck out from Endal's arms were a cruel and distinctive weapon. His katanas remained sheathed about his back as he fought with no arm except for these blades poking from his forearms.

The blades buried themselves deep into the bodyguard and Endal struck him again with a palm strike, sending his body across the hall. The other guard got up from the throw and tried to wrestle with Endal. The assassin clotheslined his opponent across the neck and took him back off balance. As the soldier hit the ground Endal picked up his cutlass and fatally stabbed him. He then continued to walk towards Tamus.

More black robed guards popped out from beyond the pillars in the far corners of the room. Endal took them on one after the other without much trouble. One came at him from the air and was cut in mid flight and hurled across the hall into wooden benches that snapped into pieces upon impact.

Three others came at him at once and were cut up by his bladed arms in lightning fast strikes. One managed to tackle Endal back a few feet but failed to bring him to the ground. Endal clutched him by the shoulders and lobbed him to one side. Another got close and tried to drive their sword into his chest. Endal strafed to dodge the blade and kicked the guard directly in the face with a flawless side kick.

Before the guard was able to recover Endal drove his elbow into his chest and the blades finished him. The one that had been thrown to one side then clutched Endal from behind. This was a big mistake for all Endal needed to do was drive his elbows back and stab the guard's stomach. Another black figure clenched and slumped down onto the floor.

Endal suddenly decided to remove his hood like it was time to reveal himself to the target. He walked onwards. A volley of arrows rapidly came from the corners of the Emperor's throne. Archers were poised in the dark edges of the hall.

Endal came over invulnerable. He had been able to dodge the arrows in reflexes incomprehensible to those that witnessed it. He hit the deck and allowed the arrows to fly over his body. As he leapt back up he hurled several knives, which had been concealed within his robe, in the directions the arrows had come from. The knife throws were fast and perfectly accurate. The blades spun past either side of the Emperor's throne and appeared to strike flesh as separate shrieks of agony reported contact.

Two more guards came at Endal who was once again walking forwards in a swift pace. He grabbed one by the sword arm and used his own sword to stab the other who had tried to flank the assassin from the side.

Endal then turned the cutlass around and thrust it into the beating heart of the guard who had been carrying it. The guard gurgled in distress as Endal supported his weight and then slowly let him drop to the floor beside him. Blood now filled a distinct pathway behind Endal from the door to where the assassin now stood.

Sylvie hadn't flinched as she'd watched the assassin get closer and closer whilst killing each of her highly trained bodyguards in effortless grace. She knew it was now literally up to her to stop him getting any closer to her beloved Emperor. All of her guards were down and only her sword was left above the floor. She bent low and raised her arms, her silver broadsword aimed directly at Endal in defiance.

'You won't pass me Endal!' she yelled.

'Won't I?' he whispered darkly.

Endal walked straight at Sylvie without any pause in his advance. As soon as he got close enough Sylvie plunged her sword forwards towards him with great force. He seemed to know the move was coming and turned to her left side to swiftly evade the steel. He swung his bladed left arm out and aimed the spiked edges at the girl's armoured chest.

She was able to bend back enough to avoid the speeding limb

and swung her sword sideways in the hope of catching his side. Endal had no chance of evading this swing and had been shocked by the girl's ability to dodge his quick strike. The broadsword struck the robed figure on the side of his waistline as the two stood facing off a few feet in front of Tamus.

Endal was forced to recoil away and clutch the sword scrape. The sharp edge had cut into his skin but hadn't gone deep. It stung but wasn't serious. Endal couldn't afford to underestimate this skilled girl and raised his arms above his head, clutching both of his katana blades, and brought them down to face her. The assassin came charging into the blonde girl and his swords bombarded her sturdy steel.

Sylvie blocked several direct strikes from him and then countered with another low poke aimed at stabbing him frontally. Now Endal had his swords out he quickly cut into the blow and knocked her sword to one side. Sylvie was knocked off balance by the deflection and her sword arm flung down as the sword's tip struck the floor.

Endal turned whilst on his feet across her outstretched shoulder with his back to her and left sword arm perched. He completed his turn until their backs were resting against each other but as he'd finished the move his sword had struck her lower back and cut through the basic light armour she wore. Sylvie howled in shock and ran forwards to get away from its tip.

The assassin studied Sylvie as she regained her stance and refocused on him. His strike had penetrated her back but the armour had saved her from a deep incision. She was bleeding but still standing. Both warriors had made the other bleed.

As they analysed one another's movements in a moment of tension Endal couldn't help but take a look at Tamus whom remained seated on his elegant throne whilst watching the spectacle unfold. This was to be the first moment the assassin had looked at his target. Tamus looked back aridly.

Sylvie didn't hold back and edged closer to her opponent as he eyed her Emperor. She allowed him to attack first and was soon blocking his katana strikes once more. She was forced to step back as Endal unleashed a swift wave of fierce swipes at the girl. Her defence held and she launched her own attack. Her powerful swing looked to test the assassin and he himself had begun to retreat back as her sword danced with his. The fencing appeared to go on and on as the two warriors danced around the hall beside the throne. Tamus was growing desperately nervous as the assassin continued to strut around in front of him.

Sylvie was tiring as her opponent's assault relentlessly continued. She'd been unable to find any weakness or momentary chance to strike through his defence. Although Endal himself had not managed to truly break through her own defence yet she knew she was getting fatigued and that the wound to her lower back was starting to sting more and more. She was getting paler and less energetic with every few seconds of battling.

They fought on and eventually Sylvie had slowly retreated back to the far end of the hall nearest the doorway leading to the stairs as Endal's assault forced her backwards.

She suddenly found herself leaning against a wall and realised she was cornered. She tried to put up more resistance but was now beginning to fathom that this was a fight between a woman and something far more dangerous than any man. She'd proved more than a match for any human over the years but Endal was no ordinary opponent and the highly skilled swordswoman knew she was truly outclassed by the dark figure beyond her sword tip.

She was breathing heavily by now and her blue eyes were weary and fearful. Endal sensed she was tiring and allured her into a sneaky trap. He let his swords down and as soon as she instinctively swung her sword with all her might at his exposed chest he raised his swords back up in a lightning pace.

One struck her broadsword side on and knocked it from her grip. It flew across the hall and smashed into a glass cabinet. With his other sword he struck. Endal slid the steel across the girl's chest. The blade's sharp edge scraped across her shoulder and right breast. It tore through her armour like a claw cutting into wet clay. The assassin withdrew the dripping blade as Sylvie fell back against the wall behind her.

The cut was quite deep and went from the tip of her right shoulder and down across her chest to her upper stomach. It stung and blood started to seep from her hacked up armour plates. Her skin went an ice cold, pale white and she lost all strength in her legs. Endal looked down at her and put one of his katanas to her throat. He kept it pressed against her skin for a few seconds and then abruptly withdrew the blade and turned to march back towards Tamus.

The assassin speedily advanced back up the blood stained floor of the hall where countless bodies now lay inert. Tamus had seen him coming and stood beside his throne with The Sword of Tamus raised high and proud.

'You have no idea what you are about to do assassin!' he shrieked angrily. 'This realm will fall back into total chaos without me! Do you really want that you fool?'

Endal continued to walk closer towards him.

The Emperor continued: 'You just don't get it do you? Are you even alive? Do you have any emotion besides bloodlust?!'

The assassin was now only feet away from the unguarded Emperor. Endal was indifferent to the Emperor's small speech. It was as if he was entirely unconcerned about the world around him and of the consequences of his actions.

'Whatever it is you truly are,' yelled Tamus desperately, 'may you rot in hell for all you have done in your sick life!'

These were to be the Emperor's last words. Endal closed in for the killing blow. Tamus raised his sword high and let out a wild yell in defiance: 'God bless Marmia!'

He launched a futile swing with the mighty weapon he held but before it had even fully come down from his raised arm Endal had stepped to his side and slid a katana clean across his gullet. Tamus stumbled back and hunched against his throne.

Blood spattered out from his cut throat in fast flowing spurts and stained the royal colours of his mighty chair. Tamus clutched his neck but it was no use. His last sight was of Endal standing before him with swords by his side. The robed figure looked like an evil demon from some deranged nightmare. His evil presence consumed the Emperor's last thoughts. He fell down to his knees and then collapsed onto the ground beside the throne. His white robe was covered in warm blood. The Emperor was dead.

Endal briefly studied the body and then placed his swords back across his back. The assassin had got his kill and the contract had been completed. He studied The Sword of Tamus, which lay beside the dead Emperor. It was an exquisite example of regal steel. He looked at both sides of the blade and then the handle. Intriguingly, he decided not to take it and placed it back down by the Emperor. He then moved it nearer to the Emperor's arm and placed the corpse's hand on its grip in the slightest mark of respect for his victim. Tamus would be remembered as the

Emperor who died holding the symbolic steel.

The assassin turned and walked back down the hall towards the door. As he reached the exit he looked to Sylvie who remained panting helplessly like a wounded animal in the far corner. She was still conscious but in a lot of pain.

Endal walked over to her. The girl's eyes rolled as the assassin closed in. She was just able to focus on him as he looked down at her with a soulless expression of coldness. Endal showed no empathy for the girl he knew had spent her whole life defending the Emperor she so adored.

Endal spoke with a rare clearness and volume: 'You may wonder why I have not finished you girl. It is because I am fond of at least one witness being able to give an account of my actions. You witnessed this day! You have a function. It is to tell of this event to Marmia and perhaps even the lands beyond. Tell this tale my child! Let them fear my name; Endal! And let them remember this day!'

Sylvie took in the message and emotionally bowed her head in complete defeat and grief. When she raised it back up the robed figure was gone.

CHAPTER X

THE PURSUIT INTO DARKNESS

Akumi was a broken girl. Her mind was completely drained by the grief of seeing her master die in her arms. She'd not only lost her father figure but another of her close friends, Harkor. The female assassin wept uncontrollably as she contemplated all that Hazati had said to her in his last words. She realised during this point of grievance that she no longer had anything to lose. She knew no one and had nothing except her sword and her training. To this assassin the Emperor now meant little. Her pain was too personal and her sense of duty faded. She also internalised what Hazati had told her; that Endal would prove unstoppable. Their mission had been in vain. She hugged Hazati softly and then finally edged back. The girl was alone and had been left with an order to do as she saw fit. Her mind was made up. She seemed to know what to do.

The girl stood and looked around her. Endal had now long since vanished into the tower and she was alone in the courtyard of bodies. The remaining standing troops were more concerned about attending to the wounded than charging into the tower. The men who had really felt a duty to defend the Emperor were now lying in the mud and debris. Akumi noticed Hazati and Harkor's horses still standing where they'd been tied. For a moment she thought of riding away and doing as master had said. But then she looked back down at Hazati. She realised she couldn't just walk away. She couldn't simply forget all about Endal. She knew she was the only one who could potentially take him on. Her belief in her skills had truly congealed now she had lost all she'd ever had. She refused to fear Endal, regardless of what even her late master had said. She refused to accept he was an avatar of some dastardly God and instead focused entirely on her own ability.

Her thoughts then turned to Sylvie. She was up there, part of

the last line of defence. In her lowest and weakest moment
Akumi had forgotten entirely about anything besides aiding her
master. Now her initial shock had passed she felt an utter sense of
failure. She'd let Endal pass.

The assassin sprung into action and ran to Hazati's horse. She
hunted through a large bag that hung from the mount. It wasn't
only Endal who could spark fireworks. She clutched several
small packs of powder much alike to Endal's red stuff and placed
them about her belt. She then charged towards the tower but was
instantly struck by the image of Endal strolling out from the
broken door. The black figure paused as he stood just outside the
doorway. Akumi stopped in her tracks and stood in the middle of
the courtyard between him and the gap in the wall that led back
into the city.

'Endal!' she screeched as loudly as her voice would allow.

Her scream echoed around the walls and whistled up the spiral
staircase of the tower.

'You may have completed your contract,' Akumi yelled fierily,
'but you won't get away with it alive!'

Endal smiled to himself. His head was still fully visible as his
hood remained drooping down the back of his robe. His long
black hair and bristly face blew with a light breeze that started to
press against him from the sky above. The clouds had opened up
and the diminishing sunlight was being replaced by a full moon
and wealth of stars. It wasn't dark yet but the light was starting to
drop. There was a reddish tone in the sky.

'Come at me with everything you have,' Akumi provoked.

Endal didn't seem concerned by Akumi although he knew she
was very skilled. He'd never fought anyone as tough as her and
Sylvie and felt ever so humbled by his human opposition on this
occasion. He hadn't expected to ever encounter anyone as skilled
as the girl that stood facing him. He knew she was able to break
his defence. He recalled his last encounters with her. Whilst he
dwelt on this Akumi focused herself on the opponent. She knew
he was exceptional. On both of the main occasions she had
fought him her life had been saved by another. The first time it
had been Jobe who had prevented Endal's katana from finishing
Akumi off in the distant pine forest. The second time it had been
Sylvie jumping in to protect her after Endal had knocked her
unconscious.

As the wind picked up strength Endal stepped forwards, towards Akumi. He raised his arm and brought down one of his katanas. The two squared off as Endal reached her.

'And just to think,' Akumi said, 'you won't even get paid for this, with Vortor dead and the rebels who contracted you safely behind bars!'

It wasn't news to Endal that Vortor was dead. He had expected the mage to fall as soon as he'd left him for the tunnels. He also didn't seem too shocked his clients had been captured.

'I didn't do this for the money,' he mocked. 'I accepted this contract because it gave me a challenge. Those such as me get bored. It was also a way of carving my name into the stone of this realm. My name will never be forgotten. It was the will of the Gods that I did this!'

'The will of the Gods?' Akumi questioned. 'Aren't you meant to be one?'

Endal laughed. 'It is my will then.'

Akumi refused to dwell on Endal's words. All she knew was that whatever Endal was he was truly evil and needed to be stopped once and for all.

The assassins charged at one another and their katana blades locked in combat. Endal was the first to strike and launched a hail of attacks with immense speed and well placed angling. Akumi was on the retreat and forced to defend. She bent low and rolled to one side of Endal then attempted to thrust her sword into his side. Endal had sidestepped to avoid the strike and continued to attack. Akumi was unable to do anything besides continue to fall back and defend herself.

Suddenly, Endal's blade came from a low angle; Akumi was unable to deflect the speeding steel in time. The sword slid across her right leg just above the knee. She flinched back with the shock and immediately felt Endal's steel come at her again with great speed. The dark assassin had opened the girl's defence up and managed to strike her twice in a row. His katana caught her in the waist and cut into her skin.

Akumi panicked and backtracked away from Endal whilst pressing down on her painful wound. Endal walked towards her without pausing. Akumi knew she had to attack or she'd face another round of strikes from her enemy. Her blade leapt out at him and her adrenaline refused to falter. Her assault did little.

Endal deflected her first three strikes and managed to knock her sword arm to her side. He drove his palm into her stomach and then jabbed her in the cheek as she bent forwards. Akumi fell over and rolled away in alarm at how easily she'd been put to the ground.

'You have much to learn girl,' Endal remarked. 'You have the makings of a fine warrior but you aren't there yet.'

Akumi sat up and got to her feet. She felt blood trickle down from her waist and right leg. Both cuts throbbed but she didn't seem concerned. She appeared to take in Endal's words; like she knew that, for his vices, he was observing things about her that were truly accurate. She had no delusions at this stage that Endal was the master and she the underdog.

'I always suspected the female of the human species would prove the tougher of the sexes when given the right circumstance,' Endal commented. 'You and Tamus' protector, Sylvie, have been proof of that.'

As he spoke Akumi refocused and shuffled back nearer to him with sword poised and stance firm. A few seconds went by as the assassins circled one another slowly. Akumi then attacked. The katanas once again danced. Endal didn't seem to struggle, like his focus was now so sharp as to make him invincible, and deflected strike after strike. Akumi didn't let up and suddenly her katana managed to snake its way around Endal's blocks and cut into his robe. It didn't stop and poked into his left breast. Endal moved back to prevent a deep incision and stared at Akumi's katana as his blood dripped from the tip of the blade. She held it outright and slowly withdrew it back to her side.

Endal came at her once again but Akumi didn't stand back. Both assaulted at once, the swordplay stepping up a level as each strike moved across the air with colossal pace. Akumi swung her katana down at Endal from high in the air but the dark assassin struck the incoming steel to her side. He then turned his blade and drove it towards her belly. There was contact. She had been swift to move back but the sword still partially entered her skin. The pain was great and she stumbled to the ground.

Endal closed in but Akumi swiftly launched a kick from her position on the ground that struck him square in the groin. He fell onto his knees and collapsed onto his back. The warriors got up in unison and although Akumi felt blood slip from her belly she still remained determined to battle on. She knew that she was weakening though and her initial fire had started to fade. She kept back.

Endal also appeared reluctant. He put his hand on his chest and looked to his palm. It was stained in blood that had not stopped gushing from his slashed breast. His waistline also still stung and bled from his encounter with Sylvie in the tower. He now felt foolish hanging around. More guards were likely coming and his state was weakening and his strength faltering. It was time to call it a day.

'We can conclude this another day my girl,' Endal grinned.

He started to fondle with something within his robe. Akumi spotted part of a bottle appear from the black pocket. She instantly knew what it was. In what seemed like a moment of mutual dishonesty and sly cunning both assassins revealed their explosive powders. Each warrior knew they'd be dancing with death if they ignored their wounds and continued to fight on. They were keener to get the quick kill at this stage, or at least the quick exit.

Endal raised a bottle from his robe and Akumi reached down and grabbed one of her pouches of mysterious powder. She was first to throw and the pouch sped across the few feet that separated the assassins then instantly erupted. It had reacted to fast movement and was clearly under some form of spell to be able to detonate with no fuse. Hazati had certainly known where to find such rarities.

Endal hadn't managed to throw his bottle in time. He'd intended to quickly light the fuse first and then hurl. The explosion went off right beside him. It seemed to be much smaller than one of his but still forceful enough to send him flying back and into the air. His body went a few feet upwards and fell back down to earth with a firm thud. His bottle bashed against the ground and the glass cracked, allowing the powder to pour out. The dark assassin was clearly hurt and didn't immediately get back up.

Akumi ran towards him with katana at the ready. Endal rolled away as fast as he could and stumbled to his feet. His face was cut and bleeding and his black robe was burnt in several places. He was less energetic than before the bang and although he had his sword raised he was faltering and appeared unable to keep it up without it swaying.

Akumi came at him full force, her blade swinging with immense speed and straightness. She was on fire and her adrenaline pumped. Endal was instantly unable to cope with the onslaught. He deflected the first few strikes and leaned back to dodge another but then became more interested in retreating than standing ground. As he stepped backwards Akumi intensified her assault and shuffled after him.

Akumi swung away until her blade fiercely struck Endal's. The two swords pressed against one another until Akumi pulled hers back and, with great speed, slid it downwards; making contact with both of Endal's thighs. Once again she'd caught his legs but this time the pain seemed to greatly trouble the dark assassin. He bent low in a reflex and Akumi's katana sliced across his left shoulder and arm as he bowed forwards. Blades still sprung from his forearms but Akumi's strike had also slid through them, cutting each of them into blunt pieces of metal sticking from his left limb.

Endal dived away to avoid further injury and fell in a heap on the ground. He rolled back to further the distance but Akumi wasn't far behind him. He got up to confront her but was now unable to raise his katana. Blood was visibly seeping from his thighs and left arm and had started to drip from his robe and flow down his legs onto his black boots.

For the first time Endal was feeling truly fearful, like he sensed he was about to be defeated. He'd never sustained so many wounds and felt as weak as he did right now. Endal knew he was beginning to lose all of his strength and ability to fight. He needed to flee. On this occasion the girl had outwitted him and there was little he could do to turn the tables.

Akumi studied him carefully as his sword arm dangled up and down.

'You are the best I have fought,' Endal said respectfully. 'I have no desire to see you die.'

Akumi was unsure what to say. 'Well, maybe I do desire to see you die!' she replied.

'I don't doubt it,' said Endal, 'but it matters not what you desire my girl. I see you achieving great things... but our paths will now separate. Goodbye, my fellow assassin.'

Endal smiled after he'd finished his sentence. Akumi was intrigued by his words. As she stood back in brief allurement over the menacing figure he made a sudden run for it and bolted across the courtyard with some final burst of energy. Akumi gave chase but as she kicked into a sprint she noticed someone coming from out of the tower behind her. It was Sylvie. She'd managed to drag herself down the spiralling flights of stairs and out into the open in hope of aid. Akumi had no choice and knew to run to the assistance of the girl that had saved her life earlier that same day. Endal was left to flee into the streets like some faltering phantom.

The female assassin ran to the tower exit and immediately supported Sylvie in her arms as she wearily stumbled around on her feet.

'Sylvie,' she said caringly, 'I am so sorry. I should have been by your side.' Akumi was beginning to cry.

'It's okay,' said Sylvie softly. 'We did all we could. There was no stopping Endal. There was just no stopping him!'

With those words Sylvie herself started to break down. Akumi placed her on the ground and noticed a bottle of water resting beside a dead soldier. She instantly handed it to Sylvie who sipped away. The blonde girl had already tied her own bandages to her wound, which seemed to help ease the blood flow.

'Endal let me live so I would tell this tale of what he did,' said Sylvie. 'He told me to give an account of his act to the realm! How can I live with myself? I let him kill our Emperor!'

Akumi hugged her as she sobbed. 'No one let him kill the Emperor, especially you Sylvie. I should have done more though. I should have…'

'Stop saying that!' Sylvie butted in. 'You did all you could. Where are the others?'

'The general, Hazati, and my friend Harkor are all dead Sylvie,' said Akumi dryly, 'along with most of the troops that defended the tower.'

Nothing could be said to this. Instead, the two girls continued to hug one another and sob in unison. It had all been too much.

A minute or two flew by as the girls aided one another. They both suddenly heard voices and rushing hooves. They looked up and spotted a large group of soldiers storm into the courtyard from the broken wall. The company of reinforcements had been on route but had clearly arrived way too late. However, one thing they weren't late for was to aid the injured. Several of them immediately dashed to the girls whilst the others attended to the mass of claimed and wounded troops.

'Are you girls okay?' a rider asked whilst removing his feathery helmet.

'Sylvie needs assistance,' said Akumi. 'I am okay. Just cuts.'

Akumi knew she wasn't really okay. Those cuts were bleeding unchecked but she refused to pay them any attention.

'The Emperor?' the rider asked.

'The Emperor is dead,' Sylvie announced.

There was a morbid silence. A few troops got off from their saddles and knelt beside Sylvie. The rider who had spoken raced off to spread the news. As Sylvie became the focal point of the men's attention Akumi got up and looked to one of their horses.

'Do you mind if I borrow that ride?' she asked a soldier.

'Go ahead,' a disconcerted voice responded.

The horse bounded out of the tower grounds and down the debris infested street. Akumi studied every angle as she sat atop the stallion that seemed perfectly able to leap over the rubble. Her aim was to race through the streets and out of the city. The white horse sped by as onlookers slowly emerged from their houses now word had spread the violence had ceased. The animal passed through narrow lanes and turned with flawless agility as Akumi navigated the complex city. This realm was in its last moments of calm and didn't even know it. With the Emperor fallen the chaos predicted by the rebels would inevitably ensue. The empire was leaderless and there was already a growing sense of desperation among the troops who had started to hear Tamus was dead.

Akumi wasn't troubled by all that was unfolding around her. Her aim was to get Endal. This was personal. The assassin knew she couldn't drop this now. It was her only plan. She rode on through the streets until the gate out of the city appeared ahead. The guards were uninterested in challenging her and let her pass over and onto the bridge that led across the lake.

Endal had darted down the streets and back into the sewer via the manhole he'd entered out from. Although he was hurt he had managed to keep a swift pace and moved through the dark tunnels without much trouble. He had reached the tunnel he'd initially entered into beside the lake and stepped over the pack he'd left in there. It still had things inside but Endal was no longer going to be needing them and dragged the bag forwards and plunged it into the water. He then dived in from the blown sewer cover. By the time Akumi had passed over the bridge Endal was about half way across the lake, swimming slowly and with great care for his wounds.

The female assassin had spotted Endal's black horse from the bridge and noticed a figure slowly pass across the water towards it from the lake. She headed straight for the horse once her ride hit the grassy hill beyond the bridge.

The weary and fatigued Endal had spotted her coming as he reached the last segment of his swim. Harwind became alert and attentive as his master finally returned like he'd said he would. The assassin forced himself onwards and reached the hillside a few seconds before Akumi's horse was able to arrive. Endal looked exhausted as he clambered up from the water and onto his black horse. His katanas were back around his back and his hood was raised once more. With his command the horse took off up the hill. Akumi was close behind on her white stallion and turned to pursue the black rider up the sloped ground.

The chase became long and drawn out as Endal's black horse did what it did best and ran like the wind. Akumi was lucky in that her chosen ride appeared able to keep up. However, distance was widening between her and Endal. As they reached the hilltop and passed by the exit to the secret tunnel they had come from to reach Brimma earlier that day it became clear Endal's black horse was not going to be caught.

The sunlight was now greatly fading and the darkness of early night crept in. The stars became brighter and the moon more apparent in the blackening sky. A cold wind started to howl as they got further and further from the city and deeper into the western countryside beyond the hill. The flat grassland of the southern Plains of Falgor turned into dense forest and bushland where only a rough dirt track kept them from snaking through trees. Endal had linked onto this path heading west.

In this darkening setting Endal and his black horse became harder and harder to make out. What was initially a distinguishable shape became a diminishing silhouette surrounded by dark tones. Now they were on the flat the black rider ahead seemed to shoot into an even greater pace but this was only clear by the amount of dust being kicked up ahead. The chase went on until Akumi sensed her horse was slowing up. It appeared unable to maintain this lightning bolt pace and, although keen, stepped down a level. It was in this moment that Akumi realised she was surrounded by black. The forest tree line blocked out the remaining light and ahead of her there was now no sign of any rider, only a void of darkness.

She brought her horse to a halt and listened carefully for any sounds. There was no noise except for that of her horse panting away as they stood on the dim pathway of the shady forest. The view ahead was entirely black. There was nothing to be seen and no way of spotting Endal. The dark assassin had vanished into darkness. He was gone, riding away into the night and back into obscurity. The myth had proved devastatingly genuine and the character of chilling fables remained alive.

Akumi felt utterly defeated. There was nothing she could do. She turned her horse around and headed back for the city. The white animal and red cloaked rider were now the only light tone in the area.

As Akumi raced back towards Brimma her eyes suddenly closed and she felt as if she was about to fall into a deep sleep. She shook her head and opened them in defiance. The momentum of the horse didn't seem to keep her alert anymore. She no longer felt the bumps and jolts being on horseback were all about.

The darkness started to devour her as her eyes yet again closed against her will. Her head bowed and her arms drooped to her sides. A couple of seconds later her body collapsed frontwards and struck the horse's back. She lay lifeless atop the animal, her head resting against their firm neck.

The ride didn't seem bothered and continued on. It passed back out of the western tip of the forest and up the hill until Brimma and the tower were again in view. Moonlight lit up the waters of the lake and the torches tied to the side of the bridge flickered in distant luminosity. Her horse halted once they'd reached the end of the hill and the beginning of the lake. It took a sip of the water and bent its head down to reach. The movement sent Akumi's limp body off from the saddle and down onto the grass beside the white stallion. She was motionless and masses of blood emerged from her clothes as it seeped down her wounds and out from gaps in her attire onto the grass and soil below.

Across the lake a party of horses sped out from Brimma and

onto the bridge. They darted over the crossing and onto the hill. They clearly had spotted the white horse standing beside the glistening water. The group headed straight towards the animal as they made across the side of the lake in single file.

The first rider leapt from their mount once they had reached within a few feet of the white stallion and raced towards the still girl. Their red cloak looked less fetching in the darkness. It was partially covered by large, white bandages that wrapped around her chest and shoulder. Sylvie knelt beside Akumi and waited for the rest of her party to catch up. Back across the lake a loud horn blew in Brimma. It could be heard for miles around. It was a notice marking a significant event. The Emperor was dead.

CHAPTER XI

A PLACE OF SANCTUARY

Friar Jamus preferred it when the sun kept behind the clouds. It was cooler and he and his monks were more able to get on with their demanding physical labours. The Abbey didn't take care of itself and with so many fields to work there was rarely much time in the day to relax. The friar didn't seem to mind. His was the peaceful life, away from the wars and battles that once filled his days. For Jamus the times of the sword were long gone. His memories chronicled a lifetime of war. His peace was now with nature.

It had been a few days now since the death of Emperor Tamus. Marmia had fallen back into a war footing. The Emperor's death had been enough to reignite the will of the rebellious factions. Prisoners were being freed from the jails and dungeons of the realm; the guards fearful of being killed by hordes of rebelling men intent on liberating their brothers in arms.

In the face of this the fate of Golandin and Arthir was unknown. Perhaps they were awaiting a visit from Endal seeking payment for the contract he'd managed to complete, or maybe they were now too interested in plotting to seize power to remember old deals. Whatever their concerns the dark, notorious assassin in question had vanished back into obscurity and away from the focus of the realm on the brink of further bloodshed. Like a faded apparition, he was gone.

Jamus rested against a small, low fence whilst watching several of the Abbey monks rake dry leaves from a pathway that led out from the stables. It was a still day; with no wind and a perfectly neutral temperature. The clouds above were a puffy white and bits of blue sky peeked out from gaps in the veil. Jamus wiped his temple and continued raking the brown leaves.

One of the robed monks walked over from the far side of the field and stopped beside Jamus. He looked up.

'Yes brother Aimis?' he inquired.

'Friar, there be a rider coming from the northern road,' said the monk.

'Oh, well thank you brother,' replied Jamus.

The remote Abbey only ever saw someone from the outside world if they had some business with the Abbey. The rural location never saw people merely passing by. The rough roads in the area led nowhere else but here. Whenever a rider was spotted it meant a visitor was coming.

Jamus put down his rake and strolled across the field onto the dirt track the rider was coming from. To the side of the pathway was the Abbey. The friar peered up the road and spotted a single horse coming closer and closer. Jamus could tell it was a white horse and as the animal moved ever closer he could tell the rider was female, with brown hair and a pale complexion. The friar was intrigued. It was not usual to see lone female riders and especially rare to see them coming to his Abbey.

The girl entered into the Abbey grounds and slowed her horse as she moved up the road. Monks continued to rake the leaves as they stood around the roadside. Several of them gave the rider the slightest of bows in welcoming. She smiled back and looked towards the friar who stood patiently waiting for her to reach him. It didn't take long.

She ordered her ride to stop and jumped down from her saddle. A katana hung by her waist from within her red cloak. Her brown eyes matched the tone of the scattered leaves. She was bandaged up around the lower torso and right thigh and had a slightly bruised face, with a noticeable cut to her cheek. It was clear this girl had been in the wars.

'Welcome my dear girl,' said Jamus. 'Are you looking to stay at the Abbey?'

The girl stepped closer and politely responded: 'Hello sir, I am hoping to stay here yes.'

Jamus nodded and studied the girl's attire. 'You seem a little young to be brandishing swords,' he said.

Akumi looked to the ground shyly. 'I am one of Hazati's apprentices, he told me of this place. He told us to come here if we ever needed shelter or got into trouble,' she said.

Jamus sprung up, now slightly more alert. 'Of course!' he remarked. 'You must be Akumi?'

'Yes, and I take it you are friar Jamus?' Akumi asked.

'Indeed I am,' answered the friar.

Jamus walked to the girl's side and made a gesture to one of the monks to take her horse to the stables. They started to walk up the path towards the Abbey entrance as the white horse was led away behind them.

'I was a close friend of Hazati's,' said the friar. 'We knew each other for many decades. Being one of his students you are also my student. I want you to feel at home.'

'You're aware he...' Akumi was cut short.

'The news has spread as far as the borders of the realm Akumi,' Jamus said. 'I learnt of Hazati's death some days ago, and of the Emperor's fall.'

They turned and headed up a small gravel path that led directly to the Abbey doors.

'I hear Tamus' former protector, Sylvie, has taken command of the empire?' the friar was intrigued.

'She was the highest ranking member of court left,' responded the assassin. 'She's in charge of things, for now at least.'

Jamus nodded to himself, clearly interested.

'I came from Brimma,' said Akumi. 'I didn't know where else to go. I knew how to find this Abbey...'

Akumi became emotional as she started to discuss the situation and dwell on the pressing issues.

'It's already getting chaotic out there Jamus,' she said forlornly. 'The rebels are reforming! The empire's grip is crumbling. Endal got away. I won't rest until I have found him. I won't rest...'

Jamus nodded and placed his arm around the female assassin affectionately. He didn't seem at all surprised by what he was hearing. They reached the wooden doors of the Abbey where Jamus cranked a bronze handle downward and pulled open the squeaky entrance.

'Come inside Akumi,' said the old friar. 'We have much to discuss.'

THE ROAD TO BRIMMA

BEING THE SECOND PART

OF

The Dawn of Tamus Tower

BOOK THREE

CHAPTER I

FOREBODING STORMS

Clouds were forming over Grange Abbey. They were dark, menacing, fluffy patches sending the message of foreboding storms. The weather seemed to represent the mood of Marmia. Once warm, sun filled, cerulean skies were now becoming dull, dystrophic vistas of the above. From the window sill of the small bedroom Akumi studied the landscape beyond the glass. She felt a deep sense of responsibility and knew that there would be no rest. For her this was the time of reckoning; her mind was more focused than it had ever been.

Friar Jamus studied her gazing out of the window as he entered the room.

'Not too spacious of a room,' he smiled, 'but it is cosy none the less.'

Akumi turned to face the old monk with a warm expression of gratitude on her tender face.

'Thank you for your hospitality Jamus,' she said, 'but I don't expect I will be here long. There is just so much to do.'

Jamus could sense stress and strain in the girl's voice as she spoke. He knew she was destined to play a key role in shaping whatever was to now become of Marmia. His duty was to watch over her and point her on the right path. Suddenly, Jamus was at the forefront of yet another struggle.

'Come with me,' he glinted, 'and let us discuss this all downstairs beside a nice fire.'

The couple walked along the narrow hallway of the second floor of the Abbey and down the spiralling wooden staircase. The warmth of the raging fire filled the entirety of the space they entered: a humble room with wooden tables and a stone floor. The fire was in the corner beside two armchairs. There was once a time Hazati would come and sit in this precise spot, sparking conversations with the friar well into the early hours.

Akumi was first to sit down, directed to the chair by Jamus. A couple of monks strolled by heading for the fields outside. The friar gave them a slight bow of recognition before taking his seat next to the assassin. She was staring into space.

'My girl, your mind must be racing,' said Jamus softly.

Akumi nodded whilst continuing to stare at the heart of the fire.

'You have already done so much for Marmia,' he continued, 'but you don't need me to tell you there is still much to do. We must ensure this realm does not fall into chaos again and with people such as Golandin probably now back at large there is a real chance it could.'

Akumi sprung up suddenly, as if out of her brief trance. 'Endal must be found,' she hissed. 'We cannot allow him to get away with what he has done.'

Jamus understood her tone and sensed a vengeful desire burning deep inside the girl. However, his wisdom told him that Endal was no longer of any primary concern.

'Endal is out of the picture,' he said. 'He won't be seen again in these parts I assure you. We must focus on those that pose a threat to the state of...' The friar was interrupted.

'My war is with Endal,' Akumi said firmly. 'My duty was to protect Tamus and since I failed in that duty I must now do what I feel is right. I must track him down and serve justice. He cannot be allowed to get away with this!'

Akumi was consumed with both anger and apprehension. Jamus could well understand this. Endal had killed many close to her and sparked this whole state of affairs into being. However, he knew that thoughts of revenge were fruitless at this stage. There were more pressing matters.

'We are in a state of war once again,' he said. 'My monks are already altering activities and acting as scouts. Several are out across the plains in search of any rebel gatherings. We must focus on the matter at hand Akumi. We must track down Golandin and aid with the defence of Brimma. That city will no doubt be attacked at some stage now our armies are in chaos and essentially leaderless.'

The female assassin was insistent and although she knew Jamus was right couldn't just drop her deep urge to confront Endal again. This had become personal and the girl was not prepared to forget about the mysterious figure that had so decisively altered her life. She spoke:

'I am so sorry Jamus but I know what I must do. There are many who will defend Brimma from any potential rebel attack and there is no doubt that Sylvie will take control of that effort. I can't be expected to go after Golandin after all that has happened. I must get Endal!'

The old friar was at odds with what to say to the girl. Suddenly, he found himself in the late Hazati's shoes; expected to order the fiery Akumi around and ensure she did the right thing. The truth was he could understand the girl's desire to go after the dark assassin and knew that there was little he could say that would change her mind. There was also one other thing the friar seemed to know.

'This will be a testing time for all,' he said. 'We will all have our own aims and I do not wish to rest too weighty of a responsibility on your young shoulders my dear.'

Akumi smiled humbly as the soft tone of the friar's voice warmed her heart.

He continued: 'I am still in contact with many able fighters whose allegiance is in no doubt. I have already sent forth several brothers to send for them and I know they will come. I will form a band of warriors whose task shall be to stop Golandin and cut through the rebel factions before they can even stage an assault on the capital.'

Akumi was intrigued by this information and felt slight relief. She wasn't alone in this, far from it.

'Then you will understand that my task is separate Jamus? I must go my own way and settle with Endal,' said Akumi.

'You must do as you believe is right my dear and I have no doubt that you know this is the path you must take,' he replied.

She gave the friar the slightest of head bows in respect and swiftly got to her feet. 'I must set out in search for Endal,' she said. 'There is no time to lose.'

Jamus was stunned by her urgency. 'My girl, you have not yet warmed your bed or eaten a thing!' he chuckled. 'And how will you even know where to look first?'

'I am sorry Jamus,' she said, 'but the knowledge that there are warriors coming to aid you in crushing the rebels has given me the justification I needed to do this. I wanted to be sure I could go on this journey. I wanted to know I was not required elsewhere.'

'You are always required,' smiled Jamus, 'but it seems clear you are seeking my blessings in this fervid disposition of yours; go Akumi and find Endal! You have proved quite his equal and I have every confidence you will get him.'

Akumi pounced on the old man and gave him a hug. Jamus laughed, patting her affectionately on the back as he sat on his chair buried in her arms.

As Akumi turned to face the door she looked down to Jamus and asked: 'Who are these warriors you have summoned?'

'Oh, they come from far and wide Akumi,' he announced confidently. 'They are strong, with firm bonds to our land, and a hatred for men like Golandin. They are varied and powerful and I have no doubt they will come.'

Akumi seemed impressed and nodded. 'Thank you Jamus,' she said. 'Now I must go. Where I am to tread I still have no idea but my intuition will guide me. I know I will find him.'

Jamus stood and stared into her radiant eyes. 'I will see you on the other side of all this,' he remarked knowingly.

Akumi nodded at the positive prediction and smiled.

'Good luck Akumi,' he bowed.

'Farewell Jamus,' she said as she walked to the backdoor.

The wooden frame cranked open and she slipped through the narrow gap that closed shut once she'd let go of the handle. Outside her horse was waiting for her. He'd been fed and watered and a large stack of supplies had been thoughtfully placed about his reins. Akumi leapt onto the saddle and without a second's delay was gone; racing back up the track into the dimming light of the woodland beyond.

Friar Jamus couldn't resist watching the young girl ride off out of view. He felt a deep sense of admiration for the girl who had managed to stand up so well against the notorious Endal. She was now already becoming somewhat of a legend herself in these parts, with rumours and tales of all that happened up until Tamus' death scattering all over Marmia. People such as Akumi, Sylvie, and those lost in battle were becoming highly praised names. Even in defeat they were deeply respected.

Jamus knew he was in a time as important to these lands as the rain was to the crops he strived to grow. The old man turned and walked down the gravel pathway towards the fields. A light shower now pervaded the landscape in a calm, soft downfall of moisture. One of the robed monks suddenly came rushing to Jamus.

'Friar, the weather tells all,' the robed figure smirked. 'The Gods are not pleased with this state of affairs; they have shifted the sunny skies for this gloom.'

Jamus appeared to acknowledge this with an ardent faith in such abstruse signs.

'We have no reason to worry my brother,' said the old man. 'Soon now a gathering of the willing will reach the Abbey and from there we will decisively crush the enemy. Tamus will not fall.'

As he spoke he thought of those that he had summoned. All old friends of his and the late Hazati, they came from the furthest reaches of the realm and had ties with Tamus that had been tested time and time again over the years. They represented a host of skills, from the arcane abilities of mages to the physical attributes of sturdy warriors. Together they would be unstoppable. Jamus smiled to himself whilst thinking about it. Now all that was required was patience. There would still be some days to pass until their arrival. All the old friar could do was wait.

CHAPTER II

THE PERTURBED COURT OF BRIMMA

The view of the heap of dead bodies surrounded by pools of dry blood was sickening beyond description. No manner of experience or training could prepare oneself for such things. As the freshly arrived soldiers saw to the piles of victims Sylvie simply sat beside the tower gates in deep, morbid despair. To her side was Akumi, gently stroking her blonde hair with affection.

Both were bandaged up like a pair of toy dummies and neither seemed able to quite come to terms with all that had happened. Akumi was tentative and couldn't resist keeping still any longer.

'I have to go Sylvie,' she said. 'I must go after Endal. I cannot rest.'

Sylvie looked up at her as she spoke. She knew that this was something Akumi had to do and wasn't about to try and talk her out of it.

'Go then Akumi. I will not allow this empire to fall. Rest assured of that,' Sylvie said.

Akumi hugged her and was gone without a moment's pause.

Sylvie suddenly woke up. She was resting in a warm bed of white sheets and bouncy pillows. She had been dreaming, recollecting on her last minutes with Akumi. After this she'd been put to rest in a dwelling outside of the tower quarters somewhere within the city of Brimma. She must have been asleep for several hours and felt invigorated and focused. The blonde girl sat up and looked towards a bedside chair. A new sword and her light armour rested beside the wooden fitting. As she studied the blade it shimmered ever so slightly as a dim sun poured light through a window to her far side.

She contemplated what needed to be done. The weapon seemed

to represent her goal; it was as if by perceiving this object she knew that there was still fighting to come. She knew that everyone would now be looking to her to lead the defence of the tower and therefore the powerbase of Marmia. If the rebel factions were able to take this city they would be in control of the realm. Sylvie was not going to let this happen.

With great formidable drive she jumped from the bed and started to place her leather tunic back around her chest. It was a fresh set of armour, coloured white with red stripes along the sides of the tunic. Her blade was clean and lighter than one would expect. She recognised the sword and briefly contemplated why it had been passed onto her of all people. Once fully kitted she caught a glimpse of herself in the mirror next to the bed. She suddenly looked regal, the armour suggesting an important status. It became obvious that Sylvie was suddenly seen as the next best thing to an Emperor. The Sword of Tamus was hers.

The girl left the bedroom and swiftly passed by the quarters she found herself in. Beyond this small thatched barracks was a bustling street of Brimma. Hundreds of citizens wrestled past one another in the narrow road filled with stalls, carriages, and armour clad guards. It was chaotic on the one hand, reassuring on the other. Sylvie stepped out of the wooden doorway and immediately came into view of the guards surrounding the exterior of the house.

'Sylvie!' one yelled. 'Are you okay?'

'I am fine Sergeant,' she said whilst walking past him.

Several guards started to follow her as she marched up the road, the crowds opening up for her as they looked on in slight awe.

'There is no time to lose,' she announced. 'I want to chair a meeting in the tower and assess our position.'

The guards nodded as they shuffled behind her. Her mind was transfixed on both maintaining her calm and coming across as a confident leader. Before long they were at the tower, mounds of bodies still plainly in view in the area of the courtyard.

Sylvie was greeted by several figures that came racing towards her in open gestures.

'Welcome back Sylvie,' said a thin man waiting by the tower entrance.

Sylvie stopped and smiled at the figure. She had seen him numerous times before but they had rarely ever spoken. He was an advisor and for years now had been on the scene, but never of particular prominence in court.

'Thank you,' she said.

The thin male was awkward looking. He was bent forwards ever so slightly and pale. His scraggly, unkempt hair and thin goatee blew around in the light breeze. He seemed middle aged but with an older, worn face.

'This is Ellis,' announced a guard beside Sylvie. 'He was an advisor to Tamus but now will act as one of yours.'

Sylvie nodded. 'I'm aware of that. I am about to call for a meeting Ellis,' she said. 'We must discuss what comes next.'

Ellis sniggered in a bizarre fashion before responding. 'Yes, let us do just that my Empress,' he said.

Sylvie was more aware of being addressed as Empress than she was of his odd behaviour. She would probably have to get used to this title.

The group moved on to a large room within the tower used for meetings. A prominent table seated up to twenty with Sylvie's chair at the head. She sat down without reluctance as groups of servants raced to alert those that would be present. As the girl sat down by herself she looked to the chair to her left. This would once have been used by General Dorwor. Sylvie would have sat to his right. How different things were now. She tried not to dwell on it.

The first figures to arrive were dressed in quite flamboyant robes. These were members of the council whom were accustomed to these top level meetings. Sylvie counted twelve of these. They represented all factions and were mixed in gender. Next to enter the room were representatives of the armies. With no general to lead them, several lower ranking soldiers were called upon, all of whom had seen Endal's assault first hand. The five of them sat together to the girl's right side. The chair to her left was still free.

As she was about to start speaking Ellis suddenly popped into the room and strolled to this spot. He sat down and looked at her with intrigue. For some reason Sylvie felt more nervous now this odd character was beside her. She tried not to think about it and spoke:

'Thank you all for coming. I am humbled to be in charge and with this duty I will remain steadfast and loyal to our realm. We cannot dwell on what has happened and instead must now plan our next move.'

There was a calm silence in the room as the girl addressed her subjects.

'We must firstly ensure the rebels do not enter this city. Defending Brimma is vital. If we lose it we lose control of Marmia. We will lose the war. Secondly, we must try to break up the enemy before they can even reform. No doubt Golandin will be at the forefront of their effort. He must be found.'

Several council members mumbled acknowledgements of this plan and nodded to themselves.

'I want our legions here in the capital. Let the rebels retake the smaller towns for now. We cannot defend every city. Instead, I propose we turn this city into an impenetrable fort.'

A council member suddenly butted in: 'Like we did to ensure the Emperor's safety?'

Sylvie's face went ever so slightly red. The truth was this town had been highly fortified and defended prior to Endal's incursion and they had failed to keep Tamus safe from his blade.

'This time we are fighting an army who will attack via more conventional methods,' she said firmly. 'This time we will hold. This time we must not fail!'

One of the soldiers opened his lips: 'If the enemy reforms in the numbers they were at prior to our victory against Twinicia we shall be outnumbered two to one, perhaps more. In the past our best strategy has always been in implementing our superior tactics and skill.'

'Yes, and we shall do this in our defence,' said Sylvie brashly.

'But to defend relies more on numbers than tactics,' the soldier replied.

Another to his side came in with conviction: 'No! To attack you need the numbers and the enemy has them!'

'Yes, but we must consider our...' another voice bickered.

'You are missing the point!' came another.

In a flash of disagreement the meeting turned into a debacle of clashing voices as the table of figures argued over the plan. Sylvie patiently stood silently for a few moments before yelling out to her subjects.

'Enough!' her tender voice was suddenly assertive.

There was total compliance and each face fell silent. She was in control.

'We can debate the intricacies of our tactics later but for now hear this: We will ignore the rebel numbers and focus on defending our empire. We will not be defeated!'

With her words came further grumblings of agreement. Sylvie abruptly shifted her focus to Ellis. He had remained silent throughout and seemed oddly calm and collected.

'Do you wish to add anything Ellis?' Sylvie asked.

He suddenly looked up, as if out of a daze.

'Oh no,' he said. 'Your plan is our best bet and I am in total agreement my Empress.'

She nodded. 'We have said all that needs saying. As we speak, Akumi, the late Hazati's exceptional apprentice, is on the hunt for Endal. We must now restore order on the streets of this city and prepare for anything,' the new Empress said. 'And make no mistake; this tower in which we sit will remain the tower of Tamus! Tamus Tower!'

'And what about Golandin?' asked a soldier. 'May I volunteer to form a group of our most elite troops to go after him? We already have an idea where he is after all.'

The soldier was referring to the fact they knew where the prison was Dorwor had put him in. They also knew the empire's prisons were likely the first target on the reforming rebels' list of objectives. The chances were he was still in that area at least but this was really only guess work.

'I will consider your request soldier,' said Sylvie. 'What is your name?'

The warrior stood up, his chair squeaking back on the stone floor.

'I am Sergeant Elgor, humble servant to Tamus!' he roared.

'Well Elgor, I will consider the request,' the Empress answered.

The proud warrior sat down smiling to himself. He seemed content with that.

CHAPTER III

THE LOATHSOME UTOPIA

The rusty iron bars looked pliable and weak enough to be pulled apart by hand. However, they were as strong as the day in which some far away fire had strengthened them. There was no use trying to bend or break them. They were faultless and the small dim cell inescapable. Light managed somehow to find its way into the bare confines of the room as it crept in through narrow gaps from beyond the underground passageway and into the basement Golandin found himself in.

He was lucky not to be in chains and at least could flex and occasionally pace up and down this despicable space. There was no one else around and only the odd rat to keep him company. Beyond his bars were other empty cages and a corridor leading to a staircase to the world above. It had been several days since Golandin had been caught and sat down with Dorwor. The rebel veteran now felt nothing but frustration and anger over not knowing what was going on. What was the fate of Tamus? Had Endal somehow managed, against all odds, to slay the Emperor? Golandin had no idea.

There was a rough and dirty bed in the far corner of his cell and the warrior spent most of his time resting on it in contemplation. The guards would check up on him once every few hours but Golandin was aware that no guard had come down now for what seemed like almost a day. He was intrigued but not enough to move from the bed. This was his world and nothing would change it now. The reality was Golandin had little confidence his plan had succeeded. He imagined Endal, no matter how tough, had been defeated by an army of Tamus troops and now lay dead in some pit in the sewers. He imagined Tamus was happy and laughing merrily up in his tower. He started to wish he'd never met or spoken with Bollam and that he'd just vanished out of the fray when it had been possible.

Golandin was so lost in thoughts of regret that he hadn't heard the commotion going on upstairs. There were several yells and the distinct sound of blades clashing. Upturned furniture slammed against the walls and voices bellowed out in fear. Golandin was indifferent to this until the sound of platemail armour smashing against the stone steps became deafening. He stood up and looked to the stairs only to spot a Tamus soldier roll down them and land in an awkward slump on the cold stone of the basement floor. He was spattered in blood and lifeless.

'What of this!' Golandin yelled in shock.

A figure suddenly raced down the steps and into the passageway. He was a rebel troop, no doubt about it. His armour consisted of dyed black leather and savage war paints plastered across his face.

'Golandin!' the figure yelled in relief.

He raced to the cell door and looked to the lock.

'He is down here!' the man yelled.

'Who are you?' asked the imprisoned rebel.

'We have come to free you sir,' the figure smiled. 'Our war is back in full swing!'

Another rebel came down the stairs and ran to the lock. He was holding a set of keys.

'What has happened soldier?' Golandin asked.

'The Emperor is dead sir!' came the reply. 'Endal killed Tamus!'

Golandin felt a surge of energy rush through him and a euphoric sense of relief. His dream was a reality!

'This is fantastic!' he screamed, hardly able to word his emotion.

As he spoke the cell door cranked open, Golandin was a free man.

The rebels raced up the steps and passed several dead Tamus troops. This outpost had been all but destroyed by the rebel troops who had converged on it in an organised assault. There were no survivors and, with Golandin the only captive, no one else to free. A fire was already raging as men hurled torches into stacks of hay and freed horses. In every direction was woodland and no Tamus troops would be coming to resist this horde. Golandin stepped forth into the courtyard as he looked around at the chaos and flames.

'It is time to claim our lands!' he bellowed with thespian presence. 'Let us march on Brimma and truly end the remnants of that vile dead Emperor's grip!'

Rebel troops cheered in every direction. One came racing to the leader's side, handing him his sword and armour.

'They kept your stuff in a safe,' the rebel sniggered.

Golandin immediately started to place his attire back on. He'd even been reunited with his pouch of gold. As he fiddled with the plates of armour he noticed a couple of troops dragging a wounded Tamus soldier before him.

'Ha! This rodent tried to run away,' a rebel spat out. 'We caught him in the woodland, he ran right into us! Thought you might want to deal with him.' There was collective laughter.

Golandin raised his large longsword and studied the old blade. He then looked down at the Tamus soldier bowed before him. He was being held in position by several bloodthirsty men.

'Any fool that fights for Tamus is as good as dead,' Golandin said smugly.

He drew back his sword and thrust it into the soldier's back with a firm downwards motion. The blade sliced into the man's torso and killed him instantaneously. The rebel leader pulled his sword back out of the troop and watched the body drop down into a pool of blood before him. There was further applause and laughter from the men around him.

'Any news of Arthir?' Golandin suddenly asked, indifferent to the murder he'd just committed.

'He was being held in a different outpost,' a rebel in the know said, 'but we've now also liberated that place. I am confident he has linked up with our main force forming up to the north-east of here.'

'Excellent,' Golandin smiled, 'and what of the assassin, Endal?'

'We have no news sir,' said the rebel. 'Nothing beyond that we know he got away and vanished.'

Golandin remembered Endal's word that he would find him to accept payment. It seemed like a distant memory but one that was now at the forefront of his thoughts.

'Whatever I have,' announced the warrior, 'it goes to Endal! And in the meantime we must find Bollam.'

A rebel came forth from the forming crowd around Golandin.

'Sir, word is Bollam was some sort of mage, he was defeated in battle before Endal killed Tamus.'

'Oh?' Golandin was intrigued.

'That is all I know.'

Golandin didn't seem too bothered by the news although was slightly perplexed. The financial implications of this were his only real concern. He had hoped the innkeeper would further fund their cause.

'Then let us press on and link up with our forces!' he concluded.

The rebel unit was then on the move. A gang of darkly clothed thugs marched off into the forest and left the fires to rage and the bodies to rot.

Surrounded by tents and men at work, busy in their labours, Arthir sat with a bottle of wine that had been handed to him in celebration of the day's news. He'd been freed earlier that day by the reformed rebel factions and had been led to this semi-permanent base of operations south of the trade city of Dwenton. The slippery character was as pleased as Golandin at the news of Endal's success and relaxed by himself in his recently erected tent in an ever increasingly intoxicated state. It had been a few hours now since this gathering flock had reached this flat terrain. To every direction were green, verdant fields and to the north, some miles away, stood the town of Dwenton. Beyond this only Brimma remained as the northern most dwelling of significance in these parts. The rebels had been swift to converge on this area.

Once fleeing bands of men were now reignited with their desire to see the empire fall. All as grim and power hungry as each other, this undisciplined army represented a horde rather than some side with a common purpose or ideal. The camp was becoming filled with every level of thuggery known to Marmia. Murderers, rapists, and petty thieves all fought under the new leader's banner. Prisoners from every captured dungeon were at large; all on a journey to reach this place of loathsome utopia. There was no cause here except a desire for power and no philosophy except to take it by force.

Arthir jostled with his leather armour and took another swig of wine. A gang of rebels had managed to steal crates full of ale on their journey to the base and had brought the stolen goods to the camp for all to consume with abandon. The signs of mass drunkenness were already showing as the horde became rowdy.

On the horizon an advanced party were racing towards the camp. Their horses were darting across the grassy fields and a prominent figure remained in front.

'Golandin is here!' a voice cried in camp.

With this announcement masses of the radical horde raced out from the centre of the dwelling to greet their leader. His plan was already coming to fruition; they saw him as the leader now Warlord Twinicia was a distant memory.

It didn't take long for Golandin to reach the outer sections of this construction site.

'Hail! Hail!' he roared from his mount.

'Welcome Golandin!' a mass greeting sounded out.

For a moment the aged warrior seemed taken aback by quite how passionate and warm his welcoming had been. The hordes surrounding him were ecstatic that he was finally with them and there was already a deep, collective sense that he was their true leader. Rumour had already started to spread that it had been he who had plotted Tamus' death at the hands of Endal and got the ball rolling. To many here Golandin was already a hero. The fact it had been Endal, a figure of whom men like these knew nothing, who had killed the late Emperor meant little for he was not here and Golandin most certainly was.

As the warrior reached the centre of the camp he got down from his horse and waved as the crowds struggled and jostled to reach his side.

'I am humbled to be so warmly welcomed,' he yelled. 'Thank you all, but there is much to do! We must secure this camp and prepare for war!'

A foray of cheering erupted as the bloodlust and euphoria of the army reached fever pitch.

'More will surely join us as the word continues to spread that we are forming up near Dwenton,' the leader went on. 'We must ensure we are safe against any possible enemy attack and will continue to allow each man that comes to join us to filter into our army!'

As Golandin spoke he noticed his old pal Arthir sitting in his tent watching attentively. Golandin smiled and raised his arms up in the air.

'But tonight we celebrate!' he announced.

Roars of celebratory cheering continued as he walked away from the spotlight and into his friend's small canopy.

'Hello Golandin,' said Arthir.

The rebel leader sat beside his friend, ever so reluctant to speak. Golandin wasn't sure if Arthir was aware he had been responsible for giving Dorwor the whereabouts of his hideout.

'And so here we find ourselves together again,' Arthir said. 'Although perhaps this time in rather better circumstances, huh?' He laughed with abandonment.

'Yes, our plan succeeded Arthir,' said the snake of a friend. 'And we will now take this land by the throat!'

Arthir sat up, placing his wine to one side. 'Any news of Endal?' he asked, eager to find out all he could of the assassin.

'Only that he killed Tamus,' answered Golandin. 'Nothing else. I know not where he is or if we shall ever even see him again.'

'He will expect payment?' Arthir pressed.

'Well he might,' said Golandin, 'but what can he do now we are all together?' Golandin smiled as his lips closed.

'No, we can't underestimate him now, not after... not after all this! He killed the Emperor after all!' Arthir spoke in an alarmed tone.

'Calm down my old friend,' Golandin said. 'Firstly, I hear the word is that Bollam, our contact from Dolsbury, was actually Vortor... a mage. He was killed in battle aiding Endal before he'd reached Brimma.'

Arthir was suddenly sharp with concentration. Golandin continued:

'I suspect this Vortor character used us to achieve a common goal we all had; to see this realm leaderless. It seems that they were both in this together somehow, I don't know. I don't honestly care. However, I do know that all this is good news for us my friend.'

'Well it better be,' said Arthir, 'because without Bollam we have no money to settle our bill with the assassin anyway. I trust you no longer possess the gold he gave you?'

'No I don't,' replied the dishonest leader, 'and this is very true, but I suspect there was more to Endal than we realised. I suspect money was not what drove him to complete our contract. I think we just managed to stumble across an entity, if you will, that cleared the path for us!'

The two rebels were silent at that remark and studied the crowds busy outside the tent. There was no doubt about the fact this situation now had a momentum of its own and was hardly under the control of either man. They were simply now riding at the peak of this wave. Where it went from here was anyone's guess.

'Now we must ensure we are safe in this position and able to repel any potential attack those fools might launch,' said Golandin. 'I am sure Dorwor has something planned now our position is known to the realm.'

'Oh...' Arthir sniggered. 'Dorwor is no more, apparently killed by the blade of Endal no less.'

Golandin laughed out loud before speaking: 'Well in that case our enemy is now weaker than even I had suspected. It seems our grand objective will be rather easier to complete than we could have ever possibly dreamed for. The gates to Tamus Tower are surely open!'

CHAPTER IV

THE RETURN OF OLD FRIENDS

The rake suddenly was less important to the old friar than it once had been. He found himself struggling to maintain even the focus to sweep the dry leaves from his doorway. Farming was no longer of any great priority and instead Jamus could only think of what was happening to his beloved lands. He decided there was little point trying to pretend nothing was up whilst he waited for the return of his scouts and messengers, and instead of raking entered back into the Abbey, in search of a half full bottle of whisky he'd been working on earlier that morning.

He found the bottle where he'd left it. It rested on the great table that took up most of the space in the dining hall. At capacity his table could seat anything up to forty monks or visitors to his household. However, he found himself alone staring at the glass concealing his favourite drop.

Just as Jamus was about to take a swig of the alcoholic beverage he spotted a figure race by the view through a window to his side. A monk was running up the path and towards the entrance. He was swift to greet the brother as the door to the hall opened.

'Jamus,' the monk panted as he entered. 'They are here!' he stammered as his breath caught up with him.

The friar nodded whilst raising his eyebrows in thought. 'Who are here?' he asked.

The monk was quick to clarify: 'The warriors you called for… all of them have come with brother Aimis.'

Jamus immediately bounded out of the Abbey and into the clearings outside. To the south a group were clearly closing in from the distant backdrop of hills. The messenger monk spoke:

'We came across them on the road heading in this direction. They were already on the way! We filled them in on what has happened and they all continued to come without any persuasion.'

Jamus seemed excited by the development. He had been waiting several days now for this party of his most trusted contacts to arrive at his Abbey. The time had suddenly come to get cracking. In a symbolic move Jamus pulled his monk's robe off from over his head and hurled it at the monk beside him.

'I am no longer friar Jamus,' he declared. 'We are now at war and I am once again a warrior. Call me only Jamus.'

The monk nodded whilst he looked on at the distant riders heading towards them.

'I am going to fetch my armour and sword from my quarters,' Jamus said. 'Once the party arrives beckon them into our hall and I shall be at our table.'

Jamus, now standing wearing only sandals and baggy pants, swiftly entered back into the Abbey. The monk placed his robe beside several stacks of hay and remained in position by the door.

Upstairs Jamus was already staring at an old wardrobe in a far corner of his modest bedroom. It was of sturdy oak and large double doors revealed skilled carvings amongst the hardwood body. The aged warrior put his tired hands to the rounded handle and slowly opened it. Inside were various garments hung up on wire frames. Most of the attire consisted of robes and simple shirts but to the right side a set of chainmail hung separate from the rest of the clothing. The dark silver glistened with the slightest of light and beneath the hanging armour rested a mighty sword; wrapped in mounds of fabric. Jamus bent forwards and clasped his steel with pride and caution. As he removed it from the wardrobe and raised it in his arms he started to pull away the protective sheets of yarn.

His was a gleaming blade as ancient as The Sword of Tamus itself. It felt heavy but Jamus refused to acknowledge this burden. He then looked to his chainmail; still in place after years of dormant storage. This was a significant moment for the man; he was suddenly arming himself once again.

Brother Aimis rolled into the Abbey grounds ahead of the incoming party. He was Jamus' most trusted of brothers and had been in his service for many years. Within the drab brown robe was a warrior of great skill and experience. He was some years younger than Jamus but just as full of wisdom. He had long brown hair and distinctly hazel eyes. Like Jamus he had sworn never to raise the sword again but times like these called for men like him to revoke such faded promises. The monk standing by the Abbey door was quick to notice the brother halt beside the pathway.

'Brother, are they close?' he asked.

Aimis dropped down from his black horse and walked towards his friend.

'Yes, they are moments away,' he announced. 'Where is Jamus?'

'Preparing for their arrival,' answered the monk. 'I am intrigued Aimis… how is it that they were already on the road?'

Aimis smiled at the question. 'All I know is that we bumped into them heading in this direction! We only travelled half the distance before spotting them coming the other way. Hah! No doubt 'tis a question Jamus will ask them.'

The monk nodded, staring into the horizon with an inquisitive expression.

'Perhaps Jamus had summoned for them earlier?' he asked.

'Well I am eager to ask Jamus that very question,' smiled Aimis.

The door to the Abbey creaked open as the monks entered into the quarters. As they closed the door they spotted Jamus coming down the wooden staircase before them. He was suddenly a warrior; silver chainmail wrapped around his thin frame and limbs. A dark green cloak tied around his back, and a black belt was strapped about his waist with his mighty sword sheathed within a humble tabard.

''Tis the Jamus of old; the warrior I met all those decades ago,' Aimis declared.

'Indeed,' bellowed Jamus.

He paused beside them once reaching the last step. 'They are here?' he asked.

'Almost,' said Aimis. 'Let us prepare at the table, our monks will guide them in.'

A lone black bird circled the fields beyond the holy place warriors were gathering. It swooped low and hovered with the grace only nature can supply. With the coming roar of racing horses it suddenly fled high into the clouds. They had arrived. Two monks riding black horses were first into the clearing outside the Abbey pathway. Behind them were five riders coming in at a slow, composed pace.

'We shall see to your horses,' said one of the escorting monks. 'Please enter the Abbey.'

The party halted beside him and the riders scanned the grounds they found themselves in.

'Nice place,' sniggered a tanned male. 'Might have to stay here some time!'

He was first to pounce from his mount. His black boots landed onto the gravel path with a thud that created a cloud of rising dust. Before long the other riders were on their feet and the gang headed for the Abbey door.

'Where is that old fool?' the voice of a larger man gargled in mirth.

'No doubt inside beside a warm fire,' the tanned male mocked.

Behind them the two monks wrestled with the horses and dragged them by the reins towards the nearby stables.

Jamus was seated at the head of the marvellous rectangular table. A fire indeed crackled beside this regal fixture. To his right sat Aimis, still robed but with a brown bandana now tied around his forehead, keeping back his long auburn hair. The other monk had vanished, not required in this place of pressing business.

As the party entered the Abbey they quickly knew where Jamus sat. The door to the room was half open and the fire was beckoning through the gap. First to appear through the widening entrance was the tanned male; clothed entirely in black with short, spiky hair and a slight mild scar down his right cheek. He looked young and full of energy.

'Fenris!' Jamus exclaimed merrily.

'Hello old timer,' the male chuckled as he made for a seat in front of the fireplace.

Next to enter the room was the larger male. He was a chubby axe wielder; with long greying hair and wavy, thinning beard. He was kitted out for a small war with a sturdy battleaxe strapped over his shoulders and a curved blade drooping from his rounded belly. Jamus sat, nodding continuously at the sight of this rough looking character.

'So you made it Rense?' he laughed.

'Oh, I couldn't resist another party!' Rense replied in his deep tone. 'If only to see your wrinkled face again!'

He took a seat beside Fenris, who faced Aimis sitting on the other side next to Jamus at the head of the table.

The third face to appear before Jamus' glance seemed like something of a contrast to the last. A striking girl entered and paused as she spotted him. She had shoulder length brunette hair with a series of dangling multicoloured braids. She looked like she was about the same age as Akumi and in many respects resembled the assassin.

'My dear Lady Yuuki,' Jamus whispered. 'I am so glad you came.'

The girl got close to Jamus and bent down, giving him a soft hug.

'Hello Jams,' she giggled.

The girl's attire was colourful and vibrant. It resembled a kimono, with a tight midriff and long dress flowing down to her ankles. She was carrying a large staff that sparkled in the light of the fire as the countless gems peppered all across its extent glistened.

'Please take a seat my girl,' Jamus said.

The remaining two figures were already now in the room, standing by the doorway and eager to greet their old friend.

One came forth: 'It is good to see you again Jamsee,' said the feminine voice.

Aimis sat up at that, intrigued by what seemed like another mildly humorous nickname.

'As it is good to see you too, Emi,' Jamus smiled. 'My how you and Yuuki have grown since we last met!'

The girl looked as young as Yuuki. They were in their later teenage years but already had more experience of life than most twice their age. Emi was dressed in shades of green with a large bow prominent around her back. Its stave rose taller than she as it pointed up at the ceiling. She had blonde hair tied back in a bun and innocent blue eyes.

As she took a seat beside Lady Yuuki the final figure emerged forth from the doorway.

'Shall we begin,' he smirked.

Jamus didn't seem quite as warm towards this figure as he had been with the rest. It was as if he saw this last guest to his Abbey as merely an acquaintance that he required for the task at hand rather than some old friend he would also happily have social dealings with.

'Yes, we shall begin this meeting in earnest once you are seated Arifor,' he remarked.

Arifor was swift to sit down beside Rense. He slightly resembled Fenris with his black attire and sword resting on his belt. However, there was a sharp coldness about this male. He looked to be in his later years, with mid length black hair rolled back over his forehead and a pale and worn face. He was quite well built and slightly taller than the other two males he had come with but walked with a hunch, meaning he seemed shorter.

The seven warriors sat by the table in silence. On one side of Jamus sat Aimis, Yuuki, and Emi. To the other sat Fenris, Rense, and Arifor. Jamus took a swift glance at all of them before initiating the meeting. He then started to speak:

'Firstly, I want to thank you all for coming. I am aware you have travelled far to reach here and before we set off you must rest and feast with my monks here in the Abbey. I am intrigued though... how is it that you were already on route here?'

Aimis jumped in. 'Sir, I assumed you had sent scouts out before me for I bumped into them half way on my journey to reach where you'd said they'd be.'

'No, I only sent your party to contact them,' Jamus seemed confused.

'No, we formed up and left for Marmia about a week ago,' said Rense. 'Word had reached as far as our lands that a plan to kill Tamus was afoot.'

'I see,' Jamus said. 'So you came without any request?'

'Of course,' said Lady Yuuki. 'We wanted to ensure his safety...'

'You are all aware that Tamus is dead?' Aimis came in.

'We are,' said Rense. 'Word reached us during our journey here.'

'It has only strengthened our resolve to see the thugs finally quashed,' Emi remarked with firm tenacity. Jamus nodded.

These five warriors had come from lands beyond the boundaries of Marmia. They were esteemed fighters and deeply admired by Jamus. In years past he had fought beside them in the wars against the hordes of thugs desperate to crush the empire established by men as noble as the late Tamus. Jamus knew that the protection of this empire meant everything to these people. They had fought to see it come into being and were prepared to fight again to ensure it was saved. The only reason he hadn't summoned for them sooner, when he'd first discovered the news of the plan to assassinate Tamus, was because he'd never imagined they'd reach the realm in time. He was so relieved to see them here before him now at this time of reckoning for Marmia.

'We formed up like old times,' Rense recollected. 'Of course, in our hearts we hoped to reach here in time to help protect Tamus. However, we knew the road was long. We are prepared to do anything required of us Jamus.'

This party of admired fighters had known one another for years and firm bonds tied them all together as a unit. They each represented some specific skill as vital to what was to come as any other. Rense and Fenris were battle-hardened warriors of men. Fenris was a skilled blade, exceptional some would have it said. Rense was a sturdy axe fighter. His strength was unparalleled in these parts and his name notorious in every inn. He was a brawler and behemoth of a figure. In contrast, Emi was a deadly tracker and expert with the bow. She could kill with lightning pace and lurk silently in shadow. Lady Yuuki was a mistress of magic. She was heralded in her parts as a Lady of conjuring. Armed with her arcane staff she could take on armies via her spells and even had the capacity to heal minor wounds for those around her. Her abilities had been tested time and time again and her venerated name was now somewhat shrouded in myth and conjecture.

Arifor was a warrior whose roots were entirely unknown. He had fought for Tamus in the war and remained a trusted member of this special gathering. His skill came with his dark abilities to lure nature and the elements into acting however he saw fit. Some would call him a shaman; others labelled him an anomaly. His talents could not be taught nor could any trace of his past be dug up. At best Arifor was a mysterious magician.

Jamus propped himself up on his uncomfortable grand chair.

'With Tamus dead the rebels are reforming in great numbers,' he said. 'My monks have been scouting the lands and finding out all they can. This is what they have learnt. They no doubt hope to strike Brimma, our capital city, at this time of weakness. They intend to capture the tower and claim power over Marmia.'

'Fools!' Rense roared. 'Not going to happen.'

'We must ensure it doesn't,' said Jamus. 'This is why I hoped you would all come. The armies of Tamus are all over the place right now. The lone assassin responsible for the Emperor's death claimed many hundreds of them and their morale is at a low with the death of Tamus.'

'Many hundreds!' Fenris was alarmed. 'I mean, I did hear that right, yes?

'Who was this assassin?' Lady Yuuki asked, deeply intrigued.

'Right now it matters not who he was,' Jamus responded dryly. 'He is now out of the picture; although for how long I really wouldn't like to say.'

'Meaning?' Fenris asked.

'Meaning I just sense we have not seen the last of him,' said Jamus. 'However, the late Hazati's finest student has gone after him… call it a vendetta if you will.'

'Akumi?' Yuuki beamed.

'You know of Akumi?' Jamus was confused.

'The last time I saw Hazati we were children,' Yuuki smiled. 'I remember playing with her when they passed by our village one day.'

Jamus nodded. 'Well, she is an exceptionally skilled swords-woman now,' he said.

'And she has now gone after this mysterious assassin all alone?' Yuuki seemed concerned.

'I could not stop her nor would I have wanted to,' said Jamus. 'She has what it takes to defeat him and almost did at the gates of Tamus Tower.'

Lady Yuuki was fascinated by those words but Jamus abruptly went on before she could comment:

'We must focus on our task. There will be time to discuss all after battle is done. Our mission, if you like, will be to track down and defeat the, now leader, of the rebellious armies. His name is Golandin and I can confirm he was one of the conspirators in contracting Endal to kill Tamus in the first place.'

'Endal!' Arifor suddenly sprang to attention like someone had struck him in the back.

Jamus was alarmed by the dark figure's sudden abrasive behaviour.

'Yes, that is the name of the assassin responsible for all this chaos,' Jamus groaned.

Arifor was silent as if still shocked by the name he'd heard mentioned. Jamus knew that signs like this coming from the shady mage were always significant.

'What is it?' Emi asked.

'I had no idea Endal was on the scene, let alone at the forefront of all this,' Arifor stated. 'Endal is a name I have not heard for decades and yet even now that name sends fear shivering down my spine.'

Lady Yuuki appeared deeply focused and spoke: 'I have also heard of this name, but from what I heard never believed the figure to be anything more than a myth!'

'Endal is as real as the sun that beams down and reflects light from the streams,' Jamus commented. 'He is as powerful as the most outlandish tale would tell. However, he is no longer around and I stress we must press on matters that are.'

'The Endal I remember was like some demigod,' Arifor said. 'He was unstoppable and fought with the pace and agility of some creature from another world. No man could stop him or even touch him with a blade. No man had a chance against him. That is the Endal I recall.'

Lady Yuuki raised her head and looked at the mage across the table.

'No, it took a girl to do that,' she smiled.

Arifor seemed to ignore her remark and remained at odds with the news.

'Perhaps that best illustrates then quite how skilled Akumi is,' said Jamus. 'She managed to injure Endal and he fled into the night.'

'He killed Tamus though,' Fenris remarked. 'She obviously wasn't that good.'

'The fact she even managed to so much as touch him with her katana's tip tells me all I need to know about this girl,' Arifor said. 'Oh, she must be exceptionally skilled.'

With sudden presence and charisma Lady Yuuki leaned forwards against the tabletop and addressed the room:

'We must track Endal down and help Akumi defeat him! We cannot let such a thing remain at large after all this!'

Jamus waved his arm at Yuuki, shunning her to sit back down in her chair.

'Now listen,' he bellowed. 'Arifor has said all that needs saying when it comes to Endal. He is some pure evil whose powers go beyond those of mortal human flesh. Akumi was insistent that she go after him and I am not going to let us split up in order to aid her in her sworn task. Our duty is to stop Golandin and prevent the rebels gaining enough strength to launch an attack on Brimma.'

Rense shuffled around in his chair eager to speak.

'The old man is right you know,' he said. 'We must defend this land, not go off on some glory mission.' Fenris smiled at the suggestion as he sat beside the chubby axe man.

'I agree... we should stop Golandin in his tracks and only then talk about going after Endal,' Emi remarked.

It was clear Yuuki was more concerned about the lone Akumi than anyone else at the table. For some reason she felt a duty to help this girl her most distant memories still pictured as a childhood playmate. In some ways it was because she admired the way Akumi had gone off alone after this revered adversary. It was the kind of role she normally brought upon herself.

'Be not forgetful of what I said regards Endal,' Arifor whispered cautiously. 'Talk of going after him is simply folly. It is akin to talking of chasing some rampant tornado in the hope of squashing it with a spear.'

'He is right,' Jamus added. 'It is up to Akumi now, no one else. We must focus on Golandin.'

The room started to calm down with the acknowledgement of the joint wisdom put forth by the two weary men. Only Lady Yuuki showed signs of opening her lips. Jamus stood up and spoke with arms raised in passion:

'And so this is the plan; to move out to the outskirts of Dwenton where reports of forming rebel troops continue to reach the Abbey. From there we shall hunt down Golandin and prevent him from leading those masses. We shall also put as much a dent in the enemy as possible and aid in the defence of Brimma against any potential attack.'

The party nodded in unison.

'And I trust Sylvie will be leading that defence?' Fenris asked.

'Oh yes! She is around all right, in fact now running the empire my scouts tell me,' Jamus smiled.

The party had all had dealings with the girl in the past during the war and it was clear from his behaviour that Fenris had deeper feelings for the beautiful blonde than he would surely admit to.

'That is good news,' he said, 'very good news indeed.'

CHAPTER V

HAMMERS AND ANVILS

For such last minute arrangements the funeral seemed well organised. Hundreds of Tamus troops lined the streets as a procession of council members, state figures, and members of court slowly walked from the bridge of Brimma to the tower gates. This was a tradition and represented the journey made by Tamus upon first coming into the city as a victor on the battlefields. The body of the late Tamus rested in a regal open coffin carried by dozens of soldiers. A mighty sword lay on the top of his ghostly pale body, which was wrapped in a white robe of state. However, it was not The Sword of Tamus. This symbolic steel had now been passed onto someone else.

Slightly behind this walked Sylvie in morbid momentum. She was accompanied by Ellis and a large group of council members dressed in their red flamboyant colours. The girl was the closest thing to a leader these people currently had and the massing crowds of citizens chanted her name in respect and allegiance further up the bridge.

Tamus had been a popular Emperor and the hundreds upon hundreds that had gathered to watch this slow march represented a truly overwhelming sight. Sylvie was struggling to keep the tears at bay although managed to maintain a firm expression of resolve right up to the tower. The west side of the encircling wall was still blown apart and rubble lay charred around the immediate streets and alleys. The bodies of the many fallen had now been carried away to fields and graveyards around the outskirts of the city. However, what still remained were the stains of dry blood scattered all over the soil of the courtyard they now trod. The pools of red would not fade no matter how much water was poured onto them by the determined troops.

The very fact this city, along with those other main dwellings darted out across Marmia, had not plunged into chaos the moment it was discovered Tamus was dead was a testament to the allegiances the inhabitants of these dwellings had toward the empire and what it stood for. However, Sylvie knew that the morale of those around her was at a low and that it was really quite a finely balanced state of equilibrium. Only the smallest of events was now required to turn this crowd into a panicking mob.

As they halted by the place in the courtyard Tamus' coffin would be sealed and taken away to be buried in the tomb under the tower Sylvie noticed Ellis smiling to himself. She looked at him as he stood to her side, slightly bent forwards.

'What is it?' she asked slightly scornfully.

Ellis looked up, instantly retracting his faint grin.

'Oh, it is nothing Empress,' he said. 'Really it is nothing.'

She didn't wish to dwell on it and turned back to face the Emperor's coffin as several troops closed the lid. The thud of stone clasping down on stone signified the end of Tamus. There was a volley of wails from the crowds beyond the walls. Sylvie looked down to the ground.

As the coffin was carried away towards the tower Sylvie recollected on her encounter with Endal and recalled everything he had said to her before vanishing. In some ways the dutiful girl wished she'd been killed by her Emperor's side. She had contemplated cutting her throat when alone in the throne room surrounded by the bodies but she hadn't done it and instead now found herself in charge.

The girl knew very well that she had put up her best fight against the assassin but ultimately just hadn't been able to stop him. A part of her wanted to face him again but she was also well aware it was he that had ultimately put her in this position. He could have killed her there and then but didn't for reasons only he could truly understand. If it were in the hope that she would tell the tale of his killing to all those that would listen Endal would surely be disappointed. Sylvie had refused to shed any light on what happened once Endal stormed those doors to anyone who had asked her. All she would say was that he'd defeated everyone that stood before him and left her in a pool of blood near Tamus. This was really all they needed to know.

Ellis turned to face Sylvie once the coffin had vanished into the tower on its way to the underground tomb.

'You must think about sending scouts out to check for buildups of the enemy,' he said.

'Yes Ellis, I wanted to get this moment out of the way first before calling for that,' she said.

'But now is the time to prepare our defences and gather as much intelligence as we can,' Ellis said.

Sylvie nodded. 'It is and I will give the command,' she said.

As the girl spoke she spotted Sergeant Elgor in the courtyard with several troops lined up for his inspection.

'Sergeant Elgor,' she called out.

He turned and raced over to his Empress.

'Yes my Empress.'

Their leader spoke: 'I want you to gather twenty of your finest troops and head out to Dwenton. Report back on what you see but do not engage Golandin if you encounter him there.'

'Right away Empress,' Elgor yelled fervidly.

He bowed before her and ran off to summon his men.

'From the reports we have the enemy is forming south of Dwenton and no secret of that is being made,' said Sylvie. 'Elgor will be able to shed light on their numbers and position.'

Ellis was silent, staring into space in thought.

''Tis a good plan my Empress,' he whispered. 'A good plan indeed.'

Sylvie tried to ignore the eccentrics of her advisor and started to walk towards the mighty tower before them.

Arthir woke up in somewhat of a stupor. His head ached and his vision was ever so dizzy. The lightweight drinker had probably had one too many swigs of wine that afternoon. It was now late evening and the camp being established all around him was starting to take up a form and identity of its own. Lines of vast canopies kept the cold winds at bay and huge erections were well on their way to being fully built. These consisted mostly of wooden, perhaps rather rickety, watchtowers that popped up all around the boundaries of this forward base. The flat terrain of grassy fields was perfect for such constructions.

Arthir got up from his makeshift bed and left his small tent. It was now surrounded by anvils and smouldering fires where countless blacksmiths forged blades and handed them out to the constant flow of new arrivals. The sound of hammers clashing against molten metal rung out and reverberated in the moonlight.

Arthir was keen to find Golandin. He walked forwards and stopped beside one of the busy weapon makers.

'Have you seen Golandin?' he asked wearily, head in his hands.

'Can't you see I'm busy here,' the fat blacksmith grumbled.

Arthir walked on, the throbbing getting worse with movement.

'Where is Golandin?' he asked a random passer by.

'Somewhere,' the man laughed as he passed by disinterested.

Arthir could sense this place was already way beyond the control of even his friend Golandin. These surroundings were alive with the beat of war drums and fervent drive each thuggish renegade had stored within. There was now no stopping this machine churning on with greater and greater prominence. In a way Arthir sought respect and acknowledgement from those around him, knowing he was one of the founders of this now mighty growth, but instead no one knew who he was. To them he represented just another shady character stumbling around in darkness.

Several hundred feet away Golandin stood surrounded by half disciplined commanders and officers. A rough map of the area and target city had been drawn up and placed on a large board in front of him. They stood on a meagre promontory of land in the centre of camp. The masses seemed congregated nearest the alcohol supplies and only the rebel elite assembled around this place of command. As the mostly bearded middle aged men stood around their leader, eager to hear a battle plan, Golandin delivered:

'Once we are ready and secure here in camp... Bollam,' Golandin laughed, 'we will first grab Dwenton. Those fools probably won't be looking to defend that town and will no doubt be focusing their defences in Brimma.'

'Sounds like a plan to me,' a bearded face grumbled whilst swigging ale.

'From Dwenton we shall simply press on north and converge on Brimma. We shall storm the bridge, break down the gates, and overwhelm the city. By the end of this week I shall be looking down on these lands from my mighty perch in Tamus Tower!'

The men laughed.

'Yes it shall be so!' came a voice in the distance. 'Golandin Tower!'

Golandin looked around for the source of the confident tone. It came from a man on horseback coming up the mound of land from the crowds beyond. He was a dark figure with a hooded head and freshly washed black leather armour.

'Who are you?' Golandin inquired.

The man jumped down from his black horse and strutted closer to the leader. He had a Vandyke beard that pointed like a tip once it reached his upper chest. As he removed his hood a bald head was revealed and grim, dark eyes.

'Twinicia!' one of the commanders yelled.

The man laughed out loud. 'Not quite,' he mocked. 'No... I am his brother.'

Golandin wasn't convinced. 'Twinicia had no brother...' he protested.

'Oh but he did,' said the bald man. 'I am he.'

'Can you prove you are of the late Warlord's blood?' another officer asked.

There was a pause as they waited for the man to reply. He stepped slightly closer to them, now right beside the map they had been studying. He eyed it and then faced Golandin head on.

'No,' he smiled.

Golandin stepped back and gave the stranger a cold stare. 'You don't even truly resemble him,' he roared. 'I can't see it anyway. You are some impostor!'

With those words the man was deeply offended and without any delay whipped out his longsword from behind his black cloak. This sparked every man around Golandin to pull out their blades and point them at the bald head.

'Take that back,' the man yelled.

Golandin slowly brought out his own sword from its sheath but suddenly ceased. He laughed slightly nervously.

'You claim to be his brother with such certainty as to warrant your story worthy of my trust,' he commented. 'Any impostor would have attempted this with more direct and impressive persuasion.'

The man smiled, slowly withdrawing his sword.

'Then you trust that I am who I say?' he asked.

'I have no reason not to,' Golandin said, 'and I can tell from your demeanour that you are a tough and experienced warrior. But if it is so where have you been for so long?'

The man stepped forwards nearer to the leader, the officers

around him now backing down and stepping away.

'He sure looks like Twinicia,' one remarked.

As Golandin studied him he too could begin to see a stark resemblance, mainly in the eyes. The figure spoke:

'I have been far away,' he said, 'but as soon as I heard of my brother's defeat I made for these parts. I want revenge and I want to see this empire fall to dust. I do not seek to claim leadership here and will happily take your orders. All I seek is a chance to fight.'

Golandin appeared convinced and patted the man on the shoulder.

'And what be your name?' he asked.

The man chuckled. 'I am Torwin.'

CHAPTER VI

THE MOUNTAINS OF CAMDOR

Akumi had been riding for several hours and the Abbey was now many miles away back across the western roads she had been travelling. The terrain had changed from flat green pastures to hilly pine forests, and vast mountains to the far west were becoming more and more prominent as she got closer to them. She snaked through the evergreens as the ascending landscape became tougher to race by with speed.

The direction she had decided to take came to her through instincts rather than knowledge. All she knew was that Endal had vanished on the road heading south-west out of Brimma and that it would have ultimately led him to these western mountains that, once past, would lead to the boundaries of Marmia. She was now way off the tracks and roads and deep inside uncharted forest.

The weather was not promising, with drizzle in the air and grim, dark clouds forming in the north. However, all the time there was still light the girl pressed on, her horse happy to slip through the trees. This went on and on until the mighty pine forest came to an end as the hills flattened out before one final flat stretch that led straight to the mountains ahead.

Being close to Marmia's western most town, Camdor, this vast range was known as both The Camdor Peaks and, perhaps more aptly, the Mountains of Camdor. These tall, white peaks formed a natural boundary between Marmia and the barren lands beyond. Akumi could only imagine where Endal might be planning on reaching once passed these formidable obstacles. The good news for the girl was that there was only one path that led through the mountains and she was aware of how to reach it. Unless Endal had got passed the peaks some other way he must have used this route. No other way seemed feasible considering how dangerous the terrain.

The assassin knew Endal was some days ahead of her. This

couldn't have been helped as she'd needed that time to recover and heal. Regardless of this the girl was driven and tried to ignore the sheer scale of what she was hoping to achieve tracking this illusive figure down.

The journey went on as the flat grounds the hills had led to turned into rocky caves and rugged upland. This was the beginning of the mountain climb. She had passed straight by the small town of Camdor, which rested further north. Akumi knew that to find the path that led up the entirety of this obstacle she would have to ride northwards parallel to the mountains until she spotted it. There was no other way. Without delay she raced off northwards beside the rocks; the drizzle slowly turning into a showery downpour.

It felt like an hour had passed before the signs of a pathway became apparent. In the distance a track was clearly visible from amongst the rocks and dry mud of the tip of the mountains. It was only a basic, snaking track but led through the safest route one could take to cross over. As she raced to reach the beginnings of this path her mind focused on Endal. Although there was clearly no way of telling the girl sensed she was at least on the right track. This was enough to keep her driven.

Before long the white horse was on the rough road leading straight up. It bent around in obtusely random patterns as boulder after boulder forced whoever initially mapped it to sway to one side. After a few hundred feet the terrain became distinctly steeper and the horse's pace slowed. After a few more hundred feet Akumi found herself surrounded on all sides by menacing rock faces and impenetrable cliff tops. The path became narrower until there was only an arms reach between either side of her and the rocks. These rocky faces darted up into the clouds and the light became faint. The rain was still streaming down and the damp, cold assassin started to shiver.

For what seemed like an age the girl pressed on up the path. Mercifully, the narrow space had once again opened out, allowing for the light of the early evening sky to pour down onto her. The path became quite straight, although now grimly steep. Her horse appeared to be coping, although moved forwards cautiously. Akumi was now many miles into the mountain range and she could already feel the effects of higher altitude on her breathing. Behind her a great view of the realm could be seen although in this failing light it was murky and obscured by darkness. Eventually, the girl knew it was time to stop; her horse likely exhausted and the time right to set up a basic shelter for the night.

Up ahead along the precipitous pathway a fire flickered amongst the rocks. Its light was entirely blocked off from the view of the assassin due to its position in among the large stones that scattered around the ascending terrain of the mountain side. Beside this fire three men were resting, looking up at the sky as the stars started to appear with diminishing light. One of the three sat upright against a rock that deflected the heat of the fire back around them. The other two were lying down in wonder at the vista above.

'Such a long way to Dwenton,' the man sitting against the rock sighed. 'By the time we reach that place I bet Brimma will have fallen!'

'It will take many days yet for them to build up strong enough to launch an attack,' said the one nearest the fire. 'We are on course and will make it before they move out.'

He sat up and stroked his bristly chin. The three men looked like farmers, with only the most basic of clothing keeping them warm and little in the way of weapons. They hoped the distant camp would sort them out with such equipment.

'Just to think,' the one still lying down mumbled, 'we might have a plot of land named after us if we prove ourselves on the field!'

'That's the spirit Owen,' the bristly faced man smiled.

As they continued to discuss what possible gems fate may have in store for them the man leaning against the rock suddenly noticed something flickering further down the sloping rock face.

'Look,' he whispered.

'What is it Taylor?' Owen sprung up.

'Looks like a fire to me,' said Taylor.

It was indeed a fire, freshly lit by Akumi with a flint she'd carried along and tinder gathered from the dry bushes amongst the rocks of the trackside.

'Who is that?' Taylor pondered.

The bristly man suddenly got to his feet.

'Get down Scot!' Taylor insisted. 'Let's see who this is before we make ourselves visible.'

They were truly in the middle of nowhere and it was unusual for anyone to set up camp for the night in such a barren place as this. The three farmers studied the fire for several minutes, locked in awe over the prospect that some mysterious figure was down there. This curiosity seemed to run deeper with the young Taylor and Owen than it did with the older Scot. He was a clumsy yet wiser figure, less bothered by the fact someone else had been caught out by the sunset.

'Oh my! Oh my!' beamed Owen. 'It's a girl down there, on her own!'

Taylor nodded to himself. They could both make out a figure now sitting beside the fire and it was clear that whoever it was they had long brown hair and a petit frame.

'Shall we introduce ourselves?!' Taylor laughed.

Scot studied the figure then leant against a rock.

'We should be careful,' he said. 'Anyone alone in these parts is either stupid or powerful. She seems pretty clued up setting up that fire and all... so I'd expect she fits into the powerful category.'

Taylor laughed in mockery.

'Common old man,' he said. 'It's just some girl, probably running away from home or something. Anyone can light a fire!'

'Fine!' Scot snapped. 'She is just some girl. What do I know? Frankly, it is not our business either way.'

'Let's just say *hi* and perhaps keep her company...' Owen suggested, thoughts clearly in his head.

'I agree,' replied Taylor. 'Beats sticking around here anyway.'

Scot made no effort to stop the two young men as they clambered down the rock face into view. He picked up his pike and trampled their fire out. The truth was all three of them were sneaky, villainous outcasts. They had been kicked out of their village beyond the mountains and had ever since been travelling on foot in the hope they could find and join the rebel ranks they had heard rumour of in a small dwelling further up the path. They had been heading in this direction with the aim of reaching Dwenton. Scot knew the two men racing ahead had only one real thought in their corrupted heads and he wasn't about to try and stop them.

Akumi was swift to notice the figures coming down from the rocks about fifty feet ahead of her. She knew they were coming for her and got to her feet. Her katana was already resting by her side and she clutched it whilst studying the incoming group. There was now only moonlight and the fire to keep the blackness of night at bay. She backed away from the flames, knowing that standing beside the fire would make it impossible for her to see them coming from beyond the light, and faded into the shadows around it.

'Hey girl!' Taylor yelled out. 'It's okay don't run off. We just want to see if you're all right.'

Akumi did not respond and bent low beside a rock near her horse within the darkness. As they reached her fire she addressed them:

'What do you want?'

'We just wanted to say hello,' Owen said.

'Yeah, didn't like seeing you alone like this,' Taylor added.

As they spoke Scot appeared from behind them. He remained silent.

'So do you want to come out from the dark?' Owen chuckled deviously.

The assassin was very quick to sense these characters were bad news. She could tell by their tone alone and their shifty behaviour that they meant her no good. The girl was also swift to sense they were not really much of a threat to her. Only the man at their rear held a weapon and it looked more like a farming tool than anything this deadly assassin would ever pick up.

'I don't want company,' Akumi yelled. 'Now please go and leave me alone.'

Taylor tutted to himself and looked to Owen.

'Up for a struggle?' he grinned.

Owen licked his lips and rolled back his dirty sleeves.

'Yeah why not?!' he laughed.

They charged for the area they thought Akumi had been cowering in. Taylor almost ran into the rock and put out his arms to cushion impact. She had vanished and her horse was no longer visible.

'Don't play games with us girl!' yelled Scot from the fire. 'Just let them get their way... then we can all move on.'

The assassin had backtracked with her horse and turned back onto the pathway beside her fire. There was nothing left lying around except the crackling wood she'd gathered from the ground. She didn't need to hang around and in a flash her white ride bolted onwards up the track.

'Hey!' Taylor yelled, running after the animal as it appeared from the blackness.

'Forget it,' remarked Scot, 'she's gone. We won't catch up.'

The girl bounded into the darkness ahead leaving only a cloud of upturned soil.

'Damn bitch!' Owen howled in anger.

'Well, at least we've now got a better fire,' said Scot.

Although not threatened by her encounter Akumi's heart raced away as adrenaline rushed through her body. She didn't like being alone and moments like this started to remind her of quite how dangerous this place she now found herself in was. She needed to keep her guard up at every turn. The rider pressed on without faltering. Even though they'd only got a short rest her horse seemed eager and able. After several minutes the roadside encounter became a memory and as soon as the lights of a dwelling house came into view Akumi's focus shifted.

The sign to the tiny inn was rusty with age and wear. It hung from an iron bar sticking out from the stone wall to the edge of the dirt track. The house didn't seem to consist of more than two floors but was large enough to suggest there were rooms to shelter the occasional passer by. Akumi studied the area before tying her horse to a fence inside a stable opposite the house. She needed a proper rest and felt confident enough stopping here; the men she'd encountered now at least a mile back down the mountain road.

The girl didn't seem reluctant in opening the rickety wooden door and entering into the abode. It resembled some log cabin with a low ceiling and several torches flaming on the far wall. Akumi's brown eyes studied the room and carefully analysed every detail. There was nothing menacing to behold. Suddenly, a grumpy voice greeted her from a desk near a petit staircase:

'Looking for a room for the night?'

Akumi, ever so stunned by the hidden source, answered as she walked towards the desk.

'Yes I am,' she said politely. 'Is that possible?'

As she spoke the assassin leaned forwards hoping to spot whoever spoke from behind the wooden tabletop. Her eyes identified a baggy brown jumper fumbling around from behind the wooden surface. The figure suddenly stood up; aware she was looking his way.

'We are empty,' the old man mumbled, 'so yeah, no problems there.'

He was a portly man with white beard and dark, worn skin. He noticed the girl before him fondling with her belt as if about to reveal some gold. She was about to speak but he was quick to interject.

'Pay me in the morning my dear,' he smiled.

'Oh okay, thank you sir,' the girl said.

'Take the first room on the right as you get upstairs,' he said.

Akumi nodded and moved on up the staircase. She was excited about the prospect of a nice warm bed and already felt the relief of being indoors away from the darkness outside.

The room was humble, with a small bed beside the wall and a table next to a tiny curtained window. A single painting hung on the timber frames; it showed the mountain range they rested on from the perspective of someone at the base. Everything looked dusty and old but it was more than adequate for the weary traveller. She pulled her red cloak from over her shoulders and removed her belt and katana. The cream sheets were soft and as Akumi sat down she felt immense physical reprieve. It was quite dark and with no reason to feel alert the assassin lay down and wrapped herself cosily into the sheets. She kept most of her clothing on although kicked off her boots, which rolled off the bedside and landed on the wooden joists.

Within only a few minutes Akumi was fast asleep and unaware of the world around her. In her timeless state of abandon an hour went by and the moon sneaked assuredly over the speckled gloom.

In the darkness of the roadside a few figures were meaningfully marching towards the door to the dwelling. The first to enter through the entrance was instantly recognised by the insomniac manning the tiny desk.

'Owen?' the bearded old man was confused. 'Thought you lot had left for Dwenton?'

Owen crept into the room with Taylor and Scot closely behind. The young farmer shuffled closer to the old man.

'Did some girl come here? On her own like?' he asked in a whisper.

The old man nodded, mouth open in intrigue. 'Yes, why?'

'She 'ere now?' Owen pressed.

The three men stood together sketchily awaiting the response.

'Well a girl came here about an hour ago,' said the old man. 'She is in her room now. Why?'

Taylor smiled to himself as Owen turned to face him. 'It must be her,' said Owen. 'She was on horseback so it makes sense she got here so much faster than we did.'

'Yeah it's her alright,' Taylor smirked. 'Unless some other girl is riding around these parts on her own!'

Owen seemed eager, as if about to make a move. 'We are going to see her,' he said to the old man at the desk. 'We know her.'

The old man didn't appear happy about the situation unfolding in his small house.

'I will knock first and ask her if she wants to see you,' he said.

He didn't like the vibes he was getting from the three men and was already beginning to suspect they'd decided to lurk after her after spotting her on their journey down the mountain.

Taylor wasn't happy and suddenly his tone altered. 'Stay out of this old man,' he warned.

The two young farmers suddenly made for the stairs whilst Scot stood staring at the portly gentleman.

'Don't try stopping them,' he said dryly.

The innkeeper revealed a brazen trait in his character by rushing from out of his space behind the desk and halting beside Scot.

'Girl!' he yelled at the top of his voice. 'Wake up!'

The sound of his deep and powerful intonation instantly sparked Akumi to open her eyes and awaken. In instantaneous reflexes she sprang out of her bed and focused. She could hear people racing up the squeaky stairs and kicking open a door to the room across from hers.

'Empty! Try that one!' a voice yelled.

Akumi grabbed her katana and poised herself in position facing her door. It was opened with furious strength and pushed back until it struck the wall. The assassin instantly recognised the farmers she'd encountered on the path.

'Don't come any closer!' she ordered. 'Please!'

Owen slowly closed in on her with Taylor behind.

'Just a little kiss…' he snarled.

'Yeah, and then the rest,' Taylor remarked.

Owen made for the girl in the hope of clutching her and wrestling her down to the bed. Back downstairs Scot and the old man were facing off but the innkeeper wasn't going anywhere. Scot pressed his sharp pike into the old man's throat and stood by the stairs.

Akumi didn't want to strike with her steel and lowered her blade as Owen closed in. She stepped back and struck him in the chest with her free arm. The strike was swift and her palm prodded into his solar plexus. He instantly felt immense pain and fell back, stumbling into Taylor.

Owen rolled to one side as his companion raced at the girl. She kicked his shin and drove her knee into his stomach as he lost balance and collapsed beside her. Akumi pounced over Owen and grabbed her boots, belt, and cloak from a bedside chair.

'Stay back!' she screeched.

The female assassin bounded down the stairs and flew into Scot as he stood facing the old man. She'd leapt into his back feet first, knocking him forwards and into the innkeeper. The old man was quick to strike the farmer's pike from his grasp and hurl him across the room. Akumi paused beside him and speedily attached her belt and cloak back around her. She bent down and hobbled on one leg whilst trying to put her boots back on. She slipped her cold bare feet into the leather footwear and tightened the laces as she and the old man backed away from the stairs and paused in the middle of the room.

The old man stood beside her clasping Scot's pike. 'Get away girl,' he spat. 'These men mean to rape you!'

She didn't seem concerned although kept her eye on Scot as he moved back towards the stairs as they circled him. Owen and Taylor appeared behind him on the steps, both rubbing their bodies in soreness.

The girl managed to get her boots laced with only seconds to spare. In a mad rush the three farmers ran towards her and the old man. The assassin appeared to predict the old man sweeping forwards in her defence and thoughtfully pounced ahead of him to his shock and surprise.

She'd sheathed her sword and bent low as Owen attempted to wrap his arms around her. The girl raised her arms and struck him in the chin with force. As he stumbled back Taylor tried to slap the girl but she effortlessly drove her foot into his chest as she jumped into the air before him. Scot watched his allies hit the deck in pain and revealed a menacing dagger from his simple rags. Akumi instantly stepped back and brought out her katana.

'Don't come any closer!' she commanded.

Scot ignored her and ran at her with dagger drawn. Just as the girl was about to deflect the blade the old man's nabbed pike prodded Scot in the face. The farmer was knocked out cold and fell back against the hard wood flooring.

Owen and Taylor got to their feet and made another attempt at overpowering their target. Akumi still had her blade drawn and tried to withdraw it before the farmers closed in. Owen didn't seem to notice her steel and as she brought it to her side he ran into its shimmering tip just as her fist struck his cheek. The cold, sharp edge embedded itself into his guts and he dropped down with his hands clasping the gashing wound. Akumi was alarmed like she'd not intended to see it come to this. She stepped back as Owen lay in an increasingly large pool of blood. Taylor stood back, eying Scot's dagger that rested on the floor beside him.

'Don't,' advised Akumi.

He ignored the girl and grabbed the weapon. He ran towards Akumi but before he'd got close the innkeeper slammed his bloodstained pike into his side. It impaled the flesh and stuck into the skin. Taylor yelled out in pain and fell back against the far wall. He dropped his dagger, clutched the pike, and pulled it from his body with a yelp of agony. This seemed to be all his faltering energy could manage and just as the old man was about to close in for another strike he dropped down beside Owen's bloody corpse.

Akumi looked deeply troubled and put her sword away. The innkeeper stood over the bodies and studied them.

'Stupid fools!' he roared. 'Coming at us like that!'

He then turned to the girl. 'Where did you learn to fight so... so like a man?' he inquired.

'I had an excellent teacher,' Akumi frowned.

As the old man pondered on her words Scot suddenly showed

signs of movement. The pike blade had only cut his forehead and his brief lapse of consciousness from the painful sever had passed. He sat up and as the innkeeper's back was turned stuck another of his concealed daggers into his lower back.

'Watch out! No!' Akumi screamed.

It was too late to warn him and he went limp with the entry of the alien dagger. Akumi reacted with immense speed and leapt forwards with katana at the ready. Scot didn't even have time to get up as he pulled his dagger from the lifeless body of the old man beside him. Akumi knew he was about to try and attack her and, without anymore holding back, she thrust her blade into her target. The katana entered into his torso and came out again as the assassin poked him with great precision. He was dead.

The isolated halfway house had turned into a bloody scene. Four bodies lay flat against the wooden frames. Akumi looked down at the old man. There was nothing she could do. He had died moments after the dagger had entered him. The girl jumped over the pool of blood that had now developed around Owen. He had bled to death. The assassin took one last peek at the grim vista of bodies as she reached the door back to the path outside. She felt deeply sickened at the fact this had happened. It was as if fighting and violence went hand in hand with the girl wherever she went. She opened the door and cautiously stepped back out into the cold.

CHAPTER VII

ALL EYES ON DWENTON

The morning came with a fresh sense of purpose for Jamus. He was first to race downstairs and grab a quick breakfast whilst his monks gathered in the dining hall. The sun had only just risen from the hilly horizon to the east and light was still dim, with that sense of early morning bombarding the senses. The night before he and his band of warriors had feasted and got an early night. Today was the beginning of the journey they were to embark on.

As the fully clothed and prepared old battler grabbed a mug of warm tea and commenced chewing a loaf of bread he'd picked up from the table Aimis entered the room and acknowledged his master. The monk was no longer dressed in a robe and now wore his light leather tunic and leggings. A brown bandana matched the colour of the armour and contrasted slightly with his pale complexion. He was suddenly a warrior once again. He knew how to handle himself and had always been respected by Jamus.

'Good morning,' Jamus greeted his friend.

'Hello Jamus,' replied Aimis. 'Are we to leave soon?'

Jamus nodded whilst biting his bread. 'We will leave now,' he said. 'No time to waste.'

Aimis' attention was drawn to the door behind him. Fenris appeared with the rest of the group standing outside in the lobby. It was clear they all shared Jamus' sentiment.

'Looks like we are ready,' Aimis said.

Jamus put his empty mug back down on the table and bid farewell to several feasting monks.

'Look after the place,' he remarked. 'I will miss it.'

He looked up at the ceiling and as he walked to the group in the lobby took in the surroundings as if to try and build a picture in his head for memory. He paused by Aimis and looked to Fenris as he stood in the doorway.

'Let's roll,' he said softly.

The gang made for the main door and passed down the Abbey path towards their horses that had been placed on the roadside by several monks and kitted up with all the group would surely require.

Jamus stopped next to his brown horse and stroked the animal's neck with affection. Lady Yuuki stood beside him, playing with her braids.

'To Dwenton then?' smiled the radiant girl.

'Yes, to Dwenton,' Jamus confirmed.

The warriors mounted their rides and instantly were moving forwards up the track leading north from the Abbey. Jamus took the lead with Yuuki and Aimis behind him alongside one another. A few feet back from them was Rense; his battleaxe prominently placed around his back and glistening with the morning light. Fenris was beside him with Emi a few paces to his left. At the rear end of the party Arifor crept forth by himself. His black horse matched the tone of his clothing and gave him a mysterious and alluring appearance. Above him some fifty feet in the air a black bird hovered and circled the group. It seemed to be following them and kept swooping back to keep directly above the dark sage of shamanism. This didn't appear to surprise or intrigue his companions.

The riders' pace increased once they'd left the initial grounds that surrounded the Abbey. They were now on the main road leading off through lush woodland of mighty birch and oak trees. The horses were now able to gallop with ease and before long they were racing forwards with great speed. There was a slight breeze that gushed through the trees and whistled against them. Apart from this the weather was ideal and the journey potentially straight forward. Dwenton wasn't too far and it was now a question of patience.

The road they travelled had been passed some days before by a lone assassin. This had been the very path Endal had crossed and killed a single foolish bandit on. This group were unlikely to encounter such cocky criminals for they were now likely too busy all trying to reach Golandin's *Camp Bollam* and enter into the ranks of the rebel forces.

Jamus felt he was on an important mission and knew a heavy weight was on him and his comrades. They were the vanguard of the forces hoping to repel the rebels. Although Jamus had no way of telling what the new Empress Sylvie was planning in Brimma he sensed she'd be more inclined to focus her forces on defending the capital. Those forces were all that the empire had to muster.

There were likely no other groups of battle-hardened warriors out to hit Golandin. They would probably not be so lucky as to encounter such hidden allies. Jamus imagined he and his riders were it. They represented the only able group capable of doing this and no one else was likely going to be appearing to aid them. A part of him was eager to get in touch with Sylvie but first they had to track Golandin and get an idea what exactly was forming up around him.

The hours rolled by and the journey proved eventless as they moved on across the road. It had blended in with the now winding terrain of hilly slopes and green pastures. The woods had become sparser and they now found themselves in open plains. The overcast sky kept the sun at bay and Arifor's black bird was lost in sweeping fog that blew above them with the breeze. The air was moist but there had not been any rain.

The party had remained silent but the repetition of the road seemed to suddenly get the better of Fenris.

'Hope you brought the beers Rense!' he yelled.

Rense chuckled and yelled back at the swordsman: 'Thought you did?'

'As long as someone brought the chocolate!' Emi giggled.

This sparked the riders ahead to add further comments.

'Oh yes,' laughed Yuuki, 'someone please tell me they brought the chocolate!'

'Or tobacco,' added Aimis.

'Well I have my pipe,' chuckled Jamus from his lead position ahead.

Their voices were only just audible over the sounds of the horses' thudding hooves. It seemed the old warrior's comment was to be the last in this line of silly banter.

'Not going to add to that Arifor?' Fenris laughed.

The old man didn't seem to take much notice and remained silent as he rode behind them.

'What's his lil' vice?' Emi pondered playfully.

'Oh I'd say he must be privy to the odd ale,' Rense roared.

'The *odd* meaning quite a few!' Fenris beamed.

Suddenly, the alluring voice of Arifor responded: 'I am privy to killing rebels,' his tone serious. 'As many as I can find.'

There was silence; his comment instantly demanding of a more serious mood. He wasn't akin to joking around and his companions knew to cease. Jamus smiled ever so slightly as he listened back whilst studying the road ahead. He'd suspected Arifor would darken the moment.

They continued on for a few more dull hours and found themselves once again surrounded by a bushy landscape as the track led into a flat, rather meagre, forest. It consisted of young trees and knee high strands of grass. The sun was now centred in the sky and could just be made out behind the white fluffy clouds. Jamus suddenly halted and turned his horse off the road.

'Let us take a rest from the road,' he announced.

The riders tied their horses to nearby tree branches and sat together in the grass of the roadside. As they sat their legs were lost from view within the tall, damp, green blades. Jamus brought out a pipe and started to fiddle with the tobacco stash he had in his belt. Aimis and Lady Yuuki sat beside him whilst Fenris and Emi shuffled beside the large body of Rense. Arifor didn't sit down and instead stood a few feet away from the group and raised his arm. All eyes focused on his mysterious bird that suddenly fell down from the firmament above them and perched on his wrist. The old man stroked the bird and strolled away further from the party.

Lady Yuuki turned to Jamus. 'He never relaxes,' she said. 'He's always this distant.'

Jamus placed his pipe between his lips and lit the contents with a piece of flint he'd rubbed against a stone.

'Arifor is a melancholy fellow,' he puffed. 'Has always been since…'

Emi was intrigued and got closer to the old warrior. 'Since what?' she asked.

Jamus blew a large wisp of tobacco smoke into the air around them and continued puffing.

'When this realm was in turmoil, before Tamus came to fight here, Arifor fought beside me and Hazati,' Jamus said. 'We fought the thugs that wanted to snatch power but in those days we were the minority. It was long before you lot came onto the scene.'

There was a slight pause before he continued:

'Arifor's family was taken from him. Twinicia discovered where his wife and children lived and sent a horde of murderers to the village. They killed them and burnt the place down. Since that dark day Arifor hasn't cracked a smile and only thinks of revenge.'

Lady Yuuki was deeply saddened by this and felt empathy for the old man she'd never truly understood.

'I had no idea,' she said. 'We always just thought it was in his character.'

'My dear, there is always a reason behind such traits in character,' added Jamus. 'Arifor has been consumed by war. He supported Tamus in the early years and left these parts once it became clear Twinicia had lost any hope of being victorious. That was several years ago if I recall right. He vanished.

'I suspect that, now he has had to come back to fight on, he is probably a little more consumed with rage than is usual.'

'We must stop Golandin!' Yuuki declared in reaction. 'We will defeat these evil criminals once and for all!'

'We must succeed,' Emi added.

'With you two at our side I have no doubt of that,' Jamus chuckled.

'Sure, they will prove effective at distracting the enemy at least!' mocked Fenris. 'The soothing sight of a couple of girls will probably do more to them than the most powerful of magic!'

'Want me to turn you into a lil' slug?' Yuuki teased.

'With an arrow for company...' Emi smirked.

Fenris enjoyed receiving the light-hearted threats from the two rapturous females.

'Well maybe I like being dominated...' he said cheekily.

Lady Yuuki pointed her radiant staff at him with eyes wide in a blasé response. Emi pretended to reach for her bow.

'Okay enough,' Jamus cut in. 'Time to press on.'

The party moved to their horses and remounted. Arifor was quick to spot them get up and swiftly moved back to his black mount. His dark bird flew from his hands as he reached the reins.

'Onwards to Dwenton,' Jamus called out, his horse already kicking into motion.

Elgor's proud horse screeched to a halt beside the brass sign. In worn letters it read Dwenton. Elgor raised his metal visor and scanned the dwelling houses immediately ahead. His men were closing in behind him in two long lines. They were dressed in heavy plated armour with helmets and shields in place and swords poised.

The journey from Brimma took only a matter of hours on horseback and the troops were now fired up having reached their destination. The northern tip of the town seemed lifeless and silent. Elgor could spot the church tower down the descending stone track. A plethora of buildings ran parallel to either side of the lane and furthered out with each turn and new street.

'Helmets on men!' Elgor ordered. 'Look sharp.'

The twenty elite troops rolled into town behind Elgor, studying every turn. They pressed down the track and moved forwards hoping to spot signs of an enemy presence. They knew the rebels were forming near Dwenton and chances were they had already seized the town.

'We must reach the Dwenton gate to the south of the town,' Elgor yelled.

The gate had been abandoned by the small garrison that had taken command after Endal's bloody visit. All forces had been called back to defend the capital. The tall southern wall could already be seen by Elgor's men as they moved down the hill and reached the central church. They had still yet to spot any signs of life in the seemingly abandoned trade town. Once bustling streets filled with traders were now ghostly quiet and uninhabited spaces.

Elgor didn't seem nerved by the silence and they pressed on by the church until the gate was visible up ahead. They'd travelled down the main lane, which split through the town like a central artery.

'Let us pass under the gate,' Elgor ordered. 'I suspect we will be seeing a lot more activity on the other side of that wall.'

They reached the pulley that remained abandoned beside the sturdy gate. The wheel required turning in order for the mighty entrance to rise from the ground. The sophisticated contraption kicked into motion as several troops wrestled with the cogs sticking out of the wheel. They resembled sunbeams on some fictitiously painted sun.

The gate had begun to rise up slowly and as it moved Elgor stood studying it. He noticed distinct damage on the surface. It looked like a blade had impaled the exterior surface at some point. Remnants of a stain of dry blood noticeably surrounded the small incision. Elgor thought nothing more of it as the entrance rose up enough to allow him to pass under it. His troops followed in two lines of ten to either side of him. The first two troops on either line carried long menacing javelins, ready to tackle any incoming enemy.

It was only a matter of seconds until the view of the flat plains to the south beyond the gate struck the troops. They raced down the track leading into the western woods of Tantria and continued onto the southern grass once the path turned away into the forest. Once they started to move onto the sward it became obvious there was a rush of activity going on ahead. The rolling fields revealed a mass of erected towers and swarms of distant figures crowding around countless tents. There was an army on the horizon and Elgor was quick to halt at the shock of spotting this overwhelming display.

'Well men,' he declared. 'There is our enemy.'

'There must be hundreds of them down there...' a troop yelled. 'If not thousands!'

By now the enemy camp had truly formed into a formidable outpost. It was clear that to get any closer would be folly and Elgor turned his attention to the western woods.

'We can't afford to get spotted now,' he said. 'Not like this.'

He removed his helmet to get a quick fix on their surroundings.

'We must move into those woods and scout the enemy position from the tree line,' he suggested.

'Golandin is bound to be in amongst that swarming mass,' a troop commented from within their metal head.

'Yes, but with the numbers that seem to be over there he is as good as unreachable,' Elgor said. 'It is as I feared. They are more numerous than even before their Warlord's fall.'

'Because they now have hope,' said a soldier. 'They are look-ing to strike us at our weakest moment.'

Elgor turned his horse and looked to the western woodland along from the southern wall and the Dwenton gate. This had been the very wood Endal and his pursuing assassins had entered into after he'd slain the garrison guarding the gateway.

'We have no choice,' Elgor said. 'We must set ourselves up in the woods of Tantria and try to ascertain the details of that presence in those plains.'

'Sir…' a troop said nervously.

Elgor turned to face the soldier and put his helmet back on.

'What?' he snapped.

'Incoming!' a bunch of his men yelled, pointing south.

Just ahead of the masses a group of figures were closing in on Dwenton on horseback. The riders had been concealed up until now as they'd been riding up the western tree line further south and had only now popped out of it and into the fields.

'There is no time to flee into the woods,' Elgor's voice wailed. 'We must hold our ground against them.'

From the speed of the incoming enemy horses Elgor could tell they were only minutes away. His men formed two lines facing the enemy head on. The lines were side by side with several feet in between them. Elgor positioned himself within the line to the right.

'As soon as they get within a few feet of us,' he ordered, 'charge them!'

He and his men were not afraid and, if anything, were eager to take on the enemy. These troops were the cream of the empire and every one of them still grieved over Tamus. This was the moment they had wanted.

CHAPTER VIII

IN THE COMPANY OF ELGOR

Torwin stroked his beard and wiped the cold sweat forming around his bald head. He was first to spot the cavalry just outside the Dwenton gate and raised his arm to bring the flock of riders behind him to a halt. They were all dressed in black armour and several had painted their faces an intimidating white with red streaks, representing blood and war. Torwin was leading this mass of undisciplined yet enthusiastic horsemen. Golandin had been quick to recognise the obvious skill and experience the late Twinicia's brother had and had given him command of this flock of cavalry. His task was to snatch Dwenton and raise a standard on the southern wall. From there the rest of Golandin's amassed men were to leave Camp Bollam and pass through Dwenton on route to Brimma. Torwin was to secure the town first.

'Time to test those blades,' Torwin smirked.

Behind him the rabble of riders studied the lined up and fully suited Tamus troops ahead. They appeared to see red and war cries rung out in uproar. Torwin was just as keen to attack but knew not to underestimate the enemy. He was aware the men around him were relatively untrained compared to the troops of the empire. He was the only true warrior in this crowd but seemed content with the knowledge their advantage was in their sheer numbers. There were fifty at his command and he counted twenty one across the field.

Back inside the rebel camp the initial chaos of construction and gathering had died down. Most of those that would come had arrived by now and been kitted out. Although the alcohol was still flowing most of the rebellious mass was now focused and eager to move out.

Golandin couldn't make out much besides the Dwenton wall and the flock he believed to be Torwin's advanced party. A few miles separated the camp from the town and without a visual aid the rebel leader soon gave up trying to suss what was happening. Arthir stood to his side, his hangover a distant memory.

'And so it begins,' he said.

Golandin nodded. 'This is the beginning of the end for the Tamus Empire,' he qualified.

Arthir noticed a rider coming from the western wood towards the camp. At first he just presumed the rider to be one of Torwin's men, fleeing before they'd even seen action. This wasn't an unlikely prospect considering how undisciplined and unaccountable most of Golandin's army truly were. However, as the rider got closer Arthir recognised the thin character bobbing up and down atop their mount.

'Here be a turn out for the books,' Arthir sniggered.

Golandin was intrigued and looked in the direction his old friend was staring.

'Aha,' the leader smiled. 'Ellis.'

Their shady contact passed into the camp unchallenged by the guards standing beside the furthest watchtower. They assumed he was a rebel seeing as he had dressed himself in black for the journey.

'I don't think I've seen Ellis for years,' Arthir said. 'Thought he'd died long ago.'

'Quite the contrary,' Golandin laughed. 'He joined the enemy and fought as a Tamus soldier, climbing the ranks until he became one of the late Emperor's most trusted. He has been our insider my friend. He has been waiting for a time like now to kick into action.'

'My oh my,' Arthir was pleased. 'I had no idea...'

'Not many did,' said Golandin. 'In fact only I, Twinicia, and a few now deceased commanders knew. With Twinicia now dead I guess only I have known in these past days.'

'So he is going to do what exactly?' asked Arthir.

'Well let us speak with him,' Golandin said.

The leader waved his arms out at the rider as he strutted up the ramshackle track that snaked through the tents and countless crates of supplies. Ellis spotted his old pal and quickly raced towards him.

'I got here as quickly as I could,' Ellis yelled whilst closing in. 'Sylvie has sent an advanced party into Dwenton.'

Golandin sprung to attention and watched Ellis leap from his horse and confront him and Arthir as the men stood on a mound.

'Good to see you again Ellis,' said Arthir.

'Yes, welcome friend,' Golandin said. 'Now what of this enemy move?'

Ellis eyed his two ancient friends. It had been many years since the weary advisor had been in the presence of men like these. They were his old war allies and this was his side. He felt a sudden surge of excitement. All his many years of service for Tamus had been in aid of this moment. He had managed to stay undetected and could now finally serve his true purpose. He addressed them:

'My friends, the new Empress, Sylvie indeed, sent twenty elite troops to scout Dwenton and this camp. I followed them from Brimma and carefully kept back. I observed them enter the town and raced across the woods to reach here. Everyone knows of this location.'

Golandin didn't seem concerned. 'My position is no secret,' he said. 'As for this advanced party...'

Ellis came in. 'I am sorry I couldn't reach here before they left but I had no time. They are now in Dwenton.'

'Torwin will run right into them then,' Arthir noted.

'Torwin!' Ellis yelled.

'You know of Torwin?' Golandin asked.

'Yes, he is the late Twinicia's brother... thought he was long gone.'

'Well that at least confirms he is as he says,' said Golandin. ''Tis good news.'

'He turned up the other day,' said Arthir, 'told us he came from far away and travelled here at the news of his brother's fall.'

Ellis smiled. 'Well it is great to know he is with us,' he said. 'He will crush Elgor.'

'Elgor?' Golandin inquired.

'Yes, Sergeant Elgor is leading that advanced party,' said Ellis. 'A naïve little thing. He believes in the empire... one of the passionate Tamus supporters.'

'Well, I wonder how passionate he will be with Torwin's blade spliced through his guts,' Golandin howled.

The men laughed in evil unison.

'So Sylvie now calls the shots huh?' smiled Golandin. 'That

former protector of the Emperor... God how I want to see that girl's face before my boot!'

'So what can you achieve Ellis?' Arthir was unsure.

'I can supply you with information and convince Sylvie to make the wrong move,' he smiled.

'Ellis will be vital,' Golandin said. 'I knew he would come... I never forgot about him.'

He looked to the hunched and pale snake. 'How was Endal?' he asked.

'Oh, I watched him from the tower,' said Ellis. 'He was unstoppable... he killed troops in droves and flung all to his side... well bar for one.'

'One?' Arthir was intrigued.

'Yeah, after killing Tamus he took on some girl, not Sylvie, but some girl... had never seen her before. She put up a good fight against him and he fled. She gave chase, and I later heard failed to catch him.'

'Interesting,' said Golandin. 'I cannot fathom whom that might have been.'

'Her name was Akumi, apparently,' said Ellis. 'Strange name if you ask me. I later found out she was one of Hazati's assassins.'

'Oh, that fool,' commented Arthir. 'I've heard the name.'

'Dead fool,' said Ellis. 'Endal claimed him and everyone else for that matter... besides Sylvie and this Akumi. Apparently he let Sylvie live.'

'Well, his contract was to kill Tamus,' said Golandin. 'That's all I care about now, although it is great to hear Hazati is finally six feet under. 'Tis the case he used to be a thorn in our side, although I never had dealings with him myself.'

'It was always said that Hazati was exceptional with a blade,' said Arthir, 'and for Endal to have killed him he surely must be truly remarkable. But we should take note of the name Akumi if she were able to, in turn, force Endal to flee.'

Golandin took on board the wise comments and pondered for a moment on where the female assassin could possibly now be. Ellis didn't seem to know and since neither he nor Arthir had ever heard of the girl their intelligence was lacking. He tried to focus on what they did know.

'The girl is not our concern right now,' he said. 'What is of our concern right now is Torwin's advance.'

Ellis squinted at the distant town hoping to catch the sight of some far away action.

'Why don't you back him up?' Ellis asked. 'I can confirm only Elgor and his twenty men are between you and Brimma. You can safely move into Dwenton now.'

Golandin shared this view and suddenly raised his arms high and turned to get the attention of several of his commanders all poised nearby.

'Move our men forwards to Dwenton! Move everyone out! Time to roll...' he roared.

Several bearded men raced away towards the tents where the bulk of the men were sitting around idle.

'Arthir,' Golandin said. 'Get 'ya horse.'

Torwin hadn't made his move yet and continued to cautiously study Elgor and his men. The ranks of rebels behind him were growing impatient and couldn't understand why their leader hadn't given the command to charge. The truth was their leader knew not to underestimate the highly skilled soldiers up ahead. He wasn't about to run into their line without a tactic.

'Let us press forwards and destroy them!' a rebel snapped.

Torwin suddenly became content with an idea he'd devised for their assault.

'We will come at them in two groups,' the bald warrior yelled. 'I want twenty with me and thirty flanking them from the right. We will converge on them like enclosing horns.'

The rebel horsemen started to mingle around as best they could. They'd never bothered with forming groups before but seemed able to form up into two crowds. Although it was clear the mathematics weren't quite to Torwin's specification he was happy with the groups. The larger mass had formed several feet to his group's right.

'Remember to hook to their right together and maintain my group's pace,' said Torwin.

The large group yelled out in response and appeared to collectively acknowledge him.

'Charge!' Torwin yelled with enflamed passion.

Their attack was initiated and the horses pounded the ground with rushing hooves. The plan seemed to be working, with the larger group scattering to the right of Elgor's split lines and

Torwin directing his group slightly to their left. The terrain was perfect for this cavalry charge, with flat fields and short dry grass acting as the ideal ground.

Elgor's men stood firm knowing the attack they'd been so eagerly anticipating was now closing in on them. If anything they were excited; they had no respect for the enemy and trusted their training over the rabble coming at them.

'Remember,' Elgor yelled, 'as soon as they are close enough I will give the call and we shall charge into their masses like a stinging blow.'

'For Tamus!' a soldier called out.

'For Tamus!' the line hailed.

A minute or two went by as Torwin's force got closer and closer. Suddenly, it was within arrow range but there were no archers in Elgor's party. The adrenaline raced as each soldier focused on their enemy now only a stone's throw away. They got closer, and closer, until:

'Charge!' Elgor roared.

The two lines kicked into action, one moving to their right towards Torwin's group, the other making for the larger mob coming from their left. Elgor didn't seem concerned by this split, although the gap was widening between each of his ten man lines as they moved towards their respective targets.

In a crunch of horse heads, swords, and men, the two rivalling groups had clashed. Torwin led his group and instantly, his large longsword struck the javelin of an oncoming Tamus troop. Elgor ripped through the first two enemies he encountered; his sword swaying through their defective leather armour and splicing across their chests. His men kept to his side and like a small machine they drove through Torwin's men. The horses naturally avoided one another, allowing them to sneak by and strike each rebel they came across from the side.

This was much the case with the other group as it hacked into the larger crowd of rebels. The ten Tamus troops smashed through the enemy, and already the first section of the rebel rush was beginning to turn around in order to chase after their advancing enemy.

Torwin's horse sneaked through Elgor's line and he swiftly turned around in the hope of racing at them from behind. As his horse completed the turn he was struck by the sight of the silver soldiers breaking up his two groups into faltering pockets of disorganised horses. In moments the two opposing forces had passed each other; all of Elgor's men still with him and reforming for another encounter.

The rebels had been cut up and many lay on the grass dead or wounded, with stray horses bounding around in confusion and playfulness. There was no way of telling but the experienced man of war guessed they'd just lost at least twenty men out of the fifty that had launched the attack.

'Reform on me!' Torwin screeched. 'Do it now!'

There didn't seem to be a great response from his men. They were individually turning to face Elgor's troops but some were more concerned with attending to fallen friends whilst others just appeared at odds with what to do. Torwin raced closer to his men and studied Elgor. He could tell who was leading the troops. A figure in the middle of the newly formed single line with a slightly more distinctive set of armour and red feather sticking from his helmet was most likely his opposite. At this stage neither leader knew who the other was. If Elgor had known he was in direct confrontation with the brother of the late notorious Warlord Twinicia he'd likely have been more fervid in his behaviour.

Torwin would now have been concerned a retreat was beckoning if it were not for the fact he'd spotted the vast hordes of Golandin's army running from the camp towards them. If he could hold long enough for the masses to reach them he might still see victory yet. He didn't want Elgor to notice the incoming army behind him but was unable to control the reaction of his men to the vista. Several pointed in ignorant openness. However, Elgor's line didn't seem to pay attention and suddenly raced forwards in a direct assault.

'Hold your ground!' Torwin yelled. 'Form together now!'

His men had half completed this order. It was too straight forward for even them to fail at. Some still bent beside fallen friends but even those seemed to know to snap back into formation eventually. Torwin positioned himself in amongst the rebels and raised his sword high. In seconds Elgor had reached them and the javelins drove into the torsos of all that had been unfortunate enough to find themselves in their way. Swords clashed again but this time it was clear the Tamus troops were looking to drop every rebel rider. They smashed into the initial front line and now hacked away like invincible automatons.

Elgor sliced his sword across the neck of one rebel and swayed to his right to avoid a swinging mace, which spun over his head. He plunged his blade forwards and stabbed the heart of the culprit. Torwin had locked horns with two Tamus troops to either side of his horse. He was rapidly finding himself alone as rebel after rebel fell and stepped back. Torwin lashed out and his longsword struck the steel shoulder pads of one of his enemies. The sturdy armour held fast and no incision was made. He managed to deflect several strikes aimed at turning him into another felled body. With great skill he then prodded his blade into the neck of one of the troops. He had slipped the blade through the gap between the soldier's helmet collar, cutting into his Adam's apple and lower jaw.

Torwin's sword embedded itself into the troop's head then pulled out as he withdrew his arm. The Tamus troop fell back and hit the grass with his neck spurting out warm blood. Before Torwin could even dwell on his kill the other assailing soldier struck him with great force. Their swords clashed but Torwin was caught off balance and fell to his side, losing his grip from the mount and falling into the grass.

Elgor had noticed one of his men fall but was too busy taking on rebels to react. His majestic blade flawlessly claimed kill after kill whilst he men kept to his sides. One rebel thug came at him on foot with a dagger in both hands. Elgor bent forwards and drove his sword into the enemy like he was executing a swift fencing movement. The victim fell flat onto their face and partially knocked into his horse.

All was looking good as Elgor then spotted only a few broken enemy troops still on horseback and in the fight. He then noticed Torwin standing on foot with sword at the ready. Elgor could tell from his attire and behaviour that he was the leader of this rabble and yelled out before his men attempted to dispatch him.

'Wait up!'

He pounced from his horse and jogged over to the bald warrior. Torwin had got to his feet and had been facing off against the Tamus soldier that had sent him from his horse. He quickly shifted his focus on Elgor and the two locked horns. Their blades smashed into one another's and danced as each deflected the

other's swing. Elgor's troops circled the fight, literally unconcerned with the remaining eight or so rebel troops retreating away
in desperation.

Torwin's assault was fierce and Elgor realised he was being
truly tested. The late Warlord's blood launched a blow from his
side that came swooping forth across Elgor's waistline. The
Sergeant narrowly avoided it and poked his sword forwards,
aiming for the rebel's chest. Torwin swayed in avoidance but the
blade tip struck his left shoulder and slid across his arm. He
didn't even flinch and tried to ignore the stinging wound as he
raised his sword in further defence. A part of him was
apprehensive as he quickly noted he was now surrounded and
alone. However, he also knew the hordes were still closing in,
surely now very close to reaching him.

Elgor circled his enemy, noticing the blood dripping from his
fresh cut. Torwin let Elgor circle around whilst remaining still.
They then abruptly clashed again with the two blades clanging
against one another and cutting through the air. Elgor stretched
his sword arm out in the hope of cutting into the rebel's
abdomen. Torwin was able to deflect the strike and managed to
slice his longsword across Elgor's right shin. The armour didn't
hold up and the blade cut across his bone with flawless precision.
He fumbled back, clearly in pain but refusing to drop his guard.

'Who am I fighting?' he asked, slightly impressed.

'Torwin, brother of the late Warlord Twinicia,' said the bald
warrior.

Elgor was stunned and suddenly felt a deep sense of duty to
defeat this vile relative of that evil memory.

'Well Torwin,' he snarled, 'I am Elgor... the name that will be
remembered as the slayer of your sickening self.'

As the Tamus troops paid attention to their leader's stand off
one suddenly instinctively turned his head only to spot the army
racing towards them from the plains.

'Incoming!' he screamed.

The panting leaders both turned their gaze from one another
and briefly lowered their swords. Elgor was clearly more
alarmed. He was unsure what to do but knew it was hopeless to
try and fend off the countless mass. There was no choice and no
time to continue engaging Torwin.

'For the woods!' he yelled. 'Retreat!'

Elgor raced for his horse whilst his men started to bound away in fear. A couple knew to stay beside their leader and lined up by his horse. None seemed bothered about Torwin who stood staring at Elgor as he ran for his ride. The Sergeant couldn't move very fast and limped as the pain and blood loss from his shin wound became unbearable. He stumbled down into the grass just before his horse. His men were concerned; knowing that he was probably too wounded to flee with them. Suddenly, the fleeing troops turned and reformed with their leader and those who had waited beside him.

'Get away!' he ordered. 'Flee!'

He knew they were going to ignore him and got to his feet as two of them leapt from their horses to help him up. The rest formed a line facing the incoming army. It seemed to go on forever, with its rear still coming out from the makeshift camp some miles away. In their deep focus facing off against Torwin's cavalry none of them had realised they had been closing in.

'For Tamus!' one bellowed.

Torwin crept towards Elgor, his eyes transfixed on the man he was so desperate to claim. He was faltering and clutched his wounded shoulder in a desperate attempt to control the blood loss. He could now barely raise his left arm. He noticed a couple of the soldiers pick Elgor up and place him on his horse. They were too late to ride away and suddenly, the first sections of the racing rabble entered the fray and converged on the line of troops. They were swiftly surrounded as the horde enclosed them from the sides and front. Torwin ran towards Elgor as he clambered around on his horse. Elgor noticed Torwin and responded by kicking his horse into action.

'Retreat!' he ordered his men, not realising they were now mostly locked in combat behind him.

He rode off; just managing to snake past the encircling masses of darkly clothed revolutionaries. The troops that had aided him up weren't so lucky and became surrounded beside the rest of their ranks. Torwin's eyes closed and he fell to his knees. His body abruptly rejected his desire to fight on and he fell into unconsciousness from blood loss.

Elgor didn't initially realise his men had been left behind in the fray and continued to race from the scene, heading towards the western woods. He then turned his head only to discover this grim reality. The line initially held firm, with the elite troops hacking down at the men on foot beside their horses. However, eventually the congregation of angry insurgents smothered them like a hand over a flame. Several were pulled from their horses and trampled in the chaos. One lost grip of his sword and found himself wildly swinging punches at his assailants. It didn't take long for the compromised soldier to receive several fatal stabs from the countless blades swinging for him.

Their grip on the situation was lost and troop after troop fell from Elgor's view as they became lost within the swarming horde. Even their horses were not spared. The agonising protests coming from the proud animals were sounds even the coldest of soldiers could not fail to despair at.

Elgor noticed the last remnants of the group of rebels on horseback reform with reinforcements and a clear intention of racing after him. There was nothing the Sergeant could do and he saw no reason in sacrificing himself in some vain attempt to seal some ardent glory. He continued to flee for the woods with as much pace as his horse could muster.

'After him!' a rebel officer yelled out from the crowds.

The riders kicked into gear and pursued their designated target and potential prize rebel catch. By now most of Elgor's men were lost but a few fought on with great strength and resolve. One had lost his horse but stood with two blades swaying out at the crowds around him. The other had managed to pull back from their former line and swung their javelin around in defiance at those giving chase.

In what seemed like unplanned synchronicity both were decisively put down. The javelin of the mounted warrior received a stray strike from a sharp blade. It snapped in two and with it the soldier's resolve. He tried to retreat but to where? Behind him further rebels closed in and in unison a volley of razor sharp points dug into his torso. He died instantly.

The troop on foot could no longer hold them back and swung around with all his might, managing to deeply cut several who instantly fell to his feet. He then felt cold all over as if an ice queen had touched him. A longsword came forth from the crowd and sunk into his lower back and stuck out of his stomach. The firm stab entirely destroyed the soldier's blood stained armour plates. His eyes closed and his body dropped down onto the pile of dead rebels he'd manage to take with him.

The hand of the killer pulled their blade from the body.

'Hurray for Golandin!' the masses around him cheered.

Golandin sniggered to himself. This was the second kill of his campaign and it felt good.

BOOK FOUR

CHAPTER I

SKIRMISH ON THE CROSSROADS

The rider taking point was beginning to realise something. As his horse popped over the ascending woodland track his old eyes were able to spot someone racing into the forest from the north-east. He was being pursued by a large group of other riders and they looked to be gaining on him.

'What's this?' Aimis asked as the rest of them spotted the display.

'Looks like a soldier of Tamus being chased by rebels,' Jamus identified.

The party had just reached the southern edges of Dwenton and were in the western woods heading north up the same road they'd hit upon leaving the Abbey. They had been too far west to notice Golandin's camp as they passed it by on the woodland track.

As they rode nearer to the pursuit it became clear Jamus was right. The distinctive silver armour of the pursued figure was instantly recognisable and contrasted with the black shades of the group behind him.

'Looks like we already have company then,' sniggered Rense.

'What shall we do?' Aimis asked.

They were already close to the town as their track started to veer off towards the Dwenton gate. They found themselves on a crossroads where one could either continue north up the woods, move east into the clearings south of Dwenton, or turn west and enter deeper into Tantria.

A few hundred feet to the east of them Elgor darted from the plains and into the woods. He suddenly spotted Jamus' group but in his panicky and injured state didn't identify them as non rebels. He tried to turn his horse to move further north but suddenly the warrior slipped from his mount in fatigue. His armour struck the ground with force. The Sergeant got to his feet but his horse ran away into the woods in a panic as the screams of the enemy riders rung out around the trees.

Elgor raised his sword and faced his attackers head on. However, his sobbing shin prevented him from moving or putting much weight on the gashing limb. The enemy, now feet away, looked ominous and terrifying to this fatigued soldier. He knew his strength was faltering and already imagined this spot in between the evergreens would be where he fell.

Jamus swooped by him and circled around. At first Elgor treated him like an enemy, his blade pointing at the rider as he moved by. However, he was quick to suss this other group were there to help. His focus switched back to those coming from the fields. They were only moments behind Jamus' party of warriors who now halted close to Elgor.

'We are with you soldier of Tamus!' Jamus yelled.

Yuuki raised her staff and spoke with great command: 'Stay back! Come no closer!'

The enemy were indifferent to the warning and came flooding in. Rense and Fenris broke up the first few and tackled them side on as they pounced from the bushes beside the crossroads. Rense wielded his axe from atop his horse like there was no burden. The enormous instrument smashed into the back of one rebel and sent them flying over their horse. They were trampled by the animal's hooves upon hitting the ground. Fenris came down the middle of two as they attempted to ride by Elgor. His sword sliced through one's waist whilst his fist struck the other square off their ride.

Emi had positioned herself back from the group and already had begun to fling arrow after arrow at the maddening mob. They drifted by her companions and silently embedded themselves into each target she'd locked her eyes on. One took an arrow in their forehead and fell back with their horse running on and away into the woods, entirely unaware their master lay dead on its back. Another flinched as an arrow head penetrated their belly. The thuggish renegade tried to pull the arrow from their body but succumbed to pain and dropped into the grass.

Arifor had vanished. He hadn't come to Elgor's side like the others but had hooked down the eastern edges of the tree line in the hope of flanking the horsemen. He'd now come up on them from the side and hid himself behind a few lush bushes.

Aimis stood beside Jamus. They had both dismounted and came to Elgor's side. The Sergeant had managed to stay on his feet but clearly needed aid. The Lady of magic was behind them with staff poised. She was transfixed with concentration; her eyes closed and her implement aimed frontwards at the onslaught.

Rense stood his ground as more and more riders came at him from every angle. To his side Fenris continued to frustrate the enemy. It seemed as if these two were impassable. Rense swept his axe sideways in an arc that knocked several from their horses and fatally crushed another's skull. With each fallen rider a horse ran away into the woods in liberation. None stuck around.

The extent of the enemy mob then started to ring home. This had only been the tip of this wild rabble. Dozens closed in on Rense and Fenris at once but, before the warriors could even react, a blinding glow formed around the bushes ahead of them. Arifor cast a bright ignoble force, which whisked from his palms like gyrating debris. Spinning specks of white hot light struck countless horsemen. It burned through skin and frazzled armour. It melted leather and flicked out into nonexistence. There were several wails of agony before what looked like a third of the attacking mob fell from their mounts, lifeless and smoking like charred slabs of meat.

Rense wielded his mighty axe and snapped a weak sword before wholly decapitating another rebel. Their head spun in mid-air and was lost in the grass. There was blood in the air and the foul smell of exposed internal organs. Fenris skewered the guts of another as he poked his sword forwards with perfect balance.

A few managed to slip past the two battlers. One was instantly dealt with by one of Emi's flawlessly placed arrow heads. Another jumped from their horse with sword poised in both raised arms. They were hoping to strike Jamus as he stood in a stance beside Aimis. The veteran warrior raised his ancient steel and repelled his assailant's sword before stabbing him as their feet hit the ground. He then shoulder barged the foolish thug who collapsed like a lone domino. Another attempted to lash out at Elgor but Aimis fatally prodded his tunic with his sword whilst Elgor ducked under the strike.

There were now only several remaining enemy horsemen who'd kept back and had watched the massacre. A couple started to flee back towards the masses closing in on Dwenton. The others were about to do the same but were suddenly hit by black shapes falling from the sky. These alien objects had an undeniably demonic presence about them. Harrowingly, they ripped through the bodies of both horse and rider and even sunk into the ground, causing wide upturns of dirt. Arifor had struck again.

Lady Yuuki had remained motionless and inactive throughout the skirmish. No enemy had got close to her and she'd been careful not to cast for she simply hated to kill and had sensed her party was dealing with it. She also hadn't been able to quite find the right moment to perform.

The girl was aware of Arifor's antics and appeared concerned and oddly troubled as his last spell lodged into her memory. The magic he'd just displayed represented a certain school of demonic arts. These deadly spells required great skill but also endangered everyone around them including her. The powers emitted by such casts excited other worlds and contaminated the air with a cold, looming haze.

'Who are you all?' Elgor panted. 'You saved my skin.'

The Sergeant seemed fearful, as if the spells they'd just witnessed had shocked him. It had been the first time he'd seen with his own eyes the powers of a mage. They were a rarity.

'I am Jamus,' said the old man. 'We are here to stop Golandin. My party comes from far and wide.'

'I cannot thank you enough,' Elgor said out loud. 'All of you.'

The Sergeant suddenly broke down. 'All my men!' he yelled desperately. 'I lost all my men to that horde! We couldn't hold them. There are too many of them!'

Jamus thoughtfully put his arm around the sobbing soldier. Everyone could relate to the grief he must have felt.

'I should have gone down with them,' Elgor said mournfully. 'I should have fallen alongside my men.'

'Dead bodies are no use to Marmia,' said Jamus. 'Nor are thoughts ardent for some reckless glory.'

'Your men would have wanted you to survive,' said Aimis.

Arifor appeared from the bushes and jogged over to the now circled group. Their horses huddled together beside them.

'More are coming,' the sinister man whispered. 'Many!'

In unison the group focused their attention to the plains just outside the woods. His words seemed ill conceived. They were overwhelmed by the sight of Golandin's army storming into Dwenton and charging towards them with freshly grouped cavalry at the head.

'Here they come!' Elgor protested. 'We must flee while we can!'

He started to limp away but was stopped by Jamus. 'You will ride with me,' he said. 'What is your name soldier?'

'I am Sergeant Elgor,' he said. 'Empress Sylvie ordered me to scout Dwenton.'

'She is well I trust?' Jamus asked.

'Sylvie is well,' Elgor said. 'She is readying the defences in Brimma.'

The group mounted their horses with Rense and Fenris helping Jamus raise the wounded Elgor onto his horse. The Sergeant could now barely keep himself upright. As he sat behind Jamus Emi thoughtfully started to wind a fresh bandage around his bloody shin.

'This can't wait any longer,' the blonde girl insisted.

Elgor was mesmerised by her as she attended to him. She was so young and beautiful. His eyes then closed.

'We need to get him properly seen to,' said Jamus.

'Well one thing is sure,' Rense smirked: 'we can't stick around here.'

As he spoke the sound of endless hundreds of screeching war cries became audible. The horde were getting close, now almost at the tree line ahead of the track.

'We should press on north through the woods and seek medical assistance in Dwenton,' said Fenris. 'There is a good hospital in the town and the rebels won't be able to snatch every building for a while yet.'

'Yes,' Jamus agreed. 'We can come in from the west and by-pass around the southern wall.'

The riders were off with great speed. Their horses would prove way faster than those of the rebels closing in and the army of men on foot were no threat to them now.

From within the masses of advancing rebels Golandin marched forwards. Alongside him Arthir smugly strutted beside countless swarms of the more hardcore and battle-hardened of the rebels. They flocked to their leader whilst the hordes wreaked chaos. The leader had no idea his wing of horsemen had been so decisively slain by Jamus' party. He'd seen them race after Elgor and the rest was unknown to him as he moved closer to the Dwenton gates.

'Golandin!' a voice wailed.

The leader was in amongst a cushioned up mass of moving men. The voice was faint under the channel of marching boots and roars of adrenaline.

'Sir!' the voice was closer.

Golandin noticed one of his officers slipping through the crowd and making for his side.

'Yes what is it man?' asked the old rebel.

'That Tamus Sergeant got away,' the officer said. 'He linked up with a party of warriors in the woods. They annihilated Brent's cavalry wing, and Brent for that matter.'

Golandin knew that one thing he was short of was trained riders and the news of this, alongside the knowledge of Torwin's initial defeat outside the Dwenton gate, seriously troubled him.

'Where are they now?' he asked.

'They fled north on horseback through the woods,' said the young, eager officer. 'A section of the army started to give chase but have now regrouped.'

Golandin was suddenly distracted by the fact they were now walking under the raised gate. The entrance to the trade town was wide open and they had now passed beside the wall and were in the town.

'There was a mage with the party,' the officer recalled. 'They cast a few powerful spells... killed a lot of guys.'

Golandin paused dead in his tracks as if he'd been told Tamus himself had risen and fought on the field against his army.

'A mage?' Golandin was deeply concerned. 'That is not what I want to hear.'

Mages and those that dabbled with any type of magic were seldom seen in these parts. It was a dying art and a knowledge base only very few had access to. Such practitioners were often therefore seen as mythical rather than always literal inhabitants of the realm. Hence, whenever there was evidence of one it sent shockwaves through the ranks.

The late Vortor had represented the last known mage to dwell in these lands and with him now gone the rebel leader could not comprehend who this unknown caster could possibly have been.

'For now we forget about this,' he said. 'I want nothing more said about mages. However, I want our western flank covered whilst we secure Dwenton. I want you to take command of this and report back on any encounters with this group of riders as soon as possible.'

'Yes Golandin,' said the officer.

'For my reference what is your name?' the leader asked.

'I am Theamis,' came the response.

The officer ran back into the crowd and was gone. Golandin focused his concentration on the dwelling houses now all around him. His men were charging into every doorway, kicking in every window, and seizing every crate.

Arthir was eager to offer his contentions: 'Our men didn't seem to hold up well against an outnumbered enemy Golandin, and with Torwin dead I can't see the morale maintaining itself like it was back at camp... especially if word of this mage spreads, which it only will seeing as that skirmish back there was witnessed by so many.'

Golandin turned and eyed his war buddy. 'On the contrary, the morale will stay high,' he assured him. 'We are capturing Dwenton as we speak and our march to Brimma will surely now prove effortless. The road to Brimma is clear Arthir. It is truly clear.'

'Plus I am not dead,' a groggy voice came from behind them.

'Torwin!' Arthir jumped.

The warrior walked steadily into the town from the gateway and stopped beside them. He had been listening to the men talk whilst resting against the stone. He was pale and dry blood stained his left shoulder pad.

'Although I would be...' he continued, 'if it had not been for a couple of half intelligent men around here. I almost got trampled to death.'

'What happened to you?' Golandin asked.

'I took on Elgor, that Tamus officer; he was a fine swordsman,' Torwin recalled. 'Got wounded, passed out. I then almost got mistaken for another body until a few of your men recognised me and carried me out of the mud.'

'Is your wound okay?' asked Arthir.

'I will live,' Torwin said dryly. 'So I hear he got away?'

'Elgor? Yes,' Golandin said. 'But not his men.'

'He fled and linked up with a party in the woods,' Arthir said. 'They all but wiped out the rest of our cavalry and then fled north.'

'I wouldn't worry too much about our lack of riders,' said Torwin. 'None of them had a clue what they were doing and I almost got killed as a consequence.'

He was clearly angry and bitter about what had happened to him and his pride was ever so dented.

'Our strength is in numbers,' he concluded.

'I don't disagree,' said Golandin.

The three rebels were suddenly interrupted by a thin, slimy looking character coming in from the gateway.

'Well, Dwenton is taken,' said Ellis. 'I will now head back to Brimma. If I go now they will never notice I left. They think I am in isolation mourning Tamus!'

'Yes that is fine Ellis,' Golandin said. 'I want you to try and find out as much as you can regarding any speak of mages and any other forces around here. It seems Elgor's company was not the only resistance we encountered.'

'I know, categorically, that Sylvie sent no others out from Brimma,' Ellis said. 'Whoever else fought with Elgor must have been doing it of their own accord.'

'Vigilantes,' Arthir smiled.

'Renegades more like,' spat Torwin.

'Well just find out what you can,' said Golandin. 'Then I want you to liaise with me again once we have closed in around Brimma. That is when you will be truly required.'

Ellis laughed and abruptly jogged back out of the town through the advancing masses pouring into the gateway.

CHAPTER II

THE PATH NORTH

Jamus struggled down the steep slope as Elgor's body pressed down on his back like a dead weight. For an old man the former friar really had the stamina and strength of a male half his age. They were sneaking down the western slope that rolled out from the woods west of Dwenton. The drop led them right into the centre of the town as northern most as the notable church spire. It was lucky for them that the dwelling had only a fortified southern side. This was really for historical reasons rather than anything else. It had always been the case that military consensus believed no strategic assault on the town would ever be possible from any other direction than the south. To the west was dense woodland. To the north the hilly country would make advance troublesome and to the east a river sneaked southward.

'We mustn't hang around,' cried Emi. 'We have only minutes to spare until that mob will have reached this part of the town.'

It was clear Dwenton had already been entered. Fires were already raging to the south along with a distinct mass visibly pouring into the gateway.

'I know where the hospital is,' said Fenris. 'It is right beside the church.'

Elgor suddenly sprung alert as if he'd only been merely napping.

'I don't need further aid,' he said. 'The bandage is adequate.'

'I fear we are now too near the enemy to go hunting for medical supplies Jamus,' Rense commented from a few feet away.

The group were loitering around the outskirts of the town; their horses standing on the gravel pathway leading further into the centre.

'We need a plan,' said Aimis.

Jamus became at odds with what to do. He'd identified Elgor's wound as too deep to be ignored and knew that in reality the bandage was only a temporary solution. However, as the old man eyed the streets around them it was clear this town was deserted. News had likely spread of an imminent rebel attack and the inhabitants likely had fled to Brimma or another northern dwelling. It was probably the case the hospital had been stripped and abandoned.

'We have no choice but to retreat further north and forget about Dwenton,' he backed down.

'We are supposed to be taking out Golandin,' Fenris grumbled, 'not keeping five paces ahead of him and watching as he seizes chunks of land!'

'What else can we do Fen?' Aimis asked.

'Kill us some more scum,' Rense spat. 'Ain't going no place else.'

Jamus felt compelled to turn to Lady Yuuki, intrigued to know if she had any ideas.

'Any thoughts?' he asked whilst staring at her.

Yuuki looked down to the ground and then the sky above. She seemed to be gnawing something over inside.

'I could kick up a fireworks show,' she said. 'It might scare them off at least.'

'Or entice them further in,' said Aimis.

It was now obvious they had to make a decision. The enemy was gaining momentum whilst they pranced up and down the lonely street.

'Let's make a stand,' said Elgor suddenly. 'Let's take up a position in one of these buildings and defend it.'

'What is the point?' Aimis questioned, keen to get moving.

'The point is we ain't runnin',' Rense smirked.

Elgor stretched out his arms as he sat behind Jamus. Something then caught his attention up the hill they'd just come down from. A single rider was racing northwards along the western woodland track.

'What the?' Elgor was confused. 'No... it isn't?'

'Huh?' Jamus pondered.

Elgor's face turned a deep bloodshot colour as if he'd just seen red.

'It is... it's Ellis!' he snapped. 'What is he doing riding up from the south?'

'Who is he?' Jamus asked.

'He had been one of Tamus' most key advisors up until the assassination,' said Elgor, 'and is now meant to be chief advisor to Sylvie, but what the hell is he doing here?'

'Come to see the action?' Emi suggested.

'No, he never leaves Tamus Tower...' Elgor contemplated. 'No, there is surely only one reason why he is here... he is betraying the empire! Liaising with Golandin!'

'Can't be sure,' said Jamus.

'Trust me I know! I never trusted him! It makes sense, he must have told Golandin I was in Dwenton! That was why the swarm left camp when they did...'

'Let's go get us a traitor,' Fenris yelled.

Jamus addressed his party with sudden authority and decisiveness: 'Staying in Dwenton will be fruitless. We have wasted enough time. Let us seize Ellis and get to the bottom of this.'

None of them needed telling and they were off again back up the hill. Ellis was only several feet ahead seeing as they'd spotted him before he'd moved beside them. He turned his head back fearing someone had just come up from his rear only to instantly spot them. However, unknown to his pursuers, further back down the roadside Theamis, commander of the western flank, was rolling men out across the woods. The advancing rebels instantly spotted them come bounding out of the town and back onto the road.

'Rebels behind us!' Fenris warned.

'Ellis is our target!' Jamus yelled. 'They wouldn't have let him through unless he was one of them.'

Ignoring the enemy presence closely behind them the riders made after Ellis. He couldn't seem to kick his horse into a greater pace and soon they were right alongside him. He brought out a cutlass from within his blowing robe and swung it around at Jamus' lead horse. Elgor suddenly leapt from the animal and connected with Ellis, knocking him clean off his mount and onto soil. They wrestled briefly but in an instant Elgor had put his sword to the sketchy character's neck and knelt over him.

'Did you inform on me Ellis?!' he screeched. 'Did you tell them my company had entered Dwenton? Did you?'

Ellis knew he didn't have any likely story at his disposal and that it was obvious he had betrayed the empire.

'Tamus is finished,' he said mockingly.

The group found themselves waiting for Elgor to do something as their enemies charged towards them from further down the road. It then dawned on the warriors that they were about to make contact unless they rode away now.

'Kill him!' Fenris screamed.

Elgor's blade was faltering as if he felt deeply troubled by the execution style kill. Jamus was close to doing it for him and started to clench his sword tighter and tighter.

'We got contact,' Fenris said.

They had waited too long and struggled to meet both the objective of reaching Ellis and getting away with it lightly. Combat initiated with a volley of arrows streaming from Emi's bow and dropping the first few thugs to gain in on them. Everyone pounced from off their horses knowing this was a battle that had to be fought on foot. Rense and Fenris raced off to the left of the road with Emi firing her bow from beside Yuuki and Aimis. Arifor, forever present but often forgotten about, walked forwards directly at the enemy advance as if totally unnerved by it.

Jamus now stood over Elgor waiting for something to happen. Ellis was motionless like a cornered rat but suddenly struggled as if tension had been building up. Elgor had been unable to kill him regardless of how costly his betrayal and stumbled off from him as he lost balance. The snake rolled to one side and ran away deeper into the woods, narrowly avoiding Jamus' swinging blade. There was a moment of confusion from the old friar as Elgor raced after Ellis. Jamus noticed his party were now locked in combat but decided to follow Elgor into the trees beyond the roadside.

Several enemy archers popped out from the bushes along the track. Emi was quick to notice and slotted one of her fine, flawless arrows into the neck of one of them. A couple fired their own but the slings were way off and slipped by high in the air. Arifor was now way ahead of the rest of them and sparking a lot of enemy attention. He didn't look like much, just a darkly clothed old man, but there was certainly an aura of power and wisdom about him. A couple of thugs came at him sword first. He snapped into some sort of furious reaction and orange glows started to emit from his palms. He raised his arms up and the light expanded out in lines and burned into the flesh of his attackers before they'd got close.

Fenris parried with several enemy swordsmen. He'd grabbed a second blade from his mount and now dual wielded with ease. He deflected a strike and slid his steel across one rebellious warrior and then another. Rense wasn't far away and drove his mighty battleaxe into the midriff of one unskilled opponent. The heavy axe made easy work of flesh and bone and the distinct sound of ribs breaking put a smirk on the bearded warrior's face.

Yuuki raised her staff and aimed it ahead at the bulk of the enemies coming in. She yelled out some archaic command with supreme presence and authority. Her staff gleamed with yellow light and a barrage of shooting ashen bulbs exploded all around the roadside ahead of them. The spell sparked instant alarm amongst the rebel troops.

Aimis sneaked forwards slightly and came across a rebel trying to hide behind a bush. They swung around wildly in front of him but the monk struck the rebel's sword grip and then plunged his weapon deeply into their torso. Another came at him but fell before he'd raised his sword; one of Emi's deadly arrows claiming him.

Ellis was rushing through the foliage like a recoiling spring. He couldn't move fast enough and panted with every step. Elgor was closing in and yelling out in anger. He didn't want the traitor to get away. Jamus was trying to keep up but lacked the youthful energy or desperate drive of either of them. He stopped momentarily and caught his breath only to realise a couple of enemy warriors were eying him from amongst the trees. The pair were standing in a clearing a few dozen feet up from the road. The rebels came at the veteran full force, hoping to bring him down. His ancient sword parried and deflected a series of strikes and then swooped around as the old man spun on his feet and came around with blade outstretched. It stabbed the heart of one of them and without delay Jamus withdrew the steel and spliced the other's forehead as they stood in a daze. The skull cracked open and the brain seeped juices that oozed down the ripped skin of the dead man.

'Ellis!' Elgor roared. 'You won't get away!'

Ellis was leaning against a tree exhausted. It was in a small natural clearing. He watched as Elgor limped towards him with sword in hand. The Sergeant was equally tired and his shin throbbed agonisingly. He was about to speak but an arrow suddenly slid into his lower back like a serpent sting. His sword dropped and he fell onto his knees. Another arrow struck his shoulder. The sharp heads managed to break through his armour and penetrated his body. He turned and noticed several rebels poking out of nearby foliage. This had either been an ambush or Ellis had been very lucky indeed.

The traitor didn't hold back and ran at Elgor with cutlass poised.

'As I said,' he sniggered, 'Tamus is finished!'

Elgor had lost his strength and could barely keep on his knees. The arrows had claimed him. The sly betrayer then slid their cutlass across his Adam's apple and pushed him back to the ground. Elgor thrashed around briefly but his gushing neck was uncontrollable. He died staring at the man he'd so virtuously not been able to finish off on the roadside.

Fenris wasn't faltering as rebel troop after rebel troop fell before his blades. Rense practically cut a man's head in half as his axe swooped down and struck their temple.

'Where is the real opposition?' he shouted out in sarcasm. 'Or is this it?'

'Think this is it my friend,' laughed Fenris. 'If you can believe it!'

No others had dared try getting closer to Emi and Yuuki as their combined blitz of arrows and balls of exploding light terrified and obliterated whoever closed in. Aimis had now dropped back, trying to find Jamus, whilst Arifor continued to toil with the enemy. He was still standing way ahead of the rest of them and effortlessly launched bolts of flaming energy into the woods. Several deer suddenly appeared from the natural habitat as if drawn in by the old man and appeared to then turn into vile vehicles for his wrath. They ran after fleeing enemy troops and butted them with their heads and antlers like things possessed. His black bird had suddenly appeared once again and hovered just above the tree canopy.

'What the?' Emi commented.

'He can somehow command creatures,' said Yuuki observantly. 'An ability I have never seen performed before now.'

Jamus almost jumped as Aimis appeared behind him. They

were only feet away from Elgor but hadn't spotted him yet due to thick branches ahead. The two former holy men pushed back the plant life and entered the clearing only to spot three rebels fumbling with the fallen Sergeant's armour, trying to loot it. Jamus struck one dead in an instant whilst Aimis slid his sword across the back of another who had tried to run. The last one stupidly tried to put an arrow to their bow when Jamus was only feet from him. He fumbled with the string but quickly felt a sword plunge into his body then slide around his insides.

Elgor laid dead in the clearing with his armour half on and half pulled from its place. Jamus bent down and closed the Sergeant's eyelids.

'This has proved a tragic day,' he said.

'Aye, this is deeply saddening,' said Aimis.

The two warriors stood beside Elgor's body in silence. Before long they were joined by the others, all victorious from battle. The rebels had fled.

Yuuki and Emi raced over to Elgor and then Yuuki turned to the group.

'What happened?' she sobbed.

'He went after Ellis and got waylaid,' said Jamus. 'Nothing we could have done.'

'His sense of morals killed him,' said Rense.

'I would have it no other way,' said Jamus.

'Is there nothing you can do Yuuki?' Rense asked ignorantly.

The girl shook her head forlornly whilst looking down at the fallen Sergeant.

'Resurrecting the dead requires masterful lore and only a handful have ever been able to achieve it,' Jamus qualified.

'Like the late Vortor,' said Aimis. 'I remember hearing he'd healed Endal.'

'Yes, well Vortor was a dark master of magic,' said Jamus. 'There are none left like him.'

Arifor was disgruntled at the name suddenly spoken. 'Vortor is no more?' he asked.

'He was put down by Akumi and Sylvie,' said Jamus. 'Apparently, they sneaked up on him. They were very lucky.'

The dark shaman smiled to himself. He'd known of Vortor for an age but hadn't ever encountered the late wizard in person.

'In fact, Vortor was chiefly responsible for this whole thing,' said Aimis. 'He lured Golandin into seeking Endal, knowing it was too risky for him to go to the Grange Abbey. Jamus would have recognised him.'

'Did you not recognise Golandin or Endal when they came then Jamus?' Fenris asked.

The old man looked troubled by the question. 'I had never seen Golandin up until that day or even heard the name,' he said. 'Up until then I'd been disinterested in the war and kept out of it. As for Endal… to me the rider that came to my Abbey on that distant day just seemed like a lone traveller; I truly thought nothing of it at the time. No one knew he even existed.'

Yuuki was clearly frustrated. She knew she had exceptional abilities but lacked the skill to bring anyone back to life. It required tapping into forces she'd never dabbled with nor had ever wished to. It was also clear Arifor had no such ability and made no comment as he looked into the trees ahead.

'We have to get moving,' said Emi. 'That snake Ellis will surely be heading for Brimma now; desperate to spread some deceitful lie.'

Jamus nodded as the eager girl restlessly fidgeted about on her feet.

'The enemy has fled but they will be back any minute,' he said. 'We can't change what happened now and have to get going.'

There was no way they could feasibly bring Elgor's bloody body with them and so they left him there lying beside his sword, surrounded by dead rebels. He would be remembered.

The party rushed back through the trees towards the road. The plan was simple: get back on their horses and race to Brimma. It was only hours away and there was now no time to waste. As they slipped through the last few branches and reached the clearing of the track it became instantly apparent that their horses had been stealthily snatched from the road. They were nowhere to be seen and instead of the sight of their vital rides there were only countless rivals to behold. They had been flanked from the western side of Dwenton and were now desperately surrounded.

'Stay close together,' yelled Jamus.

'Gather around me,' added Yuuki.

The party were pumped for further bloodshed and their adrenaline was reignited. All eyes focused on the enemy masses now pervading the roadside. Nothing could be said or done. They knew they would have to fight. It was clear this was going to be one hell of a showdown.

CHAPTER III

A MESSAGE FROM THE GRAVE

There wasn't much variety for the travelling rider bar for repetitive rock faces and the view of snowy peaks high above the track. The outhouse was now several miles away and the peak of the mountain started to turn into the decline. As this point of greatest height dwindled into a descent the view of the world beyond the mighty peaks struck Akumi. This was a view she'd never seen before and a land she'd never experienced. This was the unknown for the lone girl. It looked menacing and surreal as if it represented a contrast to the lush landscape of Marmia. There was a mist in the air that looked to be rolling only feet above the ground. However, it was difficult to make out detail from this altitude and at this stage the girl could only identify shades of colour and distinct areas of darkness.

The horse sprung into a faster pace with the relieving drop down. The whole journey suddenly seemed less imposing with this refreshing sprint. Akumi travelled down the mountain face with eventless surety. No one was around and the weather was tolerable. It was now early morning and the assassin had been riding through the night. She had only got around an hour's proper sleep back in the isolated house but was surprisingly awake. After her encounter with the wandering farmers the girl didn't want to stick around and was keen to reach the bottom of the mountain range before trying to nap again.

Her will kept her sharp as her animal moved on unfalteringly. Further hours rolled by and eventually the once ominous task of passing over the Camdor Peaks appeared almost complete. The lands were now clear, with a large lake dominating the view of beyond. It was surrounded by misty forest canopies and barren flat mounds of deforested stretches of ground. It was also now clear that at the base of the mountain, where the path would cease, were several houses forming a humble dwelling.

The assassin felt a deep sense of negativity towards this hamlet. She knew not to ever ignore her intuition and as her horse closed in on the wooden, cottage-like structures she brought them to a halt. This was it; the end of the track and beginnings of the land beyond. She had crossed the mountain.

The sheer enormity of what was now required of the girl suddenly hit her. Endal could have gone in any direction from this point. He could have passed through the forest and somehow negotiated the lake. He could have gone north and moved up parallel to the mountains. Without any knowledge of these parts or of where any dwelling was besides the small settlement ahead of her the assassin felt utterly lost and unable to make any educated judgements. This was when doubt struck her. What was she doing here?

The way Akumi saw it she had no choice but to move into the hamlet and hope someone would be able to advise her on where to head. It was a long shot but she also hoped that maybe someone there might be able to recall spotting her target passing through at some point. She couldn't afford to waste this chance of gaining information and started to reluctantly press onwards towards the houses. She regretted never asking the old man back in the dwelling on the mountain whether he had seen a dark figure pass by in recent days. She couldn't make the same mistake this time.

The assassin couldn't ignore the signals bombarding her as she entered into the hamlet. The path broke away into the grassy ground that entered into a forest ahead of the buildings. She was finally on the flat ground. Four houses made up this tiny dwelling and Akumi jumped from her horse as she reached the centre in between them. One to her left seemed the most prominent, with a larger doorway and empty crates scattered around outside. She walked over to the door and knocked without hesitation. Although it was early in the morning she hoped someone would be up and eager to answer.

There was no response and she knocked again several times. As she waited she turned and studied the other houses. There was a grim atmosphere and a silence that seemed unnaturally tense. After a minute of waiting the girl knew no one was about to beckon her in. She decided to test the door only to find it was unlocked and opened outwards with a low pitched squeak. The assassin crept inside and peeked around. The interior was drab, with fallen objects and smashed furniture indicating signs of a struggle.

Akumi decided to go upstairs; her senses were pressing on her to investigate. She slowly stepped up the timber frames but was only half way up the stairs before spotting a body lying limp on the upper floor. She felt tense and popped up into the crawlspace with sword gripped. She realised the attic space revealed further bodies, three in total. They were spattered in blood and clothed only in rags. One of the bodies was a child. They couldn't have been any older than a toddler. Akumi's face went a cold pale and her heart throbbed with emotion. This was why she'd been told not to venture into this small village, because it was the scene of a massacre.

There wasn't anything that could be done and the girl ran out of the house in a panic. The image of the dead child stuck with her and tears were forming in her wide brown eyes. She didn't want to check the other houses and just felt the urge to get away. She remounted and charged away into the natural entrance of the looming misty forest ahead. The light switched from bright morning rays to a dim, baleful shade as the girl entered under the trees. The sky was entirely blocked from view and the vines and branches wrapped around every visible surface. Akumi noticed further bodies lying in the grass just within the forest. One was a woman; her hair messily wrapped around her face and neck. Whoever had last been here they'd committed mass murder. There was no way of telling who that may have been. The farmers she'd been forced to fight? Bands of travelling rebels? Endal himself? Akumi was in too much of a state to think about it and disappeared deeper and deeper into the dense woods.

It was at this point the girl lost her cool. She stopped her horse and dropped down into the grass crying. She knew she'd get easily lost in this uncharted mass of plant life and foliage. She sensed she was surrounded by evil and horror. It beckoned on her that she was outside the lands of order and the security of the Tamus Empire. She felt utterly isolated and hopeless.

'What am I doing?' she yelled out loud. 'Endal! Where are you?'

She continued to sob and started to reflect on her fallen friends. In this moment of desperation she looked back to Jobe and how he'd saved her life in that distant clearing before Endal. She remembered Harkor and how he'd been so courageous in the face of all the odds. Her thoughts then predictably went back to her old master, Hazati. She wished so much that he was by her side. She felt like she was going astray and didn't know what to do. It then suddenly happened.

A firm pressing voice whistled around the trees. It was loud and clearly audible.

'Akumi,' the voice announced. 'I am here.'

'Hazati!' the female assassin screamed.

She got to her feet and looked around frantically. She was completely overwhelmed but didn't feel afraid.

'I am with you,' said the voice.

Suddenly, a cloudy mass formed several feet ahead of the girl from beside a large birch tree. It looked like a mini tornado but soon calmed into a misty silhouette. It resembled an arcane figure surrounded by haze and unfathomable energy.

'Hazati...' Akumi said again.

'It is me Akumi,' the voice said. 'Do not fear me.'

The girl gulped and tried to calm herself in front of this alluring presence. She knew it was her master; the voice distinct and the outline recognisable.

'You are...' she was at odds.

'I am speaking to you from beyond the reality you inhabit,' the ghostly figure said. 'I am coming from another world.'

Akumi nodded and automatically fell to her knees in awe over this supernal presence.

'I can't communicate with you for long,' said Hazati. 'Listen well Akumi. All rests with you. I know this but it is only a sense. Marmia is in danger. Brimma is weak and vulnerable.'

'What do you mean master?' Akumi asked attentively.

'You must assist with the defence of the capital,' said the voice. 'You must defend Tamus Tower.'

'But what about Endal?' Akumi pressed. 'I must find him.'

'Endal is gone,' the voice affirmed. 'He is gone.'

'Where?' the girl asked.

'You cannot reach Endal now,' Hazati insisted.

'Master, I must,' the girl protested. 'I will not rest until I have tracked him.'

There were a few seconds of silence from the mystical figure before a response came:

'Beyond the lake there dwells Endal, but he is shrouded in darkness. It is folly to venture there; his abode is infused with dark energy.'

The girl was unsure what to make of her master's words.

'He is near? He is over the lake?' she asked.

'You must get to Brimma,' the voice said. 'You are needed Akumi.'

'Master, I...'

'I am fading back, go forth and act! Farewell Akumi.'

The mysterious vista started to fade away and in a flash it was gone.

'Master!' Akumi yelled. 'I don't know what to do. Come back... come back!'

Her spirits were lifted with the encounter of Hazati's ghostly presence although her mind was still at odds with what to do. She felt spiritually overwhelmed and deeply enlightened by this acknowledgement of some other world beyond the physical. However, the girl was now unsure whether to comply with her omnipresent master's command and race back to the distant capital or do as she so fervently desired and press on over the lake for Endal. She now knew that somewhere beyond that vast stretch of water her target lay. Although she felt a deep sense of duty regards ensuring Brimma did not fall to the rebels she also couldn't ignore her intuitive drive to press on after the Emperor's killer. The girl started to realise what she must do. She made for her horse and remounted.

CHAPTER IV

MAKING FOR BRIMMA

Bolts of light struck every angle around the group of pro Tamus warriors. Yuuki had cast a powerful spell that sent sheets of exploding balls down from the ether. The fireballs formed a temporary barrier around them as the enemy forces pressed in all around.

'We must try and smash through them and move northwards,' Aimis called out.

'Doesn't look like we will be going any place soon,' noted Rense.

Yuuki was standing with arms raised and continued to hum in a trancelike state of focus. Her tall staff appeared to glow with magical energy as her voice whispered. Beside her Emi had aimed her bow directly at a target she'd designated for herself. All the darkly armoured rebel thugs looked much the same although this one seemed to be a leader. He kept calling out and pointing, with men around him acknowledging his commands. Emi had been swift to spot this and knew he was a primary target.

Fenris stood just within the magical circle of exploding glows of light and stared at the enemy beyond the conflagration. Rense was close by with Arifor calmly studying every angle. Jamus was next to Yuuki and looked frustrated, as if he felt his plan was going horribly wrong.

'I can't keep casting this,' said Yuuki. 'It will exhaust me.'

Jamus knew only too well that the group couldn't rely on her protective spell for long and started to prepare for combat.

'Stick together and press northwards through them,' he yelled. 'Move up the road and snatch horses if you spot any.'

The bolts of light suddenly fettered out and the smoky grounds started to clear. With that a volley of war cries from beyond the burning soil cried out. The rebels charged in one wild rush. Fenris brought out his blades and instantly initiated proceedings with several swinging strikes aimed at his incoming foes. Rense was beside him with axe grinding into flesh like an unstoppable mechanism. Arifor started to glow like some etheric being and jogged forwards. Yuuki was troubled by his behaviour and again showed signs of unrest about the powers he was applying. She didn't have time to dwell on it though and quickly found herself surrounded with Jamus and Aimis right next to her. The three spaced out and locked horns with their enemy. Yuuki was able to use her staff for more than just spell casting and wielded it up and down like a spear. Its long reach gave the girl a major advantage as enemy after enemy was knocked to one side by its firm tip.

Jamus stabbed one in the belly and pulled his blade out with a river of blood gushing out from the ruined organs. Aimis sliced another down the back as they ran straight past him in stupidity and confusion. Emi had managed to keep her aim and stayed a few feet back from her friends as they drew in most of the attack. Her arrow pointed directly at the figure still keeping back and seemingly directing the onslaught. He was half concealed behind a bush just off the roadside and kept poking around the foliage to get a clearer view. The sharp archer released her lethal shot and the arrow flew across the area with perfect precision. He probably hadn't even seen it coming and flinched as it drove into his right breast. He clutched the shaft in reflex but was unable to pull the arrow head out of his body and dropped down out of the girl's view.

'Theamis is down!' a voice called out from the crowd.

Emi put her bow around her back and brought out her sword. The enemy was too close for her to now ignore. Fenris was on fire and continued to floor rebel after rebel with little effort. They were clearly untrained and for such an exceptional swordsman proved little more than moving targets. Rense felt just as relaxed and made mincemeat of anyone foolish enough to get close. The group were slowly but surely moving up the roadside northwards and cutting through the attack without much trouble. However, the enemy was also behind them and moving to their sides in a flanking move. Arifor seemed to be dealing with most of the enemy coming from the woodland whilst Yuuki, Jamus, and Aimis focused on the rear. Emi kept switching although mostly stuck with the old friar.

Arifor was a terrifying spectacle and none dared close in on him. He suddenly sent streams of energy out towards his foes that glowed with a dark red. The light charred flesh and rung like a demonic chanting. If anything the dark caster was enjoying this.

It appeared to be going well and the group continued to act like one unit with a momentum totally unchallenged by the enemy who were now uneasy about charging at them.

'Keep it up!' yelled Jamus. 'Keep pressing up.'

Rense and Fenris didn't need telling and as the point men continued to wage through the masses they were pitted against up front. They were truly falling like dominoes and eventually started forming a path for the two to move through as they backtracked in droves beside them. There then came a sudden yell from behind them. It was coming from further down the body filled road.

'Torwin has entered the battle,' voices cheered. 'Torwin is here!'

The name struck a chord with Jamus. He knew it to be the name of the late Twinicia's mysterious brother.

'Keep focused,' he sounded to his group. 'Torwin is a threat.'

The bald headed warrior came racing into the fray on horseback from the rear and dropped onto his feet once he'd reached the crowds formed around Jamus' party. He had ridden up from Dwenton on his own, eager to reclaim lost pride from earlier that day. Golandin was disinterested with the battle waging on his left flank and had continued to press forwards with the bulk of his army through the town.

'Theamis is down sir,' said a rebel officer. 'We can't seem to kill any of 'em!'

Torwin pressed through the crowds and took a peek at the group continuing to press on up the road.

'On my command I want every man to charge at once!' he yelled. 'I will lead.'

His presence boosted morale and there was a clear urge amongst the rebels to follow his command. He appeared from behind the crowd and eyed Jamus and those beside him. The rebels around Rense and Fenris retreated back a few paces up the road as the attack regrouped on the veteran rebel's command.

'This is where you fools hit the dirt,' smiled Torwin.

As he spoke he looked around for Elgor. 'Where is Elgor?' he yelled.

'He is dead,' announced Theamis from the huddled mass.

He had managed to pull the arrow from his breast and bandage the deep wound. The commander of the western flank was still in the fight and wearily reached Torwin at the front of the group.

'They tried to ambush Ellis,' he said. 'We dealt with Elgor and Ellis is now safely on route back to Brimma.'

Torwin nodded whilst staring at Yuuki. 'You know, you should really be joining us girl,' he laughed. 'You look pretty damn hot to me and it sure gets lonely forever marching forwards!'

The powerful caster stared back sarcastically. 'Well you'll have the worms to keep you company after we've finished with you,' she mocked.

Torwin shook his head in rejection at the comment and raised his blade. 'Attack!' he bellowed.

The mass moved at once and raced in on Jamus' group. Fenris and Rense fell back slightly to link up with the rest and the seven warriors now stood huddled together in anticipation for this impending charge.

Emi's bow started to work overtime as arrow after arrow flung into the rushing mass. Yuuki cast bright fireballs that claimed several more. Arifor, still a haunting figure of light, carelessly danced around slightly in advance of his group and suddenly, like some force of nature, turned into a cloud of bright white mist. The mysterious fog blew into one section of the attack like an incision and the reaction was dramatic. Swarms collapsed dead before hitting the ground as the mist instantly disabled their life force. Again, Yuuki was concerned like she knew something about his powers that no one else could grasp.

The spells and arrows certainly dented the attack but swords inevitably clashed. Torwin's blade smashed against the steel of Jamus whilst Theamis attempted to bring Yuuki down. She swung her staff with great speed and it struck the young officer against the head, knocking him down onto the ground. Torwin parried with Jamus and made little headway as the two experienced fighters fenced like it were a display. Beside them Rense stormed into the bulk of Theamis' men with Fenris in support. There was now no sign of Arifor, the mist gone and no bodily presence immediately apparent. Above them the black bird vanished into the clouds.

Emi was immensely swift and glided her sword around like it

was an extension of her arm. She had an assassin's touch and killed with fatally rapid contact. Aimis was trying to help Jamus deal with Torwin but kept having to take on rebel after rebel. He wasn't troubled by the numbers but noticed their group slowly splitting away from each other. Torwin was left alone to take on Jamus whilst Yuuki and Emi stood side by side. Rense and Fenris had pressed forwards with natural vigour, which ultimately left the monk standing by himself. He swung with all his might as blade after blade attempted to infiltrate his defence.

'Fenris!' he called out. 'Regroup with me.'

The swordsman heard the call and started to backtrack with Rense. However, they found themselves split off and unable to get closer. Yuuki started to suss what was happening and her and Emi desperately tried to get closer to Aimis. They then realised more enemies were still coming from the road in what looked like an infinite horde. The caster sent more magical spells in the direction of the reinforcements whilst Emi fought with those around her.

'Keep back,' Aimis panted.

He was now tiring and without any backup continued to swing around in all directions. Jamus was lost in the crowd as Torwin continued to parry with him in stalemate. Aimis became exhausted and with a sudden acknowledgement of his fatigue let his guard down. A sharp spear then jabbed his kidneys. He turned to try and prevent further injury but was then stabbed from behind by a dagger. He gave out a whimpered cry and was then lost under a sea of prodding blades and clenched firsts.

Fenris and Rense had created such a large pile of bodies around them that the rebels were now finding it hard to step over their fallen comrades to get to them. Those that had converged on Aimis turned their focus on the pair but kept back beside the corpses. The warriors cautiously continued to reach Aimis' position only to realise what had happened.

'Aimis is down!' Rense yelled.

The announcement did nothing except further stress quite how hopeless this situation was beginning to look.

Emi prodded away whilst Yuuki continued to cast as much as her tiring mind could muster. Her spells lacked the sheer destructive force of Arifor's and were more suited for targeted battle with single opponents. Concentrated bolts of flame struck rebel after rebel as they got close.

It had been the first time the sorceress had been in such a wild situation. The enemy started to become less fearful over the sight of magic being cast as if they were now suddenly accustomed to it. However, many were still afraid and backed away from the girl in droves. The combat went on and on until it looked like the enemy were becoming more interested in watching Torwin do battle than fight themselves.

Jamus had been careful to not underestimate his opponent and kept defensive. Torwin was tiring and growing impatient. He landed blow after blow but each time his blade was deflected and his body knocked to one side. Rebels started to gather around the stand off and circled the two fighters. All eyes were on Torwin who seemed fired up and enflamed with an urge to kill this old man. He didn't know who Jamus was but could sense the figure had some prominent status about him.

'You think you will stop us now you old fool,' Torwin sniggered.

He made another attempt at poking Jamus with his ancient sword but this time Jamus parried it with such force that it sent the blade flying from the bald warrior's grasp. He looked up with sudden fear in his eyes and the old man then raised his blade and, with one swooping strike from a highly angled position, split the razor sharp tip across his torso. Torwin fell back in agony and shock and stumbled into rebel troops behind him. He face went pale as they kept him upright and his pupils rolled down until only the whites of his eyes were visible. He fell limp and lifeless without any last words.

With great timing Rense and Fenris started to hack through the gathered spectators from behind as Yuuki cast several gleaming fireworks into their grouped up mass. The rebel attack had been utterly defeated and the thuggish troops started to flee back down the road southwards in undisciplined herds. Jamus was motionless and continued to stare down at the lifeless Torwin.

'You got him,' said Emi. 'Who was he?'

'He was Twinicia's brother,' Jamus said in contemplation.

'The dead Warlord?' Rense asked. 'Wow! That will be a blow to those rebels then.'

They looked down at Torwin in unison and felt a sense of relief. This had been one hell of a battle and they were all utterly exhausted. It then suddenly dawned on the group.

'Aimis!' Jamus shrieked.

The monk was lying atop a pile of dead rebels with multiple stab wounds apparent all over his body and neck. He was gone.

'We tried to reach him,' Yuuki sobbed. 'But we all got cut off.'

Jamus bent down and embraced his monk's body emotionally.

'You were not supposed to die my brother,' he said softly.

There was a morbid silence as Jamus grieved beside his old friend. A figure then suddenly emerged from the piles of bodies with sword in hand. It was Theamis. He blindly charged at the group, blood still dripping from his bruised forehead where Yuuki's staff had struck him. Emi placed an arrow directly into his stomach and he instantly fell back to ground.

Yuuki closed in on the moaning rebel who writhed around fondling with the arrow. She aimed her blazing staff directly down at him alongside Emi who had strung another arrow ready to fire.

'No, please!' Theamis moaned desperately. 'Don't!'

He stared into the girls' eyes fearfully as they looked down at him. Jamus hadn't left his fallen friend's side and let his party deal with this. Fenris and Rense moved closer to the girls with weapons poised.

'Finish him off,' Rense grumbled at them.

Theamis was clearly in great pain and just lay limply, as pale as a sheet.

'I'm so sorry,' he flustered. 'Please don't kill me.'

Yuuki was hesitant and lowered her staff. Emi also started to withdraw her arrow. Neither girl had it in them to kill someone who'd given up. They were merciful and always gave their enemies a chance.

'It's okay,' Yuuki said softly. 'We aren't going to kill you.'

'Aren't we now?' laughed Rense. 'You silly girls!'

He raised his axe high over his head and aimed it down at the injured rebel.

'No! He is defeated,' protested Yuuki. 'We cannot kill him.'

'Bah!' Rense spat.

He turned and extracted his axe from position. Fenris was less convinced as he watched the bearded man back away from Theamis.

'We can't let him go,' he said. 'He was leading that attack! He will regroup with them.'

Theamis shook his head but was weary and weak all over and didn't respond.

'We can bring him with us,' said Emi. 'I will see to his wounds.'

It was clear both girls were slightly alarmed over quite how young the rebel looked. He was likely no older than they were and in his state of helplessness they both felt a maternal instinct kick in.

'This is so stupid,' Fenris aired. 'One second we are mourning for Aimis and the next we are attending to the enemy!'

'Just drop it,' said Jamus from across the roadside.

He was still cowering down by Aimis but then started to get back to his feet and face his party.

'We have killed enough people for one afternoon,' he said. 'This boy is no longer a threat to us.'

Emi bent beside Theamis and started to carefully break the arrow and bring out the head. She had several bandages at the ready and started to apply a makeshift tourniquet around his waist.

'So what now Jamus?' Fenris seemed angry. 'I mean you have already led us into three pointless battles and now here we are assisting the enemy!'

'Not to mention the fact we've now got no horses,' added Rense.

Jamus sensed an undeniable split in the group over the issue of aiding Theamis and tried to calm the tension.

'We will head to Brimma,' he said. 'Even on foot we should make it ahead of Golandin if we move now.'

'This is turning into a joke,' Fenris yelled. 'If we are going to be dragging him along with us it will surely slow us down.'

'We can get information from him,' said Jamus. 'He likely knows all sorts.'

'What is there to know?' Rense laughed. 'The enemy is pressing forwards in great numbers! We need to get to Brimma and find Ellis.'

'And where the hell is Arifor?' Fenris added.

Yuuki was swift to respond: 'He has been using dark and demonic powers and I suspect he has been consumed by them. They suck you in and it seems he has suddenly embraced it. That is why he is no longer in a bodily form.'

'That can't be good,' said Rense.

'No,' Jamus grumbled, 'it most definitely is not good. Let us hope Arifor will come back soon and is only partially in this etheric state.'

Fenris looked to Rense and there appeared to be some unspoken mutual recognition between the tight duo.

'Let us two press ahead,' Fenris said. 'We will move faster that way and will be able to get to Brimma sooner. You lot can escort this rebel if you must.'

Jamus nodded without comment. He then spoke: 'Go now friends and we will see you at the tower.'

Without any hesitation the two warriors ran off northwards, Fenris waving at the girls. They were too impatient and unforgiving to understand why the remaining three couldn't just leave Theamis to die.

'That is probably for the best anyway,' said Emi.

'I suspect it is,' said Jamus, 'although I am hardly in control of this situation anymore. As far as I'm concerned whatever unfolds from this point on is the result of fate.'

With encouraging synchronicity fate appeared to acknowledge the old man's words. Their horses had suddenly emerged back onto the roadside from within the woods ahead. Fenris and Rense had already claimed back their rides. The rebels had obviously only temporarily spooked them away.

CHAPTER V

GATHERING CLOUDS

Akumi had sensed a grim, foreboding presence ever since entering into the dense forest. She hadn't been following a trail nor gained any information regarding a potential route to take. Instead, the female assassin had been relying on intuition alone. She hadn't been able to turn back and had pressed on knowing full well she was likely going to be needed elsewhere. She was doing this because she knew that otherwise a part of her would always crave revenge. This desire would ultimately corrupt the girl and drive her wild with anger. She had no choice but to continue on and hunt for Endal.

By now the woodland was endless in every direction. It remained dense with thick foliage snaking around high, impending trees. There was a morbid silence and unnatural lack of wildlife. It was as if the entire area was locked in some state of limbo where life was hidden from view.

Akumi paused by a gap in the treacherous vines she had been hacking through with her sharp blade. She had been forced to abandon her horse due to the lack of space in this impenetrable environment. She took all she could from the packs tied to the animal but had ultimately been forced to discard most of her supplies.

She looked up at the sky with a sudden feeling of dread in her bones. The clouds were a brooding black with menacing fog rolling ever closer to the tree line above. A howling whistle raced through the air with the odd high pitched sound of wolves moaning in the far distance. The brown eyed girl now felt such a sense of presence around her that she raised her katana in a fighting stance and eyed every angle.

'Who is there?' she called out firmly.

There was no response except further confirmation of alterations to the atmosphere. Incomprehensible sounds rung out from the blackness above. Akumi sensed magical energy at work as if she had stumbled into some dark mage's isolated playground. Whatever the cause of this mysterious spectacle was the assassin felt uneasy and vulnerable.

She had marched on for many miles and the mountains were now a distant feature of the horizon behind her. She was running low on food and water, only drips and scraps remaining in the bags tied about her waist belt, and it was clear she now needed a good rest. She decided to creep into a sudden clearing ahead. The trees started to dwindle out to the sides of this barren flatland. The ground consisted of dry mud and countless winding twigs. There were no prominent landmarks to behold and instead of a sense of discovery Akumi felt frustration at how drab the location seemed.

The sky was wrestling with itself. Clouds rolled against each other and formed into swirling masses of churning darkness. Odd flickers of white light popped in and out of view from amongst this vast aerial torrent. It looked as if the entire sky was warping into a storm cloud or something far more destructive.

Akumi circled around the clearing, staring up at the display above. She started to remember the words that had come from the late Vortor as he died atop his tower all that time ago. Was this spectacle above her somehow linked to his prediction of dark forces entering into this realm at its weakest moment? The girl couldn't help but dwell on the late mage's warning. What was happening?

As the sky turned into a mass mid-air light show Akumi suddenly noticed black shapes coming out from the misty energy surrounding the dark clouds. She then realised that these shapes represented vile figures dancing around in circles. They looked like gargoyles but the girl could only make out the slightest of details. She was fearful and backed away from the clearing in the direction she had been coming from. She was at odds with what to do. Figures from above had begun to swoop down and glide over the trees. One suddenly seemed to spot the girl. Its eyes glowed a menacing red as its form flickered with magical luminosity. Akumi was close to running with all her pace but it was too late. The spectre swiftly flew over her head with only a few feet between them. Akumi was terrified, every primal instinct in her body yelling *flee*, but managed to keep her blade held high.

Back in the clearing something abruptly appeared in a mass of blinding white light. In a puff of energy a dark figure emerged standing on the ground motionlessly. Akumi now couldn't control her instincts and turned to fly. As her head turned and her legs kicked into motion she heard what sounded like desperate screeching. She turned back only to spot the figure in the clearing casting dozens of red magical balls of light at the countless encircling entities above. They reacted instantly and vanished back into the void of darkness in the sky.

Akumi continued to watch the figure as it remained standing in the clearing. It then suddenly collapsed onto the dry mud in a lifeless frontward fall. The female assassin raced into the clearing and pointed her blade tip at the dark figure lying before her. She was intrigued by the fact this figure had taken on the entities and felt an urge to confront them.

'Who are you?' she yelled.

Her voice was dim against the continuing sounds of howling winds and groaning magical forces above. She put her sword to one side and bent down, analysing the black robe of the stranger. Slowly, the figure raised their head up to eye the girl confronting them. Their aged face was pale and wrinkled. Akumi didn't recognise the stranger.

'I am Arifor,' came the stranger's croaking voice. 'Where am I?'

'Arifor...' Akumi remarked. 'I am Akumi, and we are outside of Marmia, far to the west.'

Arifor nodded and got himself on his feet slowly. He was clearly exhausted and confused.

'I was taken,' he said. 'Consumed by chaotic energy and dropped back into the world from beyond!'

Akumi was unsure what she was hearing. 'What is happening?' she asked desperately.

'Hold on,' said Arifor, 'you are Akumi? The assassin after Endal?'

Akumi nodded rapidly. 'Yes, but I don't understand,' she said, 'who are you?'

'I was with Jamus and his party,' said Arifor. 'We were heading to Brimma, taking on Golandin's rebel army. I was overcome with dark energy and placed into some other state of reality. I was...'

Akumi was now deeply focused on Arifor's account. Something was beginning to make sense.

'Go on...' she snapped.

'I must have been morphed to this spot by the dark energies I was harbouring,' said Arifor.

'Why here?' Akumi asked.

Arifor was not his usual mysterious self and spoke with great presence. It was as if his experience had shocked him to the point of forgetting himself.

'It seems that this area is the centre of the focus of all the dark energies,' he said knowingly. 'I was brought here because I am tapped into those forces.'

'The dark forces are being focused?' Akumi pondered with eyes open wide. 'This is a portal... it is as Vortor said it would be.'

Arifor reacted. 'A portal... yes!' he screeched. 'We must get away from here. It is dangerous for us to dwell here.'

'I must go on,' Akumi announced. 'I must find Endal... he is near. I can tell.'

Arifor appeared to be calming down as if now back in control of his faculties.

'You are no match for Endal,' he mocked. 'We should head back to Marmia and link up with Jamus.'

Akumi only half took in the old shaman's words and pondered on why her intuition had led her to this exact spot where dark energies were merging into this hub of magical power. She could have gone another way and never come across this or the mysterious Arifor.

'I will continue on Arifor,' she said. 'Do as you will.'

Akumi was unsure of Arifor to say the least. Although he had mentioned Jamus and explained how it was he had appeared before her she sensed some darkness about him. However, without knowing anything about him she didn't wish to judge him too early on and tried to remain open.

'I will watch Endal kill you,' Arifor laughed. 'Besides, it is a long way back to Marmia and I have no idea how to warp back to where I came from at will.'

'Whose side are you on Arifor?' Akumi was confused.

'Yours,' he said. 'I just can't accept you're a match for Endal.'

'Well help me then,' said Akumi. 'Stick with me and let's find him.'

'I suddenly remember where I am,' said Arifor. 'Yes... yes I know this place. Oh, Endal is near. He is very near.'

'What?' Akumi screeched. 'What do you know?'

The old man sniggered whilst staring at the dark clouds above them. His presence seemed to keep the spectres and other entities at bay.

'This location has always been the spot where dark powers focus,' he said. 'Stones were placed here hundreds of years ago, forming a gateway. Vortor knew it. Your late master, Hazati, knew it... and Endal certainly knows it. That's why I know he won't be far away. This is where Endal dwells that is for sure. He is driven by the dark forces after all.'

Akumi knew to take Arifor seriously. She had further questions.

'So this portal... was it Vortor's plan all along?'

'Vortor knew of the existence of this ancient gateway,' the old man said. 'He also knew that one day, when the realm was in chaos, there would be enough fear in the air to charge it and therefore open up the door to the dark forces.'

Akumi nodded. 'How can we stop it?' she asked.

'We must defeat Golandin and bring hope back to Marmia,' he said. 'With no threat from the rebels peace will be secured and therefore no more fear will fuel this portal.'

Akumi suddenly felt she could trust Arifor. He came over sincere in his eccentric sort of way.

'I must confront Endal...' she went on. 'Golandin will be dealt with by Sylvie, Jamus, and the rest of them.'

Arifor smiled. 'I suspect I know where Endal dwells,' he said. 'After all, I once lived in these parts. About a mile from here, just outside the woods, there is a forbidding underground complex. A hidden doorway leads into a labyrinth of secret chambers. There was a time, an age ago, when I can remember it was rumoured Endal was present there, when not away on a dark contract of his. He lurks the shadowy lair like a demon! Hidden by the shadow!'

'Lead me there,' yelled Akumi. 'I beg you...'

Arifor laughed out loud whilst inspecting his attire. 'I shall,' he smiled. 'I shall.'

The horses didn't need much persuading and bolted up the roadside as soon as Jamus gave the command. Several were left behind, their riders fallen or vanished, but their supplies were mostly salvaged. Jamus led the retreat with the captured Theamis sitting behind him. Lady Yuuki and Emi were riding to either side of the old friar's horse.

Already behind them there were signs that the enemy were reforming, but they would now never be able to catch up; with their cavalry wing in disarray and countless wounded to attend to.

Theamis had been patched up by Emi. Several bandages had been tied around his wounds and his injuries had been cleaned with cool water. He was okay as the wounds were not too deep and with the bandages keeping bleeding under control he felt slightly relieved. Once he had been bandaged Jamus had demanded Emi also tie his arms behind his back; after all, he was their captive and they couldn't afford to take any chances.

The young rebel was alert but fearful and unsure what lay ahead for him. He tested the thick rope that wrapped around his wrists keeping his forearms together from elbow to hand. The knots were flawless and Emi's rope work inescapable without hours of fondling and rubbing up against a sharp edge. Theamis ceased testing the rope and just sat watching the balding head of Jamus bobbing up and down in front of him.

The party raced on northwards for a few miles without any event. The rebels were now quite a distance away as they made for Brimma. They had remained silent, reflecting on all that had happened up until now. Theamis had spent most of the ride with his eyes closed in an effort to conserve his strength.

They had been riding for a couple of hours and Jamus knew it was time to allow their horses to rest. The road leading away from Dwenton had started to veer off from the direction they were heading and they now found themselves cutting across open fields of short grass to stay on course.

Jamus brought his ride to a halt and the girls were swift to copy.

'Let us rest for a while,' he announced.

'Sounds like a plan,' said Emi.

The three warriors dismounted leaving Theamis still sitting on Jamus' ride. The former friar then placed his arms around the rebel's waist as if to support him. Theamis raised his left leg around the horse and leapt off onto the grass awkwardly.

'How are your wounds?' asked Emi.

Theamis looked at the girl with a submissive, fearful expression formed on his timid face. It was clear he was quite nervous.

'Are you feeling faint?' Yuuki asked.

Both girls stood facing him as Jamus sat in the grass lighting his pipe. The sky was clear, with only the odd cloud passing by in the light breeze. However, to the far west it was patent dark gathering clouds were forming up; the prospect of an overcast sky was looming.

They were in a flat field. In every direction the horizon was bare and barren. Only the odd tree gave variety to the otherwise unadorned landscape.

'Don't be so nervous,' said Emi. 'We aren't going to hurt you you know. We just had to tie your arms.'

If Theamis had just been a surrendering rebel troop they'd likely have let him go on the roadside. However, they knew he had been leading the assault on them and therefore knew it was important he was taken as a prisoner and not allowed to slip back into circulation.

Theamis bent at the knees and carefully dropped onto the ground. With his arms tied around his back he found it hard to feel comfort and his wounds were still sore and troubled him.

Yuuki and Emi sat beside him with Jamus a few feet away, entirely indifferent as he puffed on his pipe. Circles of smoke rose into the air around him.

'What will happen to me?' Theamis asked.

Jamus came in. 'You will be imprisoned and tried as a rebel officer eventually,' he smirked.

The old warrior was clearly bitter about Aimis' death and the way the day had played out. He had neither time nor an inclination to reassure the rebel.

Theamis looked down to the grass and closed his eyes in despair.

'I knew I should never have got involved with any of this,' he said. 'I was so stupid.'

His voice was emotional and instantly plucked the heartstrings of the girls. They didn't like seeing him so fearful. He was young and naïve and they sensed confusion in him regards where he truly stood.

'Don't worry,' said Yuuki affectionately. 'I sense goodness in you. You won't be tarred with the rebel brush unless we believe you are truly for their cause. It is never too late to change sides.'

'She is right, please don't fear us,' added Emi.

Jamus tutted to himself and shook his head in mockery at what he was hearing. He kept his thoughts to himself but was slightly amused by the girls' level of concern over this rebel officer.

'He was giving orders back there,' Jamus added. 'He was leading that attack on us along with the late Twinicia's now deceased brother! Don't be too reassuring.'

Lady Yuuki seemed to acknowledge Jamus and looked into Theamis' eyes.

'You must have some belief in the rebel cause?' she posed.

'I don't know what I believe,' said Theamis. 'Truly I don't! I was just swept away by it.'

'Rest for now,' said Emi. 'You can relax you know.'

Yuuki nodded and gave him a slight smile. Both girls believed him and saw him as an innocent young party in all of this, just someone swept away by the rush to war and promises of power.

Several miles ahead, further up the endless flatland of fields and plains, two riders were tirelessly pressing on for Brimma. The now diminishing sunlight was sparkling against the silver axe of the lead rider and the reflecting light was beginning to annoy Fenris.

'That damn axe,' he snapped. 'Can't see where I'm going!'

Rense laughed. 'Well the sun will soon set my friend,' he said. 'We will be grateful for all the light we can get then.'

'Do you think Ellis will make it to the tower before we do?' asked Fenris.

Rense was slow to respond. 'No idea,' he sniggered. 'Doesn't matter either way. Once we arrive he will be seized for the snake he is.'

'Sylvie will trust us over him,' Fenris commented.

'Ah!' laughed Rense. 'So you finally bring the girl up. I was wondering when that little thought of yours would come up to surface.'

Fenris shook his head whilst Rense started to mockingly sing a love song in his deep, bellowing tone:

'Oh that feeling once more, my heart doth restore! In those distant halls I think only of you my darling...'

'You can't sing you foolish lump,' Fenris reacted. 'Besides, I don't love Sylvie... sure I like her, I like her a lot I guess.'

'Well we will be there soon and you can talk with her all you like... and perhaps more!' Rense chuckled.

'She is an Empress now!' said Fenris. 'It has been a long time since I last saw her. It might not be appropriate for me to even speak with her... let alone flirt.'

Rense wasn't having it. 'She is only a temporary Empress, whatever that really means! You have a chance my young, slim friend.'

Fenris smiled to himself in distant hope that Rense may be proven right. 'Well let's just hope we reach Brimma before Ellis,' he said.

'You worry too much,' said Rense.

CHAPTER VI

THE SNAKE'S VENOM

Everything was dull and silent. All the guards were poised and huddled in disciplined files with civilians long gone from the city's once bustling streets. The perimeter wall to the capital was manned by countless armour clad Tamus troops but only a handful remained around the tower. Sylvie was alone in the throne room at the highest point of the structure. She had been reluctant to actually sit on the mighty chair where Tamus once sat and instead sat on the stone floor with The Sword of Tamus resting beside her. The girl was alone and her thoughts were transfixed on the image of an unstoppable horde getting closer and closer to the bridge leading to the city gate. The mood in Brimma was morose and reserved. There was a sense of impending bloodshed.

The Empress got to her feet and strolled over to the balcony that overlooked the body of Marmia. The sun was setting and light faltering. She could make out the streets of Brimma and the southern lake. Beyond that was darkness.

From beyond the shade of the other side of the bridge a single rider came bounding towards the city gate. Sylvie could spot them from her high vantage point and was eager to know who it could possibly be. It didn't seem to resemble the armoured figure of Elgor and with only one rider present she became intrigued.

Several guards eyed the rider as they reached the sturdy gate. Archers aimed at the figure from the tall wall whilst an officer called out: 'State your business.'

'It is Ellis; advisor to Sylvie, Empress of Marmia,' said the rider. 'Let me enter.'

The lead guard further inspected the thin figure and then recognised them.

'Welcome back sir,' said the guard.

With an order the gate started to rise from the ground with

churning, squeaky momentum. Ellis raced through the gap with head bowed and pressed on up the cobbled streets towards Tamus Tower.

Sylvie had watched him pass under the gate and was now on her way down the stairs of the tower towards the courtyard. She was as radiant and regal as ever but it was clear the girl was in a state. She was under a lot of pressure and the enormity of her role had clearly started to impact her mental condition. She was strong but inexperienced when it came to leading.

Ellis entered into the tower courtyard once identifying himself to the guards scattered around the half standing wall. He dropped from his horse and scrambled towards the tower doors. Sylvie popped out of them and stood waiting as the awkward character reached her.

'Ellis?' she remarked.

'Yes my Empress,' he whispered. 'How are you?'

'I didn't even know you had left Brimma,' said Sylvie. 'I thought you were in mourning. Where did you go? And why?'

The two now found themselves standing under an infinite sheet of stars. The sun had set.

'I didn't want to announce my departure,' said Ellis. 'I felt an urge to go with Elgor and watch his progress.'

'Oh…' Sylvie was intrigued.

Ellis bowed before Sylvie in false allegiance. 'It was foolish of me but I wanted to see Golandin's army for myself,' he said.

'Well… report,' said Sylvie.

She was stressed and didn't question Ellis further over why he had not informed her he was leaving. She did find it rather odd though.

'My Empress, Golandin's army is a vast horde that one cannot accurately place a number on,' said Ellis. 'It is my sad duty to report that Elgor and his men were overwhelmed and defeated outside the gate of Dwenton. I only just managed to get away myself. Sylvie, the rebels have formed up like never before. They number in the many thousands, far outnumbering us!'

Sylvie put her hand to her chin in shock. Her eyes were watering and her voice trembled.

'Is Elgor dead?' she asked.

'Aye, he was killed, along with all his men,' said Ellis.

'Did you spot anyone else on the field?' asked Sylvie.

She was hoping that Jamus and his party may have made contact with the enemy. One of the former friar's monks had reached Brimma earlier that day and informed her of the old man's intentions. Secretly, much of the girl's hope now rested with the old monk; knowing her troops' morale was at an all time low. Ellis smiled to himself, his poison about to truly set.

'Oh my Empress, it be a dark picture I am painting; but I saw with my own eyes that monk and his party of warriors fighting alongside the enemy! I saw him shake hands with the rebels. I saw him talk and laugh with them. I saw him engage our troops and kill them.'

'What?!' Sylvie screamed. 'No! No! You can't have.'

She fell back and leant against the tower wall. Ellis walked forwards and stood directly in front of her. He placed his head beside hers and whispered into her ear.

'Sylvie, I saw it!' he said. 'It was why I left after Elgor, because I sensed I had to see things for myself. I have always trusted anyone you, or the late Tamus, have held dear but I tell you Jamus and his party are no longer our friends! They have joined Golandin. I am so sorry.'

Sylvie took his words in and tears formed in her eyes. She felt anger, despair, sadness, and fear.

'It cannot be,' she protested. 'Jamus has always been so loyal. He was close friends with Hazati.'

'He has betrayed the empire,' said Ellis.

'Who was with him?' Sylvie questioned.

'I know not their names,' said Ellis, 'but they were all in on it.'

'I don't suppose you know if Akumi was with them?' she cried.

'I don't know,' said Ellis. 'There were men and women in his party, a broad collection of snakes.'

Sylvie nodded. She was completely at odds with what to do. The very idea that Akumi, too, could have turned was enough to sicken her. She felt an overwhelming sense of anguish.

'You must give the order to let no one else enter into our city,' said Ellis. 'There are no longer any friends beyond these walls. The gate must not be opened.'

'And how do we defend against this incoming army?' Sylvie was desperate for advice.

'One thing I do know,' Ellis went on: 'They are flanking us from the east. They won't be coming from the south. Golandin knows we will defend the south with the bulk of our forces. I saw with my own eyes his troops moving east and circling around Dwenton. They plan to hit you from the east my Empress.'

'And you are sure of this Ellis?' Sylvie asked.

'I am certain,' said Ellis.

Sylvie had never known what to truly make of the slippery Ellis but now found herself associating him as the one person she could probably trust. She was impressed by the way he had risked his life to report back to her with all this information. She spoke:

'Well in that case I will give the order to let nobody else into our city, Jamus included. I will also place the bulk of our forces along the city's eastern wall where they can overlook the fields.'

Ellis placed his hand on the girl's shoulder.

'A wise move my Empress,' he said.

She looked down to the ground and wiped her tears. She was an emotional wreck and started to break down entirely.

'I can't believe they have betrayed us,' she whimpered.

'They sniffed power,' said Ellis. 'Even the strongest can be corrupted by such a shimmering prospect as rulership of the realm.'

'You are right,' said Sylvie. 'I just never expected it to play out this way.'

Ellis continued to act caringly as Sylvie sobbed beside the tower door. A guard suddenly raced up to them from the court-yard. He was out of breath as if he had jogged a great distance in haste.

'Empress Sylvie,' he announced whilst bowing. 'Two riders have passed over the bridge. They are requesting to speak with you.'

'Who are they?' Sylvie asked.

As the guard opened his lips Ellis' eyes disappeared beneath the clenching skin of his eyelids. He was venomous and eager to snap.

'One calls himself Rense, the other Fenris,' said the panting guardsman.

Sylvie straightened her posture and stepped out into the open ground of the courtyard.

'Fenris...' she whimpered softly. 'It has been so long since...'

'Traitors!' Ellis spat. 'Do not let them enter. Order them to leave and vanish from sight.'

The guard seemed to ignore the gnarling features of Ellis' disgruntled face and continued to look to the blonde girl for orders.

The blue eyed Empress was slow to speak and stared out into the night sky in contemplation. It was obvious the name had sparked deep emotions in the girl. Her mouth was wide open and her heart throbbing.

'He is in on it Ellis?' she was desperate for clarity.

'Aye my Empress,' Ellis smiled. 'They were both fighting alongside the rebels. They are rebels, now acting as spies! You mustn't let them enter.'

Sylvie gulped and turned to face the guard. 'I must confront them,' she said. 'I must know why they have betrayed us! Order the guards to seize them. Place them in the dungeon. I want to speak with them.'

'Yes my Empress,' the guard acknowledged whilst racing off.

Ellis shuffled closer to the girl. He was forced to look up at her now she stood with her spine straight and firm.

'They will deny it,' he protested. 'You won't gain anything from questioning them now.'

'I have to see Fenris,' she said. 'I want to look into his eyes.'

Ellis was at odds with what to say. The rebel traitor knew that there was a danger Sylvie would be swayed by their account over his. He also sensed an obvious emotional reaction from Sylvie every time Fenris was mentioned. This did not bode well for him.

'I will retire if you don't mind Empress,' he said. 'I need to rest.'

'Of course,' the girl replied. 'Get some sleep.'

The guard sprinted down the winding road back towards the gate. It was manned by dozens of fired up soldiers standing on multiple platforms about the sides of the solid entrance.

'Seize those men!' the guard ordered. 'Open the gate and seize them.'

'Hold it tight!' a guard yelled at the riders.

They were still on horseback just outside the gate. Behind them the lake's cold, clear water swayed with great pace under the bridge. The gateway started to rise whilst countless archers aimed for the chests of either rider.

'Don't even think about fleeing,' a guard yelled. 'You will be peppered with arrows.'

'What is going on?' Rense yelled. 'We are friends of Tamus! We are here to see Sylvie.'

'We have important news,' added Fenris. 'It is vital we are allowed to see her.'

There was no more response from the guards. Once the gateway was up several surrounded the riders and ordered them off from their horses. Both complied, knowing not to be foolish enough to resist. Their weapons were snatched and armour plates removed. They were being stripped of all instruments of warfare.

'What is this?' Rense grumbled.

'You are both to be held in custody,' said a guard. 'You will be led to the city dungeon.'

Several guards walked away with Rense's giant axe underarm. It took two of them just to carry it.

'Who has ordered this?' Rense yelled. 'We must see Sylvie!'

'Calm down,' a guard ordered.

Rense was jostled against the stone wall beside the gate and his arms were manacled in irons. As he was led into the city Fenris was grabbed with equal forcefulness and pressed up against the cold stone. He said nothing whilst they locked the chains around his wrists and prodded him to move up the roadside. They both suspected Ellis had something to do with this but at this stage neither had any idea what was really going on.

They were marched up the track and down several alleyways leading deeper into the urban dwellings of Brimma. At every stage of their march the mighty tower was in full view. Amongst the mostly abandoned thatched houses of the city a guard house stood surrounded by waist high stone walls. They were escorted into the building and led down a narrow spiral staircase. It seemed to go on endlessly, with hanging torches of golden fire the only light source. Once at the bottom it was clear they were in a cold, damp dungeon. Tiny cells sneaked up the narrow corridor, with iron bars and dirty stone walls the only things to behold. Rense was first to be led into a room. The iron door cranked open and the warrior, now dressed only in rags of undergarments, was pushed into the tiny cell. The interior consisted of a bucket, mats of straw for bedding, and a single wooden chair. The light was dim but as the cell door was slammed shut almost entirely diminished.

Fenris was put into a cell positioned next door to Rense's. He was led in and abandoned. The door was bolted and vision slit left partially open. Narrow streaks of firelight poured in through the small gaps in the door. Fenris sat down on the straw mat. Chains still locked his arms together behind his back. He closed his eyes and sighed. The two warriors would just have to wait.

Not far from the walls of Brimma another group of riders were gaining ground and making for the city. They had not been travelling half as fast as their allies but were now only miles from the lake. Jamus led the group as the rolling fields morphed into a hilly landscape of bushes and shrubbery.

'Not far now,' the old warrior smiled.

Emi and Yuuki were several paces behind him but heard his sturdy voice over the sounds of hooves hitting the dirt.

'Let's just pray Rense and Fenris got there before Ellis,' said Emi.

'Even if they didn't,' Jamus replied, 'they should have sorted things by now.'

It looked to be going well for the party. Their journey from Dwenton had proved eventless and there was an optimistic sense Ellis had been dealt with by their comrades. It was now a case of forming up as part of Brimma's defences and finally making a firm stand against Golandin.

Jamus was still frustrated and deeply saddened over Aimis' fall. Unlike the girls the wise old man did not see things being as simple as just solely relying on defending the tower. He was in no mood to start smiling with some sense of distant hope. In truth he knew the battle hadn't yet even been fought.

The landscape was now forcing the horses to slow down. They were moving up a hill that, once passed over, would reveal the gleaming lake of Brimma. The night sky shed little light on the bushes being navigated by the riders. They snaked around them and pressed further on. Jamus prodded Theamis as the tired rebel slumped limply behind him.

'We are almost there,' the old man said whilst turning to face him.

Jamus turned back to face the bushes ahead. He then looked down to his pipe resting beside his mount. It was tied to the straps of a bag with tobacco in. With the horse's pace now at a walking speed he could easily fondle with it and light up. He fancied a puff and did just that. His worn fingers started to unstring the pipe but before he was able to untie the twine a silent arrow implanted itself into his right breast. He yelled out in shock and fell back, knocking both himself and Theamis off from the mount and into the undergrowth.

'Jamus!' Lady Yuuki shrieked.

Several figures suddenly emerged from the bushes ahead. They had been well hidden under the cover of darkness.

'Rebels!' Emi screamed. 'All around us!'

Both girls pounced from their horses. Emi clenched her bow and bent low in the grass. Yuuki raised her staff and whispered ancient words whilst racing over to Jamus. He was lying awkwardly amongst thorn bushes and curled himself up in a ball with the pain of his wound. Yuuki noticed Theamis several feet away, jogging off into the darkness of the hillside with arms bound around his back. She bent down and pressed her hands against the old man's wound.

'I must get this arrow out of you,' she said in a panic.

Emi rose up from her hidden position and let loose an arrow. It flew across the darkness and impact was confirmed by a distant yelp. Her trained huntress' eyes and camouflaged green attire were perfect attributes for this encounter. She crawled forwards and fired another arrow. It slammed into the forehead of the enemy archer who had been desperately trying to spot her. A fountain of blood split from his broken skull and he fell into the bushes he'd been cowering behind.

Yuuki snapped the arrow impaled in Jamus' chest and placed the old man in her arms.

'Stay with me,' she cried.

'They must have ridden up with Ellis,' he coughed. 'He must have ordered them to ambush us. Rense and Fenris can't have gone this way. They must have gone around them by chance.'

He suddenly pulled the arrow head from his wound and moaned in agony. Yuuki placed her magical hands on his chest and forehead and closed her eyes. Her staff, already shimmering with white light, started to glow with further radiance as it lay in the grass beside her. She was locked in concentration. Jamus was being soothed by her but there was no miraculous healing.

Emi crawled through the grass and reached them.

'There are only five of them,' she reported. 'I've dealt with two but three are still sneaking around up there.'

Yuuki opened her eyes and stared down at Jamus. He was now in a deep, calm sleep. He was smiling and there were no signs of suffering.

'Bandage him up,' the sorceress said. 'I will deal with them.'

They swapped roles with instant effect. Yuuki grabbed her staff and leapt up into view of the rebels cowering in the bushes further up the hillside. She yelled out and a beam of furious orange light screamed from her staff and lit up the entire area as it glided over to the enemy position. They were lit up and in full view. Yuuki started to walk towards them with staff angled forwards.

The rebels reacted by charging towards her. In a wild rush they ran at her with swords swaying. Yuuki bent low and slid her staff across the air in an arc. It created a semicircle of blue fog around her. It hummed with serene enchantment but as the rebels ran into the haze they fell down dead in an instant. It was a painless yet decisively fatal magical spell. Yuuki raised herself upright and looked down at those she'd claimed. The blue energy vanished and the girl walked back over to Jamus.

Emi was busy applying a provisional bandage to his gushing wound. Yuuki then suddenly remembered Theamis. She ran off in the direction he had slipped away in. She knew he couldn't have got far with his arms still bound.

'Theamis,' she called out.

She raised her staff and a brilliant white light lit up the entirety of the hillside. She instantly spotted him several feet ahead trying to negotiate the thick foliage further along the rising ground.

'Don't move any further,' she ordered.

The girl jogged over to him and lowered her staff. The light vanished as she disengaged from the spell. Theamis was panting heavily and several cuts were apparent around his neck and shoulders from where he'd tried to slip through the thick bushes. The rope was still firmly tied around his arms.

'I'm sorry,' he said. 'I panicked.'

Yuuki was fired up and Theamis could sense her mood. He dropped to his knees beside her and bowed his head in submission. She looked down at him and started to regain her calm.

'It's okay... get up,' she said. 'But don't try and get away from us again. Or else…'

She escorted him back to Emi who had by now fully applied the bandage. Emi gave Theamis a quick fiery eyed glance and then looked to Yuuki.

'Help me get Jamus back on his horse,' she said. 'You can ride with Theamis. I will take Jamus.'

Yuuki nodded and helped Emi lift the old man. He wasn't particularly heavy and the girls managed to get him on the back of the mount with relative ease. Emi leapt on and Yuuki supported their captive as he clambered onto her ride. Once he was on they were off, the extent of the hillside mostly now behind them.

CHAPTER VII

RUINS OF AN ANCIENT PORTICO

The empty bottles of alcoholic beverages were stacking up on the wooden tabletop. They were beginning to gradually fall off one after the other and turn into piles of broken glass. The drunkards surrounding the dwindling supplies of drink weren't interested in conserving the fields they now found themselves in.

Golandin's horde of rebel fighters had steadily pressed on beyond Dwenton and continued moving northwards towards Brimma. Progress hadn't been swift, largely down to continuous pauses for merriment and undisciplined rests; although one thing that could be said about the army was that it certainty complied with Golandin's orders. When he stopped it stopped.

The aging rebel warrior was a mess. He thinning long hair was damp from spillages of beer and other liquids. His face was worn and tired. He stank of alcohol after constant sessions with his men. He sat beside the makeshift bar; a series of old tables that had been carried along and placed in the fields, and sunk in his arms. He was drunk and so were most of those around him. The mood was good, with a sense of victory since leaving the now captured trade town of Dwenton. However, there was anger and sadness over the loss of Torwin and of the countless number of troops lost in combat engaging the mysterious riders. Golandin had been deeply taken aback by the demise of the late Warlord's brother and so had most of those commanding his army. Conversely, to the hordes of troops eager for blood it hardly mattered.

Golandin continued to sit limply whilst those around him roared and sung in a drunken stupor.

'Golandin,' a voice barked. 'Sort yourself out.'

A warrior with thin, scraggly blonde hair crept past the drunkards and sat beside his leader.

'Wake up for goodness sake,' he went on.

Golandin raised his head and with eyes half closed studied the man sitting across from him.

'What is it Arthir?' he asked. 'You suddenly have an issue with drinking?'

Arthir sniggered; relieved his friend wasn't totally paralytic.

'This is getting out of hand,' Arthir said. 'Surely you can see that? Ever since marching out from Dwenton the majority of your army seems to have been swigging a bottle with one hand and holding a sword with the other.'

Golandin smiled in a drunken solace. 'Let them be,' he said. 'We have made good ground and have much to celebrate.'

'Celebrate!' Arthir laughed. 'So far we have observed the bulk of our cavalry get wiped out, seen Torwin fall, and lost what appeared to be hundreds of men just to see those riders get away!'

Golandin sat up and brushed his forehead. He seemed to acknowledge his old friend's concerns without responding orally.

'We have had some setbacks,' Golandin said, 'but once we reach Brimma we will hit them with the largest rebel army ever formed. We shall smash their walls and take Tamus Tower!'

Arthir looked around them as his friend spoke. All he saw was drunk, undisciplined men carrying weaponry they could ill advisedly use. Most were too old or unfit to run more than a few yards and some were so elderly it seemed pointless having them around. This wasn't an army; it was a rabble.

'We are relying solely on quantity,' he said. 'Doesn't that worry you? After seeing those battles earlier I really just don't know whether to be hopeful or not.'

Golandin leaned forwards and patted his friend on his chest plate.

'My friend, you are forgetting something,' he said. 'Ellis.'

Arthir didn't seem convinced. 'We don't even know if he made it back to Brimma,' he fretted, 'and besides, even if he did, what use is he... really?'

Golandin was swift to respond: 'Well we know he made it since we didn't find his body anywhere. He has reached Brimma, I can sense it. He will spread lies regarding our battle plans. He will convince Sylvie of all sorts of things.'

Arthir put his head in his hands and stared at the rough surface of the table.

'No my friend, it is you who needs to take advice,' smiled Golandin. 'We are on course to finally taking over these lands once and for all. We have defeated Elgor and his men, taken Dwenton, and sent chills up the backsides of all those that managed to flee. Sure we lost men but we gained ground Arthir. We gained ground.'

Arthir nodded slowly and started to inspect an empty bottle with distant melancholy.

'I am relieved you remain so confident,' he said. 'And yes, you certainly have put things in a different picture to the one I was seeing.'

Golandin stumbled up from the bench around the table and wobbled slightly as his feet hit the ground.

'That's the Arthir I know,' he beamed. 'I'll tell you what... once we reach within a few miles of Brimma I will give the order: no more drinking!'

With that he walked away into the frenzied crowds of drunkards and vanished into the darkness of the night, likely heading for one of the several large tents erected for this night cap. Arthir continued to ponder with his thoughts whilst stroking the glass tip of the ale bottle in front of him.

'Oh do keep up child!' grumbled Arifor. 'There is nothing to be poised about around here.'

The old, mysterious shaman was marching through the dying woodland like he was on a mission. Akumi kept several feet back, intentionally maintaining a slower pace in attentiveness and focus.

''Tis been a long time since I ventured this deeply into these decaying parts,' Arifor said. 'But fear not! We are close now. Real close.'

They had been moving westwards through the drab woods for what seemed like an age. The clearing where they'd stumbled across the demonic portal of energy was distant and lost under endless tall tress and bare winding branches.

Since leaving that spot nothing of any note had occurred. The woodland continued without much variety. They had bypassed the great lake near where they had come across the dark portal and continued on through the woods.

Akumi had started to feel more at ease with the strange old

man. He had told her of his past and why he hated the rebels. He had also explained all he knew regarding Jamus and his band of warriors trying to fend off Golandin. The information had somewhat relieved the girl and she felt more focused now she knew there were so many out there fighting for the same cause. In a strange way Arifor reminded the girl of her late master, Hazati. He was wise and clearly experienced with the ways of Marmia. She sensed he possessed great power and trusted he was truly leading him to Endal.

'Aha!' Arifor nodded to himself. 'Yes, yes this is it. We are very close now. The woodland is about to cease. We will enter into swampland.'

Akumi was already covered in dry mud and grass stains. She didn't care about the prospect of getting wet.

'And the entrance... it is close by?' she was unsure.

'It is within the swamps,' said Arifor. 'We have reached it.'

The assassin was so focused and alert she only partially took in the old man's words. All she knew was that she was now beginning to sense Endal was near. It was a feeling she had not felt since creeping up on him all that time ago with Jobe and Harkor by her side.

Arifor was first to poke his leg into the knee deep waters of the swamp. The trees halted as if ordered to by some divine creator and gave way for a marsh-like quagmire. The water was muddy and thick with dirt and dead leaves. The only noise came with the sounds of frogs croaking and flies buzzing around the water's surface, portending nature's presence in this grim place.

The old man trudged on through the water with his makeshift walking stick raised above the surface. Akumi studied the swamp and cautiously dipped her feet into the liquid. It was cold and movement was tough as she pushed her legs onwards. Above them the starry night sky shone freckled speckles of light down into the swamp. The moon was partially covered by clouds but shed enough light down as to be reflected in the rippling waters.

'Ah yes,' confirmed Arifor. 'The old portico is near. Oh, how an age has passed since I last saw this sight!'

After several minutes of swaying through the drink Arifor clambered onto an island of land that appeared to form a natural pathway. He eyed ahead and started to walk along the extent of the thin breadth of land. Akumi followed, carefully watching her step as she tackled the muddy terrain.

'The entrance is over there,' Arifor announced. 'Behold those ancient stone columns.'

Akumi stared ahead and spotted what seemed like pillars standing amongst marshland. It looked like a mini ruins, with stone slabs scattered all over the immediate ground. The two pillars were the only features left standing.

'There was once a building covering the entrance to the underground chamber,' said Arifor, 'but it is now only ruins. The doorway is just ahead.'

They walked on and reached the stone structures. They were featureless and chalky. Arifor nudged in between them and paused with eyes facing what looked like a wooden trapdoor. Akumi's eyes lit up as she inspected the entrance. An extent of ground had been dug like a natural slope falling into the wooden doors. They were reinforced with rusty iron bolts.

'I have never entered through those doors,' said Arifor, 'but I am aware they reveal a stairway. It leads you down into the deep! Spooky!' He started to laugh out loud.

Akumi was too transfixed to acknowledge him and knelt down beside the doorway. It was essentially a large trapdoor digging into the ground diagonally. The girl was puzzled by the handle and fiddled with the round iron ring that hung from the lock.

'Twist it and pull,' Arifor suggested.

Akumi struggled and placed her feet against one door as leverage to pull the other one outwards. It worked and the entrance squeaked open, revealing only a void of blackness.

'I have no torch,' Akumi noted scornfully.

'You will just have to feel your way down,' Arifor smirked.

'And what will you do?' she asked, the thought suddenly dawning on her.

'Oh, I will leave you to it,' he said. 'I won't face Endal. It is said he is the avatar of some vengeful God.'

Akumi shook her head. 'No!' she insisted. 'He is no such thing, I know it. I have faced Endal before. He is exceptionally skilled but only human.'

'If you insist,' said Arifor dryly.

The old man suddenly walked away from the entrance and passed beyond the old pillars back towards the swamp. Akumi was about to call out to him but quickly realised there was little point. She was on her own again.

The girl dropped into the void and poked around as her feet made contact with a stone step. Slowly, she got her bearings, realising she was standing on a series of steep steps leading down into the unknown. The walls were of stone and arced over her head with enough space for her to stand up straight. With katana poised she crept downwards. It was deathly silent and the thick air was warm and putrid. There was a smell of dampness and rot about the place and even an unearthly sense to the darkness.

For several minutes Akumi continued cautiously clambering down with astute senses plucked. Her night vision had by now kicked in but it made little difference. However, the girl was beginning to make out a faint light source further down the stairway. Eventually, she could make out an orange tint to it and the closer she got the more confident she was in identifying it as a fire burning on a torch pinned to the stone wall. The torch lit up the final segment of the stairway and represented the point of the final step. From there a tunnel led off into further darkness. Akumi grabbed the torch from its perch and held it ahead of her as she started to walk along the horizontal channel.

There were doors to either side of the passageway and distinct signs of inhabitation. Pictures hung from the stone walls and to one side were several crates. The tunnel ended with a turning that went in either direction. The space widened out and became more domesticated, with red rugs on the cold ground and further torches lighting up the interior. Akumi was now feeling a sense of being in someone else's domain.

The girl crept silently into the wider passageway and decided on a whim to turn left. She moved down the narrow space; her wet, mud stained boots dripping onto the soft regal rug, and started to shiver with apprehension and adrenaline. Her legs were soaking wet up to the knee and with every step the girl took her leather footwear squeaked with movement. Her katana was clasped in both hands and her eyes as wide as the full moon gleaming down on the outside world above.

Akumi noticed several steps leading down into what looked to be a large expanse. It was cooler as she entered into the wide chasm. The space was a vast square, like some royal hall hidden beneath the earth. Pillars split around the edges of the top level she stood on and snaked around the entirety of the floor. The assassin shuffled to the edge of the platform and looked down over the waist high wall. Below was an altar surrounded by raging torches. Several wooden benches were positioned against the walls and a mosaic patterned stone floor was partially lit up by the bristling flames. The artwork revealed dark, incomprehensible figures flying around in a mass orgy of chaos. Akumi could make out the imagery of people being burnt and cut by the flames coming from the dark creatures' palms. The mosaic was sinister and the girl felt an evil energy about it. She looked away and spotted to the far end of the floor she stood on a spiral staircase leading down to the altar. She started to head for it, all the time sensing a presence. She knew she was close.

Beyond the underground complex Arifor wrestled through the swamp from whence they came. The old man was heading back in the direction of the distant mountain range leading back into Marmia. He had no interest in assisting Akumi and didn't believe she had a chance against Endal. He was now simply eager to get back into the fight against Golandin. He was bitter and frustrated over the fact he had so far to now travel. He grumbled to himself as he kicked through the dirty water.

As he dug his stick into the mud for support a screeching howl rung out from high above him. He looked up but could only see the slightly overcast night sky. The old man was not spooked and continued moving through the swamp. There was another loud screech followed by dour lamenting. It was as if a pack of wolves were watching him in protest from within the darkness. The old man raised his arms out and clenched his fists. He'd spotted movement ahead. Silhouettes scrambled around on all sides of him. They were in the swamp and closing in.

'Be gone vile creatures!' he yelled.

He suddenly spotted an entity emerge from the waters ahead. It was a wolflike figure, with fangs and glowing red eyes. It crawled on all fours with dark fur protruding from its body and mane. Arifor studied it and then noticed countless others appearing from all sides. He looked up and marvelled at winged creatures hovering above in circled flight. He was surrounded.

'Come no closer!' he commanded.

The old man was not intimidated although he immediately knew these creatures were somehow linked to the dark portal.

They were the entities entering through the magical gateway. Arifor could tell these beings were attracted to him. He possessed great magical powers that were intrinsically linked to the dark energy that fuelled these creatures. In some ways he was one of them. A voice abruptly pounded the old man's eardrums:

'Come… join us,' it groaned.

Arifor ignored the invitation and yelled out some magical command. Light emitted from his palms and blazes of purple energy assaulted the wolf beings. Some were instantly charred by the spell, yelping in agony and dropping into the waters in a smoky heap. Others leapt high into the air and avoided his strike.

Arifor took several steps back and cast another devastating spell. Spinning black, bladelike bolts of magical matter flew from his glowing hands. They hummed with menacing pitch before striking several of the dark beings. One was hit whilst leaping in mid-air and flew back like a lifeless rag doll.

The hovering, gargoyle-like creatures suddenly started to swoop down and bombard Arifor with sweeping strikes. He bent down to avoid their razor claws before casting a shield around him. It glistened with brilliant red light but remained transparent like some thin sheet of flaccid glass. Arifor started to laugh out loud like he was enjoying the confrontation.

'You will bow down to me vile wretches of the night!' he bell-owed.

The possessed wolves and flying figures seemed to multiply in number as more and more appeared from the darkness of the swamplands. They didn't approach Arifor and several sat beside his shield, howling up at the night sky. Although unscathed Arifor was tiring, knowing he'd drained himself casting such powerful spells. He then noticed a mass of spiralling dark clouds heading straight for him from beyond the swamp. It was as if the very portal itself was on the move, destined to pause over his head. He started to chant whilst eying the wolves that continued to howl.

With intense speed the mass of electric magical clouds shot across the landscape and halted above the old man high overhead. He looked up at its infinite vastness. It was a light show and as his tired eyes stared into its expanse he felt a surge of energy pass through him. His arms drooped down to his sides and his magical shield puffed into nonexistence. He dropped down into the waters, only his torso staying above the liquid. His eyes closed tight and his head rose.

The beings around him did not attack. They watched and sung in a choir of gross cries. Arifor could feel a rush of power enter into him. He couldn't resist it. Eventually, he opened his eyes. The pupils were blood red and his skin was paler than before. He glowed in neon tones of green and slowly got back to his feet. In an instant the transfer ceased. The dark cloud had subdued him. He had been overcome by the shadowy mass of energies. Arifor was lost.

The old man started to walk through the swamp. He was unchallenged by the beings around him. He was now truly one of them. They dared not get close to the powerful mage and kept back, some fading away into the darkness. The cloud mass started to move away. Arifor was heading back towards the doorway into the underground lair.

CHAPTER VIII

TOGETHER AGAIN

The warrior's eyes opened to the sound of footsteps beyond the cell door. Fenris got up from the straw mats he had been resting on and walked nearer to the iron vision slit. He was desperate to see somebody, anybody.

In the dungeon passage two guards were escorting their Empress to the prisoners. She was in between them, an expression of devout duty formed on her radiant face.

'The big one is in ere',' said a guard beside her. 'The other one, small chap, is in the next cell.'

Sylvie nodded whilst studying the cell door.

'I will see the smaller one,' she said, knowing it to be Fenris. 'I only need to speak with one of them. They will both have the same story to tell.'

'Yes Empress,' said the guard. 'Shall we go in with you?'

'No,' Sylvie replied. 'I can take care of this by myself; and besides, they are still in chains.'

Her regal sword was sheathed by her waist belt and its tip almost scrapped across the stone ground. The guard fondled with the iron lock to Fenris' cell and pushed open the sturdy door. Sylvie stared into the widening gap only to instantly spot her captive standing right beside the door.

'Get back!' snapped a guard.

'It's okay,' said Sylvie.

She walked into the cell and stood directly beside Fenris.

'Close the door,' she ordered. 'I will knock when we are done.'

The guards complied and slammed the iron door back shut leaving the two alone in the dingy room. Sylvie walked over to the chair in the far corner and then started to pace up and down whilst Fenris stood silently. His eyes were wide open and his mouth almost dribbling with awe.

'You are...' he paused nervously. 'You are more beautiful than even I remembered.'

Sylvie blushed ever so slightly and stared into the blue eyes of her prisoner.

'You are all grown up,' she smiled.

Fenris walked closer to her, his arms chained behind his back.

'Sylvie, you must listen to me,' he said. 'Ellis... he is a...' His voice was interrupted.

'He is a good man,' Sylvie insisted, 'and has told me all I need to know.'

The blonde girl brushed her swaying hair over her forehead and continued before Fenris could react:

'What happened to you? What happened to all of you? How could you do it?'

Fenris shook his head. 'We are no different,' he said. 'What has Ellis said?'

'You have betrayed the empire we fought so hard for!' Sylvie frowned. 'How could you?'

'Wait, hold on!' Fenris snapped. 'We have done no such thing Sylvie!'

A part of Sylvie wanted to hug the man she saw before her. They were old friends and had been close for many years before her role had taken over her life and he had left for other lands. There had always been an underlying tone of sexual interest between them but neither had ever acted on it. With the years that had now gone by since they last met it was clear the very presence of either was having an impact on the other.

'Ellis saw it all,' the girl sighed. 'No doubt you came here hoping to infiltrate our city!'

'Please Sylvie, listen to me,' Fenris appealed. 'We have been engaging the rebels ever since encountering them south of Dwenton. I have fought with everything I have against them time and time again. Good men have already fallen. Whatever Ellis has said it is a lie. It is a contemptible lie.'

Sylvie was teary eyed at this point, her emotions dancing in chaotic turmoil. She continued to pace up and down. She could sense sincerity in Fenris' voice and already her stout mental pious was faltering.

'So you deny Jamus has joined Golandin?' she asked.

'What?!' Fenris yelled. 'I am shocked you could even believe it. Jamus has already lost a close friend battling the enemy. His allegiance is beyond question.'

Sylvie broke down. It was due to a mixture of stress and guilt. Somehow she just knew Ellis had fooled her. She hadn't listened to her intuition.

'I know,' she sobbed. 'I am so sorry Fenris.'

Suddenly, the girl walked over to her old friend and wrapped her arms around him.

'Ellis is trying to deceive you,' said Fenris. 'He is a snake, a sick and twisted traitor.'

'You know this to be the case?' Sylvie asked.

'He is in with Golandin,' he said. 'We saw him riding out from the rebel camp. We even engaged him at one point but he got away. Elgor died going after him.'

Sylvie slowly stepped back from Fenris and wiped her eyes.

'Elgor is dead?' she was deeply saddened by the news. 'And his men?'

'All those he commanded fell,' said Fenris dryly. 'They were surrounded by the rebel horde! They defeated the enemy cavalry but were overrun. Elgor got away only to die trying to catch Ellis.'

Sylvie was silent for a few moments. The Empress was overcome by her sense of heartfelt loss. Elgor had been so loyal, and his men so steadfast in their duty. There was nothing she could say. She just lowered her head and started to dwell on what Ellis had instructed her to do.

'He convinced me to move the bulk of our defences to the eastern wall,' she recollected. 'He told me they were planning on striking from the east.'

'There is no reason to suspect that,' said Fenris. 'Golandin's force is not so much an army as it is a mass horde. He has no such strategy. The chances are he will hit the front gate from the south in one crazy charge.'

Sylvie nodded. 'I will give the command to immediately place everyone back on the southern wall,' she said.

Sylvie suddenly raced to the cell door and knocked three times. The guards outside were quick to unlock the door and churn it open.

'Everything okay?' one asked.

'These men are to be freed,' she ordered. 'Unchain them and hand back their belongings.'

The two guards entered the cell and tackled the chains binding Fenris' wrists.

'We will have to catch up properly soon,' Sylvie smiled as Fenris was freed.

'I would like that very much, Empress,' he smiled back.

Sylvie was clearly touched by his words and eyed him with flirtatious intensity. She then abruptly raced into the passage.

'Guards, you must seize Ellis,' she ordered. 'I am making for the gate.'

The girl ran off whilst the guards entered Rense's cell. Fenris followed them, partly desiring to follow Sylvie but knowing he needed to wait for Rense to be freed.

'You are free,' said a guard as they moved into Rense's cell.

The warrior got up from the floor and patiently waited as they unchained him. Fenris entered into the cell and smiled at his friend.

'I heard the whole thing,' laughed Rense. 'These dungeon walls... pretty thin.'

Fenris nodded; relieved he didn't have to explain anything.

'We better get after that girl of yours,' Rense sniggered.

'The Empress you mean?' smiled Fenris.

'Yeah, her,' said Rense.

The guards raced off and left the two warriors to themselves. They walked out into the passage, instantly spotting their armour and weapons placed in a pile by the door to the staircase.

To the south of Brimma two riders had passed over the hill beyond the lake. They raced down the descending ground with flawless grace. They passed a sewer entrance sticking out from the bush land and grassy soil. It had once been used by Endal; the iron bars still partially bent and broken. The horses reached the bottom of the hill in little time and moved along the path leading to the bridge that led to the walls of the capital city.

The bridge was rocking ever so slightly as the gushing waters of the lake bombarded it. The winds were picking up and sending the rippling water under the bridge forth in mini waves. The riders passed over the crossing and halted beside the gateway into the city. Lady Yuuki was first to stop. Her horse's breath steamed up into the dark atmosphere of the night. Emi was close behind with Jamus resting limply about her back.

'Raise the gate,' Yuuki called out. 'We have an injured man with us, and a rebel prisoner.'

The guards manning the gate didn't initially respond. Yuuki noticed archers poised and aiming at her and Emi. She was cautious and gripped her staff, unsure of what to think.

'No one is to enter Brimma,' a guard yelled. 'Be gone.'

Emi came in: 'We must enter; we are friends of the empire.'

'We cannot raise the gate,' said a guard.

Emi looked to Yuuki in confusion. Neither had expected this odd reception.

To the other side of the wall Sylvie came racing down the street and stopped beside the gate. Behind her some paces away Rense and Fenris were sprinting to catch up.

'Order everyone on the eastern wall to reform on the southern section,' Sylvie commanded, 'and gather a party to seize Ellis. He is likely in the tower.'

An officer acknowledged her orders and raced off to comply with the command. Several guards manning the platform overlooking the bridge then turned to face the Empress.

'We have more riders requesting entrance,' a guard yelled. 'Shall we detain them?'

'No!' Sylvie reacted sharply. 'Who are they?'

The guard turned and looked down at them as they pondered outside the gateway.

'Identify yourselves,' the guard ordered.

'I am Lady Yuuki and this is Emi,' said the sorceress. 'We are with Jamus of the Grange Abbey and have a rebel prisoner.'

'Jamus!' Sylvie jumped. 'Let them in. They are friends.'

The guards complied and the gate rose with great pace as the cogs that drove it churned in motion. The riders raced through the gap and halted beside Sylvie.

'I am sorry for that,' she said. 'There has been some confusion.'

The girls got off from their horses and walked over to Sylvie. They had only fleetingly met the girl once before but knew well of her and her role as leader of the empire. Sylvie also knew of them and had heard their well-regarded names mentioned countless times in the past.

'Welcome to Brimma,' Sylvie smiled.

'Thank you,' said Yuuki. 'We are so pleased to finally properly meet you.'

Both girls bowed as Sylvie blushed. She giggled as they raised their heads.

'It's okay,' she said humbly. 'No need for that.'

Sylvie's attention then turned to Jamus. They hadn't seen each other in an age but she was deeply fond of him, the memories of Hazati still painfully with her.

'Is he okay?' she asked whilst inspecting his body.

'He needs medical assistance,' said Emi. 'We did all we could but his wound is quite deep.'

'Guards, aid this man,' Sylvie called out.

Several came forth and carefully carried him off from the horse. He was still asleep.

'And who is this?' Sylvie asked as she stared up at the figure on Yuuki's horse.

'Theamis,' said Yuuki. 'A rebel we captured in Dwenton.'

'He gave himself up,' said Emi. 'He is also wounded but it isn't serious.'

Sylvie looked into his eyes as he sat on the horse. She could tell he was nervous and noticed how he avoided eye contact.

'Don't worry,' she said to him. 'You will be treated well.'

Fenris and Rense finally reached the group from the bending road leading off into the urban sprawl ahead.

'Together again,' Rense joked as he looked to the girls.

'Jamus?' Fenris was alarmed.

'He is alive,' said Yuuki, 'but he is in no state to fight. He needs rest.'

As she spoke the guards placed him on a stretcher and started to carry him away towards aid.

'They will do all they can for him,' said Sylvie.

As Jamus was carried away the Empress gazed at the party that had now formed. Theamis had been supported by Emi and Yuuki as he got off the horse and was clasped by a guard, eager to lead him off into the dungeon.

'Treat him well,' said Sylvie.

She looked to Theamis. 'You will be kept in our prison for the time being. I will speak with you later.'

Theamis bowed and was escorted away up the street. The group of warriors then stood beside Sylvie, awaiting further words from the Empress. She was so relieved there had been no betrayal on the part of Jamus and his party and now felt confidence coming back to her. With people like these beside her there was no reason to be afraid of what was to come.

'I guess it is time to prepare for the final showdown then,' she said. 'I have ordered all my forces to gather around this southern wall. I ask that you all man it alongside my men.'

The party nodded in acknowledgement and studied the stone barrier defending the city. Due to the lake the only means for any advancing army to enter into the city from the south was the bridge.

'We must create a bottleneck,' said Rense. 'They will storm up that bridge in force. If we focus all our archers on that one spot it will surely be hell for them.'

'Why not just blow up the bridge now?' Emi suggested. 'Then they will have no means to pass the lake.'

The lake was positioned around the south and west of Brimma. It was essentially a moat keeping the vast city secure from any attacking army coming from those directions.

'We have no means to destroy the bridge,' said Sylvie. 'Trust me, we have already considered it. The problem is it is too large and strong to simply destroy.'

The bridge was a well built structure; wide and reinforced with stone foundations slipping deeply into the waters.

'There is no point even considering it,' said Fenris. 'Besides, if it were destroyed they'd flank from the east and still reach the gateway.'

'Yes, that is also why we decided against attempting it,' said Sylvie.

Yuuki studied the area around the gate. She had limited knowledge of battlefield strategy but was beginning to form an idea. She spoke:

'If we were to dowse the bridge with something flammable and then light it we would form a barrier at least, and still not destroy the bridge.'

'Light it up and watch 'em squeal!' laughed Rense.

'Light it before they enter onto it!' Yuuki qualified ethically.

'That is a good idea,' said Sylvie. 'It would hopefully deter them at the least, and terrify them at the most.'

The group started to stroll towards the gate. It was time to forge firm battle plans and inspect the ground they would soon have to defend with all their might. In the air there was an undeniable sense of the inevitability of a great standoff to come. The battle for Marmia was nigh.

THE PASSING OF THE CLOUD

BEING THE THIRD PART

OF

The Dawn of Tamus Tower

BOOK FIVE

CHAPTER I

DESCENDING THE ABYSS

There was no denying a presence could be felt. Although there had as of yet been no signs of life there remained an indubitable impression that something was lurking. Akumi didn't let this trouble her as she moved down the spiralling iron stairs. Once at the bottom she didn't hesitate and walked over to the intimidating altar. It was dusty and exuded an ancient air of age.

Apart from the altar and alluring mosaic patterns on the stone ground the hall was drab and bare. Countless torches burned in the far corners, suggesting someone was present as otherwise they'd have burnt out long ago. As Akumi pondered with this thought and continued to eye every angle her heart suddenly missed a beat. Her brown eyes widened and her lips dropped in shock. Further down the hall where she now stood, amongst the darkness of the far end, it was clear; a figure was standing gazing at her in motionless silence. The girl studied the outline. They were only a vague shape in amongst dark tones.

'Who is there?' she cried out.

The girl's katana wobbled as her nervous hands twitched in anticipation. The figure started to walk forwards towards her. Their footsteps were loud against the stone mosaic. After a few seconds Akumi was certain. The figure was that of Endal.

The black robed figure emerged from the darkness and stopped just inside the torch light. Akumi had by now got rid of her torch but those around them were enough to illuminate the area. The figure was dressed as always; the robe hiding his body and a drooping hood covering his head.

'Akumi,' said the voice.

'Endal…' Akumi shivered. 'It is isn't it?'

'It is indeed,' the assassin whispered calmly.

Akumi felt both relief at finally finding herself in front of her target and a deep dread. For some reason in this dark lair she found herself more frightened of Endal than at any other point in the past.

'I knew you would come Akumi,' Endal said dryly. 'I have been waiting.'

There were all sorts of things Akumi wanted to say and ask the notorious assassin. She wanted to curse his every bone and spit venom in his direction. She wanted to question every aspect of his being. She wanted to know how he felt knowing he was responsible for all that was now playing out in Marmia. However, her lips didn't open. It was as if she knew Endal was anticipating her every question and move.

'You fought well in Brimma,' hinted Endal. 'I was impressed.'

Akumi could now make out the face of her enemy. His black hair poured out from beneath his hood and his dark, menacing eyes captivated her as they faced off.

'I must confront you Endal,' said Akumi.

Endal said nothing and suddenly revealed his sword from within his robe.

'Do as you will,' he said. 'That is the law.'

Akumi focused herself and raised her katana. This was it. The moment was here. It was time to face Endal.

The female assassin edged into the lit section of the hall as Endal stood perfectly still. She knew there was no room for mistakes. She would have to fight with all her strength to even stand a chance against her opponent. As she eyed his sword the distinct sound of laughter echoed out from above.

'This will prove entertaining,' a figure mocked from the higher level of the hall.

Akumi looked to Endal who seemed indifferent to the voice as if it were no surprise.

'Who is that?' she called.

It became clear soon enough. The head of an old man peered over the wall and looked down at them. Their eyes glowed red and an aura of energy lit up the space around them with buzzing vibrancy.

'Arifor!' Akumi was puzzled.

'Not anymore my child,' the figure mocked.

There was further laughter as the old man crept along the floor towards the spiral stairs.

'Being followed by the dark forces I see,' commented Endal.

He didn't appear alarmed by the presence of the old mage. The truth was they were both now on the same side. Akumi looked back to the possessed Arifor whilst keeping her attention constantly drawn to Endal. This was not good. It was clear the old man had been overcome by the dark energies encircling this place. She didn't need further confirmation.

Endal suddenly vanished back into the darkness. Akumi gulped and was about to race after him but knew Arifor couldn't be ignored. She turned to face the old man as he reached the lower level of the hall from the stairway.

'What has happened to you?' she asked uneasily.

'I have been born,' the old man's croaky voice said.

He didn't even sound like the grumpy character that had led her to this sinister setting. There was no life about him. It was as if he was entirely gone, just a shell consumed by darkness.

'Stay back!' Akumi yelled.

The figure glided towards her. He was hovering several inches from the ground. His hands had begun to glow and his arms rose up. Akumi pounced to one side as a bolt of deathly white light bounded out from the old man's palms. It smashed into the stone floor and exploded with immense force. Dust erupted from every old fissure of the hall. Clouds of puffy smoke formed and debris shattered against the walls. The whole space seemed to shake with the magical blast.

Akumi cowered behind a wooden bench across from the altar. Arifor was closing in on her with his arms still outstretched. There was nothing for it. The girl leapt up and ran into the darkness in the direction Endal had disappeared. She had no idea where it led but knew it would be folly to stay within the old man's view.

The girl carefully moved through the darker side of the hall. It didn't take long for her to reach the end. Several doors led off into new sections. She had no way of telling what way was best for her and so randomly opened a door to her left. It revealed a passage leading off to further doorways. Torches lit the area brightly and kept it warm.

'Where are you going?' the old man laughed in the distance.

He was catching up with her, only feet from the entrance to the passageway. Akumi moved down the hallway and tested each door as she passed it. Most were locked but suddenly she stumbled across one that was half open. She slipped in through the gap, hoping to lose her pursuer.

She found herself in a small room. Several dusty chests were piled up in the far corner and empty shelves rested on timber frames. Akumi could tell Arifor was now creeping up the passage towards her position. She hoped he hadn't seen her enter into the room and hid behind the door, leaving a tiny gap in between the doorframe so as to spot her enemy passing. She peeped out into the passage. Within moments the humming of the energy surrounding Arifor became almost deafening. She then spotted his glowing red eyes edging up the space. She held her blade tight, its tip poking slightly out into the gap of the doorway.

The possessed old man glided up the passageway entirely oblivious to Akumi as he passed the door by. Whatever force was controlling him it had turned him into an autonomous simpleton, blinded by power and lacking the astute eye of a free being. Akumi knew she had to deal with the threat Arifor now posed. She couldn't ignore his power and took advantage of her window of opportunity. As he passed the door she pulled it wide open and popped out behind the glowing figure of Arifor. She sliced her katana across the back of his neck and stepped away. The blade had passed straight through the energy surrounding him and hacked through his skin.

Arifor paused and suddenly his hovering feet hit the stone floor. His head bent forwards and then fell from his shoulders as the movement further ripped his flesh. The deep cut had spliced through bone and throat alike. In a gushing rush of blood Arifor's body dropped to the knees and then fell forwards atop the decapitated head. The magical aura vanished in a flash and his red eyes cooled into lifeless black voids.

Akumi shuffled closer to the body. A pool of blood was building up around the broken corpse. Arifor was no longer a threat. The assassin felt sickened by the fact she'd been forced to do this. She hadn't really had a choice but that didn't seem to make a difference to how she felt. Before she could dwell any more on it she looked up and glanced further down the passage. Endal was watching her.

'A flawless kill,' he commented. 'However, Arifor was already dead.'

This was the reality. Nevertheless, Akumi was puzzled as to

how he knew the identity of the possessed man.

'How did you know it was Arifor?' she asked.

'I recognised the old man,' said Endal. 'We've had encounters in the distant past.'

With those words Endal raised his deathly blade. It shone with a golden tint in the torchlight of the corridor.

Akumi knew this was truly the moment. They were now about to face off. She jumped over Arifor's bloody corpse and got into a side on stance.

The two assassins gazed at one another. Only feet now separated them and their blades almost touched. The passageway was narrow, with little space for swordplay. It was a testing environment for the skilled adversaries. Akumi could tell Endal was waiting for her to strike and didn't disappoint. With one final deep breath of focusing concentration the girl moved in and struck.

Her katana swooped into Endal's blade. The sound of steel clashing echoed down the entirety of the passage. Endal responded by poking his steel out at the young girl before him. She deflected the stabbing motion and swung at his midriff.

Endal blocked her strike with katana pressing against katana. Suddenly, the clash then erupted into a rush of swordplay. Akumi attacked with great speed, forcing Endal to step back as he deflected her strikes. Endal then turned the tables and countered with equally swift attacks. One strike forced Akumi to bend her legs and block with sword outstretched across her width. She then attempted to strike Endal's legs from under him but he stepped back, narrowly avoiding her steel.

The dark assassin watched as Akumi got back to her feet and pressed towards him. He lashed out, hoping to stab her torso, but the girl rolled with his strike as if using his outstretched sword arm to support herself as she spun forwards with katana held high. Her blade came down as she clasped Endal's sword arm firmly. Endal dropped to his knees, desperate to avoid the razor edge. It made contact with his right breast and cut down his upper torso. He pulled with great strength and managed to release his arm from Akumi's grip. He then stumbled and fell onto the ground beneath him. His katana remained in his arm and he rolled backwards, finding himself resting against the wall at the end of the passage. Akumi had managed to seriously open up on him and he felt ever so shocked over how suddenly the girl had got the better of him.

Akumi didn't falter and drove her blade down at Endal in an effort to stab him where he sat. He deflected her blade with his own and clambered to his feet. His hood had fallen from his head and now drooped over his back. Akumi noted his facial features with newly available clarity. His long black hair and stubble were as she remembered but his eyes seemed different. It was as if they were voids of black. She distinctly remembered them being blue the last time she'd studied him up close. His skin also appeared far paler.

Just as Akumi was preparing for a new wave of swordplay Endal suddenly stepped back and disappeared behind a door beside the end of the passage. It slammed shut but Akumi kicked it back open and stormed through it. To her amazement she found herself staring out at a vast series of platforms descending further into a dark hole below. It looked like an army had once mined this entire place; turning the orderless underground into a network of manmade levels leading deeper down. Somehow light was entering into this vast expanse from high above. The moonlight was penetrating the roof of the structure and came in infinitely straight rays, leading directly down.

Endal had leapt from the level the door led out onto and hit the next platform. His dark figure was racing off towards a cavernous entrance entering into the earth. Akumi jumped down and rolled forwards across the wooden flooring below her. She then raced after him. Endal suddenly paused just outside the cave's natural entrance and turned with katana at the ready. They clashed as soon as Akumi had closed in.

The two assassins were in a dance. The colossal speed in which either struck out at the other was almost too fast for the eye. After fending off several strikes from Akumi, Endal jumped into the air and jabbed out with katana straight. Akumi hadn't expected such a grand manoeuvre and desperately tried turn her body to avoid his blade. It proved too swift a move and Endal's katana prodded into her left shoulder like a javelin penetrating a mound of earth. The girl stumbled back and put her hand to the fresh wound. It was deep and stung with movement. To her relief she was still able to raise her left arm and defiantly got back in a stance as Endal looked on. If it hadn't been for the speed in which Akumi had been able to partially avoid the devastating strike he'd have now been looking down at a body.

'Impressive,' the dark assassin remarked.

Akumi was too focused to say a word. All she could think of was killing Endal. It was becoming a blind yearning, burning deep within her.

Endal didn't seem too concerned over his chest wound although blood was now appearing on his robe and dripping down from his waist onto the wooden boards supporting them.

They circled one another, the infinite fall into blackness only feet away from either of them as they pranced up and down the timber platform. Akumi went for it and struck out with all her might. Endal knocked her katana to one side with such force that the girl partially lost her balance and stumbled forwards. He nudged down and slammed his right elbow into her lower back as she passed him. This caused her to stumble further and collapse onto the floorboards. She lost grip of her blade and rolled to one side to seize it. Endal then stepped away and vanished into the cave entrance behind them. It was becoming clear he was trying to lead her somewhere.

With this moment to catch her breath Akumi started desperately attending to her painful shoulder wound. She ripped cloth from her sodden cloak and started to tie it firmly around her left shoulder and armpit. It wasn't much but it would have to do. Cautiously, the assassin approached the opening to the cave beyond the platforms leading down into the abyss. Her legs trembled as she passed into the rocky space. There was a smell of sulphur in the air and a total lack of light. There was nothing for it. The girl entered further in, her path being mapped by intuition.

Akumi felt her way down the tunnel of rock like she was blind. There was now no light source and no way of telling what was ahead. The ground was rough, with rocks and uneven surfaces creating a hindrance at every point. She knew not to rush her descent and continued on unabated by these harsh surroundings. Before long her eyes were making out flickers of light further down. Eventually, she could make out reddish glows and shining green beams lighting up a wide space. She was intrigued and continued staring ahead only to lose her balance and trip up on a stone resting below her. Her body rolled down the last section of the tunnel in a heaping tumble. She tried her best to stop herself but in the darkness it was impossible. Luckily, there had only been feet to go and the assassin found herself falling into the space she'd been eying so attentively. Her body landed with a thud. She was cut in places but more frustrated than anything else. Akumi got up and analysed her surroundings.

She was in a room of crystals. They gleamed with every colour. Countless glowing gems glistened with bright radiance. The light was mostly of a ruby red hue, with undertones of jade and crimson. She was suddenly in a beautiful environment. There was a sense of peace about the place. She started to feel her sword drop. She even smiled in warmth as a serene harmony flowed through her.

In a flash and without warning a katana came swinging down at her from behind a large, green gemstone. Akumi pounced like a surprised cat and managed to deflect the sword. Endal came swaying out from his position amongst the mass of crystals and assaulted with immense pace. Akumi had been stunned by the ambush but soon refocused. She was forced back until she found herself pressed up against a mass of blue crystals peppering out from chasms beyond. Endal had her up against them and suddenly the two were no longer sword fighting but wrestling. Their hands clasped and their swords pointed out in varied directions as they jostled. Endal was trying to impale the girl against the sharp crystals sticking out from the rocky surface behind her. Akumi stared into Endal's deathly face as she fought against his strength. His features were lit up in a blue neon tint caused by the countless precious stones sparkling around them.

Akumi couldn't break Endal's grip and started to feel herself pressing up against the sharply edged stones. With desperation she started to drive her legs into Endal's body and managed to strike him in the groin with her knee. He moaned and bent low. She drove her knee into him again, and again, until he lost his grip over her and fell back winded. As he stumbled Akumi raised her arms high and sliced her katana down at him. It cut into his back as he lay panting by her feet. He yelled out and recoiled away, disappearing behind large, glowing crystals.

As Akumi crept forwards in pursuit of her opponent she couldn't help but dwell on an impression she was getting. Endal was proving a real challenge but somehow didn't seem quite the exceptional killing machine she'd encountered before. It was as if he had changed, no longer half as godlike and unnatural as she recalled. He didn't seem as transcendent; his status as paragon of warriors unexpectedly perceptibly contentious. His demeanour wasn't quite as before. He looked to be consumed by some force. Perhaps this explained his bleak, black eyes.

Akumi passed into the mass of giant crystals. She was lit up in tones of red and green. Her katana glowed in a dazzling lime tinge and her brown eyes reflected a thousand glistening gems of deepest sapphire. They were honed in on tracking Endal.

CHAPTER II

THE PLAINS OF FALGOR

Sylvie was heading straight for the tower. Her guards had reported locating Ellis locked inside the throne room. They had surrounded the doors but were cautious, unsure how to proceed. The Empress jogged along the courtyard and was met by several guards standing by the tower entrance.

'He has bolted the doors,' a guard said grumpily. 'That or barricaded himself in.'

'You have a battering ram?' Sylvie asked.

'Aye, but thought it best to await your orders,' said the guard.

They raced up the vast staircase that ascended the tower like a vine wrapped around a tree. The throne room was the highest point. It had been where Tamus had fallen.

'And we are certain Ellis is in there?' Sylvie questioned.

'We heard him yelling to himself from beyond the doors,' said a guard beside her. 'He's in a state.'

'Okay, this is what is to happen,' said the girl: 'I want you to break open the doors but once open only I will enter. I want to deal with him by myself.'

The guards nodded as they reached the stately doorway at the top of the flight of steps. Further guards clambered around the entrance, lined up and prepared to storm inside the throne room on command. Sylvie noticed a few holding a long wooden log. It was designed to break down doorways and rarely failed.

'Break open the doors,' Sylvie ordered, 'but do not enter. I will deal with this.'

The girl clasped her sword handle with one hand and studied her men as they prepared.

The wooden ram smashed against the majestic entrance. There was a loud pounding as matter connected. First contact proved ineffective and the guards attempted another firm barrage. They stepped back several feet and charged into the doors. The tip of the ram crunched into the door handles and the entrance started to crack and crumble. With another decisive hit the entrance broke open. A shelf placed in front of the doors toppled to one side as the doorframe snapped in sagging defeat.

Sylvie crept forwards, her guards staying back and eying every angle of the lengthy room. She stepped over the broken door and analysed ahead. The empty throne was partially lit up by the white moonlight sneaking in from the balcony.

'Ellis!' Sylvie called out. 'Show yourself.'

She moved deeper into the room, walking along the aisle between wooden benches lined up to overlook the throne. The Sword of Tamus was clutched in both her hands. As she reached her throne she noticed the balcony to her left that overlooked the city and beyond. Standing in the moonlight was Ellis. He was obliviously facing the great view and seemed unaware of her as she crept up behind him.

Sylvie walked across the remainder of the hall until she was feet away from the balcony. Prominent white curtains drooped across either side of the stone terrace. A white net blind partially blocked her view of the motionless figure. She passed through it until she stood on the balcony directly behind him.

'Ellis,' she groused.

The traitor turned his head and stared at the girl. He looked broken as if he knew the game was up.

'Yes, my Empress,' he said sarcastically.

Sylvie lowered her sword as she faced him.

'Why did you do it?' she asked.

Ellis laughed. 'I knew you'd be convinced by that stupid boyfriend of yours,' he cringed. 'As soon as I heard Fenris and Rense were being allowed into the city I knew what would happen.'

'I heard the truth,' said Sylvie. 'That's what happened.'

Ellis looked out at the vastness of the dark landscape before them.

'What a view,' he said.

'So… why did you do it?' Sylvie pressed. 'Why did you betray us?'

'I guess I craved real power,' said Ellis. 'I be not content with the kind of role I have now: that of a dogsbody.'

'All Golandin offers is chaos and mob rule,' said Sylvie.

'You'd have no more power than you do now.'

'Perhaps you're right,' said Ellis, 'but perhaps that appeals to me.'

Sylvie just frowned. She had always been ever so cautious of Ellis but the revelations now coming from his lips sickened her. For so long he had been a part of the court, advising Tamus and playing a part in the building of the empire. In reality he had been plotting all along.

'I have never been happy under the banner of Tamus,' Ellis grumbled. 'It was all just in order to climb the ranks and gain trust. All along I was planning for this moment and now it is ruined… ruined by a stupid wretch like you!'

Ellis suddenly revealed a blade from his shirt. The knife glimmered in the moonlight.

'I won't bow down to you Sylvie,' he yelled. 'Golandin may take this city or he may fall before those mighty walls in some mass ineffectual charge. Regardless, I will be remembered.'

'Ellis…' Sylvie was cautious. 'Don't…'

She could read his body language. Ellis held his knife in one hand and turned to face her head on. His face was a veil of hatred and his eyes as grim as stone. He plunged at the Empress, his arm outstretched in a stabbing motion. Sylvie raised her sword and ploughed it against his knife. Ellis immediately lost grip of the blade and watched it fly from his hand and fall into the darkness beyond the balcony. He stepped back until his body edged against the railings of the terrace.

'You are under arrest for betraying the empire,' said Sylvie calmly. 'You will be taken to the dungeon and tried as a traitor.'

Ellis started to look down at the infinite drop before him. He could just make out the courtyard of the tower grounds and several thatched roofs beyond the perimeter walls. Vertigo overcame him and he quickly turned back to face Sylvie.

'Bitch!' he wailed.

'Guards!' Sylvie called. 'Seize him.'

Without delay the large group of troops that had amassed by the throne room doorway stormed into the great hall and made for the balcony.

Ellis gave Sylvie an evil glance and spoke with venom: 'I hope Golandin burns you at the stake whilst his men rape every other woman left in this foul, pestilent city.'

Sylvie said nothing but as her guards entered through the net blinds she gulped as Ellis fell back. His tired, feeble body dropped over the railings and silently, he fell from the tower. She raced to the edge and peered down. It took some seconds before he hit the courtyard grounds with an inevitable thump. The soaring fall killed him instantly.

The guardsmen disappeared behind her as they made for the stairs. Sylvie closed her eyes and lowered her sword as she stood alone on the terrace. Although there was a sense of justice about the incident she still felt saddened by his dramatic demise. She then looked up to the stars and called out loud:

'Give me the strength to defend this city. Give me the will to fight to the last. Brimma will not fall!'

'Ah, Brimma at last!' Golandin smirked.

Arthir stood behind him as the group of rebel commanders inspected the terrain ahead. They were now only a few miles from the southern lake, and from their position within the outlying fields of the Plains of Falgor could make out the city with surety. They could also spot Tamus Tower in all its might rising in phallic connotation into the sky from within the impressive dwelling.

'The moment has come,' Golandin continued. 'We have made it to our destination.'

The rebel leader lowered an eyepiece handed to him by one of his minions. It magnified the view somewhat but not enough to prove particularly useful. Due to the darkness of the passing night they could only make out outlines of buildings but it was enough to know they were there.

'Now is the time to set out a strategy,' said Arthir. 'We must map out a plan of attack.'

Golandin started to walk away from the mound of earth offering a vantage point and back down into the rolling field. His army had been ordered to halt and set up in this spot. Vast erections were already being placed into the ground, with tents and banners scattered across the fields boasting the might of this assaulting force.

Arthir walked alongside his friend as he made for a tent beside a group of proud trees.

'I hope you are listening to me,' said Arthir.

'Do not worry,' Golandin smiled. 'For now we rest. In the morning I will brief our officers with what is to be done.'

'Well please enlighten me now,' Arthir was intrigued.

They entered into Golandin's tent where the old warrior was swift to sit down on the soft sheets placed on one side.

'Brimma can be taken from the south,' said Golandin. 'We have no choice but to come from the south seeing as that lake covers the west.'

'Why not come from the east?' Arthir asked.

'Because we would just be bombarding ourselves against stone walls,' Golandin said. 'We have no means to destroy them and must focus on the gate. That we can break down.'

Arthir sat down on the grassy ground of the tent. A single candle flickered inside, creating rippling silhouettes on the canvas as the two men discussed tactics.

'So we are relying on the bridge?' Arthir inquired.

'In a sense,' said Golandin. 'Yes, we will be storming the bridge seeing as we can't swim the lake. We shall pound down the gate with battering rams and set it alight. It is only wood you know.'

'What if the bridge has been destroyed?' Arthir asked. 'They may have pre-empted this.'

'No, you see this is where Ellis has come in,' Golandin smiled. 'Before he left us for Brimma he informed me the bridge could not feasibly be destroyed like that. It is of stone and as strong as the walls that surround the city. I also recall in my distant past being a part of attacks on Brimma in the days of the late Twinicia. The bridge always played a part back then. It will tomorrow.'

'But Brimma was never taken back then,' said Arthir. 'I associate those days you speak of as utter defeats for our cause. They were fruitless assaults on impregnable defences.'

'We are stronger now,' remarked Golandin. 'We are more numerous and our morale is high. This time our forces will smash through those gates and overcome Brimma. We shall have command of Tamus Tower by the next nightfall.'

Arthir remained ever so cynical. He recalled previous attacks on Brimma in an age long before Tamus had truly secured the realm. In those distant days when the empire's army was only half as organised the rebelling armies still failed to take the city.

'I fear we are going into this without a solid plan,' he commented.

Golandin snapped. He stood up and roared: 'Be gone with your negativity Arthir! Look where I have led us so far. We have gone from retreating rebels, without a cause and propping up some distant bar, to this! We have reached this point and we can go all the way. I assure you.'

'The only reason we are here and in this position is because of that assassin, Endal,' Arthir noted.

'Oh forget Endal!' Golandin said callously. 'He is a faint memory now. He vanished like the strange, mysterious entity he is. It was I that led this army to this point, and it will be I whom leads it to victory.'

'Endal killed Tamus,' Arthir said. 'The rest is a footnote.'

Golandin got up and suddenly pounced on his old friend with arms outright. His worn hands clenched Arthir's neck and squeezed.

'Do not undermine me,' he spat. 'I am leading this. I am!'

Arthir clenched Golandin's arms and pulled with all his might. They jostled and eventually Golandin released him.

'What the hell!' Arthir coughed. 'You are losing it!'

'Maybe I am,' Golandin said softly. 'I need sleep.'

Abruptly, the aging warrior dropped down onto the blankets laid out across the ground. He removed his chest plates and stared up at the canvas.

'Tomorrow is all that matters,' he said. 'The rest is an irrelevance now.'

Arthir stroked his neck and got to his feet. He was noticing a change in Golandin; it was as if the power he now wielded was corrupting him, eating away his mind.

'See you in the morning,' he said glumly.

Arthir walked out of the tent and was immediately approached by one of the rebel officers. They were eager to discover what plans had been forged in the tent.

'Sir, what has been decided?' they asked.

Arthir responded but it was more to himself than anyone around him:

'The great battle plan has come to this: we storm the bridge and hope to break down the mighty gate. What our few competent archers do, or where our dwindled cavalry targets, seems to be unimportant. Golandin is confident quantity will defeat quality on this occasion.'

The rebel officer and numerous others flocking around the tent didn't seem concerned and came over just as ignorant to tactical planning as Golandin. Arthir was no expert but appeared the only one even remotely concerned about the vagueness of this plan. The group dispersed and Arthir headed for his tent across from their leader's. He needed a few hours' kip before the big day ahead.

The final few drops of liquid splashed onto the stone surface of the bridge. Fenris poured the flammable substance onto the ground with the bucket clenched in both arms. They had plastered the structure with alcohol. It was all they had for the job. The smell of strong spirits tainted the air and dozens of empty barrels were hurled into the lake. Rense waited for his pal to reach the end of the bridge before moving back towards the open gateway. A foray of guards raced back into the city with the two warriors close behind.

Emi and Yuuki looked on from their position beside the gate atop the platform of the perimeter wall. Beyond the lake there still remained only the darkness of this early hour. However, sunrise was coming and there was an undeniable sense of urgency about the operation. The gateway fell back down to earth and the city was once again secure.

'That will hold them off for a while,' said Emi.

Beside the two girls was a mighty line of archers. They were the cream of the empire's troops; deadly with bows and eager to use them. Emi was in her element in this position. She was surrounded by stacks of arrows and in a perfect spot to give hell to anyone crossing over the bridge. Lady Yuuki was equally as suited for this location. Her magical powers were poised to discourage anyone attempting to storm the gate.

For the swordsman and axe wielder of the group there would be no choice but to stand around and watch the ranged attacks bombard the enemy. Fenris and Rense climbed back onto the platform overlooking the bridge. As they clambered up the ladder Sylvie appeared from the street leading further into the city.

'Ellis?' Fenris was quick to question.

'He took his life,' said Sylvie. 'He leapt from the tower.'

The guardsmen who had heard those words shook their heads in disdain whilst Jamus' party took in the news guardedly.

'He must have sensed defeat to do that,' said Yuuki. 'Otherwise he would surely have waited for Golandin to liberate him?'

'I wouldn't place any reasoning on his actions,' said Sylvie. 'He was in a state. There was no consoling him.'

'Strange all the same,' Fenris said.

'The fool is dead,' laughed Rense. 'Good riddance I say.'

Sylvie started to backtrack and looked up at her allies as they perched high on the platform.

'I must see to Jamus, and the rebel prisoner,' she said.

With that she raced back up the street and the four warriors turned back to face the bridge. Lady Yuuki suddenly lowered her head and closed her eyes. She wasn't right and showed signs of distress.

'Yuuki, what is it?' Emi was concerned.

'I just... I just sense a darkness,' she whispered. 'I can't explain it.'

Emi put her hand on the sorceress' shoulder. 'What do you mean?' she asked.

Rense and Fenris looked on in intrigue. It was clear Yuuki was coming down with something.

'I have been ignoring it up until now but I am sensing a shadow forming in the west,' Yuuki said. 'It is as if it is growing with greater power with every passing second.'

'What could it possibly mean?' Emi questioned.

'I can't say,' said Yuuki emotionally, 'but the feeling is getting greater. I also keep seeing images of Akumi surrounded by shadow.'

'Akumi... the girl who has gone after Endal?' Fenris came in.

'Yes, that's her,' Emi replied for Yuuki.

'I can't stop thinking about her. I sense she needs help,' Yuuki toiled.

'Well, we can do nothing for her now,' Rense said. 'We may as well be on the other side of the world.' He was realistic.

Emi continued to rest her hand on Yuuki's shoulder. The sorceress started to slowly ease out of her vexed moment and focused back on matters at hand.

'Forget about it,' she said. 'It's nothing for any of you to concern yourselves with.'

Emi nodded although seemed unconvinced. The gang said nothing else of it and continued to man the wall in silence.

Deeper into Brimma Sylvie was racing up the tiny roads for the hospital the guards had placed Jamus. She was on multiple errands and moved with great cause. She passed a lone guard manning the thatched house where minor field wounds could be treated and charged up the squeaking steps. Jamus was resting in a bedroom on the first floor. Sylvie entered the room and quietly walked over to his bed. The room was simplistic, with wooden floorboards and white walls. A thin sheet of glass consisted of the single window that remained partially hidden behind clean curtains.

'Are you awake?' Sylvie whispered.

The old man was motionless and in the early morning light looked lifeless as he lay under the white sheets.

'Hello Sylvie,' his tired voice said calmly. 'You have grown.'

The Empress smiled. 'How are you?' she asked.

'Sore, and remembering my age,' he joked. 'Your troops gave me all the aid I needed.'

'So you are recovering?' Sylvie inquired.

'I lost a lot of blood,' he said. 'I am still tired, so tired.'

Sylvie leant over him and kissed his wrinkled forehead gracefully.

'Get more rest,' she said.

She turned and started to walk towards the door.

'Sylvie… wait,' Jamus called. 'Ellis? What is happening?'

'Ellis took his own life,' said Sylvie. 'He jumped from the tower. Everyone is here and we are ready to defend the city.'

Jamus nodded then rested his head back down on the pillow. Sylvie disappeared through the doorway and carefully closed it shut.

Not far from Jamus, in the underground passages of the city dungeon, Theamis sat on the straw mats recently occupied by Fenris. He had been placed in the cell and left to dwell on his fate. The unfaltering rope work that Emi had used to bind his arms was still in place. It hadn't been exchanged for chains by the guards that had led him into the dingy space.

Eventually, his silent contemplations were interrupted by the racing footsteps of Sylvie as she ran down the dungeon passage with a guard escorting her.

'Leave me to speak with him,' she said. 'Wait for me to knock until opening the door again.'

The guard unlocked the cell and she entered. Theamis got on his knees and knelt down as she walked closer to him. He was tense and pale.

'Don't be nervous,' Sylvie assured him. 'No one is going to harm you.'

She was thoughtful and sat down beside him instead of standing over him with intimidating authority. Theamis took several deep breaths. He was still uneasy. However, Sylvie wasn't looking at him as her enemy. She saw him as a confused boy.

'I have come to you with a proposition,' she said. 'I want you to fight for me. Help us defend this city.'

Theamis was taken aback and didn't initially respond. The Empress was patient and sat beside him waiting for a reply.

'I just went along with it... the rebellion,' he said timidly. 'The way you have all treated me has made me realise this is the side I should be on. Yes... yes I will fight for you, Empress.'

'I was hoping you would say that,' Sylvie remarked. 'You are too young to truly understand what Golandin stands for.'

'I just followed my friends,' said Theamis. 'I didn't really know what was going on... I just got so excited by it all. It all swept me away. I feel foolish. I never really thought about what I was doing. I truly regret being a part of it now.'

'Well I trust you Theamis,' said Sylvie. 'I am pleased you will fight for me.'

She seemed genuinely pleased and got up with a smile on her face. She didn't know what she would have done if Theamis had rejected her offer. She would likely have been forced to keep him confined to the cell, destined for trial at a later stage.

'I won't let you down, Empress,' said Theamis softly.

'Well in that case I best untie those arms,' smiled Sylvie.

The girl walked behind him and started to fiddle with the knots binding his wrists. Soon the rope was unwound and Theamis could finally bring his arms to his side in freedom. Sylvie knocked on the cell door and in an instant a guard opened the brawny barrier.

'Everything okay Empress?' the troop asked.

'Everything is fine soldier,' she announced. 'This boy is no longer our prisoner. Fetch him a sword.'

CHAPTER III

THE CRYSTAL CAVES

The katana blade was first to prod every corner before Akumi stepped forwards. She found herself in an immersive environment of glowing shades. The rocks were humming, with some kind of magical intensity about them, and each offered a distinctive tone. She had moved deeper into the cave of crystalline stones and was now surrounded by huge mounds of rock. Each glistened with almost blinding light. Several even flickered as if being turned on and off by some unknown source.

Akumi continued to walk forwards, passing each spectacular specimen. Endal was alluring her even more than the intense magnetism of this unique place. The assassin noticed a gap forming in the rocky walls ahead. Another vast expanse appeared from beyond the cave of glowing crystals. She stepped out into the clearing and inspected her surroundings. The cave had led her back out onto a natural platform edging beside an infinite drop into darkness. The light from the surface was sneaking in from high above and creating distinct rays of light that individually struck section after section of the flat rocky ground in great lines.

After walking a few more feet Akumi spotted Endal. He was standing motionlessly, looking down at the darkness of the infinite fall. He was aware Akumi was behind him and turned with katana in one hand.

'Why do you keep eluding me?' Akumi asked.

Endal had placed his hood back over his head and stared down at the ground in front of him.

'Forces have come to claim me,' he said. 'They lurk the sky above and yell out for my soul.'

Akumi thought of the dark energies pervading the swamplands. They had overcome Arifor. Perhaps they were also having an effect on Endal. It suddenly made more sense.

'You are trying to evade them?' she asked.

'I knew this time would come,' he went on. 'Vortor told me of this day. It was inevitable that I would eventually be brought back into the worlds beyond. Vortor has a hold on me now. He brought me back to life and ever since I have been owned by him; his will be consuming me, his great energy coming for me.'

Akumi wasn't entirely clear about what Endal meant.

'The energies are coming for you?' she prodded.

Endal continued: 'I am an avatar for the dark forces that now surround us. An age ago they took hold of me and made me what you see before you. They are now claiming me. Vortor has a grip on me now and wishes to use me as his vehicle. I can feel myself altering. The forces wish me to lead them into the night and destroy this world.'

'And you are resisting them?' Akumi asked.

Endal smiled. 'No... I am just biding my time.'

He suddenly lifted his katana and got in a stance. Akumi reacted by doing much the same. They started to cautiously circle one another. Akumi started to notice demonic entities hovering around within the darkness of the deep lair. They were coming down from the surface high above. They were the same beings she had seen in the woods.

'They will claim me and I will become the sentience of that whirling cloud,' Endal declared; 'but we must now face off! You deserve this moment to finally confront me.'

His words sparked Akumi to do just that. She now understood what was happening and imagined she only had minutes until Endal turned into some unearthly essence. She closed in and their blades cut against each other. Endal moved with inhuman speed and his katana attacked with deadly precision. Akumi stepped back and did all she could to block his strikes. She was being pushed towards the drop into darkness and desperately attempted to turn the tables.

Her blade swung over Endal's head. He bent low to avoid her strike and rolled to the ground with his legs striking her shins. She was swept off balance and fell over sideways. Endal pounced back up and drove his sword down at the girl in an effort to stab her in the stomach. She rolled away with inches to spare and leapt to her feet. They continued to battle.

Akumi deflected countless strikes as her opponent resumed their barrage of blows. She blocked his sword as it swooped low, aiming for her thigh. She found an opening and improvised. Her fist slammed into the dark assassin's jaw as he bent forwards against her sword. He stepped back only to receive a kick in the stomach. He fell onto his back with the impact of the girl's wet boot.

Akumi attacked him where he lay. Her sword prodded at his body whilst he repelled each deadly motion. He then rolled to one side and quickly got back to his feet. Their swords locked but Akumi managed to trip Endal up by sneakily putting her leg out behind him. He fell back down and again rolled away. This time Akumi was swift to react to his retreat and had already poised her blade to strike. She prodded down at him in desperate hope her sword would make contact with her enemy. The blade poked into his back and cut through his robe. He yelled out in pain but managed to recoil further back in order to prevent deeper penetration. He quickly got up and stepped away from the girl.

'You almost had me,' he smiled.

Akumi had lightly penetrated his back but it didn't seem enough to trouble him. He showed no signs of weakening as he stood facing her. In another round of combat they were again engaging one another. Endal allowed Akumi to strike then suddenly dived into a combo of sword moves. Akumi pounced to one side to avoid his descending blade then bent low to evade a strike aimed for her neck. Once his blade passed over her head she stood up straight and jumped towards him. Her sword smashed against his with force as her feet hit the ground.

Endal was suddenly on the receiving end and stepped back as the female assassin hit him with an onslaught of blows. He deflected each of her moves in turn and without warning spun on his feet until his blade came sweeping around from his side. It slid across Akumi's waist in a perfect line. She was shocked and fell back. Endal stood motionlessly with his katana held in one arm, blood dripping from its tip.

Akumi crawled away. Her wound was serious and she knew it. Her skin was deeply cut and blood was seeping from her belly. She turned a cold, pale colour and tried her best to get up. Endal seemed to be in some form of victorious trance. He hadn't moved an inch since landing the blow and bowed his head. However, his dark eyes started to twitch as he noticed his opponent slowly getting to her feet.

'Ready to die?' he smiled.

Akumi was clearly faltering; her stance all over the place and sword barely upright. She came over absolutely calm, as if she was simply ignoring her injury. Endal didn't hesitate and closed in on the girl. She immediately backed away and fled back into the cave of crystals behind them. Endal was close behind, following at walking pace. He looked up at the flying entities now only feet from his head in circled patterns of flight.

'Soon,' he commanded. 'I am coming.'

The entities seemed to acknowledge this and extended their distance from him in total obedience.

Akumi wearily forced herself to reach the chasm of glowing stones. There was an energy about this place that warmed her heart. If she was about to die she wanted to fall here in this spot, surrounded by such a beautiful and calming natural exhibition.

'You fought well,' Endal praised as he followed her slowly.

He entered into the glowing cave and suddenly became lit up in tones of brilliant crimson. Akumi was leaning against a body sized rock. Its green hue gave her warmth and hope.

The dark assassin was only feet away, walking unguardedly towards the stone she hid behind. Akumi raised her blade in anticipation. As he passed by the rock she jumped out and attempted to splice it into his gullet. The ambush failed and Endal deflected her sword. As she arched forwards with the redirected force Endal struck her in the face with his flat palm. She fumbled backwards and retreated towards a wall of thousands of sharply edged azure crystals. The stones looked like a wall of glistening spikes. The girl paused beside them. She could now barely stand. Her skin was pallid and her limbs felt like jelly. Endal closed in with blade poised for one final killer blow. He eyed her chest and planned to drive his deadly katana through her heart.

'Goodbye Akumi,' he commented.

In a flash Akumi suddenly thought of Hazati, Jobe, and Harkor. She thought of Tamus and the blood being spilt now he was gone. She imagined her allies battling against impossible odds on the fields of Marmia. She remembered Sylvie and her despair over the Emperor's death. In this abrupt moment of deep fury a spurt of energy erupted from the inner confines of her reserve.

Endal plunged his katana towards her. Akumi deflected it with sudden agility and speed. The dark assassin's sword arm was knocked to one side. Endal was taken aback by her sudden energy. Before he could react Akumi shot her katana across the air that separated them. The razor edged steel made contact with Endal's black robe and the blade pressed into his pale flesh. Like some lethal injection it sunk into his torso just below the heart. The sword passed through bone and organ and slipped out of his back. Endal dropped his sword and whimpered in agony. Akumi stepped to one side and flicked her blade to the side. Endal's body swung with it like a limp piece of meat.

She slammed his body into a thousand piercing points. The glowing crystals impaled into his back and arms as the katana flung him into the wall. Akumi lost grip of her sword handle and let it dangle from the assassin's chest. His body remained upright but his hooded head was bowed down. Blood spattered every section of his robe and the tips of dozens of the blue rocks poked out from his devastated body. Akumi stared at him whilst panting like a dog.

'Goodbye Endal,' she wheezed.

With some inhuman strength Endal managed to speak. His broken body was lifeless but his head slowly rose up to face the female assassin before him.

'I knew not what I did,' he whispered. 'I was under a spell. I thank you for releasing me.'

His head slouched forwards. Akumi was ever so moved. She had always known Endal had been human. The truth was that for all this time he'd been under a dark spell. He had been possessed. She had finally freed his soul.

Akumi watched as the last whimpers of life faded from Endal's impaled body. His head bent down until his chin pierced itself on the tip of a stone sticking out from his chest. He was finally dead. Akumi turned and started to stumble forwards.

It only took a few feet for her to lose all energy. The girl fell down onto the rocky ground. Blood had been frenziedly seeping from her waist and stained the ground around her. Her eyes closed. She forced them back open. Her body went limp and she lost all strength. Her cheek hit the ground firmly and her eyes fought against the eyelids. Her last sight was of a blur of infinitely toned colours. Reds formed with greens and soothed her as her eyes finally gave in. They closed and she lay lifeless in a haze of wondrous light.

CHAPTER IV

A FROST IN THE AIR

It was morning. The sun had risen and lit up the cloudy sky with a golden morning glow. Golandin opened his eyes and listened to the distinct sound of birds singing in the trees beyond his tent. The warrior got up from the blankets he had rested on and instinctively grabbed his longsword. He stretched his arms with a yawn and started to attach his armour plates around his body. As he fondled around Arthir strolled into the canopy. He looked apprehensive and nervous.

'The time has come,' he said.

Golandin nodded and continued to fiddle with his armour.

'We attack at once,' the rebel leader declared.

He marched out of his tent with Arthir close behind and looked around in authoritative judgement. His countless men of rank had already formed up and were eager to take orders and raise the army. Golandin walked towards them and halted as they formed a natural circle around him. Arthir kept back.

'The moment has come to finally defeat the remnants of the late Tamus' empire!' Golandin barked. 'We are to strike Brimma from the south. We shall storm the bridge and bring down the gate. Our numbers will prove unstoppable. The garrison defending that town will falter against our might. We shall overcome them!'

There was a roar of adrenaline. The mostly bearded men in positions of command chuckled with the collective sense of possible victory to come.

'Our archers shall stay back south of the lake,' the leader continued. 'They will do all they can to pin the heads of the defenders down from behind their walls. Once the gate breaks our horsemen shall storm in with our masses behind them.'

One of the officers stepped forwards into the circle. He was eager to ask a question: 'Sir, how shall we destroy the gate?'

Arthir listened on attentively as his figure lurked in the background behind the group.

'We shall break it with a barrage from our battering rams,' replied Golandin. 'It will give way.'

The men around the veteran rebel warrior appeared content with this basic plan of action. None of them had the stomach for a lengthy briefing and were eager to get into battle.

'Raise the men!' Golandin ordered. 'Gather your individual units up and form in that field to our north. From there we shall march on Brimma in mass lines.'

As Golandin concluded the morning briefing a single figure started to barge past those huddled around the rebel leader. They were dressed in a brown robe; stained in dry blood and muddy soil.

'Can we help you?' Golandin smirked.

The figure stopped once managing to reach the inside of the circle. They stood beside Golandin with all eyes staring towards them in interest. The figure raised their arms and slowly brought down their hood.

'What the...' Arthir cried as he shuffled deeper into the gathering.

The bald figure laughed whilst he stared at those around him.

'Torwin...' Golandin smiled. 'Back from the dead I see?'

There was confusion as the men studied the man before them.

'You are dead!' Arthir panicked.

Torwin grumbled to himself and then replied: 'Not quite back from the dead! More like back from the pile of corpses your men dumped me on.'

'But you were killed... by some old man from all accounts?' Golandin questioned. 'Those whom survived the skirmish reported your fall doing battle with that group of riders?'

'I lost consciousness,' said Torwin. 'He hurt me pretty bad, but your men don't seem to know the difference between an unconscious man needing aid and a dead body! I woke up eventually and managed to control the bleeding. I then grabbed a horse and raced to catch up with this mob you call an army.'

'This is great news!' an officer beamed.

Golandin patted Torwin on the shoulder. 'I am glad you are still with us friend,' he said. 'Can you fight?'

'Well, I'm not on top form if that's what you mean,' Torwin

grinned, 'but sure I will fight. I didn't race all this way just to watch as you capture Brimma!'

The men laughed in unison.

'This is a good sign,' said Golandin. 'Torwin is back! We move out now!'

The group dispersed in a cheer as Golandin headed for the field the army would assemble in. Torwin followed behind with sword already in hand. Arthir watched them head off. He stared up into the sky.

'God give us the strength to crush down those walls,' he prayed. 'Lead us to victory!'

There was a definite frost in the air. The morning dew dampened the blades of green grass surrounding the glistening blue waters of the lake. Condensation wetted the steel of each warriors' sword. Rolling mists hovered over the cold stone fortifications. The overcast sky suggested rain. It was a grim start to the day. The lines of imperial Tamus troops manned every edge of the southern wall. The wooden platform was packed with men and supplies stacked on the timber boards. A few hundred arrow heads were poised to fly out and strike the immediate area around the bridge.

Fenris was first to wake up. He had been resting against the stone wall beside Rense as they slept on the platform. Yuuki and Emi were close by and also showing signs of rising.

'What time is this?' Fenris yawned.

'Time to spill some blood,' gagged Rense.

Several guards smiled at the comment whilst staring out into the Falgor fields beyond the lake in disciplined silence. Everyone was eager for action.

Fenris got up and looked out at the morning vista. The sight of distant tents and banners immediately sent a shiver down his spine. None of the guards seemed intimidated. The sight was old news now an hour's worth of morning light had already passed.

Rense was next to marvel at the gathering amassed ahead. The expression on his bearded face said it all.

'How far would you say that forward camp is?' he asked out loud.

'About three miles,' said Emi.

She had leapt up with Yuuki standing beside her. The scene

consisted of tent after tent, with other unidentifiable erections also darted around the fields. The initial hill sloping up south of the lake wasn't high enough to block the view of the rebel position. Their vantage point allowed them to see over it and out into the fields beyond.

Although the distance was too great for the eye alone to make out detail it was clear there was a great deal of movement going on around the position. Masses were flocking in growing numbers. Lines of rebel troops were forming up. They could even hear the faint sound of drumbeats.

'Just how many of us are there defending the city?' Fenris further questioned.

The four warriors looked to one another for an answer. None of them seemed to know for sure. The guards around them remained silent. Suddenly a voice responded:

'Two thousand in all,' said Sylvie as she came clambering up the ladder onto the platform.

'I'd say that rebel mass out there looks to be numbering double that,' said Fenris.

'And the rest,' Rense said. 'Looks to be about six thousand souls if you ask me.'

Emi nodded to herself. Her trained huntress' eyes appeared to be acknowledging Rense's observation.

Sylvie analysed the forming enemy army. At least now she knew for sure they would be coming from the south. Yuuki's eyes made contact with hers as they stood beside each other. Sylvie could sense the sorceress was deeply troubled.

'What is it?' Sylvie asked.

Yuuki bowed her head and once again closed her eyes tightly. She leant forwards against her mighty staff; her partly braided hair blowing with the gentle breeze.

'I sense Akumi is in trouble,' she said. 'Darkness surrounds her. A shadow is gaining strength in the west.'

Sylvie was concerned. With all that had been going on around her the girl had forgotten all about Akumi and her solo trek in hunt of Endal.

'Please, go on…' she said.

'I can't offer any more detail,' said Yuuki. 'It is a feeling. I know she is suffering. She is a light surrounded by a veil of darkness.'

The psychic instincts of the sorceress were detecting something Sylvie recalled had once been warned about by the late mage, Vortor. She imagined Akumi confronting Endal against all odds in some place of black magic and chaos.

'Vortor warned of dark forces rising when the realm was at its weakest point,' Sylvie said. 'He said they would strike once fear had swept the lands... once the Emperor was dead.'

'Vortor was in touch with the very forces I sense forming,' Yuuki dwelt. 'I just can't stop focusing on it.'

The others had overheard the girls talking and looked equally troubled by the mystical revelations seemingly coming to pass. However, their attention was beginning to turn back to the view ahead of them. It was becoming clear the rebel horde was starting to move as one. They were advancing.

'Looks like we are close to smashing a few more skulls,' said Rense.

The lines of guards were rumbling with slight trepidation. The rebel gathering certainly was an intimidating sight even for these disciplined soldiers.

Sylvie paced along the platform, passing behind her troops as they hunched against the surface of the wall.

'As soon as that horde enters into range of our arrows let them have it!' she yelled. 'They will flounder as soon as the bridge is set alight. Fire your arrows out across the lake and bombard them as they mass up on the other side.'

Her archers had already raised their bows and lowered their steel helmets. All eyes looked on as the enemy slowly edged athwart the fields.

Across the waters of the lake and the bushy southern hill Golandin walked along the damp grass surrounded by his men. They were as rowdy and loud as ever, showing little sign of nerves. There was a collective sense of momentum and spirits were high. A few feet ahead of the leader a gang of rebels carried a large wooden ram. A further two were being carried by other groups that led the advance.

The rebel troops were dressed in dark black leather armour. Many had decorated their faces with white and red paints, giving them a savage-like appearance. The horde resembled a barbarian charge, with no sense of synchronicity about the march.

Thousands had come and still continued to race from the tents of the makeshift camp. Up until now the force hadn't been challenged by a standing Tamus army. This was soon to change.

Torwin was a few feet behind Golandin. He hadn't been given any orders and no longer desired to lead any body of men. His intention was merely to get into the thick of it. A part of him also sought revenge on the old man that had wounded him. His face was filled with hate and ravaged by the stresses of all that was playing out.

Arthir wasn't far from Golandin and eventually walked beside him.

'Are you planning on joining the first waves of attack?' he asked his friend.

'Although I would love to, I think it will be prudent to keep back until the gate has been cleared,' Golandin swallowed. 'If I did somehow fall before that stage morale would sink.'

Arthir seemed to understand. 'I imagine Torwin will be looking to dive right in,' he said.

'No doubt,' said Golandin. 'How about you?'

'I will see how things play out,' Arthir said.

Both himself and Golandin were skilled and experienced warriors. Neither of them wanted to miss out on being a part of this vital battle. The hill was now beckoning; the initial view of the city vanishing behind the rising ground. Only the peak of Tamus Tower remained in view.

Within the city there was a sense of excitement. The rebels were now closing in and beginning to vanish behind the hill. Soon they would reveal themselves as they raced down its other side and made for the bridge. Sylvie had paced the entirety of the wall and now stood beside Fenris. She had been trying to ignore him; knowing that it was best they avoided each other in order to maintain focus. However, they were suddenly side by side. He was first to speak:

'You know, it still seems so strange being alongside you again.'

'When all this is over,' Sylvie said, 'we will have to properly catch up. I want to know what you have been getting up to.'

Fenris laughed. 'Not much exciting if I'm honest,' he said. 'Well, that was the case before linking up with Jamus at least! From that point onwards it has been one long battle!'

He turned his head to fully face the girl. The truth was he felt himself falling for her. Old emotions were coming back. He was besotted by the Empress.

'I am so proud of you,' he said; 'Taking on that demon, Endal, and commanding all of this!'

She was humbled but before she could respond she noticed several guards climbing up onto the platform. Behind them Theamis shuffled up the ladder. He was untied and geared up for war.

'Theamis reporting for duty,' he yelled out.

Yuuki and Emi were swift to react. The girls studied the young male then turned to Sylvie.

'He has sworn to fight for us,' said the Empress. 'I trust him.'

Yuuki nodded. She sensed no evil in the boy. She was able to read auras but rarely made comment regarding her abstruse findings. Emi was just as indifferent. They even showed slight signs of being pleased.

'Can you use a bow?' Emi asked.

Theamis stared down at the pile of unclaimed longbows. He nodded. 'Sure I can use one,' he said.

'Just remember,' Sylvie added: 'all those beyond these walls are your enemy now. They mean to kill every single one of us and raze this city to the ground.'

'I understand,' he said.

Fenris didn't seem interested in Theamis and continued to gaze into Sylvie's flowing blonde hair. Her blue eyes then made contact with his. She smiled warmly.

'I missed you,' she said. 'I am pleased you are here.'

Fenris was mesmerised and for a moment lost the ability to speak. Rense started to chuckle to himself as he stood beside him. He then patted the infatuated warrior on the back, snapping the love-struck male out of his brief trance.

'What did I say?' Rense laughed disparagingly. 'Ah, what we gonna do with 'ya?'

Fenris just took in the teasing without any comeback. All eyes then looked up. The sound of war cries could now be heard. Thousands of voices were chanting incomprehensible words of war. Drumbeats were pounding.

'Prepare,' said Rense knowingly to those around him. 'We've got a battle to win!'

The rebel army pressed on up the hillside. Golandin had now lowered his visor and fully clenched his old steel. Everyone was suddenly focused and serious. The initial celebratory mood of the advance had turned into an intense apprehension of combat.

'As soon as we pass over this hill I want every man to break into a charge,' Golandin yelled. 'You hear me? Charge as soon as you hit the descent. Make for the bridge!'

As long as the majority of those around him had heard the command it would likely kick into fruition. There was a collective behaviour amongst the rabble. Everyone would simply follow the man ahead.

Torwin emerged from the vast mass and walked alongside Golandin.

'Torwin is on the field!' Golandin shrieked. 'Torwin will fight alongside you!'

There was a dim cheer. The news fuelled those that had heard it.

'Torwin is with you! Brother of Warlord Twinicia! God rest his soul!' Golandin continued to call out.

Torwin was excited. 'Who is with me?' he yelled.

A mass response flooded back at him. It seemed as if everyone most certainly was. Arthir suddenly appeared. His helmet entirely covered his head, making him indistinguishable from most of the others around him.

'I will stay with you Torwin,' he said. 'I want to be at the forefront.'

'That is commendable,' said Golandin. 'You will see him spill the blood of those Tamus pigs!'

'We are coming for you Sylvie!' the rebel leader roared. 'Be afraid my girl.' Everyone laughed.

'I bet she'd be great in the right environment,' laughed Torwin. 'Like the bedroom for instance!'

'Precisely,' laughed Arthir. 'We shouldn't just kill her. We can have some fun with her first!'

Adrenaline was pumping and the mindsets of the three men brewed with an equally vicious thirst for blood. They had reason to despise those defending Brimma and held a genuine hatred for them. To these rebel warriors all the empire represented was a barrier preventing them from seizing power and ruling the lands in their own twisted fashion. Sylvie and those willing to fight beside her were the obstacle to those plans.

The rebels strode onwards as the climb started to cease. The hill had reached its peak and suddenly the rebellious flock could once again make out the entirety of the city before them.

'Charge!' Golandin ordered zealously. 'To the gate! To the gate we march!'

CHAPTER V

THE BATTLE OF BRIMMA BRIDGE

The old friar opened his eyes as his tired body lay motionlessly under the soft sheets. He felt weak but stronger than before. He had an urge to get out of the bed and proceeded to drag his legs onto the floor beside it. His armour had been removed, leaving him clothed only in white, light trousers and a grey, unbuttoned shirt. Jamus eventually managed to sit up and get out of bed.

The aged warrior stepped over to the window and examined the view. He could just make out the southern wall to the city in the distance, with countless guards manning every inch of the raised platform behind it. Jamus could also clearly make out droves of dark figures storming down the hillside beyond the stone barrier. He immediately realised the enemy had reached Brimma.

Jamus spotted his sword and armour piled up on a tabletop across from the window. He raced over to it and speedily started to gear himself back up. A spurt of energy seemed to drive him. He was still in the fight.

Not far away from the rousing warrior the mass of defending troops stood firm. Sylvie carefully analysed the rebel advance as the flocking enemy forces raced down the hill towards the bridge. The Empress could already differentiate between those leading the assault and those being led. One figure was surrounded by authoritative looking men. They massed around him as if he were a key individual. However, the distance was still too great to make out specific detail.

'Archers at the ready,' she cried.

Hundreds of bows were raised, with arrow tips aimed into the sky. The enemy were feet away from entering into accurate range.

'Prepare the fire,' she called.

Two archers were standing beside a raging fire burning inside a barrel of wooden tinder. They dipped specifically designed arrows into the flames and revealed the smouldering shafts as a thick smoke climbed into the air around them.

The burning arrows were pointed towards the flammable liquids soaking the stone body of the lake crossing. All eyes were on the bridge as the rebel advance gained swifter momentum. The enemy swarmed down the hill and were now reaching the brief clearing ahead of the overpass.

Within the rush Golandin found himself knocked and jostled by the eager men around him. The leader was intentionally holding back and paused in his tracks once reaching the field in front of the bridge. There was no sense of fear amongst those stampeding past him. The rebel warriors made for the bridge as if it were a competition.

Arthir kept close to Torwin whom by now had broken into a charge of his own, running alongside the hundreds of men making up the first wave. They were almost part of the spearhead.

'It can't be,' Fenris grumbled. 'I don't believe it...'

Rense tried to work out what was troubling his friend. He stared into the crowds across the lake. The distinguishable sight of a bald headed figure pushing through the charging flock sparked warning bells inside of him. He then noticed the distinctly pointed beard of the figure he was following with his eyes.

'Torwin,' Emi suddenly declared.

Her huntress' eyes confirmed it was him. Yuuki turned to Sylvie.

'Torwin is alive,' she said. 'We were certain Jamus claimed him but it seems he is a part of the attack.'

'Torwin... the late Warlord Twinicia's brother,' qualified Fenris.

'Aye, that's him alright,' Rense grumbled. 'His ugly behind sure is easy to spot.'

The news didn't seem to trouble Sylvie. She remained composed and continued to study the bridge. Her lips opened. She knew that in only moments she'd have to give the command. The enemy was about to storm onto the crossing.

Torwin fought against the huddle alongside him whilst Arthir struggled to keep up. The proud warrior pushed aside those around him as if battling a torrent of waters. He was keen to lead the assault and be the first to hit the bridge. His behaviour was being fuelled by the intensity of the moment. He craved glory and was being swept away by the rush of the charge.

'Move you fools! Let me through!' he protested.

Reactions were mixed but most appeared to acknowledge the menacing character before them. He barged through until he suddenly found himself at the front of the bottleneck of men forming feet away from the relatively narrow crossing. The vast horde was being forced to pour into this small space and already it seemed like chaos was kicking in. Too many feet were pounding the ground and hoping to get in front. Golandin was now way back compared to his allies. He stood alone, partially leaning against a tree just beyond the lakeside. All he could do was watch things play out.

'Fire!' Sylvie screeched at the top of her voice.

A volley of deadly arrows launched out from over the extensive wall. It looked as if a blanket of sticks had been fired, all gliding across the air as if one. Torwin's feet struck the wet stone surface of the bridge and within seconds a swarm converged onto the overpass. Arthir had only partially managed to keep close to the infamous rebel figure but also now found himself clambering onto the soaking stone.

'Arrows!' an anonymous voice wailed.

Torwin looked up only to behold the vista of a plethora of deadly sticks falling down to earth. None of these ragtag soldiers bore shields and had only their swords and arms to cover themselves against the incoming salvo.

There was nothing that could be done. The sticks of death fell to ground in silent precision and struck flesh and bone alike. The insurgents had been hit with the disciplined effectiveness of the skilled archers beyond the wall. Countless men fell as the arrows embedded into them from above. Many were hit in the shoulders and head, their light leather helmets doing little to protect them against the sharp edges.

A single arrow homed in on Torwin. It was as if fate itself had dictated its path. The warrior tried to dive forwards but too many halting rebels surrounded him. It slammed into his right shoulder and deeply penetrated his flesh. He cried out in both pain and sheer anger and fell back into a pile of bodies that had formed behind him on the stone. He stumbled to his feet and abruptly leapt over the low wall to his side. He fell into the cold waters of the lake with a loud splash and was gone.

Arthir had been shielded by the downpour by those around him. One had stumbled back and knocked him over. Their body had been peppered with arrows but none had touched Arthir as he lay hidden behind the dead. He started to desperately crawl away back into the grassy ground before the bridge. Suddenly, a second volley let lose into the sky from the walls of Brimma. Those that remained standing on the bridge instinctively started to dive into the lake, leaving a pile of dead and wounded lying on the crossing. Dozens of men hit the water in unison. The lake protested as the calm waters turned into a spray of splashing impacts.

The arrows slammed onto the bridge, further impaling the countless bodies piled on the stones. Many of them fell into the lake and made contact with the floundering bodies that desperately attempted to swim away. There was a volley of agonising cries as the whistling sticks claimed rebel after rebel. Torwin had managed to swim under the bridge in relative safety. There were narrow gaps in between the stone and the surface of the lake. As he bobbed on the water he forcefully pulled the arrow from his underwater shoulder. He howled in pain and clenched his gaping wound. The dark red tones of blood climbed out from the lesion like smoke bellowing out of a chimney and started to noticeably stain the clear liquid of the pond.

The mass attack had been utterly defeated. The rebels that had survived the bombardment were frantically swimming back towards the hillside they had come from. Others crawled from the bridge in agony with arrows stuck into their flesh. A heap of dead rebel troops lay lifeless across the overpass with further bodies floating atop the waters of the lake. Blood formed in distinctly red pools as the denser liquid rose to the surface.

From within the city wall the defenders looked on. The archers were already poised to launch another volley but Sylvie hadn't given the command. The leader studied her enemy. It seemed as if disorder was already kicking in amongst their ranks. She noticed one prominent figure standing in between a circle of panting warriors in the field. He appeared to be ordering them around, pointing at the gate and yelling into the sky.

'He must be leading them,' she said to herself.

'Yes, that's him alright,' Jamus came from behind. 'That's Golandin.'

Sylvie turned to face the old warrior. 'Jamus!' she jumped. 'You have recovered?'

'I am fine my girl,' he smiled.

The others acknowledged him with smiles and waves. All were pleased he was finally now back beside them.

'You just missed it,' said Fenris. 'A rebel massacre!'

Jamus was intrigued and popped his head over the tip of the stone wall covering them. Bodies covered the bridge and bumped into one another in the water surrounding it. To the other side the enemy seemed to be in disarray. All of them cowered back, out of accurate arrow range.

'They will strike again,' he said.

'Strike them again!' Rense requested. 'Our archers could hit them where they stand. We don't need to wait for them to hit the bridge again.'

Sylvie didn't appear to agree. 'No,' she said softly. 'Force must only be used against them once they cross the line. That line is entering onto the bridge. I want them to associate the bridge with that. I want to give them all the chance to conclude it is pointless trying to cross it and press on.'

'Most of them are civilians holding swords,' said Yuuki. 'They should be given a chance to retreat.'

'They don't look much like civilians to me,' grumbled Fenris. 'They look like a horde of savages! Those face paints and all.'

Jamus stood beside the Empress and focused his attention on Golandin. He then noticed the slim figure of Arthir scrambling through the crowds to reach the leader. He just knew it was him, a faint memory lurking in his head. They looked to be wearing the same armour as they had sported an age ago on distant battlefields he suddenly remembered.

'Arthir,' he chuckled. 'A full house it is then.'

'Who?' Rense asked ignorantly.

'Golandin's closest friend,' Sylvie qualified. 'The two go hand in hand as far as this is concerned.'

'They go back decades,' commented Jamus. 'The true essence of the rebellious mind.'

'We should target them somehow,' said Fenris. 'We could end all this with one decisive kill… or two.'

'It would be impossible to target them specifically,' said Sylvie. 'They are holding back intentionally.'

Jamus suddenly noticed the figure of Theamis standing next to Fenris. He was holding a bow in his right hand and resting his other on the stone wall pressed against his chest. He said nothing but instead looked to Sylvie as if requesting an explanation.

'He swore to join us,' she said. 'He had no real ties with the rebels. He was confused. I trust him.'

Jamus made no comment but seemed to be unsure with the idea. However, he knew not to create an issue over it and turned back to face the enemy ahead. They were once again stirring with meaning.

Across the bridge Golandin found himself on the receiving end of a bombardment of his own, only this assault consisted entirely of verbal strikes. His men were already flustered and demanding of some speech from the leader. He fought against the chaos around him and spoke:

'So they have archers! Break through the gate and fight arrows with swords! No use standing here.'

Arthir reached the leader and stood beside him trembling as if still trying to calm himself down after his dance with death.

'We will be destroyed before even reaching the gate!' he cried.

Those around him appeared to acknowledge his warning. Golandin snapped with sudden anger and slapped his friend around the back of the head. His steel helmet clanged with the metallic impact of Golandin's armoured glove. Arthir stumbled forwards and tried to compose himself.

'I never said this would be easy!' Golandin yelled. 'We will lose men. This is a battle!'

'How can we possibly overcome them?' an officer asked.

Golandin studied the mass huddled around the field and hillside. Many had still yet to even pass over the mound of ground from the plains beyond.

'Our numbers will overcome them,' he continued, 'and our battering rams have yet to even strike.'

The men manning the giant wooden logs had been overtaken by the masses of foot soldiers during the initial failed assault. They had now gathered just ahead of the bridge.

'Give the command to charge the bridge with everything we have!' Golandin commanded. 'Ensure our battering rams are protected and first to strike the gate.'

The officers bowed slightly and raced off to initiate his command. Arthir stood cautiously beside the rebel leader.

'Perhaps our archers could assist the assault?' he asked.

'Don't be foolish,' Golandin barked. 'You know as well as I do that our archers consist of a bunch of farmers more used to killing rabbits than pinpointing imperial Tamus troops hidden behind vast fortifications.'

'At least give them the order to fire,' said Arthir.

'Sure, okay… if it makes you feel better,' laughed Golandin.

The rebel horde was being woven back into a standing force as countless men in command called out for order. The battering rams were poised feet away from the crossing into Brimma and the masses huddled behind them in collective obedience. There was still a desire to attack.

The defenders peered outwards across the lake and prepared for another round of combat. The few hundred archers raised their bows and Sylvie's lips opened in anticipation.

'This will be the real strike,' Jamus noted. 'This is the one we must repel.'

He was deeply focused and unaware that beside him Lady Yuuki stood eager for attention. Her mind was elsewhere.

'Jamus,' she whispered.

The old friar looked at the girl beside him. She had her head bowed and eyes closed. Her multicoloured braids danced with the incoming breeze and her brown hair brushed across her blameless face.

'What is the matter Yuuki?' he asked patiently.

'It is Akumi… I sense she is…' the girl paused.

'Akumi? Whatever is it my dear?' Jamus was alarmed.

He knew the sorceress before him had great psychic abilities and was able to sense things few could even comprehend. His attention was drawn to her.

'I sense she has faded into black,' Yuuki said morbidly. 'I sense she has gone!'

The girl was emotional even though she'd never even met the late Hazati's finest student since distant childhood encounters.

'She has gone?' Jamus was concerned.

'I am sorry,' said Yuuki. 'I can't explain it any further. I just keep seeing this image of her lifeless body surrounded by shadow.'

Jamus put his hand on Yuuki's shoulder affectionately. He didn't question the girl any further. His wise mind already imagined what her magical insights were suggesting. Endal had defeated her. She was no more. What Jamus had feared all that time ago at the Grange Abbey had probably come to pass. He looked deeply discouraged.

'Do you think she is dead?' Yuuki asked fervently.

'If that is what you see, it would seem so,' Jamus whimpered.

The two were silent for several moments.

'Say no more of this,' said Jamus. 'For now I want everyone to be focused on matters at hand. This news will deeply upset them, particularly Sylvie.'

Yuuki nodded distantly. The two then turned back and faced the bridge.

The rebel army was on the move. Golandin had yelled out and his flock had listened. Arthir had once again joined the charge, desperate for glory. The battering rams were first to storm onto the bridge. The assaulting men were forced to tread on the bodies of their fallen comrades, arrows still freshly sticking from their corpses. Each of the three logs was being carried by six men. They were long and sturdy and those that held them were of a stocky build.

'Light the bridge!' Sylvie called. 'Before they get close!'

She had been waiting for this moment. A part of her was sickened and at odds with having to give this order. However, the girl knew it simply had to done. Arrows alone would now prove ineffectual.

The rams were half way across the bridge. They were being carried one after the other in a line. Behind the last one an endless mass of darkly attired rebels jogged forwards. The crowd went all the way back to the hillside and beyond. This was clearly an all out assault. Golandin's isolated figure was now lost from sight as the horde merged into one vast mass.

The two archers beside the burning barrel released their blazing arrows. They were aimed diagonally downwards towards the bridge's central section. The sticks of fire fell down to the stone with perfect precision. By now the rebels were huddled on the crossing with only inches to spare. The battering rams were almost fully across.

The arrows snapped against the stone but within seconds their flames had reacted with the flammable liquids soaking the structure. The fire erupted into a combusting line of glaring flame that overcame the entirety of the overpass within only moments. The attackers hadn't even had time to react.

Flames encircled those on the bridge and then conquered them. The wooden logs caught ablaze as the men carrying them were consumed by fire and dropped them. Their leather armour was caught in the blaze and instantly started to melt with the raging heat. The mass of burning flesh fell from the sides of the bridge into the water below. Many were already too burnt to salvage themselves and were lost in a firing inferno like meat in a glowing furnace.

Figure after figure dropped into the lake, instantly being soothed of fire by the reddening water. Many were only partially burnt whilst others had simply felt the heat of the flame tickle them before taking the plunge. However, many were now deformities of men and never re-emerged from the deep pond they had fallen into.

Sylvie was suddenly utterly overcome with guilt and heartfelt empathy for those fighting against the flames. She dropped to her knees and cried like a child. Yuuki and Emi were swift to console her and bent down next to her. Although they tried to comfort her they too felt deeply troubled and upset by what they were seeing. They all did.

'It had to be done,' Jamus called. 'It stopped their attack dead in its tracks.'

It all seemed lost for the enemy. The bridge was ablaze with a roaring fire likely to burn on and on. Nothing could be made out beyond the conflagration as bellowing smoulders formed a barrier to sight. It was as if the entire rebel army was lost behind the wall of flames and rising clouds of dark smoke. Jamus pranced up and down the platform as the troops around him stared into the fire. A barrage of arrows suddenly struck against the wall from beyond the smoke.

'Incoming arrows!' an archer called.

It hadn't been much of a salvo. Most of the shafts broke against the stone whilst others whistled by high overhead. Jamus had bent down in reaction to the warning but abruptly emerged back on his feet. Calmly, he walked over to Sylvie and noticed her face. She was in a state. Her wide eyes gazed into air guiltily. Hers was the face of remorse.

'You did what you had to Sylvie,' Jamus said.

'He is right,' Rense yelled uncaringly. 'They are all scumbags anyway. Let them burn!'

She looked up at Jamus and cautiously nodded her head with slight consternation.

'You saved Brimma,' said Emi. 'You commanded the empire to victory!'

'Listen to Emi,' added Fenris. 'She is right. You saved lives giving that order. You saved the lives of your people.'

CHAPTER VI

GLIMMERS OF HOPE

There was a panic. The field was dark with smoke and the flames heated the air. Golandin coughed uncontrollably as the dark, meandering haze rolled over him. The wind seemed to toil with the rebels. One minute it aided Tamus arrows, the next it directed smoke into their faces.

The rebel leader dropped to the ground and covered his face as a thick, dense cloud of smoke hovered by. Ahead of him hundreds were fleeing from the flames, breaking up from the charge. Those that had yet to pass over the hillside had halted and those that had dived into the lake were still floundering in the water as if awaiting some nonexistent aid. Some had swum back onto the lakeside and clambered onto the grass. Their skin was charred and smouldered like a trampled bonfire. Golandin noticed several of his men fighting amongst each other for a single rag of cloth. He then noticed Arthir cowering beside a tree several feet from the burning bridge. He got up and raced over to his friend.

Arthir had been partially caught by the flames. He was drenched and clearly downbeat.

'Are you okay?' Golandin asked.

'I was swift to hit the water,' said Arthir. 'I spotted the flames racing towards me. I was just lucky. If I'd have been a second slower I'd have been engulfed by fire.'

'A sick move!' Golandin cried out. 'Those Tamus pigs!'

Arthir had been moderately burnt. The flames had licked his legs as he'd pounced off the bridge. However, he didn't seem troubled by the mild burns around his calves.

'It was effective,' said Arthir. 'Got to give it to them.'

Arthir's voice was croaky and distant. He was still coming to terms with the fact he'd now had two scrapes with death in one morning.

'What now?!' cried Golandin. 'What now?!'

'We flee like the defeated ants we are,' Arthir moaned, 'and Ellis is notable by his absence might I add!'

'He was obviously discovered,' said Golandin. 'If that party we engaged near Dwenton now dwells in the city they probably exposed him. They knew we were coming from the south. Ellis would have ensured they acted on some false information and defended another section. No, Ellis is now history I fear.'

'I knew he'd be of no real use in the end,' said Arthir. 'I just knew it.'

As the two rebels spoke their troops continued to flee from the flames and stand around the hillside in shock and frustration. Many lay dead and charred in the field whilst others cried in unabated agony on the edges of the lake. The water itself was now bloody and filled with floating corpses.

There was no recourse to Arthir's suggestion. Even Golandin now looked lost for words. There was no way they could possibly put out the flames nor could they possibly expect their army to regain the morale they entered into battle with. Golandin noticed his line of archers fruitlessly firing into the smoke in the hope of striking a Tamus troop behind the mighty wall.

'Don't waste your arrows!' he yelled.

The small group of archers heard and lowered their bows. They didn't need convincing.

'So we are decided?' Arthir asked. 'It is over?'

Golandin was about to nod but reframed. He had suddenly spotted a seemingly unscathed figure emerge from the lake. Their bald head and pointed beard were a dead giveaway.

'Torwin!' he exclaimed.

The robed figure raced across the clearing under the cover of the smoke and immediately spotted Golandin waving at him. Torwin made for the rebel leader and bounded across the field with an energy nobody else around him seemed to possess any longer. He reached the veteran rebels in seconds.

'Well, what a show so far!' Torwin smirked.

'A show!' cried Arthir. 'We have been massacred. I thought you were dead. That blitz of arrows happened so quickly.'

Torwin looked into the eyes of Arthir and Golandin. He laughed out loud.

'What's this?' he asked. 'A bit of fire got your nerves tarred to shreds?'

'Our attack was waylaid by flame,' said Golandin. 'We lost many men in that blaze.'

Torwin stepped forwards into the grassy ground ahead of the trees his comrades cowered under.

'I was hit by an arrow and dropped into the lake before the bridge was lit up,' he said. 'I took a bit of a tour of their southern wall. Very nice indeed.'

'A tour...' Arthir remarked, unimpressed by his tone.

'I swam across its width and spotted an opening,' said Torwin. 'They have left a sewer entrance unguarded. The iron corrugated bars covering it have already been destroyed. It looked to me to be the work of an explosive but that is unimportant.'

Golandin's ears pricked. This was intriguing.

'Listen, as it seems you two are lost for words right now let me make things clear,' Torwin continued. 'This battle is winnable. I have scouted the sewer entrance and it leads into the city. If we form a vanguard force to enter into it, with me leading, we can breach Brimma.'

Golandin nodded; with sudden glimmers of hope sparkling in his eyes. Even Arthir was impressed.

'Gather twenty men,' said Torwin. 'I will lead them in. Now, as for this bridge, here is what should be done: call your archers and order them to fire their arrows into the fire. They will catch alight and pass through the flames. They will strike the wooden gate and set it ablaze! From there we watch the entrance burn and once the bridge has smouldered out you charge!'

'Will that work?' shrieked Arthir.

'Yes,' laughed Torwin. 'It is called physics. The fire will eventually burn the wood.'

'Cunning,' said Golandin. 'Very cunning.'

Sylvie got to her feet. The fire was weakening and the initial smoke clearing. She noticed countless figures scattered out across the field beyond the lake. Many were moving around in agony. There was clearly no rebel medical assistance to be had. Her heart throbbed with concern. She still felt immense guilt.

'Victory!' a Tamus troop suddenly declared from beside her.

They were a Sergeant. Sylvie could tell from the red ribbon tied around their chestal armour and feathered helm.

'General Dorwor would be proud!' he continued.

Sylvie smiled and thanked the soldier. She tried to come over resilient but the truth was she felt nothing besides being sickened. Perhaps the late Dorwor would have been proud of her but this thought didn't seem to aid her despair.

'The fire will surely wage on for an hour at least,' said Rense. 'I can't see them having the stomach for another assault.'

'It won't burn that long,' said Fenris. 'It will only burn for a few more minutes. Talk of victory is folly at this point.'

'Aye, but they won't hit us again!' the Sergeant laughed. 'We got 'em running scared!'

The reality was they all sensed victory but couldn't mentally declare it just yet. Something then occurred that truly confirmed Fenris had been right to warn against early calls of triumph. A volley of arrows crunched against the firm wood of the gateway from beyond the fire. All of them had lit up upon passing through the long line of flame and instantly embedded themselves into the thick lumber.

'Their archers have gone mad!' Theamis laughed, suddenly opening his mouth.

Jamus eyed the former rebel disconcertedly. 'For God's sake, we must ensure that gate isn't lit up!' he yelled.

Sylvie snapped out of her trancelike state of melancholy and peered down at the gateway. The entry points the arrows had made looked to be already smouldering.

'They must be planning to set the gate alight,' she said.

There was little that could be done. Further incoming arrows darted through the fire and slammed into the wood. Each brought with it a new ember of smouldering ash. Smoke started to form around the impact holes being created by the barrage. Without warning a fire then became apparent slowly edging its way out from the shaft of an arrow and onto the wooden gate.

'We must immediately form up en masse beside the gate,' said Sylvie. 'If it burns down there will be no stopping them. We will have to defend the road leading further into the city.'

'We need water,' said Rense; 'to stop the fire from building.'

'There is none,' Sylvie replied, 'unless you fancy running out to the lake!'

As the Empress called out for her sword bearing troops to form in lines on the road below her the gate continued to receive arrow after arrow. The enemy plan appeared to be working.

In a separate development a large group of rebels dropped into the water of the lake a few hundred feet from the bridge. Covered by the blanket of smoke that hovered over the surface they swam across its body and slowly made for a single entrance point. Torwin was leading the advance, his front crawl slightly modified due to his bandaged shoulder wound. He'd had time to see to it whilst Golandin had summoned those that now moved beside him. They were the ardent few that had been with Golandin ever since it could be remembered. They were mostly largely built, with bristled beards and aging complexions. Several carried longswords whilst others clasped spears. All had painted faces except for Torwin.

The sewer entrance was reached in no time and the group of twenty-one warriors didn't seem to get noticed by those manning the wall above. The smoke had ensured that.

'Climb into that sewer one by one,' ordered Torwin.

The rebels climbed up and clasped onto the broken iron bars for support. One by one they edged into the dark space that had once been used by a lone assassin eager to kill the Emperor. Although Torwin said nothing of it he believed this must have been the route once taken by Endal. He'd heard the story of the assassination with a keen ear.

The bald headed warrior waited patiently as his party climbed into the tunnel. Only a few now remained in the water.

'Wait for me,' a voice cried from the smoky lake.

Torwin looked ahead and studied the single character emerge into view.

'So you fancy being a part of this little elite operation?' Torwin smiled.

'Wouldn't miss it for the world,' said Arthir whilst swimming beside the mighty wall. 'It's time to turn the tables on these Tamus dogs.'

The gate was succumbing to flame. Its exterior side had been peppered with arrow heads and with each small collection of hot embers that struck the wooden entrance came further genesis points for fire. Eventually, the fires had begun to blaze and climb up the entirety of the vast door until reaching the stone archway around it. It now seemed certain that the gate would ultimately burn into ash. Sylvie had ordered her troops to form in mass lines behind it. Hundreds stood in single columns, with swords and shields poised. The winding roads and thatched houses behind them were vacant and unaffected by the chaos ensuing outside.

'Archers will bombard them with every last arrow as soon as the fires clear,' Sylvie yelled. 'Once they enter under the gateway they are to be held here. We cannot let them pass into the streets and break up. If that happens Brimma will have been breached.'

Jamus and his party remained on the platform and looked down at the mass lines of Tamus troops ready to fight with everything they had. Emi's bow was already poised ahead, with Theamis beside her. Sylvie was now on the ground next to the gate. The Sword of Tamus was firmly clutched in her hands.

'I will do all I can to form a barrier around the gate,' Yuuki declared, 'but I can't cast spells indefinitely.'

Jamus nodded. 'Do all you can my girl,' he said.

The old warrior started to climb down the ladder. Rense and Fenris followed him, both knowing they could do little on the platform and would be required in the thick of it.

The gate gave in as the fires overcame it. The thick, dark oak burned with a great orange glow. Black smoke bellowed into the air. With cruel synchronicity the bridge fire started to flicker out as its fuel source diminished. The flames faded and the air cleared around the blackened stone surfaces. Dozens of sooty, charred skeletons of men were starkly revealed as the flames gave way. Behind the smoke an infinite mass of rebels continued to patiently stand waiting for revenge and ultimate victory. Golandin now stood in front of the horde. His officers had done a good job of rallying them and distributing the news of what was to be done. Word had spread and Golandin's army was once again back in array.

'This is truly the moment!' Golandin screamed with all his might. 'Watch as their gate burns down. We shall storm the entrance and overcome the defenders!'

The army cheered in unison and once again there were drumbeats coming from within the huddle.

'Torwin will raise our standard on Tamus Tower!' the leader declared. 'We will be victorious!'

The gate was losing its form and turning into blackened ash

with a greater pace as the fire waged. Sylvie's blue eyes were lit up by the flames snaking into view from behind the thick, crackling oak. They glowed with golden intensity.

She stood in front of her men. They were several feet back from the Empress, with shields raised and helmets down. The girl stood firm with her steel held high and proud. The Sword of Tamus was the closest blade to the gate. She was to be in the thick of it.

CHAPTER VII

AWAKENING

A tranquil cerulean miasma lit the walls with sudden vibrance. The crystals were mysteriously altering colours like they were reacting to some alien energy. The air was cold and icy. If it weren't for the glowing stones the cavern would have been shrouded in the deepest darkness.

Hovering in encircling flight beyond the vibrant cave grim entities gradually amassed. They were gathering; dropping down from the great heights that led to the outside world above the surface. The shadowy creatures had even started to pass into the cave of crystals and glided above the luminous rocks. Several feet further into the rocky space a body lay in a pool of drying blood. Its pale, lifeless skin was lit up in the azure tones around it. A damp, red cloak covered most of the inert corpse.

Not far from the female's body another stiff rested against a wall of prickly crystals. Endal's bloody, mangled carcass still seeped blood. The liquid dripped from the body's countless gashes and slowly crawled down a black robe. The corpse was beginning to smell foul and fetid.

The infernal beings suddenly descended down from the black depths of the underground chasm en masse and entered into the cave from the wide entrance of the rocky natural platform beyond. They silently flew over the gleaming crystals and halted above the body of the late Akumi. More and more flying figures continued to appear around the corpse and started to huddle in droves around the diminishing space available. None seemed to take any notice of the late Endal.

The girl's corpse was being smothered by shadow beings as they got nearer and nearer to it. Eventually, the body was lost under a mass of dark figures. Their eyes glowed red in stark contrast to the blue tones around them. There was an ethereal quality to the creatures. They were semi transparent and shrouded in murky light. So many now filled the cave that there was no further room for the multitudes still coming from high above.

Akumi's body was clearly at the forefront of the dark energies' attention. Way beyond the cave and above the swamplands of this desolate land, the unearthly cloud mass rolled and churned with magical intensity and immeasurable power. It seemed to be directing the behaviour of each ungodly being that flew from its otherworldly corpus.

The female assassin's body was suddenly lifted from its ultimate position resting in a formed pool of blood. The girl had initially slipped into unconsciousness due to loss of blood but had eventually passed away where she had collapsed.

The beings danced around her and raised her into the air as if she was weightless and able to float on command. Her red cloak drooped onto the rocky ground and her legs dangled against gravity. Her body was lifted higher until it gracefully started to hover through the air towards the clearing outside of the cave. Thousands of black figures lurched around her in what looked like a display of mass excitement. Akumi's corpse was lifted higher as it passed out into the dark space beyond the cave. It was moved through the air with great pace and eventually taken over the edges of the rocky platform. Below it was now only the blackness of the infinite drop into inaccessibly deep orifices of the world.

The dark forces surrounding and snatching the body formed a giant ball of black around it, which stretched out until it almost touched each distant corner of the mighty space. The cloud of creatures ascended with great speed. Within only seconds they were starting to pop through the mass of gaps within the earth that roofed this hollow section of the underground lair.

Akumi's rag doll corpse lifted through one of the many narrow tunnels carved by the dark forces to gain entrance. Her pale face suddenly appeared from the earthy burrow and entered into the soothing sunlight of early morning. The esoteric forces guiding her continued to carry her further up into the sky above. They were heading straight into the black fog of the swirling energy whirlpool resting above the swamplands. Her body disappeared into the dark clouds as the flying entities transported her into the heart of its mass essence.

Her remains were surrounded by intense energy. Light poured

into her cadaver from every angle and empowered her every muscle. She was being healed. Her bloody waist started to gradually alter. The perfectly cut flesh reformed and renewed. Her skin turned a chirpier tone. After a few more moments she was even twitching as if reacting to a touch.

The process went on as her body hovered in the cloud mass. Her shattered vehicle had been mended. No wound remained and her brown eyes suddenly opened. Her lips moistened and her strength started to be replenished. The female assassin was lifted back down to earth as her trancelike state of regeneration reached final stages. The girl slowly descended from the clouds and ultimately landed softly onto the dry soil of a mound of earth sticking out from the swamp. Entities circled above as she lay peacefully in the sunlight.

The girl's eyes had closed back shut but suddenly opened again. This time there was a life force behind her glare. Akumi was alive. She had been resurrected by the strange energy around her. She remembered everything and sat up abruptly. She immediately noticed her lack of wounds. She felt her waist only to discover perfect, uncut skin. Her makeshift bandage still wrapped around her now nonexistent shoulder wound.

Her last memory was of staggering away from Endal's remains and falling to the ground with exhaustion in a state of hypovolemia. She then recalled what had come next. The girl distinctly remembered feeling at peace and slipping into some other state of awareness. She had entered into light and glanced into an infinity of possibility. She even recalled seeing lost friends. Hazati had warmly greeted her with straw hat in hand. Her old friends, Jobe and Harkor, had even been present. She then remembered a sensation akin to waking up only twice as exuberant. As she reflected on what had happened to her an incorporeal voice called out from the dark cloud above her:

'You have been healed and resurrected. We are at your command.'

Akumi was perplexed. The voice was calm and friendly. She wasn't sure if it was in her head or audible to anyone potentially around her.

'But why?' she asked.

The omnipresent voice responded:

'You defeated Endal. You have shown yourself to be a warrior of great power. The chaotic energies will do your bidding.'

Akumi recalled what Endal had said to her. He had been preparing to lead these massing energies into great conflicts with man. He had claimed to be a demigod of sorts. The fact she'd ultimately defeated him had clearly put her in a great light. The forces around her now seemed naturally prepared to switch allegiance to her supposed great powers.

'You will do as I command?' she asked out loud.

'Your will be done,' came the voice.

'And what of Endal? Will you bring him back to life as you did me?' she further questioned.

'Endal is no longer of any relevance,' answered the voice. 'He was defeated. You have proved yourself superior. You will lead us.'

Akumi nodded. In a strange way she didn't find this unprecedented spectacle hard to swallow. Her dance with death appeared to have given her some insight into the otherworldly realms these energies pervaded. She could accept the reasoning of the ethereal voice.

'So I was dead?' she asked.

'Yes,' said the voice.

'I... I recall meeting fallen friends,' she said.

'You passed into another dimension,' said the voice. 'We pulled you back. It would have been too late if we had waited only minutes more.'

Akumi nodded to herself. 'So... Endal,' she said. 'He can't be resurrected now?'

The girl wanted to be sure. She was ignorant to the implications of what the voice was saying.

'No one is ever resurrected,' said the voice. 'It has only occurred for you today because you defeated Endal. You will command us. We require it. Endal is gone. He no longer has any presence in this world.'

It suddenly started to make sense. This was an exceptional moment; the intense magical powers that had formed had saved her by default. She'd claimed the cloud's leader and it now turned to her for guidance. It appeared there was no sentience about this dark energy; it possessed elementary intelligence.

With the minutes that had now gone by since Akumi had awoken her mind had started to forget about her faint experiences in some other world beyond the veil. Just like gradually forgetting the details of a lucid dream after waking from a deep sleep, the girl now had only a sense of what had happened. She no longer remembered much beyond knowing she had sensed the presence of her old friends.

Akumi got to her feet and stared up into the cloud. She then looked down to her side only to realise her katana was missing. She then remembered leaving it embedded in Endal's shattered body. It was now unsalvageable; miles below her within the deep, cavernous underground chamber she had been lifted from.

'I will command you,' she yelled out to the spiralling clouds. 'Take me to Brimma! We have a battle to fight. We must ensure that the army attacking that city is defeated! That is my will!'

With instant obedience Akumi was once again carried into the air by the flying creatures above her. The wolflike beings that had remained hidden around the swamp suddenly emerged into full view. They ran with great speed and abruptly morphed into yet more of the flying entities that encircled the vast mists. The body of energy was then on the move. The great cloud rolled eastwards, Brimma its destination.

BOOK SIX

CHAPTER I

IN THROUGH SMOKE

The mighty gate was smouldering. A ravaging heat lurked in the air around the vast entrance into Brimma. The wood was all but spent as the orange flames licked every inch of the thick material. Those within the city were preparing for a grand confrontation with those eager to storm the entrance. Swords were held high and shields rested together in lines on the street beyond the entranceway.

Sylvie, Empress of Marmia, stood firm. There was a profound intensity about her stance. She wasn't going to budge. On the platform above Jamus prepared himself for the looming fight. He, Fenris, and Rense had climbed back onto the raised area; eager to see the enemy charge in all their might. Every last one of them knew this was to be a vital battle. The odds were against them but none dwelt on the numbers about to charge through the fire. All but Rense remained silent during this moment of final calm.

'What 'ya reckon?' he asked out loud. 'My guess is they out-man us three to one.'

'Probably,' replied Emi, 'but we have one huge advantage.'

'Oh?' pondered Rense.

'There are females present,' the huntress smiled.

Fenris chuckled to himself whilst Rense shook his head in playful mockery.

'Outnumber...' Rense modified. 'They outnumber us three to one! Better?' Emi just laughed.

The waging fires started to flounder. The wooden bulk of the gate was all but consumed. Suddenly, Sylvie could make out figures standing on the bridge through large gaps now appearing in the entrance. Dark smoke still blocked the majority of the view but things were getting clearer.

A section of the gate finally gave way as the heat overcame it. A bulky segment of charring wood fell against the remaining piece still standing. The impact smashed the further remains of the gateway into two pitiful parts. Both were wildly ablaze and visibly turned into ash within only seconds. The remaining slabs of oak just lay in smoky ruins; blackened and gritty with ash and smoulder. Kindlings of birch shone in radiant red before puffing out into cinders. The gate was gone.

Sylvie and the army of troops behind her instantly made out the horde formed up on the soot stained bridge. The smoke cleared and there was clarity.

'Charge!' a rebel voice wailed.

The rebellion kicked into full swing. Golandin's armour clad figure was first to lunge forwards towards those standing within the broken entrance. His platemail made movement difficult but his pace was swift. His army charged as one and fierce war cries filled the air.

Archers let loose a salvo of arrows. Emi placed two on her bow string and fired them at once. Theamis stood beside her and let his arrow fly down at the storming attackers on the bridge. The round of bowshot claimed countless rebels. Men fell and screamed in agony as the wooden sticks struck their flesh and impaled their flimsy leather armour. Several fell into the lake. Others just collapsed and got trampled by hundreds of advancing allies. Although the bombardment proved deadly the vast horde appeared to just absorb it, so great was their number.

They were now only feet from passing into Brimma. Lady Yuuki raised her arms and clasped her elegant staff in both hands. She was looking down at the attackers from the platform beside the bridge. Her soft, feminine voice yelled out some magical command:

'*Mia Folem Ex!*'

Her words were lost under the sounds of stamping boots on stone ground and waves of feral yells but this didn't seem to matter. Her staff shone white and bolts of deadly light crashed against the huddled masses below. Each individual bolt burned through flesh and evaporated once striking the stone. The intense magical force smote dozens of rebel thugs. They dropped down lifeless and were lost under the sea of stumbling insurgents.

More arrows descended on the enemy. Yuuki did all she could; casting further spells, each as terrifying as the last. She was clearly terrorising many of those sinful thugs that had witnessed her wrath. However, the advance was endless and there was no turning back for any of them now.

Golandin raised his sword high as his body swept under the entranceway. Several arrows had struck him but his sturdy armour had sent them bouncing back into the air. The first lines of his men were only feet behind him.

Sylvie stood perfectly still in the middle of the track within the city wall.

'Come behind us!' a soldier yelled out to her.

She ignored them. She wasn't afraid to be at the forefront and could instantly tell the figure charging towards her was Golandin, leader of the rebellion and heart of the revolt.

'Death to the empire!' a voice yelled from the mass rebel crowd that now passed under the wall.

In through smoke the rebels came. Sylvie's archers continued to fire at those still coming from the bridge whilst Jamus and his party were on the move. Yuuki remained on the platform and chanted to herself with staff raised high. Behind her Fenris leapt from the wooden scaffold and dropped into the mass rush storming through the gateway below him. Rense was swift to follow but fell with far less agility and prowess than his ally.

Fenris landed on his feet, with dual scimitars poised to hack at anyone close enough. He had managed to land in a clearing to the side of the gateway, only feet from Sylvie. Rense dropped beside him and smashed into a group of empty wooden barrels. They crumbled with impact. The sturdy figure got up and instantly started wielding his mighty axe. Fenris broke into the horde with his swords slicing at every limb he could reach.

Golandin ran at Sylvie without fear and suddenly the two were pitted against one another. The Empress of Marmia was battling the leader of the rebellion. The rebels passed the figures by and crunched into the first line of Tamus troops. Their shields had absorbed the impact and their swords poked out and thrust into the crowd.

Sylvie's steel slammed against Golandin's longsword. The blades pressed together with great force. Neither withdrew. Golandin then raised his left arm and struck his armour clad elbow against Sylvie's unguarded cheek. She stumbled back and Golandin deflected her blade to her side. He then barged into her body with his shoulder. The steel plates struck her chest and she fell to the ground. Golandin laughed.

'So this is all the once mighty Tamus Empire can muster for an Empress!' he mocked. 'I will be doing Marmia a favour by slaying you my girl.'

Behind them the Tamus troops battled against the horde still sweeping in through the gateway. Their line had held but the sheer numbers now accumulating around the track were forcing them to step back. One lost their shield against the tide of men pulling and striking at the line. He bent to pick it up but his head was swiftly decapitated in full view of those around him. A rebel blade had managed to connect with his neck.

Fenris and Rense had gained a lot of attention. Their position just beside the gateway meant they were able to ambush the enemy as they stormed in. However, the bodies now surrounded them and many entering in were turning straight for them. Fenris danced against the sea of swords prodding at his agile frame. He struck one from a bearded rebel's hand with one sword and spliced down their chest with the other. A haze of blood steamed out from the figure as they dropped to their knees and fell forwards into the dry soil of the track.

Rense swung his axe with such momentum that it knocked a whole group of insurgents off their feet. Another charged towards him. He raised his axe into the air and drove it down vertically towards the assailant. It hacked into their face and split their head down the middle. The skull smashed like a vase being dropped onto a rocky surface.

On the platform Emi fired arrow after arrow. She must have claimed dozens by now. Theamis had seemed just as dedicated but his arrows no longer left his bow. He was now watching the battle play out around him. His fearful eyes looked down at the ground below. His bow dropped onto the wooden timber boards and his sword hand clasped his blade handle.

Jamus had remained on the platform but now clambered down the single ladder. He found himself right beside Fenris but wasn't interested in aiding him. His eyes were homed in on Sylvie across the other side of the track.

The Empress had managed to fend off Golandin's mighty longsword as she lay on the ground after receiving his shoulder barge. She rolled to one side and got back on her feet. The rebel leader continued to come at her with swarms of advancing thugs behind him making for her troops. He swung his steel high, hoping to make contact with the girl's head. She crouched down to evade it and jabbed The Sword of Tamus into the aged warrior's torso. His armour appeared to soak up the strike and he slammed her blade to one side with his clad arm.

'No use you wretched dog,' said Golandin. 'My armour is too strong, forged by great blacksmiths of the past. It has never failed me.'

Jamus stumbled through the crowds, embedding his sword into one rebel whilst clambering across the track. He'd finally reached the Empress.

'Golandin!' he yelled from behind the rebel leader.

The armour clad commander turned to face the old friar.

'Jamus?' he smiled from under his helm. 'I remember you!'

As Golandin spoke Jamus had swung his sword forth towards the figure's ribcage. Golandin made no attempt to parry it. The blade jabbed into his armoured tunic but failed to penetrate the steel. The rebel then launched his own strike. His longsword came at Jamus. The old warrior was poised to deflect it but Sylvie had leapt in from behind and done it herself. She then slammed her sword handle into Golandin's helmet and kicked him in the back of knee. He dropped down onto his knees, the clanging of steel ringing in his ears. The Empress desperately plunged her sword into his back but the blade merely slipped down the side of his armour.

Jamus poked his steel into Golandin's chest but to no avail. The rebel got to his feet and ran into the crowd of insurgents like he needed a breather.

'I will go after him,' Sylvie insisted.

Jamus was panting. His wound was playing up with all the antics he'd forced himself to perform. He had his back turned to the mass of enemies slamming against the lines of imperial troops.

'He must be finished,' the friar yelled. 'Once and for all!'

They were about to move on but Jamus suddenly felt a cold shaft of metal enter into his lower back. He howled in pain but his moans were soft and fell silent. A single rebel had targeted him as they came bounding out from the mass horde. Jamus fell to his knees.

'Jamus!' Sylvie cried.

She stepped forwards and instantly thrust her sword into the rebel. He'd had no time to react, still trying to pull his blade from Jamus, and felt her sword press into his heart. He cried out and fell down dead.

Jamus dropped onto the muddy track. Sylvie bent down and pulled the scimitar from his back. The blade was stained in blood. The old friar was silent but his eyes were wide open. The Empress knew there was nothing she could do. Jamus looked into her eyes as she propped up his head. He had no energy to speak. Sylvie suddenly got up and raised him, his arm wrapped around her shoulders.

'I have to move you away from the battle,' she said.

With steadfast strength she supported his failing body and dragged him away from the track. She headed straight for the first building she could see; it rested further north from the gateway beside the track her troops were fighting on. She passed by her men as they valiantly struggled against the tide of rebels and dragged Jamus up the porchway steps. The home was empty and silent. Once inside she placed Jamus on a dormant bed beside the wall of the small room. There was nothing else inside besides a dusty cabinet of ornamental plates.

Sylvie tore cloths from a blanket and tied them around the old friar's lower back. He had now lost consciousness but was still alive. It seemed like nothing but it was all she could do for him. The girl then raced out of the house and cried out loud for medical assistance. To her amazement two of her guards ran out from their line without delay.

'Jamus is hurt,' she whimpered emotionally. 'Do all you can for him.'

The guards ran straight into the dwelling house whilst Sylvie stroked her sword handle and eyed the battlefield ahead. She ran straight back into the fray.

On the platform Emi and the line of archers continued to fire down at the oncoming enemy force. It seemed endless; droves still charged up the bridge with others still yet to step away from the field beyond the lake. A group of men on horseback lurked the lakeside like they were still waiting for the moment to advance. All had now crossed over the hill.

Emi was low on arrows. She'd used up all of her own stash and now borrowed a handful from Tamus troops beside her.

However, no more could be spared once this pittance had been depleted. All of them were close to running out entirely.

Yuuki was panting against the stone wall. Just below her graceful figure Rense and Fenris continued to wage war with the enemy. The sorceress was exhausted, she'd been summoning spell after spell with as much might as she could muster. She was now quite drained.

Theamis was still near them but was at odds with what to do. The former rebel had been paying attention to the situation around him. He was in deep thought. Below the platform a group of rebels suddenly barged past Fenris as he struggled against the numbers surrounding him. They started climbing the ladder onto the wooden podium.

'I'm with you,' Theamis screeched.

The young male was abruptly switching sides again. He sensed all was lost for the defenders and believed he'd now be better off reaffirming allegiance to his former masters.

The insurgents scurried up the ladder. The first to reach the platform was instantly booted back to ground by Emi. She'd fired her last arrow out towards the bridge and dropped her bow. The girl was now brandishing her trusty huntress' knife.

'Don't be foolish Theamis,' she yelled in reaction to his call.

He continued to stand on the plinth with sword drawn.

'They are overwhelming us,' he yelled. 'It's no use!'

Lady Yuuki regained her posture and stood to Emi's side as more rebels attempted to prod their way up the ladder. Yuuki jabbed her staff into one, sending them flying off the ladder. Emi kicked another's sword from their hand and started to vehemently shake the delicate ladder with all her might. Yuuki joined in and soon the cords that bound it to the platform were faltering. Rebel after rebel lost grip and fell to earth. The ladder was at least ten feet high making the drop potentially perilous.

Down below Rense wrestled with several attackers that had started attempting to manhandle him. In the jostle he dropped his axe. Fenris was too busy spinning his blades around in desperation to help. Hundreds now surrounded just them; all poised to either climb the platform or join the fight against the Tamus troops lined up further along the track.

The ladder shook continuously as the girls ensured no one reached the archers above. Theamis, noticing the rebel crowd's eyes, suddenly plunged at them. His allegiance was switched and he wanted to be seen fighting for the rebellion. Both girls stumbled forwards and fell from the podium directly into the maddening horde.

'For Golandin!' cried Theamis.

The coward's glory lasted only seconds. The line of archers had finally ran out of arrows and drew their swords. They turned towards him and edged in; all had seen his treachery. He crept back until his feet negotiated the final inches of the platform. Swords plunged and he stumbled back to avoid them. He fell onto the ground beside the joists holding up the wooden stage.

Emi and Yuuki had kicked and bitten their way out from the enraged crowd. Rense had been lost under a pile of assailants in the far corner beside the entranceway wall. Fenris was hopelessly encircled and being prodded at like a weakening dog. The girls backed away until they stood to the side of the wooden platform. All looked bleak as the crowd raced at them until the line of archers pounced from the podium and landed on the rebels in a mass group of falling bodies.

Suddenly, the entire platform broke away and snapped as if faltering under a great weight. Theamis had slid his blade across each wooden support. Those that hadn't taken the leap into the revolting crowd fell with the wreckage and disappeared into a pile of broken timbers. Around twenty of them perished under the pile of ruins as they fell with the crumbling platform.

With the rebel crowd now occupied taking on the archers Emi and Yuuki turned and raced after the traitor. He had ran away towards the urban section of Brimma; slipping the net of Sylvie's defences.

Golandin's armoured figure stood mightily in the middle of the fray. He joined the rebels trying to break through the ranks of Tamus troops defending the track into the city, and ultimately into Tamus Tower. The column of soldiers had been all but surrounded, with a vast pincer of rebels attacking on both sides. Spearmen poked at the troops whilst they bent under their mighty shields and fought back with their swords. Many had fallen victim to the spears and blades that hacked at them from every angle.

Golandin had kept back but now walked closer towards his enemy. As he reached the line several Tamus troops lunged at him with their steel. He took the arm clean off one of them, his blade slicing through their silver armour. The other had missed him and felt Golandin's longsword cut into their gullet. They fell in a bloody mist. The other scrambled around for their arm in a wild panic. Golandin plunged his sword into their back as they bent forwards trying to pick the limb up.

'Break through the line!' the rebel leader called out triumphantly. 'This is the opening!'

With the two pivotal troops down there was indeed a gap. In only seconds the rebel horde broke through it like a cancer corrupting a pool of cells. This was the moment the tables started to turn.

Golandin led the breakthrough into the imperial column of soldiers. Their lines broke away as if being brushed aside by a mighty wave. Discipline and skill could do nothing against this vast mob. The Tamus troops were just too outnumbered.

As Golandin hacked through the retreating soldiers a single figure suddenly pounced through the air towards him. It was Sylvie. Her blonde hair waved with her downwards momentum. The Sword of Tamus was pointing straight for Golandin.

Her attack had come from nowhere. She had been lurking behind her men. Golandin raised his sword but it was too late. Before he'd even managed to point his blade towards her the girl had sunk her sharp weapon deep into his heavy chest plate. The speed and strength behind Sylvie's manoeuvre had given her sword enough power to penetrate straight through the warrior's armour. Her blade tip stabbed into his solar plexus and ripped through his tissue. He called out in desperate pain and fell back with her force as she ploughed into him from above.

CHAPTER II

THE GREAT VICTORY

The manhole cover launched into the air and slammed against the cobbled stones of the street. Torwin climbed out of the sewer and shuffled across the urban lane for cover. He sneaked into a side alley and scanned every inch of ground ahead.

'Looks clear,' he called.

His party clambered up the iron ladder and popped into the street one by one. Arthir was third to appear and raced over to Torwin without delay.

'The tower!' Arthir decorously declared. 'We have stumbled right in front of it!'

Torwin nodded and studied the impressive structure. The black tower rose into the sky in menacing decadence. The omniscient construction resembled nothing either man had seen before. Now they were so close the sheer enormity of it struck them.

'Behold Tamus Tower Arthir,' Torwin said; 'our new home!'

The last revolting warrior appeared from the manhole and grouped up with the others in the street. Torwin stepped out from the alley and started to jog towards the tower. The wall surrounding its courtyard was only a few hundred feet away.

'To the tower!' Torwin ordered.

The party broke into a charge with Torwin and Arthir at the front. A few of the selected rebels carried a rolled up banner under their arms. The plan was to hang it from the highest point of the tower to mark a great victory even though none of these men really had a clue how the battle further south of the city was now playing out.

Within minutes they had reached the wall of the courtyard. They came from the very side Endal had once assaulted from; the section of the wall he blew still missing from the perimeter. Torwin passed through that gap and his party raced up the courtyard unchallenged. There were no guards anywhere but the southern gateway.

Further down the street a lone male scurried past the thatched dwellings around him. He was being closely pursued by Emi and Lady Yuuki. They had raced after him through the narrow streets of the city and carefully ensured they didn't lose him. Theamis had nowhere to hide and knew the girls were onto him. He clasped his sword and turned to face them head on. He'd have already been claimed by Yuuki's ranged magic if it were not for the fact the sorceress was drained. As the girls caught up with him they both noticed the darkly clad figures of Torwin's party passing unchecked through the wrecked wall into the tower grounds ahead.

'The city has fallen,' cried Theamis. 'Look! They are already storming the tower! I had no choice but to switch sides.'

Neither girl looked impressed. Yuuki leant on her staff with scornful eyes focused attentively on him. She looked livid and eyed him as if she desired to extirpate him on the spot. Emi looked equally enraged and clasped her knife in her left hand.

'You almost killed us!' she said. 'Knocking us into the rebel crowds like that!'

Theamis knew he'd played his card. There was no longer any turning back. He raised his blade and raced towards the girls.

They reacted by running towards him at once. Theamis swung at Emi once they had reached each other. She evaded his strike and edged towards him as his blade arm passed across his side in completion of his swooping arc. Her dagger sunk into his belly as she clasped him by the neck. In her heart she had never truly trusted him.

He dropped to the cobbled stones and moaned in agony. Emi pointed her knife down at him as if about to finish him off. Yuuki stood beside her.

'Please don't kill me,' he whimpered frostily.

Both girls knew his wound would prove fatal. He was in immense pain and blood percolated from his stomach. The merciful thing to do was put him out of his agony. Neither girl liked seeing someone so desperate.

'Rest,' Yuuki said calmly. 'Be at peace.'

The sorceress knew of the spiritual nature of their reality and took refuge in that knowledge. She soothed the warrior with a calming light that poured out from her palms and looked away as Emi forced herself to finish him off. She raised her knife towards his torso and stared down at him.

'Please!' Theamis cried out, blood dripping from his lips.

Emi toiled with her emotions. She aimed the blade at his chest, but slowly her knife withdrew to her side. She couldn't do it.

'Why ever did you attack me?' Emi shrieked. 'You shouldn't have come at me like that.'

Theamis had proved to be a very foolish character. He no longer had the strength to speak. Yuuki knelt beside him and thoughtfully stroked his forehead.

'There is nothing we can do for you,' said Emi softly. 'I am sorry.'

A magical glow continued to relieve him. It danced around his body in a transparent haze. Within seconds he was gone. His body lay limp and his eyelids curled shut. Theamis was no more.

The girls turned their attention to the tower. Both seemed slightly demure after the male's demise. The group of figures had vanished behind the wall surrounding Tamus Tower. They could just make out the street passing up the side of the wall they had entered from.

'There looked to be many of them,' said Yuuki. 'We should warn the others and form a group to repel them.'

Emi was in full agreement. They ran back down the street towards the gateway. They just hoped there would be enough troops to spare.

The gateway was drowning in bodies that had been savagely tramped underfoot by the advancing rebel militia. The entirety of Golandin's mob had now passed under the entrance and fought against the hopelessly surrounded Tamus troops. Sylvie was struggling against the enemy presence around her. She had landed atop Golandin after stabbing his chest but the figure had crawled away behind the crowds of rebels like a wounded animal. Sylvie had been unable to chase after him due to the numbers surrounding her.

Together with her troops beside her the Empress was locked in combat. Her sword slammed into body after body. Blow for blow the rebels were being massacred by the skill and discipline of her forces, but those forces were now dwindling under the pressure.

With every passing second a Tamus soldier appeared to fall down.

Nearer the gateway Rense had managed to hurl an entire group off from him as he fought against those pinning him against the stone wall. He picked up his axe and continued to wield it with great might. Fenris had managed to keep an entire crowd at bay but he was clearly exhausted. Behind him the dozens of archers that had pounced into the enemy were busy fighting sword for sword against the insurgents. Many of them had been killed; they were surrounded and their armour less sturdy than that of the troops with Sylvie.

Rense broke through the crowd in the hope of reaching Fenris. He could just make his friend out bobbing in and out of view behind a mass of savage warriors. Almost every rebels' face was painted white and red. As the large man fought through the swarm his axe crunched into the spine of one rebel and snapped the bone. He launched his fist into another and knocked their eyeball into the socket. With his arm outstretched he suddenly felt the sting of a spear slot into his left thigh. He yelled out and swung his battleaxe in a full circle around him. It cut across limb and bone like some possessed wheel. A scimitar swirled through the air and pierced his side. The shock of the blow stunned Rense and he dropped his axe in reflex. He pulled the blade out of his waist but as it left his skin another spearhead sunk into his guts. Another then cut into his back. Without warning his body was then hacked at by countless swords. The proud warrior had been opened up and the insurgents took advantage. He cried out but his voice was lost under the brutal sounds of battle. He fell to the ground as a flock of rebel warriors continued to stab him with continual thrusts of their blades.

Fenris lost the grip of one of his swords. It flew into the air and was gone. He cut across the neck of one enemy and then deflected a swing from another. A bearded opponent came forth and managed to stick their dagger into his thigh. Fenris reacted and impaled the rebel on his blade. It stuck into the corpse's insides and could not be recovered. As the body fell to earth Fenris found himself standing with no weapon. The rusty dagger cut into his leg deeply. He pulled it out and hurled it into the crowd. He expected this was to be his last moment and closed his eyes in defeat.

The last remaining Tamus archers suddenly broke through and struck his body from behind as they fought against a group pressing them back. Only twenty remained standing after the pitched battle against the crowd. They had smote masses of the enemy and bodies now piled up across the entirety of the space around the gateway.

Emi and Yuuki appeared from the sprawl ahead and ran down the track nearer the action.

'They have flanked us somehow!' cried Yuuki.

'The enemy has entered the tower!' Emi added.

'We must defend the tower!' Yuuki concluded.

Sylvie had heard them and immediately fell back, snaking past her men as they locked horns with the enemy. So many bodies now lay around them it was making it tough for the enemy to advance further. They tripped on the corpses of the fallen and the wounded rolled around in despair.

Sylvie reached the rear of the troop column. Thankfully, the enemy had still not managed to entirely surround them.

'I need ten troops to help defend the tower!' the Empress yelled.

Immediately, a group nearest her at the rear came forwards and ran with her as she linked up with Emi and Yuuki on the trail.

'They must have come from the sewer,' said Emi.

'At least twenty of them,' said Yuuki.

'I can only spare ten troops,' Sylvie replied. 'The rest are needed to fend off this attack. I must stay here and help hold the line. I cannot abandon my men. You must stop them!'

The girls knew they would have to make do with the numbers that were available. Every other troop was locked in combat and unable to break away. There was no time for questions and they ran back up the track with the troops racing behind them.

As they faded Sylvie noticed an isolated group ahead of her troops just in front of the gateway. They were bearing the full brunt of the assault head on. She then spotted Fenris doing battle in the middle. She charged towards them.

Fenris had picked up a spear and used it to prod at his assailants. He was weary and faint from blood loss. His right leg was dead like a slab of meat and forced him to rest all his weight on the other. The archers around him valiantly battled against the murderous thugs bombarding them. The Sergeant that had earlier declared victory on the platform was one of them. The cuts on his face and arms signified quite how wrong he had been.

Sylvie leapt into the fray without fear. She appeared to Fenris' side after knocking a mass of rebels to the ground with her wild volt. She instantly thrust her symbolic sword at the enemies closing in around them. Suddenly, the Sergeant received a deadly blow to his neck from a knife that had been hurled towards him. He fell onto the pile of bodies beside his feet. With every Tamus bowman that fell at least five rebels had been claimed. It had proved to be a massacre for them but still their numbers seemed vast. Minutes of battling went by until eventually Fenris realised only he and Sylvie were left standing. The group of archers had finally been wholly engulfed by the greater numbers that surrounded them.

Sylvie was a thing possessed. She showed no fear as adversary after adversary came at her. Her sword cut them with fatal precision whenever they got near. Fenris was now on his knees with fatigue beside her. He continued to jab his spear out towards those nearest him but they were no longer staying back. Several closed in but in that moment the remaining Tamus troops stormed into the rebel horde in one final desperate move. Their lines had been broken and their column gradually weakened down. None still held a shield but battled with their swords and pole arms with great velocity. They had seen their Empress surrounded and had made this charge in an attempt to save her.

Their counter appeared to work and the enemy fell back against the might of their disciplined assault. They linked up with Sylvie and Fenris and pulled them out from the centre of battle. Both were exhausted. Fenris dropped his spear and slipped into unconsciousness as his body was dragged behind the Tamus line. Sylvie was clearly shattered but remained on her feet with steadfast resolve. She bent beside Fenris and made sure he had not left her. He meant so much to the girl and in this moment of concern the extent of that emotion struck her.

A single guardsman noticed the Empress' concern for the warrior and started to apply a bandage to his wound. She was grateful and got up slowly. Her men had pulled the enemy back into the immediate area around the gateway. So many of them had fallen it looked as if less than half their initial number was left standing. She suddenly heard a voice cry out from the bridge:

'Move aside! We are coming up the bridge!'

Sylvie frowned. The voice was Golandin's. He was now on horseback, with a large group of cavalry behind him poised to charge. The rebel leader had obviously managed to somehow recover from his injury.

Sylvie studied her troops. There probably only remained a few hundred of them. Many were wounded and had crawled away out of danger. A tiny handful of troops gave medical assistance to the immeasurable casualties but even these troops boasted the cuts and bruises of the conflict. Sylvie could only estimate that at least a thousand of her troops had died in this bitter combat. Hundreds more were wounded. She imagined the enemy had probably lost three times that over the course of the battle.

The crowd of rebels fell back and formed a gap in the gateway large enough for the cavalry to storm through. The line of troops held firm as Golandin's black horse trotted up the bridge. Many of those behind him were carrying javelins; their tips pointing menacingly towards the defenders.

Fenris was carried away by a single guard eager to please their Empress. His body was cut almost everywhere and his leg was a bloody mess. Sylvie tried her best to forget about him. She knew the battle was still far from over. The horses on the bridge were beginning to stir.

With all eyes on the bridge the riders kicked into motion as Golandin's lead horse started to gallop forwards. The crowd of rebel infantry had edged to the sides of the stone overpass in a desperate clamber to avoid the trampling hooves. Several still fought against the line of Tamus troops but were swiftly being put down.

'There looks to be about fifty of them,' a guard said to Sylvie. 'Alas! Will be a nasty one!'

Sylvie looked at her remaining huddle of soldiers. Around two hundred and fifty still stood firm. The wounded had mostly all made it back to the line of houses where Jamus had been placed. This was all that remained of her once two thousand strong garrison. They were exhausted and their armour plates stained in blood and dirt. As the horses raced up the bridge Sylvie called out:

'For Marmia!' she bellowed.

There was a cheer from her men but within seconds the cavalry had struck. Golandin's lead horse slammed into the line; his sword swinging down at the troops from his mount. He broke into the huddle with dozens more right behind him. Javelins stabbed through the armour of the first troops in line. One penetrated straight through a guard and continued back until cutting into the neck of another. Some of the riders were instantly prodded with long spears and fell from their mounts. Others slammed into the line so fast that they flew from their horses and straight into the guards. They were stabbed where they landed.

The charge smashed through the exhausted line of defenders. They fell back but were being waylaid by the horsemen as they poked down at their prey. Sylvie was feet away from Golandin as he pushed through soldier after soldier. He spotted the Empress and swung down at her once by her side. Sylvie knocked his longsword away from her and jabbed her sword handle into his leg. The strike was ineffectual and Golandin continued to attack her. A guardsman appeared to his side and attempted to pull him from his mount. Golandin struck them in the helm with his iron fist and managed to sink his steel into their shoulder.

Sylvie's blade danced with his once he'd pulled it from the dying soldier. The swords struck one another continuously. The clang of steel striking steel was piercing and prominent. Suddenly, the remaining mass of rebels on foot charged from the gateway as the last horse passed them by. Within seconds they too were attacking the remaining Tamus troops.

All was looking lost for the defenders. The cavalry had devastated their formation and the rebels were now engulfing them from every angle. Some groups of thuggish insurgents even ran straight by them and started to mercilessly attack the piles of wounded resting by the buildings on the roadside. Those who had been giving aid to them tried to defend against the assailants but were put down by the rush of bloodthirsty scimitars. As the wounded troops lay helpless they were stabbed and cut, kicked and beaten. The rebels had no sense of morality.

Sylvie fell back as Golandin attacked her with a volley of powerful strikes. She couldn't find a weakness in his ancient armour and hadn't managed to dismount him.

'You truly are about to die,' laughed the rebel leader.

At that precise moment a vast black banner suddenly fell and drooped from the soaring tower in the distance. It had been dangled over the throne room balcony and could be seen with clarity. It was a long cloth placard. A forbidding white skull flapped with the breeze. It was surrounded by dark red symbols representing flame.

'The banner!' Golandin cried. 'The tower is ours! Torwin has taken the tower!'

'Torwin...' Sylvie muttered to herself.

The rebels cheered and fought with even greater determination. Sylvie turned her head to take in the view. Her heart sunk. It was clear the rebel banner was indeed flying from the mighty structure. She just hoped Emi and Yuuki were close to liberating the tower.

With her backside turned in a brief lapse of focus, Golandin suddenly plunged forwards and scraped his blade across Sylvie's back. It cut into her cloak and slid down her skin. She recoiled and fell to the ground. Golandin leapt from his horse and stood over her victoriously.

He looked around them. He watched as piles of wounded Tamus troops were systemically executed by stabbing blades. He noticed the remaining few guards left standing being utterly surrounded and lost behind his horsemen and infantry. There looked to be less than a hundred now still battling. He suspected at least a thousand of his men were still in the fight. Victory seemed certain. He raised his sword into the air and cried out:

'Victory! I declare a great victory!'

Sylvie looked up at him as he stood in full splendour. Her skin was pale; the gushing wound stung and took the strength right from her. Golandin looked down at her menacingly. He kicked The Sword of Tamus from her weak hand and raised his longsword in both hands as if preparing to thrust it down into the centre of her chest. She lay on her back and stared up at him submissively. It seemed to be all over. The battle was lost. She wished to fall beside her men and wouldn't have wanted her death to be any other way.

Around her guards continued to battle against the swarm. With every blood soaked minute that went by there were fewer and fewer of them standing. By now many of the rebels on horseback had advanced deeper into the city and some even started to hurl flaming torches onto the thatched roofs of the buildings wounded guardsmen had been placed.

'Goodbye Empress,' Golandin laughed. 'I am in charge now.'

His steel descended. It dropped towards her chest as he bent forwards holding the handle in both hands. Sylvie's eyes were closed. She was ready to die.

With only inches to spare Golandin's mighty longsword was suddenly knocked to the side. Its tip stabbed into the dry soil beside the girl's body. Fenris had risen from his slumber and staggered to the aid of the Empress.

CHAPTER III

THE BLACK BANNER

'Stand aside my lasses,' a guard said, 'I will take care of this.'

His steel boot slammed into the partially barricaded doorway to the tower. The impact broke through the entrance and rattled the doorframe. With a further shoulder barge the opening broke inwardly; a single wooden cabinet shuffling forwards against the opening doors. The token blockade had been placed there by Torwin's party.

Emi was first to pass into the tower lobby with Yuuki close behind, whose glowing staff partially lit up the morbidly lit space. The guardsmen swiftly poured in and rushed towards the giant staircase that wound around the tower.

'They have already raised their banner,' said a guard. 'We must reach the throne room.'

'It was so foolish not to guard the sewer,' said another.

'We needed everyone by the gate,' said Yuuki. 'We couldn't afford to split our forces up.'

Regardless of what any of them individually thought it was now too late to dwell on what ifs. The enemy had seized the opportunity and breached into the city. At this stage they could only presume the sewer had been their method of entry.

Flickering torches lit the steps. Regal banners hung from plain stone walls. They were mostly of scarlet fabric. The party dashed up the stairs and prepared for a bitter confrontation with the vanguard enemy forces.

Within the throne room the rebels ransacked every inch of the regal hall. They were pillaging all they could; several had smashed into a glass cabinet and snatched countless gleaming gems. Others tried to prise valuable stones from the sides of the prominent throne with their sword tips. Torwin and Arthir were on the balcony staring out at the city. To the south thick smoke had started to rise into the sky. Fires were being lit on thatched rooftops. The rebels could just make out insurgent horsemen buzzing around the southern wall unchallenged. A large group seemed to be overwhelming any last resistance near the gateway. It looked to be all over. The distant signs of victory created contented smiles on the warriors' faces as they stood on their high perch.

'I do declare that it seems Golandin has succeeded in defeating the guards,' smiled Torwin. 'Looks like we have pulled it off!'

As he spoke their dark banner flapped below the terrace. It was tied to either side of the wall bordering the balcony and hung like a giant sheet rolled out onto troubled seas.

'Brimma is ours!' Arthir exclaimed. 'I almost can't believe it, but it appears we have taken the city.'

'The defenders have been overrun,' said Torwin. 'Golandin is no doubt on his way to the tower.'

'What a great moment this is,' said Arthir. 'We have triumphed!'

In the throne room the elite of the rebel forces continued to grab all they could. They scurried around like rats picking through leftovers. There was suddenly a loud thud against the doorway. It was already partially damaged from earlier frolics with the late Ellis but the rebels had surrounded the doors with all they could. Benches, cabinets, and ornamental shields pressed against the entrance. With the thunderous strikes against the door ringing in the rebels' ears they all drew their blades and gathered around the doorway.

'We got company!' one yelled.

Torwin and Arthir bolted into the room from beyond the curtains of the terrace. Both had swords at the ready.

'Looks like they are going to try and remove our banner,' Torwin said knowingly. 'We mustn't let them pass us. Golandin has taken the city; their occupying force has been conquered. They are desperate. We shall hold them off!'

'Golandin will soon storm up from behind them no doubt,' Arthir added. 'I suspect the rest of them are racing this way as we speak.'

Torwin nodded. 'Let us ensure the banner is not spoiled,' he said.

Those beyond the doorway continued to pound at the barricaded entrance. Torwin and Arthir crept closer to their allies whom stood in a mass huddle preparing for a decisive show-down.

Outside of the throne room Yuuki studied the doors. The guards smashed against it with their swords and bodies. Emi was patiently waiting to one side.

'Stand aside,' the sorceress announced. 'I will clear our path.'

The guards stood back as Yuuki's staff pointed towards the entrance and edged down the staircase in a single file. The tip of her staff beamed in a radiant amethyst tint. The surroundings shone with a cascading heliotrope hue.

'Cover your eyes,' the girl warned.

A powerful surge of light exploded from her staff and obliterated the materials it made impact with. The doorway blew wide open; the objects propping it shut slid across the room and crumbled into broken slabs of wood. The light glistened as it entered into the room and then flickered out into a memory. The enthralling spell had cleared the way.

The guards stormed into the room before Yuuki and Emi had even opened their eyes. The rebels were shocked by the magical breach but not enough to waver. These were the battle-hardened elite. Keeping the black banner flying from Tamus Tower meant everything to them.

The guards made straight for the group of rebels of whom were twice their number. Emi and Yuuki were right behind. Torwin was first to tussle and thrust his blade forwards towards the incoming foes. The two groups slammed into each other like a great crash of carriages. Arthir's steel struck against a guards-man's blade with great force. He was alive with passion.

Emi swiftly pounced into an enemy's body foot first. Her flying kick knocked them backwards. As they stumbled she thrust her knife into their chest. The rebel fell to the ground. Yuuki swung her long staff around as several targeted her. The long weapon was akin to a large pole and smashed one across the jaw and prodded another in the belly. She then swung it low and swept one from their feet.

Torwin disarmed a guard and drove his knee into their groin. They bent low in agony. The fanatical rebel was swift to stick his sword into their back and claim his first kill of the skirmish. Another came at him from the side but was swiftly stabbed in the torso by Arthir as his slim body popped up from behind Torwin.

The guard clutched the fatal incision but soon fell to ground lifeless.

Torwin shuffled forwards and claimed another, then another. He was on fire and flawlessly deflected everything that came at him only to then sink his sword into each and every assailant. Arthir kept beside him. A guard attempted to strike him but the ardent veteran avoided the blow and dug their sword into the guard's neck. They dropped down as the gushing throat spilt warm blood.

Only four guards remained. Emi had been pushed back by a group of five rebels and desperately fought for her life as they pinned her in a far corner of the room. Yuuki had continued to stand her ground against several eager to strike her. The remaining guards gallantly battled the rebels. One spliced his steel across an insurgent's chest before poking the blade through another's abdomen. Another of the guards managed to trip a rebel up and sunk his sword into their chest whilst they lay against the floor. Torwin suddenly came from behind and stuck his own sword through the soldier's back. They cried out and dropped dead.

Yuuki noticed Emi's predicament as she swung her staff around in desperation. The female huntress had now been pressed against the stone wall. Three rebels pinned her arms whilst another savagely tore at her green attire. She had managed to stab one of her attackers dead but the group of sturdy men had proved too much for her as they closed in and wrestled her back against the wall.

'My my...' one zealous rebel laughed. 'What a feisty thing we have here!'

'Get off me!' she wildly protested.

Her arms were pinned above her head with the rebels' dirty hands pressing against her wrists tightly. Yuuki could do nothing for her. She herself was surrounded. Her staff kept them at bay as she swirled it across the air. The rebel men were also more cautious of the sorceress, knowing she had some magical ability about her, and kept back.

The last three Tamus guards faced off against Torwin. With himself and Arthir there were now thirteen rebels left standing. Four were dealing with Emi and five surrounded Yuuki. Two were standing beside the rebel leaders. The guards attacked at once and drove their blades towards the figures that confronted them. One rebel thug felt the sting of a sharp blade tip pass into their lungs. The other rebel managed to sink his sword into a guard as they, too, dug theirs into him. Both fell down dead together. Two more rebels had fallen.

Torwin smote one guard, his blade breaking through their helmet and disabling the brain. Arthir's sword caught the stomach of another whom fell down with the pain. Both men cowered over him and stabbed his chest in unison. Only Emi and Yuuki now remained.

'Stay back!' Yuuki screamed. 'I'm warning you!'

The girl was breathing heavily and clearly on edge. Her arms were limp with fatigue. She could now barely clasp her staff. The men around her laughed.

'Hear that?' Torwin mocked. 'She's warning you!'

There was further laughter. The eleven remaining rebels seemed to be in high spirits.

'Please stay back!' Yuuki cried.

Torwin turned and looked towards Emi. She was still being pinned against the hard stone. She kicked and spat but to no avail. Her foot suddenly then caught the man fondling her in the face. He stumbled back.

'Wretch!' he yelled, his lips bleeding.

He callously drove his fist into her belly with great force. She squealed in pain. Her tunic had been ripped and the bare skin of her reddening stomach was in full view.

'Don't kill these two,' Arthir said. 'Seems a waste; particularly if it turns out Sylvie is no more.'

His corrupted mind was thinking of only one use for these girls. Torwin was just as wicked.

'Good thought,' said Torwin. 'Although I'll have that braided haired one first! She looks particularly fruity to me.'

He was staring at Yuuki. The sorceress suddenly yelled out some magical command and a faint beam glowed in her hands. Torwin hurled his sword into the air directly towards her. It spun with great pace and slammed into the magical girl like a throwing knife hitting its target. Just as it cut into her lower body her palms fired a jolt of light towards one of the surrounding rebels. It burned into their body and instantly killed them. Yuuki stumbled back and fell against empty wooden shelves. Torwin's sword stuck into her flesh.

'Well, I guess I won't be ravaging her after all,' Torwin said dryly.

CHAPTER IV

IN COMMAND OF THE SHADOW

Fenris was clearly no longer fighting fit. His sword dangled in the air and his strikes lacked any vigour. Golandin deflected his feeble movements as he stood beside Sylvie's limp body. They duelled for a few seconds but the veteran rebel soon managed to knock Fenris' blade from his grasp. The young warrior was exhausted and had forced himself to race to Sylvie's side. Golandin didn't hold back and dug his longsword deep into the valiant warrior's waist. Fenris kept himself on his feet but it was now fruitless to resist. Golandin pulled his blade out from the fleshy section of his torso and then sliced it across the love-struck male's body. The razor edge slid across his skin and deeply cut the tissue. Fenris fell back and hit the ground with full force. He managed to land beside Sylvie and put his cold hand on hers.

'We have defeated them sir!' a rebel yelled to Golandin. 'There are none left standing.'

'You hear that Sylvie?' Golandin laughed. 'Round everyone up and make for the tower!'

The rebel officer acknowledged the order and ran back towards the crowd of insurgents. They had finally brought the last Tamus troop down in a blaze of prodding blades and poking spears. The horde had overcome the outnumbered men of valour.

'And now it truly is time to say goodbye,' Golandin said whilst looking down at Sylvie. 'There be no one else left to run to your aid Empress!'

The fires now burned most of the thatched buildings around the track uncontrollably. Rebels were about to enter into one of them; its roof ablaze but the building still intact. Inside, Jamus lay helpless and weary on a bed.

'I was going to keep you alive,' Golandin went on, 'for a bit of fun… but now I have you at my feet I cannot control this desire I have to see you die!'

Sylvie's blue eyes were still open but she was weak from the wound to her back. She felt limp and once again closed her eyes in anticipation of the killing blow. Golandin raised his sword.

A piercing sound of high pitched howls suddenly bombarded everyone's eardrums. It echoed against the stone walls of Brimma and got louder and louder. Golandin looked up into the cloudy sky and instantly spotted a black mass rolling over the mighty city. Dark, infernal clouds marched over Brimma from the western sky and soon hovered over where he stood. Bolts of lightning enraged the mass orgy of energies as it halted above. There was panic. The hundreds of remaining rebels cried out in mass terror. Even Golandin was unnerved by the bizarre vista.

Horses kicked their riders off from their backs and fled away across the bridge en masse. All eyes looked up as thousands of hideous creatures suddenly descended from the black cloud mass. They fell down with an otherworldly pace as if they had been sped up by God themself.

'What manner of ungodliness be this?' Golandin cried out.

Sylvie had no clues but suddenly felt an intuitive sense of hope. Without being told the girl just knew this boded well for her. She looked at Fenris whose hand still pressed against hers. He was alive but too wounded to move. She stretched her arm out and clutched The Sword of Tamus, which rested a few paces from her. Golandin was too busy staring up at the dark entities racing towards him to notice her movement.

Perched high in the air within the cloud mass a lone girl commanded the terrifying force. Akumi had reached Brimma.

'Defend the city! Rid the streets of all those that desire to rebel against our realm!' she cried.

The entities appeared to know whom to target as if they had access to the thoughts flowing through every person's head. There was nowhere for the rebels to hide.

The menacing, winged beings swooped over the rebels' heads. The insurgents formed up into a mass huddle of terrified men. Those that had broken up from the main crowd were soon claimed by lunging claws. Hundreds of the beings fell to earth and commenced to morph into the wolflike creatures that had roamed the distant swamplands of the west. All had red, glowing eyes and a hundred razor sharp teeth.

Men fell in droves. They were victims of swooping claws,

which hacked through flesh and ripped bodies into unidentifiable pieces of meat. The wolves leapt into the huddle of remaining rebels and proceeded to massacre them like they were pieces of mutton placed there for disposal. Bodies were chewed open and gnawed at. Blood exploded into the air with every rebel that felt the wrath of the dark forces.

The rebels that had entered into the building Jamus lay in hadn't got far. A wolfish beast ripped one apart as they stood in the doorway. Another ran into the room and cowered beside Jamus as he rested. His feral face paints were no longer the most intimidating thing in Brimma. As he bent by the bedside the wolf stormed into the room and pounced onto his trembling body. The creature bit into the man's face and chewed on his eyes before turning his head into a splattered pulp of mashed flesh. Jamus stirred as the creature departed.

Golandin fruitlessly swung his sword in the air as a winged entity hovered over him. The blade touched the creature but seemed to pass through its leg as if the entity was some deadly chimera that lacked corporeal reality.

Sylvie slowly got to her feet as Golandin battled against the encircling creatures.

'Be gone!' he yelled. 'What is this foul sorcery?'

'Golandin!' Sylvie called out, her blade held high.

The rebel leader turned to face the girl. He appeared amazed by the fact she had risen to her feet. Before he could react the girl had driven her steel down at his sword arm with all her strength. The ancient blade cut through his armour and severed limb from body. His arm fell to the ground with sword still in hand.

He screamed in shock and looked into the Empress' eyes as she staked him in the stomach. The sword caved into the armour plates and dug into his ribs. She pulled it out from his body and he bent forwards until he was bowing before her. His armour had been breached by the mighty blade now being swung by an Empress in all her majestic might.

'Your rebellion has failed,' Sylvie declared. 'Farewell Golandin.'

He yelled at the top of his voice as The Sword of Tamus hacked into the back of his neck. The steel passed through his collar and throat with flawless momentum. His decapitated head fell to the ground beside Sylvie's feet and his broken body dropped to the bloody soil.

Nobody appeared to acknowledge the moment. The dwindling rebel crowd was too petrified to even notice their leader had been killed. The wolves and winged beasts devoured them like a well oiled mechanism. Sylvie could tell none of the entities were interested in targeting her. She bent down and supported Fenris' head as he lay bleeding.

'Stay with me,' she said. 'It will be over soon.'

Sylvie forgot all about slaying Golandin and focused her attention on the warrior in her arms. She felt enough strength coming back to her to be able to see to the male's wounds. She noticed a pile of bandages resting beside a fallen medic and grabbed them. As she started to wrap the cloth around his chest the extent of the bleeding became apparent. Fenris was pale and clearly close to death. Sylvie's eyes watered as tears formed. She resiliently continued to apply the bandage but it was a token exertion. Fenris stared into her emotional blue eyes and opened his bloody lips.

'I love you,' he whispered.

His eyes closed and his head went limp. Sylvie burst into tears and hugged his body.

'I know,' she cried. 'As I loved you.'

At the tallest point of Tamus Tower Torwin shrunk behind the drooping net before the terrace. Arthir stood beside him trembling with fear.

'What are they?' he asked.

'I have no idea,' said Torwin. 'I have never seen anything like it.'

They were looking up at the darkened sky above the balcony. From their mighty vantage point they could even make out a single figure sitting within the black cloud.

'Is that some demigod?' Arthir pondered: 'Here to punish us all for our crimes?'

The lone figure sat within the fluffy dark mists as if floating on fog. They certainly looked to be in command of the swirling cloud mass. Several flying entities suddenly soared across the balcony. They were encircling the tower in droves of hundreds.

'Judgment!' cried Arthir. 'This has to be some heavenly intervention!'

'Whatever it is,' Torwin said, 'I'm not sticking around.'

The rebel backed away from the terrace and walked towards the broken doorway of the throne room. Emi had been bound hand and foot by the rebels and placed on a bench in the middle of the great hall. Her arms were tied behind her back with thick rope and her tattered clothing blew with the breeze coming from the open balcony.

Yuuki was in the far corner where she had fallen. The rebels assumed she was dead. Torwin's sword still poked out from her body.

Torwin gathered a few things from a pile of loot the rebels had created. It consisted of everything they had found in the throne room that might be of worth. Gems from the cabinets, old swords, manuscripts, and even plants stacked up in a heap beside Emi as she writhed around against her bonds.

'I don't know what's going on out there,' Torwin said, 'but I'm not leaving this city without taking my fair share of booty.'

Arthir continued to gaze out through the curtains beside the balcony.

'They might be on our side,' he said timidly. 'We don't know for sure if we should be fearful of them or not.'

'I just know it's time to leave,' Torwin said. 'We've made our mark. Presuming Golandin has defeated the defenders at the gate this city is ours now anyway, and there ain't anything no damn demon can do about it!'

As Torwin spoke Yuuki started to stir. She had briefly lost consciousness but it had been more down to her own exhaustion than the injury to her waist. She carefully pulled the sword from her body and put it on the floor. It seemed to be only a flesh wound. She felt strong again; as if some nearby energy source was fuelling her with an immense charge of magical reserve. The black cloud was indeed giving the sorceress power. She could sense the dark energy over the city but also could feel the presence of Akumi. It warmed her heart. She instantly knew Akumi was in command of the shadow. Her intuition told her so. Akumi had overcome all the odds and reached Brimma. Yuuki's deep concerns regarding her state no longer pervaded her mind. Akumi was alive and truly now with them in the fight.

The remaining rebel warriors gathered around Torwin. They all appeared confused and nervous. All eight of them stood beside him, with Arthir still staring out at the marvel in the sky beside the balcony.

'We are with you Torwin,' a rebel confirmed staunchly. 'Let us help you carry the loot.'

Torwin didn't reply. His mind was transfixed on placing as many gems into his black sack as possible. He no longer cared about anything else besides his own share in the spoils. Arthir gawped towards his allies as they desperately clutched all they could.

'Where will you go with all that?' he asked. 'You can't possibly leave Brimma now!'

Torwin smiled to himself. 'Like I just said,' he spoke firmly, 'if we are to assume we now control the city it won't matter who comes and goes.'

Arthir wasn't convinced. He was starting to sense a devious streak coming from his ally.

'So, you're sure this little departure of yours has nothing to do with this great spectacle outside?' he inquired. 'It seems to me you're running away all of a sudden.'

Torwin didn't rise to Arthir's comment and continued to jam all he could into his thick sack.

'The road to Brimma has proved a tiresome expedition,' he said. 'It has led us to a very perilous destination it would seem, and considering I have already been left for dead twice during this little campaign I am no longer in a mood to stick around.'

Arthir was beginning to intuit a new ambition driving Torwin. He was ensuring he was to get all he could out of the situation now presenting itself.

Torwin started to tie his sack up. As the rebel got to his feet from clambering around the pile of precious objects he suddenly noticed Yuuki rising in the far corner. Her staff was gleaming with vengeful red tones. He had been about to walk over to her to seize his sword before departing the throne room.

'She rises,' Torwin grumbled. 'How sweet!'

In that moment Arthir abruptly screamed in absolute terror from beside the terrace.

'They are coming in!' he shrieked.

Torwin and his remaining party of rebels turned to face the exterior platform. Winged beings hurtled through the curtains and ripped the dangling cloth from the ceiling as they passed. Dozens stormed into the throne room and darted across the expanse of the regal area in circular patterns of flight. Torwin grabbed a sword from the hand of a rebel beside him and focused on the creatures flapping about the air.

'What is this?!' he cried out.

Arthir retreated back until he stood beside the group of rebels. The infernal creatures fell to the floor and suddenly transformed into wolf beings. Yuuki was not alarmed and stepped forwards with her staff pointed towards the rebels huddling in the middle of the room.

'What do you want from us?' Arthir asked ignorantly, his voice trembling.

There was no response from the wolves as they crept closer towards them. A figure then pounced into the room from the terrace entrance and landed on their feet beside the dark entities. Her brown eyes throbbed with intensity.

'Akumi!' Yuuki screamed excitedly.

The sorceress knew it was her. She'd seen the girl in her mind and felt a deep respect for the trained assassin.

'Who are you?' Torwin asked.

'Your rebellion is over,' Akumi said.

The wolves dived into the air and fell onto the rebel group in a mass attack. One rebel was instantly beheaded by the powerful jaw of one of the creatures; another was slammed so hard in the chest by the impact with a wolf being that they crumpled onto the floor as if a hammer had lain waste to their insides. Torwin jumped forwards in avoidance of the attacking fangs. He found himself facing off against Akumi. Behind him his black sack was already being split open by a ravaging set of glowing teeth. Yuuki noticed Akumi wasn't holding a sword and quickly grabbed one from the ground beside a fallen enemy and hurled it across the room.

'Akumi! Catch!' she yelled.

The assassin caught the sword by the handle as it glided towards her. It was a katana blade; likely once stolen from a true warrior by the fallen rebel that had carried it into battle.

Arthir dropped to the floor and crawled away to a far corner of the room nearest the ruined doors. Yuuki had spotted him falling back towards the doorway and confronted him where he sat. He looked up at her; his face a void of hatred. His hand reached for his sword, which rested against his thigh. Yuuki pointed her animated staff directly at his head.

'Don't!' she cried, staring at his fiddling hand.

A wolf plunged from the fray towards the veteran rebel. Little did Arthir know that his cause was already lost and his old friend Golandin a spoilt bloody mess of remains. He rolled to one side and avoided the descending claws. The wolf had plummeted into the wall and cracked the stone. Pallid powder rose into the air.

In the middle of the room the last six rebel fighters were brought to the floor in a lethal combined assault by the dozens of creatures massed around them. Their bodies were effortlessly torn into separate parts of bloody slabs of fresh meat. They hadn't even managed to raise their blades.

Arthir noticed Torwin facing Akumi. The two were staring at one another with swords poised. The wolves didn't appear to target his ally, likely knowing their leader wished to confront him herself. Arthir was petrified as every creature in the room turned their red eyes on him. He looked to Yuuki. She was standing with her staff ready to strike but held back. She knew Arthir was already about to meet his fate.

The sly rebel seemed utterly finished. The dark figures crept towards him menacingly. Torwin was too occupied to even notice, or care. Arthir then suddenly spotted Emi sitting up on a bench a few feet from him. She was still struggling with her bonds and desperately wriggling her arms around behind her back. Yuuki hadn't had time to free her.

Arthir ran forwards and grabbed the girl from behind as she sat facing towards the incoming wolves. He pressed his sword against her helpless throat and pulled her backwards until her tied legs were dragged from off the bench and hit the floor.

'Stay back!' Arthir called out. 'I will kill her if you get closer!'

Emi was defenceless and submissively allowed herself to be hauled back further until Arthir hit the cracked stone surface of the wall beside the doorway. The creatures looked to understand him and with some elementary intellect stood back.

To the other side of the throne room Akumi continued to circle Torwin. She didn't want to underestimate her opponent and paid careful attention to his meticulous movements. Torwin was hesitating as if he sensed the girl was skilled. He was also unsure if she were even human. He had been recollecting over how she fell down into the tower from the looming dark cloud above, where she had sat like some omnipotent goddess.

'Your fight is over!' Yuuki asserted. 'Let her go right now!'

Arthir was a bag of nerves but didn't back down. His sword pressed against Emi's delicately thin section of skin. She was motionless and rigid. The old rebel was sweating profusely. Suddenly, a girl ran into the hall from the broken doorway with sword in arm. Sylvie had reached the top of the tower. Dry blood stained her back and splattered every inch of her attire. Even her hair was blotted with the thick tinges of dark red. Her watery eyes said it all.

With her entrance came the final clash. Torwin suddenly closed in on Akumi and swung his blade towards her throat. Arthir watched his ally attack with Emi still held firm in his grip.

'Have it you vile witch!' Torwin yelled at the top of his voice.

His blade came at the girl from high in the air but she gracefully blocked the strike with her katana and twisted about on her feet until the deadly steel spun around and stuck into Torwin's chest. The razor sharp blade pierced his flesh and dug deeply into his throbbing heart. He dropped his sword and gazed into his killer's eyes. White froth foamed out of his mouth and his eyes lost vision. Akumi bent forwards and placed his body onto the ground slowly as it propped up against her katana. She lowered her blade until his back softly hit the royal carpet leading up to the throne. With a swift movement Akumi then pulled it out from his lifeless corpse.

Arthir wailed in despair. He couldn't believe how easily Twinicia's brother had been put down.

'Golandin is dead and your rebellion is crushed,' said Sylvie. 'Let Emi go and I will show you mercy.'

The Empress looked across to Akumi whom had walked towards them and stopped beside the dark beings doing her bidding. They were breathing heavily and moaning as if desperate to kill the final rebel. Hot steam blew from their twitching, semblant noses.

'These creatures are at my command,' said Akumi. 'I will call them off if you let Emi go.'

The seminal rebel was at odds with what to do. He was being offered the chance to save his skin and surrender to his sworn enemy. He had no wish to die and knew it was now pointless to resist. It was all over. However, a part of him refused to accept Golandin was no more.

'Golandin can't be dead!' Arthir yelled. 'He can't be.'

'I killed him myself,' snapped Sylvie. 'This very sword took his head from off his shoulders! Now give yourself up!'

He felt utter desolation and despair over the news of Golandin's death but was now too preoccupied in his own predicament to let it linger in his mind any further. He knew he was at the mercy of the girls surrounding him. Akumi could at any moment order her army of ominous beings to attack him, Lady Yuuki could effortlessly floor him with a deadly magical strike, and Sylvie's wrath might smite him where he stood.

'Let Emi go!' Yuuki commanded feverishly.

Arthir's mind was made up. He stared into Emi's light hair as it pressed against his chin. She smelt of flowers. He breathed in the scent and calmly lowered his sword and let go of her arms. She immediately dropped forwards and rolled away until she reached Yuuki's feet.

Sylvie edged closer towards Arthir. Yuuki bent down and started to untie the knots that bound Emi's wrists and ankles. Akumi continued to stand beside her minions of infernal creatures.

'Drop your sword Arthir, son of Alrin,' Sylvie ordered calmly.

She knew of Arthir's murky history and dredged up the name of his late father from the memories she had stored of briefings with General Dorwor in the distant past.

Arthir smiled and looked down at his sword. It represented his resolve to fight on. Dropping it down onto the floor would mean he had truly surrendered. It would prove a symbolic action. He was hesitant.

'We came so close, did we not?' Arthir asked those around him.

Emi's arms were finally free. She grabbed her huntress' knife from where it had fallen and slid it across the rope that tied her ankles. The twine broke then split away from her legs and she got back onto her feet.

'Yes,' Sylvie answered after a few seconds of delay. 'You certainly did come close to ensuring this realm would fall back into utter chaos!'

'Your rebellion would have lasted as long as it took for another to gain momentum and then overthrow you,' said Yuuki.

Akumi nodded whilst the others spoke. 'Marmia needs leadership,' she said; 'strong enough to ensure there is order and peace. Your cause was doomed from the start; all it offered was further bloodshed.'

Arthir took in each comment with careful scrutiny. Perhaps they were right. In his heart he knew it had all been down to the cravings men such as he had had for power. In a stark realisation he suddenly grasped the full implications of what that power would have meant: responsibility, and a duty these virtuous figures around him were so passionate in carrying out.

'I am lost for words,' he said.

Akumi whispered commands to the wolves, ordering them to continue to hold back. Sylvie was still staring at his sword.

'Drop your blade Arthir,' she said. 'We won't harm you if you surrender.'

Arthir looked up and smiled with sudden intrinsic surety.

'My Empress,' he said softly, 'I would only harm myself if I did.'

He suddenly turned his sword in on himself and sunk it deep into his abdomen. He fell against the wall and slid down it until he sat touching it with legs straight on the floor. The four female warriors raced to his side. They were all taken aback by his grave, momentous action. Sylvie knelt beside him. He was dead within seconds.

CHAPTER V

AFTERMATH

Jamus studied the illusive, shady creatures converging around the track into the city. They hovered the air in droves and dived to the ground, with fatal implications for those they had targeted. Hundreds of the wolflike figures continued to churn through the diminishing group of rebels left standing. Barely a hundred of them remained; the once mighty rebel army utterly devastated.

The old friar forced his tired, feeble body out of the room he had been resting in. A bloody corpse lay beside the bed; its severed limbs resting feet away from the torso in separate pools of blood. Jamus stumbled out into the clearing of the trackside. Not an inch of ground was left spare. Endless piles of bodies lay on the land around the gateway. It was the scene of a great massacre. The battle had proved vicious and gruesome. His weary eyes scanned the scene for fallen friends. He had no idea who was left alive.

The courtyard emerged from the doorway as Sylvie ran out of the tower. The girls had bounded down the mighty flights of steps once it had become clear Arthir was gone. They'd ripped the black banner from the balcony and let it fall to earth. The wolf beings had continued to lurk the tower but the girls hadn't dwelt any longer in the throne room and now found themselves back on the ground. Once in the square around the structure conversation finally kicked in.

'I am so pleased to see you Akumi,' Sylvie said joyously.

They hugged and soon after Yuuki came forwards to face the assassin. Although they hadn't met since childhood the sorceress felt an affinity with the girl.

'I am Yuuki,' she said. 'It's so great to finally meet you.'

Akumi felt humbled. She then looked to Emi, another new face for her.

'Hello Akumi,' said the huntress. 'I am Emi.'

For a few moments the girls started to bombard Akumi with questions regarding what was going on and what she had achieved. Yuuki was the only one who seemed to resist the urge to initiate the verbal probing. They were all downtrodden and emotionally exhausted but still remained focused enough to converse. Akumi was about to answer Sylvie and Emi's burning questions but suddenly thought of someone close to her.

'Where is Jamus?' she asked.

'He is resting in a house near the gateway,' said Sylvie. 'He was injured.'

No further words were necessary. Akumi started to jog away. The others were close behind.

Jamus dragged his feet and watched the dark creatures do their bidding. He didn't seem troubled by them. He could tell they were targeting the rebels. He remembered how the wolf had not attacked him back in the room but had fled once slaying the insurgent. It appeared he was safe.

The fires that had consumed several of the buildings on the roadside had by now naturally smouldered out. The roof of the house Jamus came out from was all but gone but the stone walls remained standing. The smell of smoke overwhelmed the friar's lungs.

As the old warrior stood dazed four figures came rushing down the meandering track from the direction of the great tower. Akumi led them. She was quick to spot Jamus and ran towards him with immense pace.

'Jamus!' she exclaimed merrily.

The old man turned to face her. Within seconds she had playfully clasped her arms around his shoulders and kissed him affectionately on the cheek.

'My dear Akumi,' Jamus whispered, 'I am so relieved to see you are safe.'

'I have so much to tell you,' said the assassin.

'I don't doubt it,' laughed Jamus. 'I trust these creatures have something to do with your arrival?'

Akumi nodded. Her eyes were wide with intensity.

'I defeated Endal!' she announced, as if dying to finally tell the world.

The others stood next to her. Sylvie smiled at the news but her mind was elsewhere. Yuuki and Emi were clearly most pleased. They knew all about the notorious character and of his role in all that had played out. His demise seemed like justice done.

'I can't explain it well, but an energy force was building around him,' Akumi continued. 'It was awaiting his instruction. It turned to me for direction once I had killed him.'

Jamus knew more than he let on about the dark forces following the girl's command. He had known all about Vortor's warnings of an army of infernal creatures forming to destroy the realm.

'So it seems Endal was even more integral in all of this than we thought,' he said. 'He was to lead these forces. My guess is Vortor knew the assassination of the Emperor would trigger this energy to form. It all comes together.'

'I felt it,' said Yuuki. 'It now makes sense to me. You overcame the shadow and took ahold of it.'

Akumi was listening but also started to notice the vista further down the track. The creatures under her command were still meticulously carving into the wailing cluster of rebels. She couldn't watch any longer.

'I command you to stop!' she yelled; her mind focused on the energy that permeated through her. 'Cease and go back into the cloud!'

There was an instant recognition of her order. Every last entity that roamed the city started to move into the sky. The wolves flashed back into winged beings and joined the ascending mass. For a few seconds the sky itself was blackened by the vast accumulation of dark figures.

Sylvie stepped forwards and faced the small group of rebels that remained. They were bundled together in a thick pile. All of them were utterly petrified and as pale as sheets.

'Tamus Tower is secure!' Sylvie shouted emphatically. 'Brimma remains under my control! Your cause is lost and your leaders are dead. Be gone and never again plot to overthrow the empire!'

Jamus was pleased by Sylvie's decree and smiled as the group of no more than sixty men ran away in terror and defeat. They bounded up the arrow infested bridge and within seconds were gone from sight.

The battle was over. Sylvie faced her allies. Jamus was faltering on his feet. Akumi was first to step forwards and help him stand upright.

'You must rest,' she said.

'What now?' Sylvie suddenly broke down. 'Look at this!'

She burst into tears and dropped to the ground. Yuuki and Emi ran to her side. The realities of the aftermath were starting to ring home.

'Fenris died in my arms,' Sylvie cried, 'and look at how many now lie dead and wounded around us!'

All were shocked and moved by the announcement. It was news to the rest of them that Fenris had fallen. Only Akumi knew not of his identity.

'And what of Rense?' asked Emi.

'I fear he, too, was lost!' Jamus expressed.

'We need to gather up assistance from outlying villages,' said Emi emotionally. 'Your citizens will come back to Brimma now they know there is no threat.'

'But my army?' Sylvie screeched. 'It is no more!'

'It has been a bloody day and our loses have been great,' Yuuki said morbidly.

Jamus sat down and bowed his head. He was weak but managed to speak:

'All that matters is that this realm did not fall into chaos. The future of every man, woman, and child rested on the outcome of this battle. That future has been secured.'

Emi and Yuuki sat beside Sylvie. All of them were now silent and absent. The sheer enormity of the morning's dramatic events had now overcome them. Only Akumi remained standing.

Above them the mass of dark, looming clouds continued to swirl and hover with foreboding presence. Akumi looked up at the spectacle and walked away from the group. Jamus raised his eyebrow and studied the girl. He sensed she was about to speak.

'It is my command that you resurrect and heal all those that fought today in the defence of Brimma!' Akumi yelled. 'Bring all those back to life that still dwell in this realm!'

None of the group had expected anything like this. Even Lady Yuuki was speechless at the magical implications. She had no experience of anything as grand as this.

Akumi continued: 'You brought me back from the dead! Now I

ask that you do the same for those that fell here today!'

Jamus was alarmed. The revelation that Akumi had been resurrected by the forces in the air changed everything.

'Akumi!' he cried out. 'You are under the shadow! It is within you now!'

Akumi didn't grasp his meaning. She was too focused on the stirrings above. The clouds were coming down to earth.

'Those tainted with the mark of your enemy shall not be saved!' a voice came from the clouds.

'It speaks!' cried Emi.

There was no time for debate. Jamus hadn't been able to express his concerns forcefully enough. The air became consumed by a dark fog. Howling gales erupted and blew around every crevice of Brimma. The black cloud sunk until the city was within its grim body. Thousands of black beings descended onto the mass of corpses. Emi dropped to the ground in fear and covered her ears. The piercing blare of spiralling energy sounded like some bellowing storm bombarding them. Yuuki's staff glowed red with an acknowledgement of the powerful forces around her. Jamus sat motionless.

Akumi stood firm as her command was carried out. She felt like a goddess; able to order the mystical energy at will. Sylvie had raced to where Fenris lay. She had no idea what was going on but believed Akumi's words. Her eyes gazed down at the body of the fallen warrior.

After a few minutes the cloud suddenly rose back into the sky high above Brimma. The dancing swarms of entities faded back into the foggy backdrop and followed the cloud. The city was promptly visible again. Akumi stared at the bloody field of battle. She refused to dwell on Jamus' warning. All she desired was a fair end to this bitter episode for all those that had fought so fearlessly against the enemies of the realm.

The command had been carried out. In one momentous moment many hundreds of the fallen started to stir. The wounded got to their feet. The dead opened their eyes. Even the fallen horses were rising.

'Not all were healed,' said Akumi. 'Only those whose spirits still lingered have been given back life. Many have passed too deeply into other worlds beyond our own.'

Jamus studied the girl as she spoke. He was confused. He knew

Akumi wasn't aware of the full implications of her unique condition.

Hundreds of Tamus troops were alive once again. They slowly got up one by one in a constant flow. They were weary and staggered around as if half drunk. There would surely be some explaining to do.

Sylvie watched Fenris carefully. His face was still pale and lifeless. For a moment she feared he was one of those that had been too far gone to save. She then noticed his eyelids stirring.

'Fenris!' the Empress cried.

He opened his eyes and smiled with intrinsic warmth. His wounds were healed and his body strong.

'Did I lose consciousness?' he asked. 'Are you okay?'

Sylvie laughed with joy at his ignorance and hugged him as he lay perplexed.

In the distance the large frame of a bearded warrior emerged from a stinking pile of rebel corpses. They picked up a battleaxe and glanced across the dirt rack. Rense was on his feet.

Jamus slowly strolled towards Akumi. He was stunned by what he had seen. He was amazed yet at the same time apprehensive. Akumi smiled as he reached her side. She looked exhausted and troubled.

'What is to happen to me?' Akumi asked.

She had sensed an alien energy within her growing with every minute that had passed since she had risen from the distant swamps. Jamus' brief comments had sparked something inside of her to question the reality of her current state.

'Akumi, I don't pretend to know much about these things,' said Jamus, 'but I fear you have yet to fully grasp what has happened to you. Please explain to me exactly what occurred.'

As they spoke Emi and Yuuki came closer and listened attentively. Sylvie remained beside Fenris. The two were standing with arms clasped around each other. Even the Empress' wound to her back had been healed.

'I fought Endal,' said Akumi. 'He gravely injured me but I managed to lure him into a room of crystals. There I was certain I would fall but a rush of energy came to me. I let him think he'd won. He plunged his blade towards me but I managed to strike him, and then hurl him against a wall of the crystals. I killed him but then fell down; my wound was too serious and I died.

'I recall waking up and being informed I was in command of the cloud. It had already consumed Arifor, the mage that was with your party. Endal said he was preparing to lead the dark cloud into battle against us.'

'Arifor was with you?' asked Yuuki. 'What became of him?'

'Yes, he appeared before me,' Akumi said. 'He said the dark forces he harboured had warped him to the cloud. He was taken over by it in the end and I was forced to kill him. He was a shell of his former self and was trying to kill me.'

'Akumi, please listen to me,' Jamus spoke firmly; 'you don't have long until the energy growing inside of you overwhelms you as it did Arifor. Endal was acting as the avatar for this great power. His body was being taken over by it. Once he died the energy sought another carrier. The role has now transferred to you.'

Yuuki was deeply troubled by the information coming to light. Her intuition confirmed the old man's words were accurate.

'What about all these people that have just been healed by the energy?' she asked out loud.

'They will be fine,' said Akumi knowingly. 'They have been resurrected but it was at my command. The energy has nothing to do with them. It is within me. It chose to enter into me and claim me as its head.'

Jamus said nothing in response. He could tell Akumi knew this to be the case and no more words were necessary. As the four stood silently swarms of Tamus guards started to pull away at the wreckage of the wooden platform beside the southern wall. Within the broken piles of wood dozens of guardsmen were protesting and battling to free themselves. Rense was aiding the efforts and lifted a mighty slab of lumber; revealing a thankful troop pressed against the debris.

Akumi was teary eyed and looked at those around her. 'All that's important is that everyone is alive,' she said. 'The cloud has at least ensured that. It has now come to an end. I will leave before I am consumed by this darkness.'

'Surely we can do something?' Yuuki asked. 'Command the cloud to leave this world and go back to wherever it came from for good. Order it to leave you!'

'It won't abandon me,' replied Akumi. 'I can just sense it is a part of me now.'

'It is relying on her,' said Jamus. 'It won't depart her now.'

Jamus was strong again; his wounds healed by the cloud, and knew he had to act. He could sense Akumi was already considering taking her own life. Her tone was dark and her face absent of joy.

'You will come back with me to Grange Abbey,' he furthered. 'There I will do all I can to banish this darkness and free you from its grip.'

Sylvie appeared to the old man's side with Fenris holding her hand. They were gleaming with happiness and delight.

'Thank you so much Akumi,' Sylvie said elatedly.

'I don't pretend to know or understand what has happened,' Fenris added, 'but it seems to have all worked out!'

Rense abruptly jumped into the group from behind Fenris and patted him on the shoulder.

'Seconded,' he laughed. 'All back together again!'

'It looks like hundreds of guards pulled through,' said Emi, 'thanks to you Akumi.'

'The rest were too long gone,' said Jamus. 'Even forces as strong as these cannot reach the spirit once it has truly moved on from this mortal coil.'

'Life forces linger on after death,' Yuuki added. 'Eventually, they pass over. Those that have risen are those whose souls still remained here.'

'Yeah...' Rense sighed. 'What she said!'

Sylvie was beginning to realise Akumi was far from okay. A weight rested on her shoulders and she was in no mood to relax. The assassin walked over to Jamus and then looked to everyone as if about to address them. She spoke:

'Our struggle is over; we have succeeded in defeating Golandin. Marmia has prevailed against those that wished her harm. I must now leave you. My mind is slowly being corrupted. I can feel it. The cloud above us will not leave me.'

'She is to come with me to my Abbey,' said Jamus. 'There I will do all I can.'

'We will come with you,' said Fenris.

'No!' Akumi snapped. 'I don't want you to witness me fall. I can already sense changes inside of me. Please let me go with Jamus alone. I am sorry.'

Sylvie raced to Akumi's side and hugged her. She knew the

moment had come to once again say farewell to the female assassin.

'You have done so much for Marmia Akumi,' said the Empress. 'Please do all you can for her Jamus.'

The old friar nodded. 'I shall do all I can, Empress,' he smiled astutely. 'And I trust you shall ensure Marmia prospers like she deserves to.'

The Empress sensed Jamus had every faith in her ability to rule the lands. She humbly looked to the ground before the wise old man.

'I will not fail Marmia,' she announced.

Jamus was confident Sylvie had it in her to lead the realm to greatness. He again nodded and turned back to the female assassin.

'It has been an honour meeting you Akumi,' said Lady Yuuki.

Akumi bowed her head in reaction to the touching sentiment. She then looked to Jamus with the corners of her eyes.

'We best move now,' he said calmly. 'We don't have much time.'

The old man started to make for the gateway. Akumi didn't hesitate and emotionally gave the party of warriors around her one last glance as she jogged after him. The cloud above appeared to roll in the direction she was moving like an invisible rope connected her to its vibrant mass.

As Akumi sped away Sylvie faced her fading figure and stood motionlessly with her head slightly bowed. Within seconds everyone else had joined her. They stood in a line of respect for the girl that had saved the realm.

'Jamus will know what to do,' said Fenris. 'She will be okay.'

'She defeated Endal, and turned the tide of this battle,' said Sylvie respectfully. 'She saved us all. I owe everything to her now. She mustn't leave us! She must be okay!'

Yuuki nodded to herself as the Empress spoke. Their hopes rested on whatever plan Jamus had. The sorceress could only imagine what that could possibly be. Her eyes continued to focus on Akumi attentively. She then furtively slipped away from the line with meaning.

'Goodbye Akumi,' said Emi softly.

'She's certainly something,' added Rense.

They continued to watch the girl fade from view. All heads

bowed as she passed onto the bridge and was gone. The humble moment of admiration lasted only for a short while but it meant the world to this small band of companions.

CHAPTER VI

THE RIDERS OF THE CLOUD

A group of horses had formed in natural assembly just beyond the hillside. Jamus paused once he'd reached the top of the rise south of the lake. Akumi wasn't far behind him.

'We can grab a pair of horses,' said Jamus, 'then ride for the Abbey. It will be the fastest way.'

Akumi reached his side and looked at the fearful animals. It was clear they were already backing away further down the fields with the coming of the cloud. Within seconds of it reaching the hill directly above its leader the horses bolted. There was no use trying to catch them.

'They are too afraid of the cloud,' Akumi said. 'I have a better way.'

Jamus was intrigued and studied her as she looked up at the darkness above them.

'Raise us into the cloud and take us southwards,' Akumi ordered.

The fog descended and the two travellers felt their bodies being lifted into the air.

'Leading this thing has its perks I see,' Jamus smiled.

'Well it seems silly not to use it for my own gain,' said Akumi jokingly, 'for now at least, while I still can.'

They climbed the air as the haze of thick cloud lifted them as if it had clasped them by the arm. They appeared on a blanket of fog and sat side by side with the world below them. The ground was passing them by with great pace. The Falgor fields south of the lake of Brimma were soon crossed. Vast forests shot by in the blink of an eye. They felt a great sense of acceleration.

'I have never experienced anything like this,' Jamus said. 'In all my years I have never felt such a sensation as this.'

'I can't imagine anyone ever has,' Akumi replied. 'No one has ever been in command of this energy, not even Endal got the chance.'

Jamus was in amazement over the situation he found himself in and took in every last angle of the mighty view below. They were perched so high that the horizon visibly curved in the far distance. The cold air resisted the pace as it pressed into their faces against the swift momentum of the cloud. Swarms of birds flew to one side in avoidance of the potent incoming force.

They continued to travel southwards with immense speed. Those below that had caught a glimpse of the alien spectacle as it rushed across the plains mostly cried out in terror and fled from its path. Nothing like this had ever been witnessed in these parts.

After several minutes the riders of the cloud were close to the Grange Abbey. The long distance they had travelled had been covered in a fraction of the time it would have taken them if riding by horse. What took hours on the ground took merely minutes for this great mass of condensed power.

'We are already close,' said Jamus. 'The Abbey is only moments away from us.'

Akumi wasn't surprised. She had already experienced the immense speed of the cloud when it had taken her from the distant swamplands of the far west to Brimma.

As Jamus had noted the Abbey was soon in full view. The cloud halted above the monastic retreat. The sight of the homely location instantly formed a smile on Jamus' face. They had moved due south from Brimma but the cloud had also been mentally directed by Akumi. She hadn't spoken but the energy within her had read her thoughts and followed her mental lead, such was the link between it and her. They started to descend as the foggy haze around them dropped to the grassy ground.

'There is no time to spare,' said Jamus. 'I must gather all of the monks. Every mind is required for what we are about to attempt.'

Akumi still had no idea what Jamus was planning. She had faith in the wise friar but feared the grip around her was already tightening; her mind and focus slowly starting to fade.

They pounced from the fog and landed on the grass of the flat field just outside of the Abbey house. The monks who had been working in the frugal grassland retreated away from the alluring energy. They had no idea what they were witnessing.

Jamus ran towards the doorway of the Abbey. Gradually, the fearful monks scattering around the holy grounds realised their friar was back. He paused near the entrance once he'd raced up the gravel pathway and overlooked the field.

'This is a matter of urgency my monks!' he called. 'Gather up in the hall immediately! Gather everyone up!'

Those that had heard him knew to spring into action. They raced off to fetch the others and several converged beside Jamus. Akumi stood silently; the cloud still carefully following her with every step she made. The winged beings were nowhere to be seen. It was as if they were currently all hiding within the cloud.

'I can feel a vast force bombarding me!' Akumi announced abruptly. 'It's so powerful!'

The girl suddenly dropped to the ground in front of the monks.

'Help her up and take her into the hall,' said Jamus.

The monks complied and carried her arms around their shoulders then dragged her through the doorway. Jamus studied the cloud before entering the building. It was vibrant with flashes of lightning and thunderous roars of energy. Something was happening.

Lady Yuuki cut through the fields with as much pace as her horse could muster. She had managed to calm one down near the bridge of Brimma and claim it as her ride. With the cloud gone the animals no longer seemed as alarmed. The sorceress was heading for the Grange Abbey. She knew roughly where it was, remembering well the journey her party had made when heading to the capital. Although she was aware of Akumi's request that none of them should follow her Yuuki couldn't help herself. She had an urge to assist them and sensed her presence would be required.

Back in Brimma Sylvie was commanding the efforts of her men. She had ordered all the troops whom had risen to assist the wounded rebels. Hundreds of them rolled around the gateway grounds in agony and desperation. The cloud had healed all of the imperial wounded but had left the rebels to writhe in pain.

'Treat them well,' Sylvie ordered as she watched her men scramble around before her. 'They require our aid and we will give it to them.'

Fenris was beside her. The two were holding hands. They were very much in love. There was no longer any question about it.

'That is quite commendable,' said Fenris. 'Although I very

much doubt Golandin would have issued any such order if it were us now floundering on the ground under his sword.'

'I suspect not,' said Sylvie, 'but that is irrelevant. It matters not what he would have said or done. All that matters is that these men are given our assistance. They are no longer our enemy. Many of them are seriously injured, those creatures tore them apart! We must help them.'

Not far from the two lovers Emi stood with Rense. They were leaning against the southern wall beside the wreckage of the fallen platform. Both of them appeared restless.

'She certainly can be stealthy when she wants,' smiled Rense. 'One minute she was beside us, the next she was gone.'

'She cares for Akumi,' replied Emi. 'She has fretted about her ever since we left for Dwenton.'

Rense nodded whilst stroking the bloody tip of his mighty axe.

'She wasn't going to comply with her request,' Emi continued. 'She has clearly headed off for the Abbey. She believes she can help her.'

Rense looked to Sylvie and Fenris. They were walking hand in hand around the smouldering houses of the trackside.

'Looks like they've become a couple,' he laughed. 'I knew it was on the cards.'

'And you know what that means...' Emi smiled. 'Emperor Fenris?'

Rense laughed out loud. 'Well I guess someone's got to do it,' he beamed.

Their thoughts then turned back to Akumi. Both turned their heads and stared across the bridge beside them.

'Well, it doesn't look like we're going to be needed around here anymore,' said Rense. 'It seems silly hanging around.'

'It certainly does...' said Emi predictively.

'I say we follow Yuuki's lead and get to the Abbey,' Rense suggested. 'With me?'

Emi smiled and took in a deep breath. 'Sure,' she said. 'I'm with you.'

Akumi was placed on the surface of a hefty tabletop. A large group of monks surrounded her with brown robes covering their bodies and thick hoods concealing their heads. Many had placed lit candles beside the girl's body. All of them seemed to know what Jamus was planning.

The old warrior entered the hall. He had removed his armour and now wore his old robe. He looked humble and back to his holy self.

'We must prepare faster!' he yelled.

'We are gathering all that is required friar,' said a monk.

As they spoke the sky above was blackening. The menacing cloud was expanding and erupting into a fervent mass of vivacious, pulsating mists. A great miasma was encapsulating the Abbey. The dark energy was throbbing with greater strength. A wind howled against the thin panes of glass to the far side of the hall.

'The cloud grows stronger with every passing minute,' said Jamus. 'Alas! If we do not succeed in banishing it from Akumi's soul it will consume her and turn her into a shell of her former self. She will no longer control the cloud. It will then be the cloud commanding her; the ultimate desire of this wretched design.'

'I have never been a part of a banishing ritual,' said a single monk. 'I fear I lack the knowledge to assist you friar.'

'All of you must do as I say,' said the wise friar. 'That is all that is required.'

Akumi's body was stretched out on the wooden table. Her arms were placed outstretched past her head and her sleeves pulled up her arms. Several monks started to dab blobs of black paint on her bare wrists. One then rolled a wet brush across her forehead and stroked it in between her eyes.

'Mark her chest,' ordered Jamus. 'A line down her torso, in between her breasts.'

Akumi was unconscious and pale. Whatever was happening to her she was now too weak to resist it. As the monks started to unbutton her cloak from around her neck and rip the fabric of her top a terrible shriek came from outside. The dark silhouettes of the flying entities suddenly jetted across the coloured panes of glass. The infernal creatures were stirring. The cloud was sensing resistance.

The holy men did not falter as they tore the assassin's top. Once the fabric split her bare chest was in full view. A monk painted a black line across her torso from the neck down. It moved in between her breasts and stopped at her belly.

'These liquids are blessed,' said Jamus, 'and consecrated for this very purpose. They will protect Akumi from the forces desiring to enter her.'

Candles encircled the girl as she lay atop the table. Each thick, white stick of wax glowed with a radiant, flickering flame.

'Gather around the table,' ordered Jamus. 'Circle around her.'

The group of twenty monks stood around the table. Each was beside a candle; their robes partially lit up by the pale light within the dingy room. Jamus leant forwards and drew a circle around Akumi with the dark paint. The brush stroked against the old wooden surface of the table without protest. The old friar then stepped back and joined the circle of monks.

'We will banish the cloud from Akumi,' he panted breathlessly. 'We will order the cloud to leave her. We will then compel it to vanish from these lands for good.'

His monks were silent and prepared for whatever esoteric battle they were about to initiate. They bowed their heads and crossed their arms within their drooping robes. Jamus was about to begin.

'It has been an honour fighting alongside you both,' said Sylvie. 'I understand your desire to go after Yuuki and catch up with Akumi. I wish you luck. I would come too but I must now stay in Brimma and help with the clearing up.'

Rense and Emi nodded in unison. It was obvious the Empress now had her work cut out dealing with the aftermath of the battle. Rense looked to his old friend Fenris.

'I trust you will be staying too?' he asked jokingly.

'My place is by Sylvie's side,' replied Fenris. 'I now desire nothing else but to be with her.'

Sylvie smiled and the two clenched their hands together ever so slightly tighter.

'Ah! 'Ya love-struck weakling you!' Rense teased.

'We are going to help the guards bury the dead and assist to the injured,' said Sylvie. 'Once this is done we will be busy planning how best to move on from this dark period of Marmia's history. We will ensure the citizens of this land learn of our victory and we shall get on with the business of ruling the empire.'

Emi and Rense could sense great passion in Sylvie's voice.

'We?' smiled Emi.

'Indeed,' said Sylvie, whilst staring into Fenris' eyes; 'You are looking at your future Emperor, after all.'

The four bid their farewells to one another. Rense shook Fenris' hand and Emi hugged Sylvie. They then split apart. Rense and Emi raced for the bridge.

Sylvie and Fenris watched them as they vanished across the sooty overpass with arms around each other. Fenris turned to face the blonde haired Empress. She caught his glance and they immediately kissed. The Empress had found her true love. The realm was strong again.

CHAPTER VII

BANISHING A DARK PRESENCE

The old friar chanted an archaic word of command. There was an undeniable energy about the arcane language he muttered in the candlelight.

'*Salek Meanthra Esto*,' he bellowed as if it were a mantra. '*Esta Valek*!'

The monks were motionless and locked in meditation.

'We must combine the circle,' cried Jamus. 'Clasp each other's hands!'

The circle of monks brought their arms out from their robes and clutched the hands of those beside them. There was a rumbling in the air.

'You will leave this girl!' Jamus cried. 'You will free her from your grasp! I order it. I order you to go back to the world whence you came!'

There came a mighty response in the form of hundreds of deathly entities pounding against the four walls of the humble house. The winds picked up as if a vortex were forming around them. The cloud focused all its energy on this single space.

'Be gone!' Jamus roared with great command.

The window smashed open. Countless fragments of coloured glass fell against the stone ground of the hall. A vile air entered through the narrow opening.

'This girl does not belong to you,' yelled Jamus. 'She is protected by the great seal of our holy creed!'

The friar suddenly sensed a great presence. Although the cloud was converging on them it lacked true sentience. However, there was now a charisma in the air. It was as if a ghost had entered into the proceedings. Jamus was in a cold sweat. He was already fatigued. The dark energy was targeting him.

'There is a presence,' cried Jamus. 'I sense it.'

The monks did not budge as droves of winged spectres flowed

into the hall through the broken window. Suddenly, an apparition formed in the air above Akumi. At first it resembled only a black mist but soon it fashioned itself into a hovering figure. The manifestation spoke:

'You dare challenge my will!' the dark figure howled.

Jamus looked up at the ghostly figure. 'Vortor!' he grumbled nervously.

The monks were in a trancelike state of focus and did not move. The circle held firm.

'My powers still stir in this realm Jamus,' Vortor's apparition said. 'They are what now surround you. They were hijacked by this wretch of a girl! She took the role of avatar from Endal! She defeated him!'

The black mage was wild with anger and his voice bitter and twisted. Jamus was stunned by the dark wizard's presence but it did not impact his resolve.

'You failed Vortor,' Jamus said. 'Marmia won't be destroyed by your dark spell. Whatever this twisted magic is you have dabbled with it won't prevail. It won't consume Akumi. Your fury will not be realised! Her body doesn't belong to you! She is to become no avatar!'

Vortor screamed with frustration. His transparent figure floated across the tabletop as the flock of dark entities continued to hover over the monks. Akumi's control over the cloud was slowly fading. Vortor was beginning to take over her mind and use her body as his host but the creatures in the hall were nevertheless unable to attack Jamus and his monks. Their ancient ceremony gave them all collective protection against the infernal masses.

'You can't do a thing can you?' Jamus laughed. 'You rely on this girl's body for your dark cloud to do your bidding. Your plan has failed. Be gone!'

Akumi's back suddenly arched as she lay against the table. Her body rose into the air with her head dropped back against the neck.

'She will fall into my grip,' Vortor insisted. 'I am taking over her soul!'

'No!' Jamus wailed. 'You will not take her.'

The two minds were wrestling for control of the girl. Vortor's otherworldly presence enticed the dark cloud to continue attempting to overcome her whilst Jamus' righteous ritual battled to keep the darkness at bay. The two rival forces seemed to be swaying with dominance. It looked as if it could truly go either way. Vortor's presence remained in the hall as the mystical battle waged on. Time appeared to speed up as the magical forces locked each involved mind into a deep focus. Eventually, three demanding hours had passed with no signs of abatement. It seemed to be a stalemate.

Lady Yuuki entered into the outskirts of the fields within the Abbey grounds. She had ridden with great pace and made the distance in good time. As soon as the vast, dark cloud came into view from behind passing trees her horse halted in terror. Yuuki pounced from her mount just as it turned and bolted away. Her staff started to glow again with acknowledgement of the pervading energy. The sorceress jogged up the path towards the dwelling.

Once she was near the Abbey house her presence was felt by Vortor. The dark cloud was beginning to take full hold of Akumi against all of Jamus' efforts. The girl was gradually becoming a minion to the dead mage. Vortor now had enough of a hold on her to instruct the cloud using her as his mouthpiece. Somehow, the late mage had found a way of influencing this physical world from the place his spirit now dwelt.

At the evil ghost's command a scurry of the grim creatures coming from the cloud targeted Yuuki. She now stood just beside the fence squared around the perimeter of the house. The sorceress spotted dozens of flying spectres converging on her from the sky. She raised her staff and focused. She wasn't shocked by the reception. Her honed intuition had warned her of something like this.

The sky was black and the air thick with rolling mists. The red eyes of the flying beings beamed through the fog like fires through dense smoke. Yuuki's staff turned into a pole of bright lime light. She held it in both arms and swung it overhead as the first entity swooped by her. It was alarmed and recoiled from the magical power pulsing from her staff.

Another attacked only to retreat with equal consternation. Several then came at once but all fled as soon as they got close to the green energy glowing from her staff. Yuuki opened the tiny gate and walked up the pathway towards the Abbey door. She was eager to enter.

Behind her several of the wolflike creatures suddenly emerged from the field beyond the low picket fence. Yuuki turned to face them and called out a magical command. Bolts of green light flew out from her glowing staff and plunged into the entities' gloomy, miasmic auras. They protested in high pitched howls and fled away deeper into the field. Yuuki opened the door to the Abbey house.

From the sounds of commotion the sorceress could tell where to go. She raced down a narrow corridor and pushed open the doors to the hall. She instantly spotted Jamus surrounded by his monks seemingly wrestling with the forces around them. The girl ran further into the hall and halted beside the friar.

'Jamus!' she exclaimed. 'What is happening?'

Jamus was too focused on maintaining his deep concentration to reply. His eyes were closed and his sweaty palms tightly clasped the hands of the monks to his sides. The protective circle was faltering against the power of the cloud. Yuuki noticed a black figure hovering over Akumi's arched body. She could instantly tell it was an ethereal presence and one of great influence.

'And so the wretched Lady Yuuki joins your side Jamus!' Vortor screeched. 'You do not deserve the reputation that precedes you my girl!'

Yuuki was enthralled by the apparition. She aimed her glowing green staff directly towards it.

'I trust you are Vortor!' she yelled. 'Your time has come and gone! Do not dwell in this realm. Be gone to the world of spirit!'

Vortor laughed mockingly. 'You dare confront me sorceress!' the dark mage was fervid. 'You will feel my wrath!'

Every last entity that now roamed the hall attacked Yuuki at once. She bent low and raised her staff. Just as before the creatures retreated one after the other once coming close to her shining, magical rod. Her magical presence and exceptional power acted as a shield. The spectres dared not come closer. They wailed in vivacious protest but were unable to claim the sorceress.

'You can't win Vortor,' Yuuki insisted. 'Leave this realm for good!'

There was a mighty wind that swept in from the window. It

swirled around the monks and instantly blew out the flickering candles. Yuuki focused and once again pointed her staff at Vortor's ghostly figure. His face could just be made out from within the veil of dark mist. His robed body was transparent and occasionally flashed in and out of existence. She closed her eyes as the green light glowing from her staff grew greater with intensity. She was summoning all her strength.

Rense and Emi had arrived. Their horses refused to move any further and stopped precisely where Yuuki's had. Emi dived from her ride before it kicked her off. Rense hadn't been as swift and was knocked from his horse's back as it raised its front legs. He fell to the grass with a thud. Both horses then turned and fled into the woodland along the roadside. Emi looked down at her bearded companion and giggled.

'Stupid creatures,' grumbled Rense.

He got up and jostled with his axe as it rested across his back. He looked further on from them into the fields. Several hundred feet ahead the black cloud had amassed over the Grange Abbey. Countless entities vividly encircled the building and gathered in packs in the grass around its fence. It was a menacing, bleak scene.

'What do you think?' Rense asked.

Emi scanned every inch of the view ahead. Her bow was at the ready.

'I think it would be foolish to get any closer,' she said. 'We should avoid gaining those creatures' attention. Let's hold back in that tree line.'

She pointed to a series of trees resting on the outskirts of the woodland surrounding the Abbey grounds. From there they could overlook the fields around the dwelling.

'But what if they need our help?' Rense was reluctant.

'What can we do against those things?' Emi pondered. 'Nothing! We need to hold back.'

Rense acquiesced, sensing Emi was right, and followed her lead. They moved westwards beyond the roadside and crept along the tree line beside the edge of the northern field. In the distance the flock of wolfish creatures hanging around the fence suddenly seemed to stir. They had noticed them; their blood red eyes glowing feverishly through the haze.

Lady Yuuki's staff blinded those around her. The monks bent their heads even lower to avoid the powerful light. Jamus was intrigued by the girl's actions.

'The cloud is too powerful Yuuki, even for you!' Jamus warned. 'Vortor is taking over Akumi! I can't hold him back for much longer. He will consume her!'

Yuuki was not startled. Her mind was transfixed on saving her ally. She yelled out:

'*Collas Teremath*!'

The powerful light coming from her staff surged forwards towards Vortor. It touched against the dark smog surrounding him and within seconds encircled him. He was lit up by the spell. A white light gleamed around his entire figure. It continued to pour out from the sorceress' staff.

Suddenly, Jamus could sense the force attacking him weaken; it lessened as if it had split its focus all of a sudden. Akumi's arching body dropped back down onto the table. She had been partially levitating and hit the wooden surface loudly.

'Be gone!' Yuuki cried. 'You have no place in this realm anymore!'

Rense was first to spot the flock of wolves racing towards them. He grabbed ahold of his axe and prepared for combat.

'Trouble!' he yelled.

Emi sprung to attention and put an arrow on her bowstring. She aimed it towards the creatures as they got closer. She was leaning against a tree that partially concealed her camouflaged figure. Rense stepped out from the tree line and held his axe forwards.

'Looks like these things no longer like us!' he said.

'Akumi can't be commanding them anymore,' Emi suggested. 'She must be free!'

The ghoulish creatures crossed the field in moments. Rense was close to swinging his axe towards the first one in the group.

'Step away!' Emi cried. 'Get back in the trees!'

She fired her arrow at the one Rense was about to engage. The sharp arrow slid across the air and passed beside Rense in a whisper. The arrow tip plunged into the creature and entered through the haze surrounding it. There didn't seem to be a reaction. The shaft was lost in the darkness and then emerged behind the vile entity. It had passed straight through them and harmlessly fell to the grass upon coming back out.

The archer panicked and desperately grabbed hold of another arrow. Rense swung his enormous axe into the body of the first creature to reach him. The steel slipped straight through the misty haze. The wolf was clearly illusionary; that was at least until it decided otherwise. Suddenly, the being became clearer. Its mighty mouth of teeth widened and its eyes went dark. Rense tried to sidestep away but it was too late. His axe fell to the grass as his large body was pounced upon. Sharp claws plunged into his chest and teeth clutched his neck.

'Rense!' Emi screamed.

The warrior fell back and was ripped open by the creature. Others soon converged on his body and tore limb from limb. His head was entirely devoured within seconds and soon only a bloody pool of chewed, unidentifiable organs remained.

Emi was terrified and knew her arrows were useless. She ran away into the woodland behind her. The dark creatures were not fooled and pursued her in their mass huddle. One by one they faded into the dense canopy of the forest.

Vortor was in a desperate rage. His etheric presence could do nothing against Yuuki's focused power. She continued to surround him with her energy. Something seemed to be happening. Jamus yelled out further commands ordering Vortor to leave. His monks hadn't moved. Akumi suddenly stirred. Her pale skin showed signs of colouration as if blood was beginning to fully flow once more. Her fingers twitched and her body started to convulse in light trembles.

'She is coming back to us!' Jamus announced.

'You cannot resist me!' Vortor screamed. 'I command you!'

Outside, the cloud started to tame. The immense energy was wavering. The intense winds ceased and the air started to cool.

'You will never come back into this world!' Yuuki cried. 'You are banished!'

'Be gone! You are not welcome here!' Jamus added.

Vortor's presence suddenly cried out in great despair: 'It cannot be! No! I will break your spell!'

The late mage screamed in frustration and defeat as Yuuki's shroud of light surrounded him. It had locked him in place and eroded his strength and resolve to stay lurking in this realm beyond his. Jamus' circle had managed to ensure Akumi was not lost to his dark spell.

As Vortor floundered above her Akumi abruptly opened her eyes. She was back and truly alive with energy. Vortor's grip on her was lost. She no longer commanded the cloud. Its hold on her had finally ceased.

'Akumi rises!' Jamus declared. 'You are finished Vortor!'

'No!' Vortor shrieked in one long exclamation.

'Find peace in the spirit realm,' said Yuuki. 'You are no longer welcome here.'

With those words Yuuki's spell looked to suddenly take its toll on the ghost of Vortor. His presence faded. The entities cowering above him vanished in an instant. Akumi could just make out Vortor's troubled face from within the powerful light encapsulating him.

'Farewell Vortor,' she said softly.

He was gone in a whimpered flash. Yuuki withdrew her staff and the light ceased. There was a warming calmness to the air. The magical showdown was over.

Emi dived into a bushy section of the woodland. Thick shrubs rolled beside the trees. Her feet crunched against a blanket of brown, dry leaves that had fallen down from the tall branches above. She crawled deeper under the foliage and turned to locate her pursuers. She was terrified and breathed heavily. Her sharp eyes studied the section of woodland she had come from. She expected to spot hordes of the wolf beings storming through the trees but after a few seconds it was clear nothing was chasing her.

She bravely clambered out of the bushes and walked back in the direction she had fled from. Her small knife was poised in her right hand. All appeared clear. Several birds sung high above her and the sun suddenly lit the wilderness up with soothing light as it emerged from behind a fluffy cloud.

She sensed an unexplainable calmness about her surroundings as she continued forwards. Eventually, the girl had cut back through the wood and found herself right back on the tree line. She looked across towards the Abbey. It was the very quintessence of a serene sight. The green grass rolled and swayed with a cool breeze as a blue sky revealed itself above.

The dark cloud had gone and with it the army of infernal creatures. The energy had passed and no trace of it remained. It was as if it had never existed. Once it had become leaderless, and lost its grip over Akumi, it had lost its power; with Vortor cast out of the realm there had been no one left to direct or influence it. It had lost all contact with its host and was vanquished.

Emi stood silently in reflection and then noticed Rense's bloody remains at the corners of her eyes. There was nothing left of him besides the mangled residue of his corpse and the blood splattered grass around it. She bowed her head and wiped away the tears that inevitably came from her watery eyes.

CHAPTER VIII

A SOLEMN DEPARTURE

The hall was filled with joyous cheers. There was a great sense of relief at the passing of the cloud. Jamus sat himself down on an old wooden chair, utterly exhausted. His monks broke into song and hugged one another indiscriminately.

'We did it!' one cheered. 'The cloud has vanished!'

'Our circle held!' another applauded.

Yuuki walked over to Akumi as she sat up on the tabletop. The sorceress thoughtfully placed her cloak around her shoulders, allowing her to conceal her bare chest from view.

'How are you feeling Akumi?' Yuuki asked.

Akumi wrapped the material around her body like it was a cosy blanket.

'I feel fine,' she smiled, 'thanks to all of you.'

Akumi turned to face the sorceress and affectionately hugged her as she dropped from off the table.

'The darkness has passed,' the female assassin said. 'It has gone.'

'Yes,' smiled Yuuki. 'For good.'

Akumi was ecstatic and noticeably her chirpy self once again.

'And so it is over,' she announced. 'The threat to Marmia has passed. We prevailed!'

Yuuki nodded rapturously. 'It's hard to believe,' she laughed joyously, 'but you're right. It's finally over!'

The elated girls joined the group of monks in blissful merriments. They then noticed Jamus slouched in his chair in the corner. He looked feeble and wilted. His monks had also started to notice his state and crowded to his side. Akumi snaked past them and leant beside his chair. It rested against the wall near the door of the hall.

'You did it,' she said. 'You rid us of the shadow. It no longer has a hold on me. Thank you Jamus.'

'The circle held,' said a monk.

Jamus continued to sweat. He was breathing heavily and clutching his chest. He looked into Akumi's eyes.

'You should be thanking Lady Yuuki,' he stammered. 'She trapped Vortor's presence and locked him into a ball of light. He lost control of the dark energies he relied so heavily on and was expelled from this realm. He couldn't overcome her powers.'

'But you ensured Akumi wasn't lost to his dark cloud,' Yuuki insisted humbly.

'Ah, but you defeated Vortor my dear,' Jamus smiled. 'You saved Akumi. I only held his spell at bay for a short while.'

'I don't understand,' Akumi said; 'he let me take command of this energy? Surely he wanted Golandin to defeat us?'

'He hadn't expected you to defeat Endal,' said Jamus. 'He hadn't prepared for it. His mighty cloud, in which all his otherworldly power focused, naturally turned to you for leadership once Endal was no more. From his place in the world of spirit he could do nothing to intervene. It was only when the dark energy started to consume you that he could appear. He used your body as a means to manifest.'

Yuuki nodded in confirmation of the old man's words. Akumi seemed to understand.

'His plan failed,' said Yuuki, 'and he will never again be able to come back into this world. He relied solely on those forces, which he had likely played a role in forming, to maintain a foothold in this realm. He has now gone for good.'

'Yes,' said Jamus, 'and with Golandin defeated, Endal history, and Sylvie in charge of the realm I'd say our struggle has truly come to an end my children.'

His words sparked euphoric roars from all around him. Akumi continued to genuflect by his side and thoughtfully stroked his tired hand as it rested on the arm of the chair. Yuuki came closer to him and placed her staff on the table to her side. She kneeled before him and stroked his other hand. Suddenly, the door to the hall opened. Emi raced in.

The monks only just recognised the young girl. They recollected on her presence at the Abbey during the initial meeting those Jamus had called for had once attended. It now felt like an age ago. Akumi and Yuuki were amazed to see the huntress and got up to greet her.

'You came?' Akumi was confused.

'I had to,' said Emi. 'We couldn't cope with not knowing what was to happen to you.'

'Who else came?' Yuuki asked.

'I came with Rense,' Emi burst into tears. 'He was killed by those evil things before it all vanished. He's back in the field.'

The joyful mood of the hall became soured as if suddenly tainted by a sinister poison. Jamus acknowledged the news by bowing his head low as he sat.

'Rense fought for Marmia and died defending her,' he said. 'Many were lost fighting for the realm. They shall all be remembered, and respected.'

Yuuki aided Emi as she sat down beside the great table in the centre of the humble chamber.

'So it is over?' Emi asked the group emotionally.

'The cloud has gone for good, and Vortor will never return,' said Akumi.

'Vortor?' Emi questioned. 'The mage that you and Sylvie killed?'

'His spirit still lingered in this realm,' said Yuuki. 'He was waiting for his dark forces to form; relying on them to maintain a grip on Marmia.'

'The struggle is over,' Akumi smiled.

'I trust Sylvie is busy dealing with the aftermath of the battle?' Jamus asked Emi.

'Yes,' Emi sobbed, 'as is Fenris. They are very much in love. Fenris is to be the new Emperor. Sylvie said it herself.'

Everyone was pleased to discover the news. Akumi was especially happy to hear it. She cared for Sylvie and the thought that she had now found a companion to aid her in ruling the realm warmed her heart.

Jamus smiled to himself as his face bowed low out of view. He was genuinely relieved to learn Sylvie was no longer alone. It all seemed to be in place. His tired face rose until he was able to see the crowd around him. Emi sat on a chair across from him with Yuuki by her side. Akumi remained bowed before him. His monks huddled to the other side of his chair.

'That is great news,' he said softly. 'Marmia's future is secured.'

Jamus raised his body as upright as possible as if about to

further address them with all his might.

'Those that have survived must ensure this grim saga is never forgotten,' said the old friar. 'The future generations of this realm must learn of this episode. You must therefore tell these sorry tales; the tales that mark the dawn of Tamus Tower and all it stands for. This great day represents the beginning of a prosperous Marmia.'

'Yes,' nodded Yuuki, 'from now on Tamus Tower will symbolise order and advancement. The late Emperor's name shall never be forgotten. All of what's happened; the death of Tamus, the fall of Golandin, and the passing of the cloud, has ensured that the path of progress is clear. This story will never be forgotten Jamus.'

The old friar smiled weakly and then suddenly let out a great moan as if he'd been winded. Akumi sprung up and put her arm around him.

'Are you okay?' she cried.

'Friar, are you injured?' a monk asked from the crowd.

Jamus sat upright and rested his head against the wooden frame of the chair. He looked absent headed and drained of all strength.

'I am fine,' he said. 'My time has come to an end. The era of men such as me has passed. This land we have fought so hard for will now enter a new phase. The age of peace is upon you, the days of the sword will pass. A time of progress is at hand. Your generation will see it so.'

The wise old man closed his eyes and smiled. 'You will see it so...' he said.

They were to be his last words. His head slouched forwards and his body fell limp in Akumi's arm. Jamus had passed away peacefully in the old armchair. There were no words. Akumi hugged him whilst his monks dropped to their knees in respect and acknowledgement of the passing of this great seminal figure of their realm. His words had plucked a nerve inside all of them. They knew it was as he had said.

Emi sobbed alongside Yuuki as the sorceress dropped to the ground. With Jamus gone the three females felt lost and leaderless.

'He has joined Hazati,' Akumi cried whilst pressing her face against the friar's chest. 'We must ensure Marmia prospers. It is now up to us to see her grow.'

Eventually, the monks had taken Jamus to be buried in the Abbey grounds. It had been a meek, solemn affair but one in which there had been a real sense of calmness. His death marked the end of this bloody episode in Marmia's history. Akumi stood alongside Lady Yuuki and Emi in the tranquil, green pasture as the monks chanted in admiration of their fallen idol. Jamus was revered and his memory surely destined for greatness.

Rense, too, had been buried and placed beside the friar. What remains there were of him had been gathered by the monks and put into a coffin. Soil now covered them and modest plaques marked where they lay.

In time the chanting and prayer came to an end. The monks scattered away and dispersed across the fields and Abbey house. The three girls looked at one another as they stood on the grass beside their fallen friends' resting place.

'What will you do now?' Yuuki asked Akumi as she stared down at the plaques.

'I hope to settle down,' said the brown eyed girl, 'perhaps even go back to Brimma, for good. I will pass on the news of Jamus and Rense's deaths to Sylvie, and inform her that the cloud has passed. I wish to help her, and be there for her. I also hope to raise a family in that city eventually…'

Yuuki nodded whilst leaning on her tall staff. 'You will find peace,' the sorceress smiled. 'I have seen it.'

Akumi was warmed by the girl's psychic insight. She looked to the others.

'What will you two do?' she asked.

Yuuki and Emi glanced at each other. Both of them seemed to know.

'Marmia is free,' said Yuuki, 'and the empire will flourish under Sylvie's rule. I am to go back to my homelands; where I can spread the word of our victory to those that would otherwise never know of it. I am no longer required in these parts and want only the chance to live my life without ever again seeing bloodshed.'

Akumi understood and looked to Emi. The huntress nodded with Yuuki's words.

'I too will depart these lands,' she said, 'and return to my home. I also hope to settle down and find peace. I want nothing more than to put down my bow and blade for good.'

With those words the girls hugged and respectfully bowed before one another in admiration and appreciation. Emi and Yuuki prepared to move in one direction whilst Akumi set her course back for Brimma.

'Farewell Akumi,' waved Yuuki.

'Farewell,' Akumi concluded whilst waving back at them.

They grew apart as the distance between them increased with every opposite step. Within minutes Yuuki and Emi were lost behind the trees meandering around the track leading southwards from the Grange Abbey. Akumi headed northwards up the narrow path she had now trod and journeyed numerous times.

Eventually, her lone figure faded into the woodland surrounding the rolling fields. As she walked along the ramshackle trail tears unstoppably trickled down her guiltless face. It had proved an emotional saga but in her heart she recognised that she had accomplished all that had been required of her. She thought of Hazati for a moment. The female assassin had not failed her late master.

The immense losses of life the realm had suffered had not been in vain. The girl knew it had all been for the benefit and security of their land. She continued to traipse along the dry, muddy track. The sun glistened down on her from above and the birds perching in the tall trees sung with effervescent carelessness. There was a sense of closure about the moment; with the passing of the cloud a great new era was about to begin.

www.ingramcontent.com/pod-product-compliance
Lightning Source LLC
Chambersburg PA
CBHW020924020726
47495CB00002B/327